LIKE A FOX TO A SWALLOW

LIKE A FOX
TO A
SWALLOW

ELLA VOSS

Copyright © 2021 Ella Voss

The moral right of the author has been asserted.

Apart from any fair dealing for the purposes of research or private study, or criticism or review, as permitted under the Copyright, Designs and Patents Act 1988, this publication may only be reproduced, stored or transmitted, in any form or by any means, with the prior permission in writing of the publishers, or in the case of reprographic reproduction in accordance with the terms of licences issued by the Copyright Licensing Agency. Enquiries concerning reproduction outside those terms should be sent to the publishers.

Matador
9 Priory Business Park,
Wistow Road, Kibworth Beauchamp,
Leicestershire. LE8 0RX
Tel: 0116 279 2299
Email: books@troubador.co.uk
Web: www.troubador.co.uk/matador
Twitter: @matadorbooks

ISBN 978 1 800460 77 5

British Library Cataloguing in Publication Data.
A catalogue record for this book is available from the British Library.

Printed on FSC accredited paper
Printed and bound in Great Britain by 4edge Limited
Typeset in 11pt Minion Pro by Troubador Publishing Ltd, Leicester, UK

Matador is an imprint of Troubador Publishing Ltd

To The Women Of My Family

Contents

Acknowledgements   ix

Prologue: Luca   xi

PART I

1	Helen	3
2	Alma	8
3	Cinderella Fights	12
4	The People's Queen	24
5	Red Claws and Almond Eyes	37
6	Tanker Blue	47
7	Cold as Stone	53
8	Before Midnight	62

PART II

9	In the Fog	73
10	Green Paws	79
11	The Cut-Out-Heart	88
12	The Little Swallow	100
13	Three Birds	104
14	Drinking Games	113
15	Shards	129
16	Behind the Blue Door	147
17	Half the Story	156

PART III

18	Penises	171
19	Not in this Life	181
20	Morning Glory	190
21	A Man Like My Dad	195
22	Monkey Theories	203
23	Seventeen Pictures	208
24	Running in Circles	218
25	Summer Solstice	222
26	Boxes	233
27	Betrayal	241

PART IV

28	Belated Wishes	255
29	Gone Girl	263
30	Helen Calls	274
31	Like a Fox to a Swallow	277
32	Legacy	294
33	Officially Invited	301
34	Serenity	304
35	A Walk in the Park	308
36	Like A Bird in the Sky	317

Acknowledgements

Writing a novel is a long journey, a full five years in this case. The challenge is that while an author oftentimes is an island, it still takes a village to write a book.

I am therefore forever indebted to my dear friends from across the world who have spent endless hours test reading and discussing the final drafts with me. A heartfelt thanks to Linda Martin, Elisabeth Wellington, Robert Colman, Vivian Zhu and Jennifer Schiffrin. Many times, I felt you had more faith in the story than I had – and everyone who has ever attempted to write a book knows that this is priceless.

I also owe a special thanks to the different teachers and mentors I met along the way – without your insights and encouragement I would never have pulled through. Thank you Julia Cho and the entire team at Hedgebrook for creating such an amazing space for writers, your support on the first chapters was vital to embark on this project. A big thanks also to Rita Banerjee for her relentless on character building and plot structure, to Alexander Chee for the encouragement to keep going after only reading a first wild draft and to Lisa Yarger for giving creative writing a home in Munich.

Last but not least, a big, heartfelt thanks to my writing group, the backbone of my writing life. You have been there from the first page to the very final version, you have been my harshest critics and biggest cheerleaders – and I am forever grateful. I can't wait to read all your wonderful books in the making and look forward to many more fun projects with Elena Kotsiliti, Simone Heller, Sonia Focke, and Moushumi Sen Sharma.

Prologue

Luca

End of August 2001, Vittuone (Milan)

He was found in the early morning hours, his body leaning over the steering wheel, the neck bent sharply, folded like a piece of paper. Two officers, a senior *commissario* and his apprentice, noticed the tyre tracks in the grass on a routine patrol, and then saw the car wreck. A convertible Fiat 1500, wrapped around a tree trunk. The wide *avenidas* of Vittuone, leading towards the city of Milan, were framed by well-trimmed pine trees, with an accurate distance of half a kilometre between them. It was a precise hit and the old tree had given in. Its crown touched the ground.

They officers called for an ambulance and then circled the wreck. The cabin was badly mangled. The apprentice moved closer and finally went down on one knee, to be able to see the man's face in the dim morning light. It was his first time seeing a dead man. The eyes were closed, the lips parted.

"There is almost something peaceful about him," he said to his colleague. He admired the vintage Rolex on the dead man's wrist, resting on the steering wheel, then pushed his hand on his knee to stand up again. He took a deep breath and diverted his gaze for a moment.

It had been a warm summer's night; even now the air was mild with a faint fog lingering over the fields. For a moment, he daydreamed of arriving at a party in such a convertible and with the same watch. Then it struck him that the watch was still ticking, and the thought made his stomach turn. He jerked up and leaned forward.

The *commissario* looked to the other side, ignoring the retching sounds of his colleague.

"What could have gone wrong in a life like that... for the one who had it all?" he whispered to himself. He took off his hat, as if he were in church, then remembered that he was not and put it back on.

They began to take notes of the position of the car, walked back and forth to measure the distance from the road. With the light growing stronger, the birds woke for their morning concert. A flock of swallows rose to the sky.

And while the wailing of the ambulance grew louder, neither of them noticed the vixen and her cub, emerging on the edge of the field. She stopped, the wreck and the men blocking her way. She sat down and blinked, then led her cub back to shelter, forced to try another path.

Part I

1

Helen

4 January 2017, London (United Kingdom)

Helen Kings drove her aching toes deeper into the cap of her high heels, so the pain would distract her from her growling stomach. Over a phone call, she had forgotten to eat before leaving the office. Beer is food, she tried to tell herself, but cold beer on an empty stomach gave her cramps. Actually, nowadays her body punished her for every sip – and accepted milk only lactose-free.

"We got our kids a Labradoodle for Christmas." A shrill woman's voice forced Helen's attention back to the phone screen in front of her nose. After a new log house in the mountains, the screen now showed three perfect children, cuddling a curly little puppy.

"Awww, that is adorable," Helen said, pushing her toes a little harder. The senior partner who had initially agreed to meet Brenda and Mitch, two attorneys from California who brought in lucrative work, suddenly had to prepare for a hearing, and that's where Helen came in. On the bright side, this was not an endless dinner, just drinks.

"It is, isn't it? I mean, sure, he is a handful, but the kids are, they are like, so happy!" Brenda said, drawing out the 'o' in 'so'. "Do you have any pets?"

"No, no time for pets. I have a daughter, but I don't think she's happy…" Helen said, beer on an empty stomach was indeed a bad idea.

After an uneasy pause, Brenda started to giggle hysterically. "Oh my, Helen, you are so funny! And one wouldn't know you have a daughter, look at that flawless figure!"

Mitch dived even deeper into his Foster's Extra Cold. Too many landmines in women-weight-conversations.

"Oh, now I'm flattered." Helen scrambled for the only possible response: "You too!"

"Thanks! But seriously, what is your secret? Superfoods? Workouts?"

"Just no time to eat between work and family…"

Though she was being complimented here, Helen felt her pulse rise. With US colleagues, maintaining professional boundaries was close to impossible. As soon as they sat down, they felt the urge to boast about their husbands, kids and boats, whereas Europeans only looked for a more or less subtle way to mention their diplomas. Brenda had surely spotted that she wasn't wearing a ring.

"Tell me about it! Although it is all a matter of organisation. Me and my husband, we do a lot of home-office. That helps tremendously! Mitch," Brenda tried to loop her colleague back into the conversation, "how do you and your wife manage?"

Mitch then went on a real stretch to make his housewife-working husband arrangement sound modern. Of course he was all for women having a career: "It is just that Suzie really likes children and playing the piano and this is the best way for her to do what she really wants."

Helen let her gaze wander across the room.

The Cittie of Yorke had already been serving drinks to lawyers when Thomas More rose against the king. Its high arched ceiling and dark wooden interiors carried a masculine smell of beer and smoke. To Helen, the pub was basically a forest of dark suits. Even if she went up on her tiptoes, despite the heels, she was still shorter than most people. The artful blonde knot crowning her head gave a few extra inches, but it did not help with the view. Upon passing through, she spotted a few familiar faces. The senior barrister who had been among the first she had worked with at the beginning of her career, another one who had been hitting on her for a while, sending her juicy mails without cc'ing his boss. She always kept a healthy distance to colleagues; anything else would be highly unprofessional.

She gazed along the counter where the barman handed over one pint after the other – and there he was. Out of nowhere. Leaning on the bar, with that smile; that confident, loving smile; and he looked her right in the eye. As if it had only been yesterday that she had found herself in those eyes, and not in a different life. His gaze still tore her shields down like nothing else. She felt an urge to walk over, but she knew he would vanish as soon as she moved.

"Well, I think the most important thing is that everybody is happy, forget stereotypes. Don't you think? Helen?" Brenda looked in the same direction towards the counter and then back at Helen, a bit puzzled by her absent-mindedness.

"Yes, definitely." Helen nodded, trying to cover up her lack of attention with a sympathetic smile. Then Mitch changed topic to their last family vacation to Australia. Brenda frantically agreed that the South especially was *amazing*. Helen had never been to Australia but she assured them that she would go soon. When she glanced over to the counter again, he was gone. The pub suddenly felt like the loneliest place on earth.

"Guys, I will call it a night," she suddenly heard herself say.

"What?" Brenda and Mitch said in unison and disbelief.

"We just got here, like, thirty minutes ago!" Brenda's high-pitched voice rose over the noise of the crowded pub and a few heads turned.

"I know, I know. I'm sorry. My daughter has a test coming up and I need to check on her before bedtime. You know how teenagers are… But for the world I did not want to miss catching up with you guys. It was so great to see you!"

What else could they do but match her toothpaste smile and return her hug? In any case, they were back to their phones before she had even slipped into her coat.

*

As she stepped out from Clapham Common Tube Station, for the first time that evening, she felt the biting cold. City life around High Holborn was such a hustle; it seemed to have no weather. Men wore the same suit all year long. But here in the calm of Zone 2, the January night crept under your coat and into your bones. Her breath rose in the air like dragon's smoke.

Helen turned north. She passed a Starbucks, a Boots, a keymaker in a cramped little booth, and the Sainsbury's with a beggar sitting in the entrance to catch a bit of warmth. Not always the same one, the guild seemed to send them in rolling shifts, alternating between an old man exposing a stub for a foot, and a Romani woman with one of those anaesthetised babies lying lifeless in her lap. One block further down was the local library, a run-down building in some sort of *Hundertwasser* style, with asymmetric windows and round edges, giving that corner the charm of an intellectual outpost. Turning right and off the main road, it was a ten-minute walk to Helen and her daughter's domicile. When people at worked asked their inevitable "Where do you live?" and she said "Clapham Common," people might well imagine her in one of those Victorian mansions stretching out south alongside Clapham Common Park. Where the local butcher had painted tiles and bacon hanging from the ceiling, pretending to be a part of an eighteenth-century Paris, and where the shop next door seemed to survive on selling one bottle of organic cactus tree oil a day. She liked them to think that, and it worked as long as one had no guests to find out they only occupied a small aprtment in the basement and lower ground.

Off the main road, Helen hastened her step and stomped her heels, letting any rapist know what he was up against. These were clearly the wrong shoes for running and the streets lay dead at this hour. Sometimes she faked an important call on the way or even arranged for an actual one with a late-working associate. The houses stood narrow and cramped, but it was still real houses with little front yards. At some point, it had probably been a charming area. Today, most of them had dirty drawn curtains; many even broken windows, and the emergency boards and foils to fill the holes often became permanent. The houses keeping up the spirit belonged to relocation firms which had the funds to renovate. Islands of joy in a desolate sea, bright windows and people dining in the alcoves. She passed in front of a house which had a *Vote Remain on June 23rd!* sign, fixed with a wire to the front gate. The house next to it used a Union Jack as a makeshift curtain. Times were changing.

A good hundred metres further down, Helen was about to step out of a particularly dark patch, where a dead street lantern was matched with two houses with broken windows, when the branches of a bush ahead of her suddenly creaked and rustled. Helen's heart skipped a beat. Whatever this was, it was no more than five metres ahead of her. She wanted to run but stood paralysed instead. Before her adrenalin level had a chance to rise enough to fight back, the culprit stepped out into the open. It was a small red fox; he had probably been hunting for food in rubbish bins. He lowered his head and began to cross the street. Halfway he stopped and locked eyes with Helen. For a few seconds, they stared at each other, both equally tense. She had never seen a fox from so close, with his bushy tail and those piercing yellow eyes, even in the dark. A creature of the wild. Then he disappeared into the hedge on the other side. A dog started barking – maybe he could smell the intruder.

She paced the last metres to her home as fast as she could; enough of the dark and cold. As Helen turned the key, her nose immediately caught the smell of takeaway pizza. For her, the eternal smell of guilt.

2

Alma

4 January 2017, Vittuone (Milan)

The library windows faced the park, but this night in early January was so dark, there might have been no world at all. Ever since Alma Carneggio had moved to Vittuone as a young bride, more than forty years ago, the park had not changed. She knew that close to the window, on the terrace, stood a Venus figurine, carrying an amphora over her shoulder, but it would not spill any water until spring. Next came the boxwoods surrounding the flower beds, and finally the pine trees framing the meadow in the back. But tonight clouds covered the moon; the night swallowed everything. Inside, sitting by a secretary desk in the warm cone of light of a Tiffany lamp, it felt to Alma as if she was the only person awake in the world. Sad and superior at the same time.

In her morning coat and slightly hunched, she shifted the photograph from one hand to the other, in the same rhythm in which she shifted in her armchair. Sitting in the same position was difficult. Her hip would start aching and the pain would move up her spine until it resulted in a massive headache. Finding a bearable position had become the dance of her days. She was terrified of the day when painkillers would no longer take her out of her misery. Even now she barely left the house, if it was not for a doctor's appointment or to renew her perm.

She put the photograph down and inspected the envelope it had come in. Sometimes she carried it with her for a few days. For the pleasure of having a secret, or out of fear. Accepting the letter made her nothing less than a traitor. She felt the softness of its rosé paper and the marks of its journey to her. The upper-left corner of this one was a bit kinked, the sides slightly scuffed. The stamp showed the Tower of London. The return address was always the same. The mother apparently still used her maiden name; the only addition had been a doctorate title many years ago. Every year, she knew what she would find inside. The envelope contained a card and a photograph. Nothing more. The same simple white card with the words 'Thank you' in an elegant black print. This was the seventeenth photograph she held in her hand. The penultimate one. They were not numbered or anything, Alma simply knew. She was sixty-three, so this was the year the girl had turned seventeen.

This one showed the girl in a rain jacket and her blonde hair put back in a ponytail, a backpack over her shoulder. In the background, one could see water, probably the sea. The girl lived in London. That was basically all she knew. Perhaps this one had been taken on a school trip. She looked rather tanned, something she could not have gotten from her mother. And in England, they might need rain jackets even in summer, from what she heard. She looked straight into the camera with a smile that would melt everything. A smile like a resurrection, almost surreal.

Her throat felt dry all of a sudden. The teacup from her afternoon tea was still on her desk; the maids had not yet cleared it up. A lucky oversight. The tea tasted stale, but it calmed down her throat. For distraction and to calm her mind, she lifted the cup into the light. Her late father-in-law had admired Ginoris' porcelain. An Italian family enterprise, just like the Carneggios were. It was one of the classic series with an orange Chinese temple on white porcelain. She had never liked it. Either you go for Italian craftmanship or you want an exotic Asian decor; in which case you get a Chinese one. But who was she to know.

She opened the lower-right drawer in the secretary desk's front. In a place where other women might have kept love letters from a secret admirer, she kept those cards. She spread out all seventeen photographs in front of her, like a game of tarot. In the first photo, the girl was lying in her crib, as adorable as any baby. In the second, she was learning to walk, held by the hands of an invisible adult (the grey pants in the background suggested that it was an old man). In the third, she was sitting next to a sandcastle in a sunhat, lifting a shovel up in the air. In the fourth, she was riding on a pony guided by another invisible adult. There was her first day at school; a proud girl in a British school uniform. From then on she turned more and more into a young lady, standing in a park in front of a flower bed, fully aware of being photographed and wanting to please. Glimpses of a happy life and a mother's pride.

On top of her secretary desk stood a framed photograph, taken on her niece Francesca's wedding, on the terrace of this house. She held the latest photograph of the girl next to it. At that very wedding she had met the English woman; and only this once. A big family affair held on their property. A few days before the big event, Luca had announced that he would bring a girl from university. That had caused quite a stir; the seating order of the banquet had been made weeks ago.

Luca was, of course, not aware of all the effort which goes into such festivities. Men were never aware of these things, for them it was a given that things at home ran smoothly. And it was her fault; she had raised him like that after all. So Alma took full responsibility for this pre-nuptial chaos. They shook their heads and laughed about naughty Luca, always good for a surprise – and arranged a seat for her at the 'remote-family-friends-table', far away from precious Luca. Alma knew a thing or two about etiquette. And in this house, any woman had to make it past her; nobody waltzed in here just like that.

"Don't worry about the English girl," her sister Clara had told her, following her gaze. "Men always go for the exotic thing, but they always come home to eat." It had made her laugh at the time. It was true; even as a toddler, Luca had a thing for blonde women. He could even forget the ice cream in his little hand and his father would pinch his cheek and say: "One day, we will find you a blonde woman for sure." It was not quite what they did in the end.

With a sigh, she put the photographs back into the case and closed the drawer. The tight feeling in her throat would stay for some more days. The feeling of a stone pressing down on her chest was with her almost all year round; probably she should see a cardiologist about it. She leaned back in her armchair and closed her eyes for a moment. Exhausted from the encounter, she fell into a light sleep.

3

Cinderella Fights

4 January 2017, London

"I'm home," Helen shouted from the hallway. No answer, as expected. Peeking inside the living room while stepping out of her shoes, she saw the young lady sitting on the couch. Another episode of *Two and a Half Men* was running. (How many did they make of that?) A pizza carton and a deranged salad bowl (some vitamins at least) were piling up on the coffee table. Emmy was done eating dinner, she sat with her knees pulled up and arms wrapped around them. A common pose these days, as if she had to seek shelter from a world so hostile to all her dreams and hopes.

Helen took off her coat, too tired for an argument but what can you do? She moved her aching toes; the left big toe showed a slight trace of blood. She massaged it carefully; the blood had already dried to a small crust. With a cushioned plaster, it would be fine tomorrow.

Emmy did not look up as she entered. It was tempting to walk right through to the kitchen and make some pasta for herself, as if she had not noticed any disturbance in the force. But simply ignoring the storm until it turned into a hurricane was a dangerous option these days. But a tea, she was entitled to a hot tea before entering the ring, and filled the kettle with some water. Ever since they had returned from the Christmas holidays, they had not spoken a single word. When Emmy had agreed to spend Christmas *and* New Year with her grandparents in Kent, Helen had daydreamed about mother-daughter conversations under the tree, sharing a laugh when thinking of past Christmas Eves. But it turned out that Emmy had simply overlooked the implications. On day two she kicked up a fuss because she was missing out on the shopping trip of a lifetime with her girl pals on Boxing Day and a New Year's sleepover.

"I am never allowed to have any kind of fun in life!" Emmy had yelled at her.

"Life is not all about looks!" Helen had yelled back. "And besides, why can't they wait until you are back for the shopping trip – if they are such *great* friends?" And that was when the door slammed in her face.

On New Year's Eve then, her own mother brought up one of her classics. She pointed at Helen's legs and said, "Are those compression stockings? You are sitting all day. You have to look after your veins! Our family is not blessed with strong ones. You wake up one day and you have bloated legs, full of water! Irreversible!"

Her mother had a wonderful way of making the future look bright. "Mum, forget it. I am not wearing compression stockings every day, how would that look?"

"Life is not all about looks!" came the instant feedback from Emmy, and then: "I won't have that problem. I have my father's legs." The provocation was too obvious to be picked up – and it had been silence ever since.

The kettle clicked, signalling finalisation of its task. Helen watched the teabag infusing the water with auburn swathes, then she gathered some strength and sat down next to the ball of fury. "Okay, so what is it that makes you look like the world has come to an end?"

"The one thing I know is that you would not understand!" Emmy snapped back. A poster came to mind which Helen passed every morning in the Tube station. It showed a distressed mother in a room which looked like an exploded toy factory. The caption said: *Parenting. Often annoying. Always important*, and then it gave the number of a hotline. Maybe she would be their next customer. She inhaled deeply and said, "Try me, I'll make an effort."

Emmy leaned forward a bit and put both feet on the ground. A bit hunched still as she was sitting on her hands, but lowering the defences, a good sign to start with.

"Well, thanks to you, I will look like a complete idiot on Ali-Saa's birthday party. That is established now, and I'm better off not going then!" Emmy hissed.

Oh well, at least this was an old and familiar enemy, a battle often fought. Behind the most recent drama, Helen had already suspected a group of girls in Emmy's class, and especially a style guru named Ali-Saa (not just Alicia, as if the name itself were a trademark). Designer brands were the talk of the day, favourite pullovers suddenly became impossible to wear, and the beauty products in the bathroom had tripled over the last months. All while her pocket money had stayed the same. Emmy had always been astonishingly calm and sensible for her age. The one that steered away from girl fights at school and understood that one ice cream a day was enough – wise like a tiny adult. These tantrums were a whole new side to her.

"And why do you think you will look like a complete idiot?" Helen decided to play along and ask.

"Ali-Saa and Sadie went out shoe shopping with their mums and they got real Louboutins! And guess what: there was no discussion at all, because *their* mums wear them too…"

Helen had gone to great lengths to get Emmy into one of the good schools on the north side of Clapham Common Park. The school fees ate up elusive holidays and a better car as she did not want to sit her baby in a public school between teenage pregnancies and rampant alcoholism. And now her schoolmates were picked up by mums in SUVs and whisked off to private villas in the Seychelles for holidays, as modestly shared on Facebook or Instagram. It had been years since Emmy had brought friends home and Helen had a suspicion as to why.

"Well, if they think it is appropriate to spend such a fortune on something which at the end of the day is also made in China…"

"Oh, Mum, no, they are not! They are real and they will wear them forever. Why are you saying that if you don't even know a thing about fashion?"

"What I mean is that in the end, the price is out of proportion to what it is..." Helen tried again, but Emmy was all fired up tonight.

"It is not just the shoes! They go to a professional hairdresser the morning before, and I have seen the pictures and it looks damn cool. That birthday party will happen only once, and I will look like a stupid kid next to the others – and why is that? Because you just don't get it! You are saying, one Saturday afternoon is enough for such a stupid thing as shoe shopping, and you won't give me the money to look on my own, and if we don't find anything that day you would just get me the second best stupid shoes that are right there – you have done this before! And that is why I always look like a weirdo next to the other girls. And I will never get a professional hairdresser or make-up in my life because you say it is a worrying trend if young girls only care about their looks. But mu-um, it is fun to look good... and it is not a bad thing. Not everybody who looks good immediately turns stupid..." Then she finally had to breathe and the breathing almost turned into a sob. It was heartbreaking, actually. At that age, it sometimes feels as if your whole life depends on a single party. And if it feels that way, it is somewhat true.

Helen remembered how she had once missed a birthday party because she had the flu – and as she got back on her feet, her crush was dating another girl and her best friend was no longer a virgin. Emmy was still sitting strangely on her hands, rocking her body back and forth; she really seemed to be in great distress.

"I want you to be happy, of course." Helen began her detour. " ...I think all I meant is that I do not think one should exactly copy the lives of girls like *Ali-Saa* and Sadie. It is just *one* party. Imagine all the things you could buy for that money, like, for example..." Helen was about to list some activities for the months between college and university, hoping to get to the topic of 'university' eventually, but she did not get that far.

"But I don't want *all the things I could buy for that money*! My feet are not growing anymore. I had good grades all year and I swear I would wear these shoes for the rest of my life and never ask for any others!"

"Yes, well ..." Helen tried again. It was not just a matter of principle. Especially after Christmas, their budget was a bit too tight to buy another round of gifts.

"I know they are very expensive but look, I said I would pay half the price of my savings, and I don't want any birthday gifts this year. I also care less about the hairdresser so we don't have to do that... Please, Mum!"

She probably really meant it; this had been going on for weeks. And to be fair, Emmy had never been the kind of kid that would nag all the time for more of this or more of that. Her own mother had driven her mad at that age, with her own striking logic: *If orthopaedic shoes are the best, why not start with them when you are young instead of waiting until your feet are ruined by the fancy ones?* How she had longed to ruin her feet with fanciness, although in her day, that would have been Adidas sneakers (with a much too thin sole, not good for the joints) and not those absurd high heels for several hundred pounds. Those were bone-breakers indeed!

"I guess I am just generally wondering whether people who care that much about good looks can make good friends..."

"Oh my God, Mum! Have you ever been to a party? It is almost like you don't want me to have friends!"

"Of course I have," Helen felt slightly offended, "but seriously, you don't want to be loved for your shoes..."

"It is fun to look good. You just know nothing about that! I am seventeen and I am the only one who has never been dating anyone! And why is that? Because you keep me home all the time. But Mu-um, I will be careful, I won't end up in the same mess as you..." Then Emmy stopped herself. For a second it looked as if she would cover her mouth with her hands. But then she kept sitting on them and the fighting spirit returned to her eyes.

Helen sighed. Their budget really was tight but there was a way she could make this work. Emmy should not feel like the Cinderella among her friends, having to pray for a miracle to be able to go to the ball. Helen took a deep breath.

"Look, that is not very fair, it is really not that I'm against happiness... I just want you to understand that shopping is not a life and death matter. Shoes are a fun thing, nothing more, nothing less. But maybe we can go this Saturday and take a look at the shoes you want, but we have to take a realistic look at what we can afford. We are simply not as well off as…"

But Emmy cut into her speech: "Really? This Saturday? Promise?"

"Yes, promise, but only this Saturday! You can make a pre-selection, and then we can take a look… how does that sound?"

"Okay, cool!" Emmy said and got up right away, probably to chat with her girl pals in her room.

"Hey, if you have to order junk food, you can at least clear up this mess," Helen shouted after her, frustrated as she had expected some excitement, at least a grateful smile for the concession made. Emmy gave her a strange look, then she awkwardly walked around the table again, picking up the rubbish with her back to Helen – instead of just reaching for it from the other side. But when she moved on to the kitchen, Helen nonetheless caught a glance of her hands. Where yesterday there had been short nails with transparent lacquer, there were now long red claws, with a small rhinestone embedded in the upper corner of each nail. She had never allowed any flashy nail polish – and school regulations were on her side. Helen's heart started pounding so wildly, she could feel it up in her throat. The spectrum of her imagination ran from *They have just stayed at Ali-Saa's and had their nails done by an older cousin or so* up to *She is smoking marijuana and got involved with a cheap nail spa which is actually a front for human trafficking.*

Was she now supposed to yell at her? Ask her where the hell she had been? Only to give Emmy a chance to respond that she was almost eighteen and her life none of her business? *Well, you can forget about that, young lady*, Helen thought, her initial panic giving way to anger.

"Wonderful little bit of artwork you've got there. You know, when I was sixteen, I was crazy about manicures, until I found they destroy the structure of your nails with all the chemical stuff," she said calmly, not taking her eyes off the TV. Emmy stared at her for five seconds, then she stormed down the stairs and banged the door to her room behind her.

Great, the shoe wars had just escalated to a new level. Whenever there was a chance for a reconciliation, things only seemed to get worse. She looked at the teacup in her hand. She remembered exactly how she had bought these cups together with Emmy from a Japanese couple who imported porcelain and sold it on Spitalfields Market. Emmy had loved the pink cherry blossoms and could not get over the fact that there was no handle. She had pushed her baby through all the beautiful parts of London – the East End or Brixton – where people dressed in *sarees* and *kurtas*, the air ripe with smells of spices and incense. It was the compensation for all the travelling she had wanted to do but could no longer afford. If one would ask Emmy now what she would think about spending a weekend with her mum at a flea market, well, the answer would be all too clear. When had this cute little girl turned into an angry woman with red claws?

She stretched out on the sofa and closed her eyes for a moment. When she opened them again, she saw on the red blinking light of the answering machine. Of course, she had not called her mother to confirm their safe arrival after the holidays. And now a little guilt trip had been recorded for her. This was finally too much; she deserved a break.

*

The bathroom downstairs was a tiny windowless room, so damp that it required regular checks for black fungus. Anything but glamorous; but after a troubled day, the best way to retreat from the world. She took off her clothes and let them form a pile around her feet. While the hot water rose and steam began to fill the room, she inspected herself in the mirror. Her hair used to be naturally blonde, all those peroxide girls used to envy her for that. But over the last year, even in this bad light, she found some silver streaks. And her face seemed to always look so tired, even after a week of holidays. She placed her hands on her hips and pinched the soft white flesh. At least her hip size had not really increased. She cupped her breasts with both hands and lifted them up, but the result did not impress. Her breasts were so small, she would look terrible with a big bum. Her figure only worked as long as she kept it lean.

Emmy was probably right about her father's legs. She had not gotten her looks from her mum. To begin with, Emmy never looked as pale as her mother. Even in winter she had a healthy golden tan, as if a bit of Italian sun had been saved forver under her skin. She had Helen's green eyes, but she had been spared Helen's hawk nose, although Luca loved to run his finger over it and called her 'Birdie'. And unlike her slender mum, as soon as she turned fifteen, she began to fill in. For her age, she had almost motherly breasts and full hips, which made her anxious about her weight. A child with the curves of a woman. Helen sometimes saw old men turn for her in the bus. Perverts everywhere.

When she looked at her baby now, she could easily see the one woman she longed to forget. That overflowing femininity, the *Madonna*-like face. A younger version of the woman who had refused to shake her hand, the one time she had visited their estate. The hot water steamed over the cold glass and her image vanished.

"You look as beautiful as always, Dulcinea," he whispered in her ear. She could immediately smell him. The remainder of his aftershave, not at all fresh and yet so sexy. He always smelled like that when they returned home after a long night. "Don't let these women's magazines get to you..." She turned and saw him sitting on the edge of the tub. In boxers and a white T-shirt, a streak of his full brown hair hanging in his face.

"You charmer... no one gets any younger. Only you never seem to change..." Helen chuckled and tested the water temperature with the tip of her toes, dangling her leg right next to him.

"To me, there is no change... look at these perfect thighs. Your mother is crazy..." and with a boyish gesture he pushed his hair back. Maybe her leg made him nervous.

Helen laughed and switched off the tap. She poured some jasmine foam bath into the water, then lit two candles and switched off the light. The guttering flames reflected from the tiles. He just sat and watched her every move. In their intimate moments, they had always been good at talking. Because it felt so safe. "You know, the real question is: why can't I enjoy a night in the pub, like the rest of London...?" she said, and let her body sink into the water. His gaze followed her, as if she were some desirable treat. "Hey, eyes here, I have asked you a question," she teased him. This was so much more fun than taking a quick shower!

He laughed: "Honestly, Dulcinea, I would not have lasted a minute in that place... Stuffed shirts everywhere... we always found a way to avoid these people, remember?" The candlelight made his tanned skin look even more desirable.

"That is true. *You* did, to be precise..." He had an amazing talent for disentangling the truly fun people from the Brendas and Mitches of this world. A city like Geneva was packed with the ultra-rich, tired expats and diplomats, all roaming the streets for excess. He just laughed right in their faces when they started to talk about their boats and houses all over the world. And with his boyish charms, nobody ever got angry. He loved to sit by the bar and chat with the barman about the music that was playing or all the types of whisky that there are in the world. Other people would join them, and suddenly there was a plan as to how to make this evening memorable.

She only needed to look at him, and she was back in her heyday, feeling the exhilaration and the sensual body of her early twenties again. "Remember the night we met a songwriter who was in the middle of a recording? How we all went back to the studio and listened to a jam session? Or that night we ran into a group of ballet dancers and followed them to the after-party of the premiere?" He smiled; she could see on his face that he also remembered every minute of it. The warmth of the water embraced her body up to her neck and she finally felt her stiff muscles let go. He sat down on the edge of the tub and dropped his hand down into the water, close to her hip.

"That Azerbaijany painter caused me a few sleepless nights, though, now I can admit it... when she kept inviting you to her *atelier* and all that... with those high Russian cheekbones and her smouldering looks. The only talent I could display was accurate law recitals..."

"Oh, come on, you know I only had eyes for you..." And that was true. In all this carnival which evolved so naturally around him, he was her man. He made sure that she sat or stood close to him; he kept a hand on her leg, drew her close for a kiss or whispered something in her ear, so that everybody knew she was his girl. And as in her previous life, she had been the nerd in her class; she could not believe her luck.

Although she was coming close to the blonde, skinny stereotype of an attractive woman, her success in dating had not been overwhelming. Her long hair over the fragile shoulders and the piercing green eyes easily attracted prey, but the fish did not stay in the net. There was something about her dry sense of humour and her bluntness. *You don't talk like women usually do*! was never a compliment but the beginning of the end.

He moved his hand in the water; the waves he created swept gently over her shoulders. He had chatted her up as she waited for the tram. A tipsy blonde elf, a little lost for direction after a 'pub orientation' by the law faculty. She always thought that she must have looked a lot more like a party girl than she actually was that night. And then he did not ask for her number but just stepped into the next tram. When a few nights later, miraculously, they ended up in the same bar, she knew he was her fate.

"And you have ruined me for other men. Look at the guys you meet at those after-work drinks. Any date is destined to bore me to death!" Now she could see him blush, even in candlelight.

"I am not taking any responsibility for that…" With his other hand, he pushed another streak of hair out of his face before he took off his shirt. She let her feet play with the foam.

"No, you don't have to… It is just that there is no real passion here… *We should not rush into this… I am the type of guy who needs time for his friends*… always seeking distance and control before things even get started…"

Luca laughed, throwing his neck back. "Oh, *Madonna*, I can totally hear them say that… It sounds terrible." From the first day, he had been so open about being attracted to her, without playing any games or protecting his ego in the slightest. He was that kind of guy. He'd jump for joy when something excited him, and by the same measure, his face showed when he got hurt – or bored. He never pretended to not care and was not beneath telling her with an open look, *I've missed you!* when she came back from the toilet.

And although he was passionate, he never followed any of the classic dating paradigms. There were no candlelit dinners, no Valentine's gifts, no 'firsts' of any kind. Yet being with him was always romantic. For the first time, she had experienced this deep urge to be around someone to feel truly alive.

"I wish I would have cared for you better. Ironic, huh, that it is me thinking that… I should have listened better when you talked about your family…" when they lay in the dark, he had sometimes started talking. *My grandfather was a success, my father an even bigger success. What when I am first to fail? What am I good for then…?*

This had been their common cord; what held them together was more than sex and going out: it was the desire to breathe and break free from home, to find their true devotion in life. His life dreams were always bordering on the fantastic. Living in Manhattan and trading in art, sailing around the world, leading a basic life in a hut in the Pyrenees with a flock of sheep. It was a fun game. She knew, he loved her for listening and building on each vision, whatever it was. At that age, she could see herself in all of this – if she were with him. It did not have to be a house with kids right away. But at some point, it would end there, somehow.

It was several months into their relationship when it dawned on her that he could in principle easily fill a dinner conversation with his own family's houses, boats and planes. His apartment was so tiny and always such a mess, he never wore designer clothes, or even ironed clothes for that matter. It was worn-out jeans and plain white T-shirt every day.

"Dulcinea, I loved my parents, and you know that. I've told you so often…" he always used the same staple comment to end the discussion. His look was withdrawn now, his hand out of the water. This mother who only ever badgered him as to whether he would come home and whether he was going out with someone. Only to be able to interfere right in time, of course, if it were someone inappropriate. How selfish could one be? Wasn't all this pressure and hypocrisy exactly what he was running from?

When she looked up again, he was gone.

Oh well, she was obviously in a gloomy mood today. First, she ditched a pub night, then she chased away her daughter and now the lover by talking parents. On other nights, she easily seduced him to climb into the hot water with her. Nobody puts up candles to fight. She leaned back and closed her eyes, tried to focus on the smell of jasmine, tenderly pressed her hand between her legs, but it turned into nothing more than a sterile massage. The moment had passed.

When the water started to get cold, she twisted the drainage plug with her feet and listened to the gurgling sound of the water.

4

The People's Queen

5 January 2017, Vittuone (Milan)

When Alma opened her eyes again, first the shape of the fountain and then the pine trees became visible. Every morning, the world re-emerged in a divine transition, not to be noticed by mankind. Even when she stayed awake and stared into the park like a spectator at a movie screen, she could never pinpoint the exact moment of change. The world suddenly returned and she could not tell whether it had just happened now or a moment ago. She switched off the desk lamp; a faint grey light filled the library. Enough to find one's way but not enough to keep a depressed soul from suicide.

It was always quiet out here. Over the summer, a flock of swallows populated the park, lending it some song and motion, but in winter they moved south. Vittuone had once been a village with cows and sheep surrounding the estate. Now it had grown into a satellite town of Milan, but they were still far from the daily commotion of city life. Only on Sundays, people took their dogs for a longer walk and appeared alongside the park. Some tried to peek through the hedge.

Alma looked at the fountain. In winter, the Venus figurine was covered by a wooden *casquette*. One winter, the frost had been so strong that it had bitten off one of her arms. They only noticed it when they removed the cover in spring. Ever since, Alma always had to think about that open wound on the figurine's shoulder, whenever she looked at the *casquette*, hoping for the other arm to still be there. Her late father-in-law had bought the estate. Built in the seventeenth century, it had been a summer house of a branch of the Medici family. Like her husband, he was never interested in mingling with the high society of Milan; he wanted to be close to the main factory plant near Vittuone, which made them one of the biggest employers in the area. She had in the past overheard people calling their estate the 'Castle of Vittuone'.

With a suppressed moan, Alma got up from her chair. Her hip had gotten stiff during her nap. The oriental carpet in the centre of the room had a golden-blue pattern in the middle and a frame in royal blue. She often paced along that border, keeping her feet on the blue frame, as if it were the cloister of a monastery. After four rounds, she paused and held on to the back of the armchair, carefully lifting up one knee, and then the other. An exercise recommended by her sister Clara. Clara was five years her senior and insisted that it would just take some gymnastics, with other boring old people, and her hip would be fine. "You just need more body strength! You are sitting there like the tower on Piazza dei Miracoli!" she kept saying. But Alma refused to join senior Pilates; she did not feel up to it.

In the past, she and Clara used to agree on all matters. Whether something was appropriate or scandalous, to be taken seriously or to be discarded, she could always bank on Clara. But since Clara's husband had died two years ago, things had changed. Her sister had taken to travelling the world on all kinds of cruise ships and organised bus tours. A cousin once said to her that Clara had started booking before the coffin was closed. But Clara gave nothing to such tittle-tattle. "Life is too short to care about people's talk," she would tell Alma. From her trips, she sent all sorts of weird stuff to her sister. The last postcard came from Greece; Athens, to be precise. Alma had put it up on her desk. It showed some sort of clichéd oil painting of Dionysus, surrounded by young women in an orgy, feeding him grapes. The faces of the women were cut out of the board and all the old ladies of the bus tour peaked through from behind, laughing with their fake teeth. Clara of all people, who had claimed all her life that all it takes for happiness is 'Home Sweet Home'. Tourism was a shallow feature of modern life, almost like something that had to be confessed in church. Clara, who had certainly always been a little jealous of all the 'home' with which Alma was surrounded.

Her eyes wandered back to the family photograph on her secretary desk. Even on such an official occasion, Luca always managed to look dishevelled. It made her smile, how even a perfectly ironed shirt would look messy on him, one corner hanging out of the belt. It was a classic, her running after him in the morning because his shirt was tagging out of his pants or because he had chosen one with stains. And he would change or get things in order, half annoyed, half grateful, planting a kiss on her forehead. On her husband, a suit always looked like a second skin.

He had introduced the English girl at the reception, like any other friend he had ever brought home. She remembered her blonde hair, the sharp nose and the bony figure. They had only one brief conversation, about an internship in New York or something. The things these modern girls talked about. There was something disturbing about the girl's friendliness, a bit like that of an atheist towards the Pope: polite and respectful but not bothered by their paradigms at all.

Clara did not know about the letters and the English girl. Only her and di Marco, the family lawyer, knew. The letter ritual had started soon after Luca had passed away. All she wanted was to leave her skin and disappear – and could not. In those days, she had stopped sleeping, and whenever Giacomo worked late, she would sit by the kitchen window and gaze over to the office building, hoping for the lights to go off. And one night in early January, seventeen years ago, the lights did not go off, but the motion sensors in the courtyard suddenly came to life. Tense and exhausted from hours of waiting she had jumped off her chair and rushed into the yard. So unrestrained, it was almost childish. The grey stone and the white sycamore tree reflected the light so strongly that she was almost blind for a moment. And when she stood in the spotlight, her hair dishevelled, she noticed to her embarrassment that it was not her husband who had left the office, but Dottore di Marco, her husband's confidant. His flawless designer suit and the well-trimmed hair made her look even more like a mad woman, the cold wind roughing through her hair.

"Oh, I thought you were… I'm sorry…" and she had already turned around when she suddenly heard his footsteps come back over the gravel.

"You might want to have this…" and without any further explanation, he handed her an envelope in light rosé, then turned on his heels and got into his car. The gate opened and he disappeared into the dark. The following year, she had stayed posted in early January as a matter of hope. And as the motion sensors came on, she saw di Marco's gaze wander towards the kitchen and she raced to the back door. There was never enough time for an awkward silence he had already turned on his heel and the lights of his car flashed up, signalling that he had unlocked it.

When she looked up and outside the window again, the morning light had vanished. It was as bright as it would get on this winter's day. The silence of the morning was disrupted by a rustling sound, as if someone was walking through autumn leaves. It was car tyres making their way through the gravel in the front yard. Soon she heard distant chatter across the foyer, followed by a clanking of plates and cups in the kitchen – the maids were making breakfast. The ultimate sign that she had survived another night.

*

The library was in the east wing of the estate; the house framed the park in an L-shape with its eastern and northern wing. To get to the kitchen, she passed through the gallery and the entrance hall with the big fireplace which Giacomo's family liked to call the *Foyer*. They did not heat these halls with their high stone walls in winter, and the fire had not been lit in more than two decades. Alma hurdled through them before the cold could creep into her bones. When she entered the kitchen, Flavia was about to remove the night's shroud from the oven, and Maria was clearing out the dishwasher. It was warmer in here than in the library and it smelled of coffee. Alma felt her shoulders relax.

"*Buongiorno, signora*, did you sleep well?" Flavia said, moving back and forth between worktop and table, always doing at least two things at once.

"Of course, Flavia, I hope the same is true for you," she responded as cheerfully as possible.

Flavia was the one that nowadays tended to all the needs of this house. Often at her own discretion, but she knew her place in this house. Maria was Flavia's first cousin and ten years her senior. At sixty-two years of age, she was a year younger than Alma, but she could easily be taken for seventy. Hard work and obedience had hunched her back, her face was wrinkled, the hair grey already, and a pair of thick glasses sat on her nose. The cousins had been hired together, and ever since, Alma had shaken her head at how different they were. When Alma entered the kitchen, Maria would not just turn her head; her whole body would make a slow turn, to verify who had come in – although it had to be Alma. Only then would she say: "*Buongiorno, Signora* Alma," with a little bow, then slowly dive back into the dishwasher. Her husband had complained so many times: "I go to work and she is about to vacuum the staircase. I come back and she is still trying to disentangle the cable."

Their breakfasts had started one winter, when the nights were long and dark. Her feet had carried her towards the light, and she had sat down by the small kitchen table, as if she had never sat anywhere else. At first, Flavia and Maria had barely dared to move, unaware of the protocol for this situation. But Alma pretended to not notice any of that. She picked up the newspaper from the serving cart – which was ready to be wheeled out to her breakfast table in the dining room – and started reading to them, whatever she came across. And they soon got used to her presence and the breakfast with her became part of their routine.

Her husband did not grow tired of joking that she had turned into some sort of *people's queen*. It had been a stern principle of the Carneggio household to take all meals in the dining room, and staff were only addressed formally. Conversations with them were about orders or their shortcomings. (*How does one not see the difference between a soup and a dessert spoon? If I don't do everything by myself...*)

Alma kept one hand around her coffee cup, just to feel its warmth.

"Oh, Jesus," she said, without looking up from the paper. "Still every day refugees drown in the Mediterranean... such a shame. Where shall this end?"

"Yes, all these poor people, where do they want to go?" Maria said, but nobody had an answer for her so she bit into her *cornetti*.

But what Alma enjoyed most was not the papers but the maids lamenting about their husbands. Maria's husband had a drinking problem and kept losing his job, Flavia's husband claimed to have a back problem and stayed on the sofa all day, same as her two sons. And the best part: they were men, you could do nothing about it. Of course, Alma never shared a single thought about Giacomo Carneggio; she knew where to draw the line.

At 7.30am, the trio was interrupted by the brief appearance of the man of the house. When he was not travelling for business, he passed through the kitchen at exactly this minute, to take the back door to the office building. He was not a breakfast man; as he liked to say, he needed to get things done to start the day. Not waste time by sitting around with his wife. And as every other morning, Maria jumped from her chair, offered her seat and an *espresso* or a piece of *patisserie*. God knows why she did that; he rejected the offer every single time. Today, he was wearing a dark grey suit, a tie stuffed in the inner pocket of the jacket. There was a reminder for Alma: "Good morning, ladies! We have the dinner at the Marchesas' tonight. I hope I won't be running late. The distributor from Indonesia is stopping by this afternoon. We leave here by six!"

And before she could even nod, he was out of the door. She would not see him again before six. "The biggest luxury is to have lunch at home," her late father-in-law used to say. But that phrase had lost all meaning. He preferred that Flavia bring his lunch to his desk, and she had stopped complaining about this more than a decade ago.

As if the maids felt caught, this brief trespass usually marked the end of their breakfast. Flavia placed her cup on her plate and as soon as she got up, Maria would follow. They would resume their chores and Alma would be on her own again. Sometimes, she started reading another article, then they would be too polite to leave right away. But this never got her more than a few more minutes of company. Flavia was already getting a mop and a bucket out of the cupboard, when Alma suddenly had an idea: "Flavia, I will need you today, because of the dinner."

"Of course, *Signora* Alma," Flavia said, and returned mop and bucket obediently. The house-cleaning could wait; what was there to clean anyway, with only Alma being around?

*

The dressing room was adjacent to their bedroom; her mother-in-law had it built. Two of its walls were covered by majestic cupboards made of dark oak; the third side had a large dressing table of the same wood with an oval mirror on top.

"If I may ask, what exactly is the occasion this time, *Signora* Alma?" Flavia asked, pulling the curtains aside. The sunlight revealed a faint layer of dust on the mirror.

"The usual couples' dinner with the Club Unione people. But mind you, the fact that it is private does not mean that it won't turn into a fashion show... Sara Picone will certainly parade the latest Bulgari. Can it get anymore nouveau riche?" Alma rolled her eyes. "My mother-in-law would have been appalled... I am glad I had such a good teacher in her."

Her mother-in-law had been of aristocratic blood. Not necessarily rich, but well revised in noble decorum. She would never have gone downtown to shop for a dress; that was for the plebs to do. She had a tailor come in and got all her clothes made according to her wishes. Alma gladly followed in this tradition; nothing rendered her more insecure than those elegant boutiques. While Alma took a seat in front of the mirror, Flavia opened the wooden cupboard doors for them to take a look at Alma's *garderobe*. A damp smell of mothballs instantly filled the room.

She watched Flavia walk up and down the coat rack, along the dresses of her life. To the very left was a garment bag which still contained her wedding dress. She had kept it to pass on to a daughter at some point. Then came a long rack of dresses in pastel colours, as worn by young women. Only at the right end were the few dresses she would fit into these days, all kept in rather dark autumnal colours.

Appropriate for her age, and hiding that she had filled in around the hips, as she had a hard time to move.

"Times are changing, Flavia, I can assure you of that. Even the people at Unione are no longer the same…" Flavia now inspected the dresses on the far right.

Alma's late father-in-law had managed to get accepted into Club Unione of Milan, a traditionalist social club founded by influential Italian aristocracy, with names like Sforza, Borromeo or Visconti on the members' list. Her father in-law was no Visconti, but he was much recognised for his entrepreneurial skills. Turning a small paper mill into a global brand for luxury paper, he had become a much respected man in the region.

"I still remember the one time he sat next to Count Gaddo della Gherardesca who had just been on the cover of the latest *Capital*. Everybody came to congratulate him, and you know what the guy said? 'Well, my friends,' he said, 'this is not much of a thing for someone whose family has already been mentioned in Dante's *Divine Comedy*…'" Alma laughed and placed her hand gracefully on her chest. Back then she had looked up '*Gherardesca*' as well as '*Dante*' in the library. And she could be sure it would be the same for Flavia.

"Here in Italy, we still believe in tradition. All the power in this country has been vested in a few honourable families, for centuries. The names at the top of the list never change. They are the backbone of this country…" Alma pontificated, a speech she had heard a hundred times from her husband. Women were not eligible as members and only rarely invited for social occasions – to her relief. But her husband disappeared regularly to the Club with his father, attending lectures and salons, making the connections to foster their wealth while she stayed at home. Now, these people were the only social contacts they had left.

"What about this one?" Flavia asked, pulling out a knee-long dress in navy blue.

"Probably the only one that still fits!" Alma sighed.

"Don't be too hard on yourself, *Signora* Alma. You haven't changed that much…" Flavia always tried to be kind, but she had no idea what she was up against.

"You should see the other women at those dinners! The women especially have changed so much. Nowadays you have to look thirty-five forever. Sara Picone and Chiara Marchesa may look young from behind, but you should see their tired eyes in their ironed faces. Sofia Casadei seems to be more of a traditional woman… though her lips also look a bit unnatural lately…"

Flavia took the dress from the hanger. Her hands were dry and wrinkled. When closing it on her back, Alma felt her calloused fingertips through the silk. A sensation, long forgotten yet burnt into her soul. The hands of her mother had felt the same, touching the white silk of her wedding dress.

Alma looked at herself in the mirror. The dress was a little tight but it was still acceptable; she could still breathe while sitting down. Flavia made her try.

"My mother was a simple woman, you know," she heard herself say to Flavia. "'*If you only pray enough, God will send you a husband,*' she used to say, no need for sinful thoughts in all these bars and cafés. And you know what, she had been right: God delivered my husband to the doorstep."

"You were a very lucky woman indeed," Flavia said, without looking up from the dress, pulling it into shape and checking for stains.

Alma was tempted to reiterate how she had met Giacomo, yet even she knew that Flavia had heard the story a hundred times. The Carneggio family had been to a wedding of distant relatives on a Saturday, and on Sunday, they went to the same service that Alma and her family attended every week. Giacomo spent the Holy Mass doing what most of the guys did: standing outside the church and smoking. Alma sat on the church stairs to look after her little cousin who had no longer been able to sit still. Giacomo was twenty-five back then and she was nineteen.

"I think we are good here for now, Flavia… I will call you if I need help getting dressed later…"

"Very well, *Signora* Alma," Flavia said, and retreated, and Alma could not help feeling that Flavia's light step indicated relief.

*

When she woke from her nap, Alma touched her neck, then carefully turned her head from side to side. It felt tense but the tension did not seem to be growing into a full-blown migraine today. With another yellow pill and a bit of luck, it would stay like that and she would be able to make it through the dinner. So often she had to cancel invitations at the last moment, because she could not risk breaking down in front of everyone and embarrassing her husband. Giacomo almost expected her to appear in her bathrobe at the top of the stairs, to tell him he would have to go without her.

It was past four o'clock, so she had a bit more than an hour left to get ready. Upstairs in the dressing room, Flavia had laid out her entire outfit for her. Her shoulder wasn't too bad, either; she could even reach behind with the hairspray today, so she sent Flavia back down.

When she was finished, she checked her appearance in the mirror. She had managed bravely to hold her act together, but now her nerves flared up. She felt her neck muscles harden again and the nausea came back, together with a feeling of pressure on her stomach. This feeling, as if you have to vomit the next minute, accompanied most of her outings. She touched her hair and applied some more spray. Her *coiffeur* used to say, *You look like a second Sophia Loren.* Her perm in hazelnut-gold framed her face in a similar way. Her fur *stola* would also have suited the Loren. She loved to run her hand through it and watch its glowing effect, because the underfur was a lighter brown. Maybe she should have held her breath; the hairspray seemed to make her feel even more nauseous. She held on to the wood of the dressing table and took a few deep breaths. In days gone by, her mother- and grandmother-in-law had sat here; the thought used to give her strength to face whatever evening lay ahead of her. Though lately, she felt, she had let all of them down.

She was about to get up, when downstairs the phone rang. That was a rare occasion in this house; most calls went straight to the office – or to her husband's cell phone for that matter. Giacomo had suggested many times putting a modern system in place, with a portable phone in every room. But what was the point? So she could speak to Clara from every room in this house?

Alma heard Maria's heavy footsteps coming closer. "*Signora* Alma, the phone, it is for you!" she shouted from the door. Lately, she often spoke in a much-too-loud voice for standing so close. Maybe she was getting a little hard of hearing.

"Who is it?" Alma whispered in a conspiratorial tone, waving her in, hoping that Maria would get the hint.

"It is a *signora* Ana for you," Maria shouted back, and now one could hardly yell, *Tell her I am not home!* in response. Alma sighed and took the phone.

"Carneggio residence."

"*Signora* Alma, is that you?" an energetic young voice came from the other end. It sounded familiar but Alma could not place it. "It is me, Ana? From the Trustee Board of the Pinacoteca di Brera?"

Alma's mind was searching through all the faces she knew, from fundraising dinners and boring receptions, but she could not recall an Ana that would have a reason to be so informal with her.

"You may remember me from the last meeting on funding the midsummer events. I was in charge of the marketing committee back then…"

A vague image came to mind – a woman in her early fifties, wearing some of those extravagant designer glasses, the hair coloured aubergine and the clothes at least one size too small. At least. Her breasts seemed to fight against the blouse and burst into a fleshy cleavage; embarrassing.

"Yes, now I remember… How can I help?" Alma tried the most sympathetic voice she could master, while massaging her acidic stomach.

"Ah, wonderful… and my apologies, I must have taken you by surprise. It is not that we usually chat over the phone, right? You see, since this year I'm in charge of fundraising… And we are currently finalising our schedule for this year. I saw that you were a regular sponsor of these events. We haven't seen you around for a while and were wondering whether you would still enjoy to take part?"

Indeed, they had sponsored the art museum for the past few years.

What her husband liked most about the Pinacoteca was that they displayed a board listing the sponsors in the entry hall all year round. Other than that, he had little interest in art in general and receptions or *vernissages* in particular. Few husbands had; it was mostly the wives attending. And there were never any chairs to sit on. Clearly, if they want old money, they should think about that.

"This is very kind of you, to think of us," she began. "Indeed, my husband always stresses that families like ours have a social responsibility, so I will consult with him regarding your kind request…"

"Well, I am happy to send you the brochure on what we have planned for the next year…" the voice continued with unbroken enthusiasm.

"As I said, this is a decision on a financial matter and it therefore rests solely with my husband. And by the way, I am no longer of the age to stand at endless *vernissages* with long speeches."

"Oh, *signora*, I remember you. You are not that old, are you? How old are you?" the voice continued cheerfully.

Was this woman insane? Alma punished this comment with silence. There was a nervous hum on the other side; obviously, someone was looking for a way to gain sympathy points. Alma sat up straight and pressed two fingers down on what she believed to be her liver; sometimes it helped.

"I don't know if I told you already, but I knew your son, like, I met him several times…"

Alma froze and let go of whatever organ she was squeezing there. "What? How? Are you sure you are not confusing him with someone else?"

"But no, Luca Carneggio was a familiar face in the Pinacoteca… he used to come to one of my workshops… I am so sorry for your loss. It is always the best who leave us too early…"

"When? How old was he, when was that?" Alma was trying to make sense of what she heard. The boy had lived in her own house all his life and she had not known that? Or was this woman just making it up?

"Like, some twenty years ago… I was giving weekend classes, in the *atelier* of a friend at the time… I hung a note in the Pinacoteca and a few people always signed up. He was a surprise, though… mostly it was ladies in some sort of midlife-crisis age. Younger than we are now," she giggled.

Despite her initial shock, Alma regained composure. This was not a conversation to have with a stranger. "I doubt my son would have had time for that," she said coldly.

The silence on the other end also indicated discomfort; maybe it had finally dawned on the woman that she had crossed a line.

"Are you ready to go?" Giacomo shouted from the foyer up to the dressing room. They were already running late and she did not want him to get angry.

"Well, I am very sorry, but I have to leave now…" Alma cut her off.

"Of course, *signora*. Then I suggest I just give you a call in a few weeks' time, when you've had a chance to discuss this with your husband…" Ana finally signalled retreat.

After she'd hung up, she stared at the phone in disbelief. Probably that woman just wanted attention to get more money. Some people have no shame and make things up as they go! Why listen to people with aubergine hair? Giacomo would laugh at her, or get furious, so better not to mention it at all.

At the last moment, she turned around and reached for the small silver tin on her nightstand. Without a glass of water, her well-trained throat swallowed down one of the small yellow pills and an anti-acidic for her stomach. The Marchesas were about to become grandparents for the second time, and the youngest of the Casadeis had recently graduated from medical school. Although the doctor had told her it would take more than an hour until the effect kicked in, she immediately felt lighter. More prepared to talk about other people's sons.

5

Red Claws and Almond Eyes

5 January 2017, London

The next morning, Helen woke to the muffled sound of a hairdryer, hissing through the bedroom wall. Gone the days when she had to drag her semi-conscious baby to the bathroom, worried whether she would ever get her to school on time. She rolled on her stomach and pulled the blanket over her head. As soon as she was surrounded by the warmth of the blanket, she could smell him again. It was different to last night; less aftershave, more sleepy. It would be easy to give in and indulge in some morning love making, but she would be late for breakfast, and she really wanted to talk to Emmy before she left for school. To at least try to get to the bottom of those red claws before she got a letter from the principal.

Getting dressed was a quick routine: the same dark costume every day with a white blouse; she owned a dozen of them from different brands with only minor variations. The biggest effort was tying up her hair in a flawless bun to last all day, so that her hair wouldn't bother her at work. She used a trick with a little cushion to make it look more majestic. Before pushing down the door handle, she checked her appearance in the mirror. "Don't go, Dulcinea," she heard him whisper from the bed.

"Not everybody is born with a golden spoon in his mouth, you lazy man," she teased him as she pushed down the door handle. The smell of coconut shampoo hit her a split second before she would have collided with her daughter in the hallway.

"Ooh, sorry," she squealed, and jumped back. Emmy steered past her, a silence like thunder trailing behind her. The actual thunder then came with the bang of the front door. Starbucks would take care of her girl's breakfast today.

*

At 9.30am, Helen was washed out of the Central line at Holborn station, together with a huge swarm of working Londoners. Other than most Londoners, Helen actually loved the commute to work. Sure, if the trains were overcrowded it wasn't pleasant, but most days there was something meditative to it. All the Londoners streaming through the veins of the system, giving the big city a pulse. On the escalator, she would read the announcements for all the shows and concerts she could not afford, next to the ads for anti-cough and caffeine tablets. It was the only time of the day when she did not have to think and could relax; following the stream of people was enough.

Stockham & Barns had existed since 1889 at Red Lion Square, occupying the entire northern front of brick houses. Its outside appearance was much more regal than the inside. The firm continued to expand and the building was flowing over with files, bundles of paper piling up in every corner and on the staircase. The coffee machine, humorously called the 'watering hole', was placed into what used to be a walk-in cupboard in the aisle. At a time when even shoes and hats got their own room in here. It was the only point of social interaction in a place where people were otherwise silently brooding over their likes. To reach her desk, Helen had to climb over and above an obstacle course of bundles every morning, as her office was cramped on the top floor under the roof. To save time, she kept her own kettle in her office, although this made her even more invisible than her single-mum schedule already did. Helen was the shy deer rushing through on the ever-same trail at dawn and dusk, when no lions were around.

On the staircase, the air grew colder with every step, and the last flight of stairs creaked horridly. The narrow walls were covered with oil paintings that the partners had removed from their offices or meeting rooms but hesitated to throw away. Too naked, too colourful, or simply too ugly. No client ever came up here. Her favourites were a painting of some sort of Francis Drake in a screaming yellow suit, including the tights, who smirked at a Baroque naked lady in a fruit arrangement on the opposite wall. She called them Francis and Babette, and whenever she passed by, she thought of a line for them to tease each other with. Like: *I'm glad, Babette will make it through the winter so well, despite only eating fruit.*

It was obvious that the labour law department was not held in high esteem. Not exactly the financial powerhouse of the firm, as one of the senior partners had kindly remarked in a management meeting. The only reason they kept it, was to appear as a full-service practice. The rooms Helen and the one other partner occupied were those for the servants and maids of the past, and that was the level of their comfort. The view was nice but the walls were badly inclined; the seasons were felt inside as much as outside. As she reached the 'attic door', she heard an only-too-familiar high-pitched giggle and coarse laughter, which could be mistaken for coughing by the untrained ear. The staple background noise to her work. The department's assistants, Albertine and Gemma, could probably work part-time and get the same amount of work done, only by cutting the chit-chat down by half.

"Good morning! Everything good in here?" she said, knocking against the wood of the door frame. Somehow she felt obliged to chat a bit upon arrival, but she was always at a loss.

"Good morning to you!" Albertine responded. She was leaning back in her chair, as always not even pretending to be busy. Today, she was wearing nothing but a tight blouse and a short black skirt, the long legs crossed elegantly. That girl never felt cold. Gemma could not answer; she was wiping away tears of laughter and trying to catch her breath. Most of the time when Helen walked in, Albertine and Gemma were discussing Albertine's dating profiles or other nonsense on her phone. Gemma had turned fifty last year. One of the senior partners had told Helen that 'she was quite a flower' when she started as a sixteen-year-old apprentice. Now they called her 'Ms Walmart' behind her back. Albertine was clearly the current flower of the firm. A twenty-something university dropout, petite and yet fleshy in the right places and with almond-shaped eyes framed by a carefully trimmed black bob. A bit like that woman in *Pulp Fiction*. Every other day, Helen found a male colleague at Albertine's desk who had nothing better to do than inquire whether (a) Albertine had Asian ancestry, because of her eyes or (b) where that orignal, yet beautiful name came from.

"Oh my, what made you two laugh so hard?" Helen feigned a bit of interest.

"This one is killing me," Gemma gasped, pointing at Albertine. "That little cutie says to me, out of the blue, she says, '*Gemma, if I had only twenty-four hours to live and I could choose one thing to do, I sure as hell would not choose sex, too boring!*' At her age, she says that!" And she burst into laughter again, her bosom shaking up and down like in an earthquake. Helen wondered when was the last time that she had laughed so hard? She could never figure out how these two had so much to share – Helen suspected Albertine simply liked to share her adventures with some kind of momma-bear who was no competition at all. She laughed faintly and then moved on to her desk, before Almond Eyes would get the idea to ask her about her last twenty-four hours.

In her office, a pile of files waited for her in the middle of her desk. It looked exactly as she had left it. She sat down and opened the first one to read the other party's court submission, but after a few lines her thoughts wandered off. After more than a decade, the reasons why people got fired or wanted to fire others kept repeating. There was nothing in there strong enough to keep her mind from trailing back to Emmy's red nails – or that sensation in the bathtub.

On page 3 of the document, she began to shiver; the room was awfully cold. Probably the heating had also been switched off during the holidays. It was time to wheel out that old electric heater she kept behind the door for the extra cold days. It made an obnoxious noise, smelled like burnt hair and it dried your sinuses up like hell – but it was better than typing in your coat. Helen sighed; perhaps to start the year on the right foot, she'd better give the heater a head start and then come back in, when the office was mildly warm. Also the plan for this year was to be a bit more social, so why not start the day with a coffee?

"Yaya, me again," she muttered, as she passed by Francis' and Babette's surprised faces. The office was still quiet; maybe some colleagues had taken an extra week of holidays. The machine was already releasing the final droplets of coffee into a flawless milk foam bonnet, when one of the doors popped open. Helen braced herself for all sorts of New Year chit-chat but this time she got lucky.

"Happy New Year – how have you been?" a familiar voice said. It was Eric Thompson; obviously, he had gotten here a lot earlier than her, which was no surprise. His dark hair looked dishevelled, as if he had roughed through it with his hand while thinking, and the grey suit was crinkled as if he had slept in it. It was a common topic between Gemma and Albertine whether Eric Thompson (or any other partner) was an attractive man. Gemma found his charms 'a little rustique, he does not look exactly well fed and rested', while Albertine found that 'well, if you prefer Daniel Craig over Pierce Brosnan, he's totally your thing'. Helen liked Daniel Craig better. Eric Thompson was perhaps not as athletic, but although one could tell he wasted no time in the gym, neither did he waste it on food.

He had been one of the youngest in the history of the firm to become partner, because no one worked harder or longer hours on a case – and had the energy to be the last guest on every after-work event. Some said he had a second battery he could switch on after everyone else powered down. They had started at about the same time at the firm, but it took Helen six years longer than him to become a partner. Initially, Helen found him rather tiring. All this talk about him doing everything for the firm had annoyed her no end. It was a different game with a nursing wife in the background, wasn't it? For many years, Eric Thompson was another reason why life wasn't fair.

"Happy New Year to you!" She smiled back and picked up her cup. Over the past year, they had worked on a few bigger projects together – mergers often involved tax as well as labour law matters, and surprisingly he had become her favourite colleague to work with. He valued her opinion, and although Helen usually left the office early to be home for dinner, he never treated her as if she put less effort into the project. And Helen was happy to spend half the night in front of her laptop on the kitchen table – to keep it like that. It was Eric's praise of her work which finally led to some sort of recognition of her work in the firm.

"How did you spend the holidays? Went to the snow or someplace else?" he asked, putting his cup down for a refill.

"No, Christmas time is family time. The best time to wind down, switch off your phone, you know…" Not bad, she'd managed to make an awfully dull and tense week on a couch in Kent sound like a spa retreat.

"That does sound fantastic indeed… I had to come in on the 27th. You won't believe it, the Candler & Sons case came back around – and of course it could not wait a day. It was just tax stuff, so I did not have to bother you, luckily."

"Oh my God, those troublemakers! Was it very bad?" This client was known for calling at the most ungodly hour with something he should have brought up weeks ago.

"It was okay, just the one day. I stayed until something past midnight and then it was a few follow-up emails until New Year's, don't worry…"

Two assistants had approached the coffee machine, the end of Eric's sentence drowned in the slurping noise of the milk frother and the clinking of cups and spoons.

"Why don't we go to your office? I'll give you an update…" he suggested, already moving towards the staircase. That was a little odd, given that his more fancy office was right next to the machine. Babette and Francis were even more astounded when Helen marched up the stairs, escorted by a gentleman carrying her coffee cup. She managed to wink at them without Eric noticing. The door to the assistants was half closed but she saw Albertine looking up from her phone, lurking for the unusual social interaction on this floor.

He placed his cup on her desk and rubbed his hands together, like one does when standing at a campfire.

"A bit fresh up here, don't you think?" he said.

"Yea, and sorry for the smell," she said, shrugging her shoulders.

"Every winter around this time, I start thinking I should get a new heater – and then it is suddenly spring."

"We should bring this up in one of the partnership meetings. I mean, they could at least sponsor a state-of-the-art heater… I'm surprised you are not typing in your coat," he said, staring in disbelief at the rattling little monster under her table.

"Yes, that they actually could." It was nice that he cared, yet she did not want to appear as if she could not fight her own battles. "So how did your holidays go, apart from the interruption by the Candler guys?" she said, to divert the discussion.

"Oh good, really good. I mean, I always look forward to the holidays and then you are also kind of grateful when it's over. We had both my and Karen's parents over at our house – which, you know, is great for the kids, but it then also becomes a bit of a madhouse." He took a sip from his cup and looked aside, as if reliving a madhouse moment. Eric lived in Acton Town with his wife and children, right next to his parents – how perfect. With all the charms and comforts of a small town, kids learning how to ride a bicycle on the street, and yet conveniently close to the city centre. After one of the kid's birthdays, he had shown her a picture with a fireplace in the background and a kitchen equipped with one of those designer ovens, which look as if you could throw a piece of wood in them, and brazen handles.

"The family stuff is always a bit intense for me," Eric said with a boyish grin. "For a change, one of my old school mates was around, visiting his parents. We went for drinks one night, like in the olden days, that was good…" and his face brightened up a bit.

That wife of his had a hell of a lot of patience. With a husband married to his work, who took a break from family after a few days to get drunk with a friend. She didn't know much about Karen. He once mentioned that they met during his first year at Oxford. *The perfect time to meet your spouse,* as he had said. Helen could not help imagining Karen, waiting by the fireplace next to the Christmas tree, for her hard-working husband to come home. Him being moved by the gesture, and although he was tired, they would make love while everyone else in the house was fast asleep…

"...but the best gift was actually the gift I gave myself this year..." Right on time, she focussed her attention back on him, before he could notice her being absorbed by some soft porn, starring him and his wife. Those morning visions of Luca were always dangerous.

"It's a book by David Attenborough called *The Private Life of Plants*..." he said, and there it was, that spark in his grey eyes. That was what Helen really liked about the breaks with him. He took a true interest in absolutely everything, and he somehow found the time, despite his job and his family. He would put his cup down, as he needed both hands when talking about the voyage of the Caribbean eels or the shortcomings of the US electoral college. He was also the only person she still discussed Brexit with, because he always found an interesting angle to it.

"Oh, that sounds a bit like this new *The Hidden Life of Trees*." Helen had seen that one on a poster at Holborn station when riding up the escalator.

"Exactly, but Attenborough's book is at least as interesting – and he came up with the whole theory first. But I could not put that on my wish list, of course. I would for all times be the weirdo in the family..." The image of the love-making by the fireplace disappeared. "The premise is that plants communicate and socialise very much like animals. Or humans. It just goes unnoticed. It is fascinating, like a glimpse into a different universe. It will totally change the way you look at your potted begonias... But sorry, I am talking too much..." and suddenly he looked a bit embarrassed.

"No, I think it sounds intriguing," she said in all honesty, and his face brightened up again. "Is there anything about plant parents handling wild teenage daughters?" Helen had not planned to say that. Not to someone like Eric, who had a phone full of happy family pictures.

Eric had to laugh. "Oh my, that bad? Enlighten me; maybe I can learn what the future of parenthood holds."

"It is normal, I guess, nothing too dramatic. Life at home right now is a wall of silence and a lot of banging of doors. Her girlfriends suddenly decided to go shopping on Boxing Day without her, while we were at my parents, and she wanted to die. Also, she needs to have shoes which cost some people's monthly rent, or she cannot leave the house anymore. Please don't look puzzled. I have put all the facts I have on the table…" For a second, she thought about telling him about the red claws and that she basically did not know anymore where Emmy spent her days, but then she did not. It was such a cliché: the single parent losing control. Nobody needed to know that.

"Sounds like a tough fate indeed," he said, with a face so serious, it made Helen laugh.

"I know, right? If shoes now become a life and death matter, I will have her shortlisted for a brain scan."

Eric chuckled at the idea, but then his eyes softened. "Come on, don't be too hard on her. It *is* a life and death matter. I would never have dated a girl that takes the shoe question lightly," he said, and jokingly glanced under the table. She instinctively pulled her feet back and a giggle escaped her throat. She immediately bit on her tongue. If he started flirting with her in the office, she would certainly not play along; that was one of her golden rules. As a single mum, she had to be even more careful than others. Thank God he skipped over her teenage reaction. "It is important for kids to find their place. You need to be part of the mainstream, keep up with the Joneses before you can step aside and do your own thing…"

"You think?"

"Sure, it was no different in my school. It just has to stop at some point. The brain should come back…" he smiled. His grey eyes had a way of looking right through her. With that, he got up and collected their empty cups. "Gotta catch a telcon in five minutes…"

"Have fun, I also have to finish a brief entitled *Revenge is a dish best served cold*, and give it some legal basis…"

He laughed and turned in the door frame. "I am sure you can do that. See you tomorrow for coffee then?"

"Sure, oh… and leave the door open. I've got to head over to the girls…"

She heard Eric pass with a "Happy New Year, ladies!" and, of course, Albertine immediately roped him into a conversation. She could not hear exactly what they were saying. Eric was talking and the girls laughed. *What a charmer*, she thought with a smile. She waited for him to make his way down the stairs before she went over herself. Albertine had confused the plaintiff's and the defendant's addresses. This happened a lot, but she did not want to ground her in front of Eric.

Back in her office, she put the coat back over her shoulders and tried to focus on the submission again. If they had asked her for her call for the last twenty-four hours of her life, today, her honest answer would have been: "Sex, definitely."

6

Tanker Blue

5 January 2017, Vittuone (Milan)

After a thirty-minute drive, the car took a left turn off Corso Vittorio Emanuelle and left the shiny boutiques of the main street behind. Behind the modest fronts of ancient houses, the upper class of Milan discreetly celebrated its luxury life. The car slowed down and the porter waved them through so their driver could enter the inner courtyard of the Marchesas' *loggia*. It seemed to fit by the centimetre; horse carriages must have been narrower than today's cars. At the door, the maid took their coats; her stiff face could not hide that she despised working an extra shift. The car drive had not helped Alma's stomach; she felt nauseous and tried to breathe deeply and calmly without anybody noticing. The noise of chatter and glasses clinking came faintly from the salon; apparently, they were the last to arrive.

Holding on tight to her champagne glass, Alma inspected the dining room which had last time received them in a gentle mauve. Chiara Marchesa's passion was to redecorate the interior of the *loggia* – and then host a dinner as an inauguration for the new ambiance. It was now dark as a cave, almost swallowing up the candlelight from the dinner table. Two figurines of Italian greyhounds were flanking an antique Biedermeier *armoire*. She remembered the dogs from last time, but in this ambiance, they looked a lot more like hellhounds.

"What an innovative colour! Perfect for fine dining!" Sara

exclaimed. She clearly could not afford to disagree with someone like Chiara Marchesa.

"It is called Tanker Blue. I immediately knew this is something!" Chiara beamed with pride.

Sara leaned forward and whispered in a conspiratorial tone, "I admit, when Chiara first told me about it, I was really sceptical. But now I'm so in awe! And we are all too young to be boring, aren't we?" and they all burst out in excited laughter. Only Sofia looked a bit sour as she had not been part of that inner circle. The thought of spending hours in that room was plainly depressing.

"Alma, darling, what do you think? Doesn't it look like a whole new space?"

"Yes. As if I have never been here before." Alma got some approving smiles.

The men still gathered in the salon, most likely discussing global economy or local politics.

"Vito, aren't you lucky to have such a talented wife?" chirped Sofia towards Vito Marchesa. "Without us, men would still be living in caves," and she tilted her head to the side, in a hopeless attempt to sound like a feminist and a schoolgirl at the same time.

Alma saw Giacomo swallow hard. This was not the kind of talk he liked: women spending the money of their hard-working husbands, and then asking for a compliment instead of being grateful and quiet.

From glancing at the knives and forks, she could tell that she would be trapped in Tanker Blue for a five-course menu.

The *amuse-gueule* was served, a tiny square of *filet du lapin* garnished with grilled octopus on a mirror of red cranberry sauce – according to the chef Vito and Chiara had hired for the dinner. He would appear before every course, hiding one hand elegantly behind his back. Alma looked down at her plate where an octopus was strangling an innocent rabbit while drowning in a pool of blood. The men returned to their discussion of the latest tax reforms while Sara praised some wheatgrass smoothies which were about to change her life. She noticed that Giacomo looked pale, he let the others do the talking tonight. He only nodded and smiled every now and then. Maybe he was working too much for his age.

With the second course, the conversation inevitably drifted to children and grandchildren. And it was Giacomo who, without hesitation, triggered the most painful landmine in the field.

"How is your youngest son doing, Lorenzo? Didn't he just pass his final exams and is a fully qualified doctor now?"

Lorenzo put down his glass. "Yes, he did, with honours! And to our big surprise, he announced last week that he has very different plans. He will join *Médecins Sans Frontières*, starting in Ghana already next month."

Alma held her breath. Ghana, the end of the world; that was as good as losing a son, wasn't it?

"Unbelievable! Young people are so much more out and about these days, so different from our generation!" Chiara clapped her hands together; she even looked happy about all of this.

"I know literally nothing about Ghana…" Sara added with a giggle, as if it was fun not to know.

"You should be very proud of this courageous young man. Let's have a toast to Paolo!" Vito said. He even got up to raise his glass and everybody followed. Alma stumbled to her feet. Giacomo smiled and raised his glass with the others.

The conversation then went on to the inner politics of Africa. The ladies were all pro feeding poor African children. Sara argued they were even more happy than we were in our materialistic society. Coming from Sara, this was, of course, nothing but a theory.

"Wouldn't you have expected him to stay near you? After having raised and nurtured him for all those years?" Alma suddenly blurted out. Everybody turned their head. They were not used to her speaking up like that. Giacomo looked away, Chiara and Sara exchanged glances.

"Well," Lorenzo said, "of course we would have liked that. But we always had a feeling. He was always so passionate about travelling and exploring foreign countries." And still, Giacomo said nothing.

"Yes," Sofia chimed in, "and we want our son to be happy first of all."

"Of course," her husband added, "happiness is the most important."

And he raised his glass to another toast; glasses were clinking, hearts flowing over with joy. Alma felt her stomach cramp and some bile shooting up. She massaged her stomach with her left hand, under the napkin. The bile burned in her throat and she reached for her glass. But when she swallowed, with all the tension inside her, the water got in the wrong tube. She gagged silently to bring the water back up to then bring it down discreetly, a hand covering her mouth. But her body was already fighting against this gulp of water aiming for her lungs. Alma bent forward and made a gurgling sound, pressing her lips closed. Sara jumped to her feet with a scream: "Oh my God, Alma!"

The next convulsion was stronger; it forced her to cough from the bottom of her lungs, and it erupted wildly. She pressed her hand in front of her mouth, but it was of little use. The water burst out of her mouth and all over her blouse and the table and still her throat would not stop cramping. She had to bend forward to cough her lungs out, and the worst was that it sounded like vomiting. Her dress, her plate and the tablecloth, all had gotten wet. Lorenzo stood next to her and patted her back. Everybody was up on their feet now; Chiara called for the maid. Sofia gave her a fresh napkin to clean her face.

"It is all right, darling, don't worry," Sara kept saying. The words were kind but her voice revealed disgust. Alma just wanted to disappear; tears were running over her face from the effort of coughing. When she finally looked up, she saw her husband standing on the other side of the table. He had not moved. When he sat down, as if on a secret command, everyone moved back to their chairs, as if they all had overstepped a boundary.

"Feeling better?" Giacomo asked with a polite smile and she nodded.

The maid cleaned up the table and restored everything to order; the group resumed chatting as if nothing had happened. A sautéed lamb was followed by a sorbet which was followed by a white fish and then finally came the dessert. Giacomo barely touched the fish and only ate half the dessert. He looked even paler and a light layer of sweat appeared on his forehead; he touched it off with the napkin from time to time. Vito tried to tempt Giacomo to a dessert wine but to her surprise, her husband declined. As a good host, Vito insisted several times, but Giacomo remained firm on that. He claimed an early business meeting the next morning; and there was also the rain. Vito and Emilio kept pointing to the temperatures above zero, but Giacomo stayed firm. At least she would be spared an hour or two in the ladies' salon.

*

After a repetition of the hugging and kissing ceremony, they finally walked out to the car. It had started raining heavily and as soon as the car pulled out into the main street, the driver had to slow down, navigating carefully through the roads which had turned into streams. She looked over to her husband. Water ran down the car windows, painting teary shadows on his solemn face.

"You are not feeling well tonight, are you? You look a bit pale…" she finally dared to say.

"I am fine," he said in a quiet voice, and to her surprise, without any resentment. "Just feeling very tired today…"

The sudden softness in his voice softened her too. "Maybe you have just been working too much lately," she offered.

"Yes, maybe…" he nodded, then he looked out of the window again.

"So…" Alma said, following an inner impulse, "shall we paint our dining room in Tanker Blue? Because we are *too young to be boring*?"

Giacomo chuckled. "Oh, that colour. Oh, *Madonna!*" He shook his head in disbelief.

"*Madonna*? Since when do you say that?" Now she had to laugh, hearing her husband use Maria's favourite phrase, and it made him laugh too.

"It was so depressing, wasn't it? I think that was also why I almost choked on that water, it got me so tense," she said, still seeking his absolution.

"Yes, that could well be why." He nodded and his laughter calmed down. He just stared out of the window again, and then he said in a harsh voice, perhaps harsher than intended: "If you ever came up with such a renovation project, we would have to have a serious conversation!" And there it was again: that tone, forever patronising and in charge. Nobody was allowed to move a finger without his permission. Alma turned away. His hand traversed half the distance between them, but then he stopped and let it slide. The moment had passed.

When she turned her gaze back to her husband, his head lay against the headrest, the mouth slightly open. He had fallen asleep. Asleep, with all the traits of his face relaxed, he looked so alien to her. She had noticed that already in the first days of her marriage, when she was often wide awake after making love while he was sound asleep. The sleeping Giacomo she did not know. The quiet and reminiscent Giacomo she did not know. And he too had grown old over the years. When does one stop noticing such things while living in the same house? His hair was grey but still full, just like his father at his age. His cheeks hung as if there was suddenly too much skin for his face, and deep wrinkles on his forehead marked the worries of his life.

When the car stopped in front of their house, he woke up. Alma used the head start to get into the house first and went straight to the bathroom to change. This house, she thought, is Tanker Blue, even if no one ever paints a wall in here.

7
Cold as Stone

6 January 2017, Vittuone (Milan)

Alma was woken by the wind howling and the blinds rattling against the windows. She turned her head to the nightstand: 4.30am. Two glasses of a heavy red wine with the dinner, also an aperitif, and then one more painkiller before going to bed should have been enough to put her into a coma for six to seven hours, which was as close as it got to sleeping like a normal person. But with all that noise, she was wide awake. She stared into the dark; there was clearly no point in even trying to get back to sleep.

This time, she almost did not need the flashlight to find her way. The landing and staircase were dark as always, but as she crossed the salon and then the foyer, the silver moon lit up the wild night. And it was a loud affair at every step, with the wind keeping up a cacophony of noises. It hit the house in irregular gusts; the strong ones cascaded up to a howl that sounded like a woman's voice before it ebbed away, only to gain strength again. The howl was loudest around the foyer's fireplace; Alma would not have been surprised to see the ashes being blown into the house. Through the high windows, she saw the park trees move wildly back and forth, painting lively shadows on the stone. They crept over the walls, appeared and disappeared without any rhythm, whipping away all clear lines of objects. Alma walked slowly, making sure she would not hit anything. No piece in these halls had moved for a hundred years; yet everything seemed on the move tonight.

The shadows were also dancing in the library, hunting each other across the old bookshelves. She gathered her courage and stepped forward to switch on the little lamp on her secretary desk, and their dance stopped at once. She let out a deep sigh and sat in its light for a bit to calm down. It was still there, even in the stormiest night, the island for her thoughts. The hip was not too bad this morning, actually. She rearranged the cushions a bit. No, not that bad. She sat down again, her thoughts wandering back to last night's dinner.

How eloquently her husband had commented on a firstborn son moving to Africa. The mere thought of it made her pulse rise. As if he were this liberal 'Oh-as-long-as-you're-happy' kind of father. He had reigned with an iron fist. Never violent, never raising his hand against anyone, he did not have to.

Outside the house, he always knew what people wanted to hear. And yet, people were never drawn to him as they were to Luca. Luca could hand a plate of cake to his ever-expanding Aunt Imacolata and say, "Only if you promise me you do a few sit-ups tonight," and get a girlish giggle in return.

Perhaps Luca should have done the same, she thought, with a tear running over her cheek. Should just have gotten up one day and told his dad that he was moving to Africa. Because it was his vocation, full stop. Perhaps they would be a happy family still, reunited at least on Christmas Eve. Alma shrieked as the storm peaked in a violent howl. It was ridiculous for an adult woman to be afraid of a storm, wasn't it?

From the day he was born, Giacomo had made it clear that his son would never ever go to a university, a great privilege. Academics knew nothing about the real world, he often said. All the tricks of the trade he himself had learned from his father as an apprentice in his own company, a family tradition. He believed the close bond he had with his own father was the reason for the tremendous success of their business.

Since he was a little boy, Luca had listened attentively to his father's plans and what he would teach him. How he would slowly gain the clients' trust and how then all the employees would look up to him. He listened with the patience of a loving son. He had adored his father so much, never wanted to disappoint him. His grades were never amazing, but this was also because he knew he would never have to write a single job application in his life. After his graduation, Giacomo generously paid for a three-week holiday for Luca and two of his best friends to Mexico – the boy should also have fun in life. There had been a picture of the three, holding surfboards at the beach, tacked to the wall over his bed for years.

After school, most of his friends left the town to study. Luca started to work, was taken to client meetings and trade fairs all over the world from day one. His father loved showing him around as the next generation and with Luca's lovable nature, he was showered with compliments for his promising son. At night, Giacomo told Alma about all the things Luca had said or done during the day. Never before had her husband shared so much with her, had seemed so cheerful and delighted.

But this happiness was short-lived. In the second year already, things became more difficult. Everything had been experienced for the first time. Luca was still charming and sociable, everybody's darling in the company. But apart from that, his interest was fading. He did nothing more than he absolutely had to, sneaked out of overtime work as often as he could. He made new friends, who knew where from, and they were certainly a bad influence. Cars would stop in their yard, sometimes even after ten and during the week. Young men would yell from across the gate to pick him up, music blasting from the speakers of their cars. These youngsters looked nothing like the children of people they knew. He never introduced them; it seemed to be different faces all the time. He began to arrive late and hungover at work, trying to hide it like a teenager. Giacomo tolerated all of this. Probably he was also hoping it was a passing thing. He often told her she had spoiled him too much; the boy was too soft.

A knock pulled her out of her thoughts and sent a cold shiver over her skin. Was there someone outside? It took her a moment to understand that the noise came from the wooden finger of a light branch which the storm had blown over the terrace. When she pointed the lamp to the terrace door, it still visibly dangled against the bottom of the window, making small knocking noises at every gust of wind. *You have always been a nervous chicken*, she heard Luca say. And it was true; she had always been the one to shriek only because someone entered the room. Just a small branch, nothing more.

Since Luca had been such a popular young man, they had expected him to soon go out with the prettiest girl in town. Alma's lady circles had a clear list of candidates in mind. But it never happened. Not at high school and not in the years before Geneva. There must have been girls, certainly, maybe even lots of them. Rumours of Luca's love interests were a constant. Alma remained a much sought-after source of information, still the inevitably popular mum of the popular kid. But she never knew anything. Sometimes, when the ladies were so eager for exciting news, she even made them up, blew up small facts to little anecdotes because she was enjoying the attention so much. He had been seen with this and that girl in a café, then he had been hanging out several times in a row with her brother, the brother potentially only acting as a wing man, etc. It was difficult to come up with a story of some substance. Obviously, although the world was his oyster, there was nothing serious going on.

At some point, she had been worried that he might have found himself a girl at the beach, among those weird friends, perhaps from another city? He insisted on going every single weekend, no matter what dinner or family function was taking place at home. But after some weeks everything went back to normal. It was hard to tell where it had all gone wrong.

Then one of Luca's friends from school, David Oliega, suddenly moved back to Vittuone. Mr Oliega was the local paediatrician, a nice person. David was very eager to make it in life, but not the brightest star in the sky. He had pursued law studies in Rome, but after the second year he suffered a nervous breakdown. The family moved him to the more sheltered realm of a private university in Geneva, Switzerland. Everybody knew that those private schools basically sold their degrees, and Giacomo never tired in pointing this out. What an embarrassment for the entire family! But for the first time, Luca began to argue with his father. He wanted to go with David. Hardly a breakfast passed without the brochure of that university on the table. The fee should be deducted from his salary, so basically he would pay for it. It would be good for him to study a bit, his English and his French would improve, and so on and so forth. Just a one-year course, just the one year! Alma could still hear her son's voice, begging his father at the age of twenty-two: *Just this one time, Dad!* Something about it had been so heartbreaking. She could not put her finger on it at the time, but she usually left the room during those discussions. And in the end, her husband gave in.

Why did the young feel such a strong urge to leave their home? Alma had never had any interest in studying or going abroad. There was a girl from her school, back in the day, who had gone to Zurich as an au pair. When they met her at Christmas, after church, Alma's mother asked her if she had met her future husband over there. The girl had looked bewildered, said, no, she had not. What a waste of time, her mother had said. The branch sent another knock-knock noise as the storm rattled against the window, but she was used to the sound by now.

Her boy leaving the house left such a void in her life. It was not her marriage but Luca's birth which truly changed her life. Suddenly she was someone in this house; she was Luca's mother, and never alone. In the first months, he would cry as soon as she detached him from her body, and she got praise from her in-laws for being such a devoted mother.

Her late father-in-law believed in elite institutions to raise a child; that was a family's task. They sent him to the local nursery and school, making up for what was missing in the curriculum with home schooling. With Luca, she had given birth to the prince of the village. And everybody fell in love with Luca; he was always laughing, the kind of child that was never shy and threw himself at everything he could find. Games, food, people; he was always in the middle of it.

She had seen the women from her coffee circles suffer so much, even cry in a café, a public place, when their babies left the house. And it was absurd, to raise a child only to then be left alone again.

That would all never happen to her, or so she had always thought. Where else would her son be loved more, where would he get all the food he loved and every wish granted? But if it was unavoidable, this was perhaps the best option among the worst. It was just a year, and studying was better than getting drunk every night. Second, Ms Oliega could also keep an eye on the boys – in case Luca would not call as he had promised or would be as vague and mysterious as he was before about all the weekends and beach trips. So in the end, Alma had also given in to this idea of visiting a private business school in Geneva.

And then the light went out. From one day to the other, the world stopped turning. She had never been able to understand it. A part of her was sure he was still around; she could physically feel his presence.

Alma leaned forward and opened the drawer, to take another look at the new photograph. That beautiful female version of Luca. Although, upon closer inspection, the face also reminded her of the few photographs she had of herself at that age. How peculiar, her finger followed the line of her round chin, like her own.

In a parallel universe, they had just returned from London, from visiting their grandchild after Christmas, showing around the photos on their phone – and complaining about the British food. *What would happen*, she thought, *if I pulled out one of the photos at the dinner table and said: This is my granddaughter?* What could he do? What could he *really* do?

Alma closed her eyes for a moment. How often had she turned all these thoughts around? What if they had not let him go? Today, things were so different – or had they even been different back then? *Doctors Without Borders* … who would have thought that chubby little Paolo Casadei would turn out to be such an adventurer? No wonder he was unmarried still.

The epiphany came so suddenly, that her heart skipped a few beats. The girl could come here! All on her own! Why had she never thought of this? She was a young woman now, and with that backpack and all, she could simply appear at her doorstep, unannounced. Looking exactly like she did on the photograph. Fate could sort things out and she would not even be to blame! But would the girl know about her father's family? Would her mother have told her? Well, if she could travel the world, she could probably also find out by herself. A lot was on the internet these days. Perhaps she even had a right to know? She remembered vaguely that she had read somewhere that children could even sue the mother in court to force her to reveal the identity of the father. Where was that? Probably not England; she would have remembered that. How could Alma not have realised things might get out of hand, no matter what arrangements had been taken! And what would Giacomo say? Would he chase her away? Or would she meet the girl in secret for some days, and then reveal her arrival to her husband when there was nothing he could do about it? Somehow, she could not really imagine any of that.

Without noticing, she had gotten up from her chair and was pacing along the blue frame of the carpet at an unknown speed. Wasn't it most likely that the girl hated her and would only come to confront her? It was absolutely most likely. She changed her running direction, now circling the carpet counter-clockwise. Clara always said that young woman was lucky she came out of it so well; not every family could pay her such a generous sum. But was that how the girl would see it?

Despite its high ceilings, the room seemed much too small all of a sudden, claustrophobic even. She went to the terrace door to get some fresh air, the weather outside totally forgotten. When she pulled the handle, the storm finally saw his chance to conquer the house and the door flung open with force. A gust of wind pushed inside the library and whirled up the papers on the secretary desk. She staggered as she had not expected such impact and stumbled backwards. Holding on to the door so as not to fall, she gathered herself and managed to lean against the door with her body's weight to push it closed. Her hand still on the handle, she looked outside in disbelief. A force from an invisible sky and yet almost stronger than her. Her hair was dishevelled from the wind and so was the room. She tightened her morning coat and started to pick up papers from the ground.

When finally everything was back in its place, she sank exhausted in her armchair but her breath would not calm down. She tried to count backwards from a hundred but it only seemed to get worse. "*When you are upset, write it down,*" Clara had told her every so often. Clara herself had written a diary ever since she was fourteen or so, although their mother had always been against it.

"What if someone finds it and then everybody could read your foolish thoughts?" she had scolded Clara, holding the journal up in the air.

"My thoughts are not foolish. Perhaps *your* thoughts are foolish!" Clara had screamed, and banged the door shut, right in their mother's face.

She had always been the wild one. Alma had never fought like that, not even close. Perhaps she could write a letter? But Clara would be back from another Mediterranean cruise soon. The calendar showed a red circle around the 7th of January. They would speak on the phone anyway; it would look stupid if she wrote a letter two days before.

She leaned back in her chair. The light blue of dawn had started to mingle with the silver moon. The naked branches looked like arms reaching up in the air, praying and begging, like a choir of banshees. She tried to imagine the girl, packing her bag in London, sitting in a train, asking people for directions to their estate. She closed her eyes and listened to the noises of the wind. Its song was more of a constant wailing now, with less violent peaks.

*

When she woke again, it was bright daylight outside. She lifted herself up in the armchair; how long had she been asleep? The clock showed 7:55, so it had been more than two hours! Maria and Flavia must be wondering already where she was, thinking she was sleeping in after the dinner party. But no, this did not make sense. Giacomo must have left the house a while ago. He would have told them that she was up already. What a mess!

After this outburst of emotions, she needed to go to the bathroom before entering the kitchen. Brush her hair; perhaps to put on some make-up. The storm had calmed to a wind. The banshees now saluted her quietly as she passed through salon and foyer, waving back and forth in a slow and heavy manner. When she reached the top of the staircase leading to their bedroom and dressing rooms, the wind stopped for a few seconds. It fell quiet. The landing lay dark ahead of her, the smell of sleep and unmade beds hanging in the air. The door to their bedroom was closed. Nobody had left the room, apart from her.

And suddenly, she knew. Before she could form the thought, she knew. The paleness, the cold sweat on his forehead; the pieces of the puzzle raced together. She ran inside, the room still dark, and her husband motionless as she had left him. She crawled onto the bed; she got hold of his arm then found his hand. Even under the thick duvet, it was cold as winter's stone. She shook him, touched his cold face, pressed her cheek against his chest to feel him breathe. Finally, she fell on her knees, and as she kneeled next to the bed, a scream left her body. First a hoarse one, weak and stuck in her throat. But with each breath, it grew stronger, broke more and more out of her lungs until finally she screamed at the top of her voice and from the depth of her own self: "My husband is dead! My husband is dead!"

8
Before Midnight

30 January 2017, London

The weeks of January floated by more or less uneventfully. At dinner, all Emmy ever talked about was the party of the year, but at least she talked. Helen had finally given in and freed up a budget for Emmy's glamorous shoe-shopping. In the end, it was Eric's comment on keeping up with one's peers which warmed her to the idea. This shopping-frenzy was nothing but a phase every teenager went through. And when she was real honest, there actually was money she could use. Every month for the past seventeen years, a transfer of a thousand pounds appeared on her bank statement. Discreetly passed on to her from a UK escrow account. She had saved every penny of it. As soon as it arrived, it got transferred to a separate savings account. She had vowed to touch it only for college or university fees, if needed. If it ever came up, she would simply tell Emmy she had put it aside over the years, which was also true.

Sometimes she imagined sending the entire sum of money back to them, with a bang, on Emmy's eighteenth birthday. Having discarded her like a gold-digger, how could this not make them feel ridiculous? It would surely be enough for another Bulgari *collier* for the old witch. But she would keep it, for the sake of safety. Nonetheless, using the money to buy her daughter a gift felt as if *they* were giving her baby a treat that she herself could not afford. But this was an exception. Only the money for the shoes, only this once.

The final compromise had been a pair of Louboutins, high stilettos in an almost transparent silver-glittery material and with a peep toe. Helen had almost fainted at the prices, while Emmy swore an oath that she would wear them until the end of time. They then settled on no whorish make-up at all – another TV documentary on teenage pregnancies had made Helen stay firm on that – and a simple H&M dress. There were a few tears, but the shoes were the real fetish and she did not put up a hard fight for anything else.

Eric had stopped by several times for coffee breaks; bright moments in an otherwise gloomy winter month. Albertine's neck seemed to get longer every time he walked into her office, but there was nothing to gossip about. Helen was careful to not overstep any boundaries here; no more flirting and teenage giggles.

It turned out that Eric equally enjoyed sharing the troubles of parenting life. This was a new side to him. Before, things had always been 'all good' and there was no more insight than the random photo on his phone. It was probably healthy for every parent to get a bit of perspective on things. Eric's kids, Jameson and Sara, were four and seven. Currently, they seemed to have switched sexes. While the younger, Jameson, had lately insisted on a princess crown for a kid's costume party (and been subject to some cruel *kindergarten* mobbing – no transgender tolerance among five-year-olds), Sara was rather loud and breaking or losing everything entrusted to her. Her mother had her signed up for ballet classes and she surprisingly enjoyed them. Eric now worried that the young girl was heading towards the biggest disappointment of her young life, while his wife apparently spent sleepless nights imagining her clumsy daughter being ignored by the eligible bachelors.

"That is also a bit exaggerated." Helen frowned. "These things are changing nowadays. Girls don't have to act like a princess anymore to find a man… don't you think?"

"I guess so… but in any case, do figure out who the guy of *your* princess is!" He took a sip from his cup.

"Oh God, don't say that. That is, like, my worst nightmare." Helen's shocked face made Eric laugh.

"You don't want her to be the weirdo that gets kissed last, do you?"

"No, of course not..."

He smirked at her with that boyish grin Helen liked, though he mostly looked overworked these days. The ironing board at home was apparently still not working properly (even Gemma had commented on Mr Thompson's 'pyjama-bottoms and wrinkly shirts'). But the few extra greys in his full black hair suited him; another way in which life wasn't fair.

Of course, Helen had already suspected that Emmy's chatting on the phone was mostly about boys, but rather other girls talking about boys. She did her best to keep Emmy busy with after-school activities, choir lessons, the art club and what not. She could not really get into trouble that way, could she?

In any case, Helen decided not to address this topic before the party; the ice was still thin.

*

And then, on the last Saturday of the month of January, the big night was finally here. Emmy was beaming with happiness she walked up and down in the living room in full attire. The way you only look when all good things can still happen to you. In that moment, even Helen found that the shoes were worth the money. Her girl placed her feet so consciously in these glittery, almost immaterial – and yet so material – shoes. The sulking and insecure teenager was gone. And her father would be so proud; she could almost see him give her a kiss on the forehead.

"Your Highness, the horse carriage is waiting for you!" she said with a bow.

And although this was a pretty lame joke, Emmy played along. "Thank you, James, does it come with four white horses?"

There was a little disruption when Helen expected the princess to put on a winter jacket – it was still the end of January. But the fury that flared up in Emmy's eyes within seconds (Mum is about to ruin everything at the last minute!) made Helen back off.

"No one looks like a princess with blue lips," she tried to argue, but even she could see that the puffy red winter jacket was Mummy's choice, not a fashion choice.

With a final bow – to restore the good mood – she opened the front door and Emmy stalked out, rolling out the new walk to the world.

The deal was that she would drive her to Ali-Saa's place ("Just drop me off, Mum, DON'T come inside!") and pick her up again at 2am. This had been another hard bargain, as apparently, "All the other girls are allowed to stay overnight!" Thank God she had managed to call one of the mums, and that one had never heard of any sleepover and planned to pick up her daughter at 1am.

Ali-Saa's house was at the south end of Clapham Common Park, a few minutes' drive and close to school. It had a front yard big enough to park the Bentley next to the Mini Cooper. A big *18* sign was hanging above the door in screaming pink.

Helen could not help but say: "Really? Now that is not childish in your book?"

But Emmy was smart enough to not pick up on this. With a quick "Bye, Mum!" she left the car and ran towards the door. As the door opened, Helen heard a bunch of girls screaming as if Emmy were an entire boy band. Plain ridiculous. Helen sighed and turned on the engine. Gone the days where she arranged play-dates with her friends' mummies. These people, she did not know them at all, and Emmy obviously liked it that way. What can you do. One year more and she would go wherever she felt like, anyway.

Back home, Helen needed a plan to keep her eyes open until 2am. The few girlfriends she still had from university were hardly ever available on weekends. Those quality times belonged to their families, or dinners with other couples. She had thought of cleaning the house, but that was a depressing plan for a Saturday night. And it would then be even more depressing to have the entire Sunday wide open and no plan to show for it. In the end, she settled for a movie night. She had ordered a bunch of DVDs from this 'Movie Lovers' service where you pick a movie online and they send you the DVD together with a return envelope. Emmy had freaked out when she found the envelope in the mail. That kind of thing was so over, ever since there was Netflix.

She had just finished the first movie with Jennifer Aniston finding love in yet another beach house, when the doorbell rang. That was so unexpected and unusual that her heart skipped a beat. It wasn't much later than 10pm. Her first impulse was to stay still, pretending no one was home. Hide under the table perhaps. She held her breath and waited, waited to hear footsteps move away from the door. But instead, after some seconds, she heard a male voice shouting, "Ms Kings, are you home?" And then a muffled coughing, which in a million she would have identified as Emmy's. She was up on her feet and at the door a second later. At her doorstep was a young man of about twenty-five years of age, and with the same caramel complexion as birthday queen Ali-Saa. Next to him was Emmy, fighting hard to keep up on her feet, her dress quite *dérangée* and with some wet stains on the front. Only one shoe was left on her right foot; the naked left one was dangling in the air, so as not to touch the cold ground. The young knight had swung one of her arms around his neck and fixated it with his left hand, while with his right arm he held her by the hip to keep her upright next to him. Emmy's complexion was a terrifying palish green.

"Hi, I'm Amir, Ali-Saa's brother. I was chaperoning at that party and your lil' girl here tried to impress us by having a bottle of vodka down her throat. Like, faster than you can think. She started to throw up in my mum's bathroom, so I was told to drive her home

"A bottle of vodka on her own?" Helen screamed. "What kind of chaperone are you?"

"Listen, ma'am, I just risked having my brand-new car covered in puke." And with these words, he took Emmy's lifeless arm, pushed her a little sidewards while sidestepping a little closer and placed it around Helen's neck. With the words, "Tag, you're it," he left the scene.

Amir was a fit young man. It had looked so easy to hold up and control Emmy, who seemed to have bones made of rubber. But Helen was a tiny woman, lighter and even a bit shorter than her daughter. Emmy's sense of coordination or any kind of body control was totally gone. She leaned with her full body weight against her mum, and they would both have fallen to the ground if Helen had not grabbed the arm around her neck with one hand, while reaching for the door frame with the other and managing to push one foot against it to somehow stabilise them. Emmy's breath reeked of alcohol and sickness, and Helen had to turn her face to resist the urge to throw up too. She gasped for breath and struggled to hold her tight enough so that they could walk inside.

"Come on, baby, pull it together. You are home, baby. It is going to be fine."

Emmy made a moaning sound as if being tortured but otherwise barely reacted. Perhaps she knew where she was; perhaps she didn't. The bathroom was only a few metres from the entrance door – but it seemed to be miles away. Sometimes Emmy moved a foot in the right direction, then she shifted back like a pendulum. After a few metres, her knees gave in and Helen had to lean her against the wall to gently sink to the ground with her, so that she would not hit her head. She sat on the floor and gasped for breath, covered in sweat, and they were only halfway. Emmy leaned her head back against the wall for a moment, then she made a sound as if she would throw up right there in the corridor, but nothing more than a bit of drool ran out of her mouth. In a seemingly bright moment, when Emmy opened her eyes and looked at her mum, Helen managed to pull her up to her feet again. It was unbelievable how heavy a body would become if its muscles were not cooperating at all. Way too heavy for a mother alone. All Helen wanted was to pull her to the bathroom, sit with her over the toilet until she had thrown up everything, until all the poison had left her baby's body. Then it would be better. Then she would get back to her old self.

Two metres from the bathroom door, Emmy's knees gave in again and they would almost have collapsed, but this time Helen shouted at her. She regained some consciousness and strength, at least for two more metres so they could half sink, half fall onto the bathroom floor. Helen was now completely covered in sweat, her shirt also showing some stains from Emmy's drool. It was a tiny bathroom, a guest toilet rather, not made for a sit-in in front of the toilet. Emmy was leaning against the tiles, her sweaty forehead resting against them. Helen got up to stand behind her and held her by the shoulders, reaching for a hairband to get her hair out of the face, the beautiful hair out of the beautiful face. Emmy had come to sit too far from the toilet to lean over it. Helen tried to pull her a bit closer but to no avail.

"Come on, honey, spit it all out, you will feel better. I know you feel sick." Smelling the toilet block from so close almost made Helen throw up. But Emmy was beyond all that. She did not understand what was going on; she could not react. As soon as she felt she was being pulled, she instinctively fought back. The more Helen pulled her, the worse it got. In a final wild movement, she tried to withdraw her shoulder from her mother's grip, and her head would have hit the wall if Helen had not instinctively held her arm between the tiles and her forehead.

Emmy was no longer part of this world. She had to throw up, or this would end badly, was all Helen could think. In a second attempt, Helen grabbed her under the arms to pull her over the toilet. Again, she pulled against it and moaned something like, "Wanna lie down, Mummy."

There was no chance and so she gave up for a moment and let her baby's body sink down on the little carpet before the toilet. With her eyes closed, Emmy lay still for a moment. *A break, perhaps we just need a little break*, Helen thought, fighting for her breath to calm down. What would be the most sensible thing to do next? Should she call an ambulance? How does one know when that's needed? Her thoughts were interrupted by a gurgling sound. Emmy's body started convulsing, in an attempt to throw up while lying down. "No, get up, get up," Helen shouted, and pulled her up, in panic. If she threw up like that, she might simply choke to death. Her panic made Helen stronger and she managed to get Emmy's face over the toilet with one strong pull, taking the bathroom carpet along as well. But when hanging over the bowl, the convulsion was over; only some more spit drooled out of her mouth.

After some time, her body started to struggle back to a lying position. Helen's arm was about to go numb so she let her sink down. Then Helen remembered another documentary on alcoholism in English boarding schools. One of the doctors on site had explained that one should lift the student's arm in a slightly bowed position over his face and then let it drop. Basic instincts would command the arm to move to the side and land right next to the face. If that failed and the student hit himself in the face, the poisoning was serious and one had to call 999. Helen raised Emmy's arm and let it drop. It landed more or less gracefully next to the princess's head. Thank God.

She made another attempt to wake her, to pull her up, but Emmy was hanging in her arms like a bag of potatoes, and Helen had to let her lay down again. While her movements had been strong, though close to a spasm until a moment ago, she now seemed rather narcotic. Like a wild animal that someone had shot with an anaesthetic. Helen was so exhausted that she could not have fought with her much longer. Emmy lay there as if she was fast asleep, her breath shallow and faint. Helen lifted her arm again. It slammed hard on her nose.

Part II

9

In the Fog

January to March 2017, Vittuone (Milan)

The second night after her husband's death, Flavia had called for a doctor. She and Maria had stayed overnight, and woke from Alma's screaming. She screamed until she had to vomit, and she vomited until no liquid was left in her body. The mere thought of standing by the open coffin again, and this time all on her own, was more than Alma could handle. The doctor had known her for years. He used to frown upon the high doses of tranquillisers and painkillers; every time she asked for a new prescription, she had another excuse. She had lost half the package or her handbag got stolen. But seeing her in this state, he finally dropped all reservations. Letting her sink into a deep fog seemed more merciful than worrying about her liver ten years from now.

The silver blister with the colourful pills in it became the only cheerful thing in Alma's bedroom. A yellow one in the morning, a blue and a pink one at noon, and then none until at bedtime it started all over again. But then again, when was bedtime, for a person who refused to leave the bed?

The worst moments were the hours when the numbness faded. When the pills' embrace subsided in the early morning hours and her mind raced free, she clearly heard her husband breathing next to her. Flavia moved her to one of the guest rooms but it only helped a bit. The room had a canopy bed, made of dark oak, with a baldachin of white linen. It had been in the house when her late father-in-law bought it, but they had removed the heavy piece; it was too antique for their modern bedroom. This bed was free from memories, but sometimes, at night, Alma saw a body press through the white linen above her. And when she finally dared to ask, "Who is there?" the body would roll over and Luca's head would appear, look over the frame down on her in her bed. Sometimes blood would drip from his forehead. Or it was Giacomo's silent grey face. Neither of them ever spoke, no matter how much she begged them.

One morning, she woke to a cramp in her lower leg. When she looked down, she saw Baby Luca, clasped to her calf, begging to be saved. She wanted to get up, stretch out her arms and hold her child, but could not move. In those moments, all she could do was reach for the blisters and take another yellow one, although Flavia had arranged the doses for her in little containers labelled Monday to Sunday. She did not even care to live until Sunday.

Only every other day, Alma had to dose down and make herself presentable. Visitors came to the estate, to console her, out of real concern, or simply following a convention. Her sister Clara stayed with her the weeks after the funeral, to help with the guests – but maybe also to make sure she did not embarrass the family. She could hardly stand upright with all the Valium in her system. Some of the local visitors she remembered. The doctor's wife, the mothers from Luca's old school. They may have held warm memories of the times when she was still around, but others were clearly hoping to ply the soft-hearted widow for money. What other explanation was there for a visit from the newly elected mayor, or flowers from the head of the local table tennis club?

A few relatives attended the funeral, despite the fact that the Carneggios had been absent from most family gatherings for a good fifteen years. She needed to be reminded of their names, and most of the children she had never seen before.

The estate had hardly been host to any guests in years, and now Flavia and Maria were using all the representative porcelain in rotation, bringing in coffee, tea and cookies and squeezing Alma's hand before leaving the room. Alma stared at the cups and plates while guests struggled for the right words. The more impertinent ones asked *so* many questions: how did this happen, had she noticed anything in the days before, did he suffer from a serious heart condition, had he been ill during the night? She told them all the same thing, one day he was walking around and everything seemed fine and the next moment – gone, just like that. Alma had heard all of their phrases over and over again, seventeen years ago. Now she was the one who had to come up with answers. Those shoulders she used to hide behind were gone.

Clara took over the conversations most of the time, as she noticed her sister's blurred vision. The visitors may have just put it down to grief. Alma appreciated Clara's presence as long as there were guests, but as soon as they had gone, her sister kept going on and on about the house being so depressing and empty and that she needed to move in with her. Ordering her, almost like a ward sister. Alma was in no state for making decisions. And so she simply agreed. Yes, yes, she had to move, of course, just not right away, but once she felt better. And Clara told every visitor with a bright smile that arrangements were being made for her sister to move in with her, and then everybody felt better.

The Unione ladies had an ethical code in place which obliged them to check on widowed members. Although widowed *and* childless might be something they had never encountered in their circles before. One week, Sofia Casadei; the next, Sara Picone; then Chiara Marchesa and then the rotation started over again. And they all arrived with their own prescription. Chiara Marchesa knew about a retreat for the grieving, in a beautiful villa on Capri, and even brought a printout from their website. Sara Picone suggested to hire a yoga guru, a spirit guide to "take care of your soul" as she put it. Finally, Sofia Casadei recommended therapy, a grief counsellor. Of course, Sofia knew someone who knew someone that was a luminary in the field; that could handle "a tough case" like Alma's. That was always the message: she was a *case*, a patient who needed to be talked into treatment.

No one just sat and cried with her.

And they all echoed Clara. When she was 'stable' again, she had to decide 'what to do with the house'.

She never felt hungry. She almost forgot what appetite was and only ate because she figured it was easier to eat than to quarrel with Flavia and Maria. Why were they all so eager to see her happy and energetic right after she had buried her husband next to her son? She had every right to stay in bed the whole day. The way life had treated her, Alma felt she owed nothing to anyone.

Apart from receiving a few guests, there were no chores or legal matters she needed to tend to. As a diligent businessman, Giacomo Carneggio had sorted out his succession and will with his lawyer. Everything was taken care of. Unlike Alma, he himself had been aware that he would not live forever. Every other day, di Marco showed up with documents in a leather folio for Alma to sign. He tried to elaborate a bit on the contents of each document for Alma's better understanding, but she would sign them right away, looking right through him.

Weeks passed, and since Alma did not show any signs of an imminent nervous breakdown – and also because the ladies had better things to do than tend to a hopeless case – the house slowly fell quiet again. In her sober moments, what shocked Alma most was not how much the sudden death had changed her life, but how little her life had changed. It was as if the house had never left the state of shock and grief which had followed their son's death. They had accommodated it just enough so that things looked normal from the outside.

On the days when Clara briefly returned home to take care of her own affairs, Alma took at least one extra pill in the afternoon. As long as she was awake and alone, no room was safe. One day, she entered the living room and she saw him. Not as a child, but as a young man, in the blue shirt he had been wearing the day he died. As she moved towards him, he turned, and Alma saw that big bleeding wound on his forehead, blood dripping into his collar. She screamed, but when Flavia and Maria came running, he was gone.

Another day, Alma saw Giacomo standing at her bedside. He looked at her with so much pain. In his hand, he held the wooden box from her secretary desk.

"I would have told you," she shouted, and tried to get up to take the box from his hands, but then she woke. It was still dark outside. It was only a matter of days and she would not be able to tell a dream from reality. And what difference did it make? In either, she could not save them. Or herself.

Ever since that night, she had not gone back into the library.

"You can trust me," she whispered into her pillow. "I will not go behind your back. I never would have. I will burn that little box, I promise."

But he would not believe her. As soon as she fell asleep, there he stood again.

*

Until one morning in early March, Flavia entered her bedroom to put an end to this half-life. Alma was lying motionless, unable to summon the strength to get up. But unlike the days before, Flavia did not tiptoe around her, or place herbal tea on the bedside and leave. This morning, she pulled the curtains aside, clapped her hands together, and said: "That is enough, madame. Now it is time to come back."

Flavia took the Monday to Sunday containers and opened the drawers of the nightstand. She grabbed all the blisters and walked straight to the bathroom, not waiting for any reaction.

"Enough with those yellow and blue candies," she shouted, her voice sounding hollow from between the tiles. "They are all from the devil. No good for anyone. For the funeral maybe, but not every day. Dangerous, *Signora* Alma. *Very* dangerous."

It sounded like a crackling firework when she squeezed all the pills out of the blister pack. Alma imagined them forming a happy lentil soup in the toilet bowl before she heard Flavia pull the flush.

"That *dottore* is also from the devil if he gives you this! He is no good!" she said back in the bedroom, raising one finger in the air. "From today, you have to come to the kitchen at seven for breakfast, like you used to. The croissant is there and the papers are there, and all you have to do is sit with us."

She looked so determined. Alma did not dare to contradict. For years to come, Alma would wonder how Flavia's husband could manage to sit drunk on the sofa even for only one evening.

10

Green Paws

31 January 2017, London

At four in the morning, Helen sat outside the nurses' room at Lambeth Hospital, waiting for Emmy's discharge papers. She had a hard time keeping her eyes open despite the plastic chair's backrest protruding painfully right where her spine wanted to rest. The disinfectant in the air made her throat feel dry, and the urine smell lingering in between was nauseating.

The last few hours had been a rollercoaster of emotions. The moments before the ambulance arrived, with Emmy lifeless in her lap, had been the worst of her life. Minutes had felt like hours, trying to stabilise her baby in a lateral recumbent position which she could not really remember, shaking her and shouting her name, but no response. The paramedics had immediately assured her Emmy would not die, but Helen only believed them when she opened her eyes in the ambulance, even though only for a few seconds.

The worst night of Helen's life was a routine event for the Saturday night shift of the hospital. Emmy finally threw up and was then put to bed with an infusion. As Helen's panic faded, a wave of anger roared up in her. She had to run for the restroom and bite her fist in the stall to not scream out loud. How could her daughter have done this to her? What was she thinking, to treat her young life like that? Helen counted back from fifty before leaving the stall, her left hand showing serious bite marks.

Helen was not the only parent waiting in line. There were five others waiting to take their offspring home again. One of them, a slightly obese woman in leggings and a Snoopy T-shirt (and nothing else despite the freaking cold temperatures, not even a bra, for God's sake) talked incessantly to Helen about her boy, Milford. Quite a name, Helen thought, for someone who was the next big thing in the Man U hooligan scene. It was apparently the third time in four months she had come to pick him up here. No school, just booze, just like his father, and on and on she went. It was hard to tell whether all this upset her or whether she was sharing some fun facts. Helen wanted that woman to disappear, and yet undeniably, they were sitting in the same line. After all the compromises on princess shopping and hairdos, that was the thanks she got!

Finally, the nurse stepped out and called her name. She handed Helen a big envelope, full of insurance forms. After two infusions and a final check of her vitals, they were good to go home.

Helen walked down the corridor a few metres where Emmy was sitting on the edge of her hospital bed. The hospital was full and there were many beds out in the corridor

"It is just easier for us to look after new cases at night," one of the nurses explained with a shrug when she caught Helen's gaze.

Emmy was dead pale and silent. Still in her cocktail dress, Helen's shawl hanging over her shoulders, she looked defeated. *Let's hope she is embarrassed*, Helen thought, and at the same time felt a massive relief that her baby's face was not of such a frightening green anymore. Helen's eyes followed her daughter's gaze and that was when she realised that Emmy had no shoes on. Her bare feet were dangling in the air. Her nylon thights were torn and the one princess shoe she had brought home was probably still lying somewhere in the hallway. When the ambulance finally came, no one had thought about the moment she would have to walk out of the hospital into a cold winter's morning.

"Oh, honey, how will we get you out of here?" Helen sighed. "You can't even walk up to the taxi like this…"

"I'm fine," Emmy mumbled, but obviously she was not.

"No, you're not. Wait here, honey. I don't want you to catch a cold on top of everything," she said, sounding more annoyed than she had intended.

Those fucking shoes. Only one of them could not even be sold on eBay. Helen found a nurse pushing trays into a serving trolley. Breakfast was about to be served. When she asked the nurse whether there were some slippers she could borrow, all she got was a bewildered: "What do you mean, 'borrow'?"

"Okay, sure. I mean, I would also buy them…"

"You always have to grab some shoes when someone goes into an ambulance," the nurse said, raising one finger in the air, and it made Helen's pulse rise like hell.

"Happens all the time. We are not running a shoe store here."

"Thanks so much for your help," Helen said sarcastically.

She was about to turn on her heels, when the nurse added, "Maybe they have some slippers in the shop downstairs."

In the foyer, she found the small shop selling snacks, newspapers, everyday stuff for patients and a few gift items. When she asked the vendor, an old Bengali man with thick glasses, for slippers, he raised the familiar finger and said, "People always forget to bring shoes. You always have to grab some shoes when someone goes into the ambulance."

"I heard that before. Now, do you have any?"

"Sorry, we are all out. A popular choice in winter months."

But Helen's desperate look must have made him think harder, because his face lit up: "Ha, I think I have got something for you!"

He walked over to the shelf with the gift items and pushed his arm through a tight row of teddy bears and heart-shaped cushions. "These have been around for years! I don't know why. Very good against cold feet!"

With a bright smile, the man held up two gigantic plush paws in bright green, with talons of mossy felt on the front. Shoes one might buy to cheer up a little boy going through a dinosaur phase. The marketing mistake here was probably the adult shoe size. But what choice did she have?

In the lift she started to think that maybe this was also a good lesson. This is what happens if you mix with the wrong crowd; they turn you into a monster.

When she got to Emmy's bed, the girl was still sitting in the exact same position, too weak to move an inch. She looked at her baby's feet and suddenly remembered how proud and deeply happy she had looked, posing in her new shoes. Life had not been fair to Emmy, , no matter what stupid thing she had done. And now, on top of everything, parading her around in green dinosaur feet was not right. Following an impulse, Helen said, "I found a solution," and slipped out of her ankle boots and held Emmy's arm to get inside them without losing her balance. Then Helen slipped into the monster paws, as that's what mums do. Emmy looked at her in disbelief. If she were not so exhausted, she surely would have laughed. Helen tucked her arm under Emmy's to stabilise her.

"They are very warm, you know. Now let's get out of here."

It turned out that in a hospital, people have better things to do than notice other people's paws.

Emmy dozed off in the taxi right away. Helen had never seen the streets of London so empty. There might as well have been an apocalypse and the two of them were among the few survivors, together with the men from the bin lorry. They reached home in a record time of twenty minutes. Nobody saw them exit the taxi; the monster mum and the fallen princess.

Neighbours had surely seen them leave, though, the ambulance with the blue lights in front of the house, lighting up the street. When Helen walked out next to the stretcher, she had seen some of them coming onto the street, nosy – or worried perhaps. An ambulance in front of a house where nobody was above eighty years old was worrying. Perhaps they were not even surprised. The girl, so often alone at home, no family around, the mother working late. That was how it happened, everybody knew.

Neither of them spoke a word as she closed the door behind them. Emmy still looked like death and Helen felt so drained. They would talk, but later, not now, not just now. Emmy changed into her pyjamas with her mother's help – no nagging, no "I can do this, I am not a toddler anymore." A minute later, she was fast asleep, looking so peaceful and innocent in her little bed. Helen gently pushed a streak of blonde hair out of her face. Like a baby, gone into a deep sleep that no noise or touch could disturb. It had always fascinated Helen how you could even pick up and carry a baby without waking it. So much trust in its world, it would not open an eye to check whether it was being carried away by a lion. All Helen could do now was watch and wait for what happened next. She put a bottle of water next to the bed and left the door open, just in case.

Then she wandered a bit between kitchen and sofa, not sure whether she should have something to eat or lie down and sleep. Actually, she was pretty sure that she needed to sleep, for three weeks in a row ideally, but she did not dare to. What if Emmy's sickness came back? What if she had to throw up again and would not wake up? Was that even possible? She really should have asked the doctor more questions.

Her eyes fell on a pile of envelopes on the kitchen counter. Throughout the week, she had been so busy that she had just gathered the envelopes from the ground, which Emmy always generously overstepped. When Helen came home in the evening, they usually formed a mosaic with her sneakers. Paying bills was a typical Sunday occupation, maybe the right thing for some distraction.

Most envelopes were advertisements, only one invoice from the dentist, and she was about to throw the pile into the bin when her hands stopped at a white envelope. A silky paper with a black frame and a black cross next to her address – and she recognised the feel of it immediately. It was a private letter. That kind of paper was not used on a large scale, and she had felt it before, many years ago. This was finally too much for one day. Her knees gave in and she found herself sitting on the floor, again. Little silver stars sparkled in front of her eyes. Her hands cramped into fists, almost folding the envelope, but the card inside resisted. For the first time she was grateful that her daughter never bothered picking up the mail.

Seventeen years ago, Baby Emmy kept her awake at night. And there she had found it, the same white envelope with a black frame and a cross next to her address. The lines inside the card had been so formal, to the extent of violence. *We hereby inform you that ... has passed away unexpectedly. ...Please rest assured that we continue to honour all legal commitments made ... kindly ask you to do the same.*

Where seventeen years ago, Luca's name had been printed, it was now his father's. For a moment, she almost felt pity for the old witch. Life had not exactly been kind to her. Losing a child was the hardest thing, even for the cold-hearted. Now she had lost her entire close family, and she was not the type of woman that could stand on her own. But well, it was certainly not Helen's job to write comforting words in a condolence card.

She stared at the card; the letters began to dance in front of her eyes. Sometimes it said Luca; then his father's name reappeared in black print. And the dance of names unlocked a secret door inside her chest; she had not even known it was there. She pulled her legs up and pressed a cushion against her chest to calm herself down. She took three deep breaths but the racing heart would not subside. It was dead silent in her house. Only the refrigerator shuddered every now and then, as if it felt cold itself. A deep despair, the loneliness and the fear of the last few hours now surfaced, and the emotion washed her away. How alone she had been; more alone than anyone should ever be. Too alone to hold onto her sick baby, too alone to know what to do, nobody there to ask, nobody there to help and nobody there now to listen and console. Nobody knew but her. And now, the family she had been hiding from her baby was dying. Though she had never planned to reveal them to Emmy or seen any merit in their existence, the irreversibility of that decision suddenly made her shudder. She had treated them as if they were dead, and soon they actually would be. The chance for Emmy to see where she came from would be lost forever, because of her.

And she had also failed in finding her a new family. All her attempts at dating had failed badly. In all possible ways. There had been the guy who was still unmarried because he could not settle for anyone and dated more than one woman at a time – WhatsApp helps a lot with that. The divorced guy who turned out to have anger management issues and ended up yelling at her at night so that Emmy woke up and got scared. Painful to admit that she waited up to that point to break up with him, so much she had longed for a family. So eager she had been to send that noble family a picture of Emmy, clearly from her wedding, from a new address and under her husband's name.

What if she had simply failed in all this? What if she was simply no good in raising a kid? What if her parents were right and there were actually just a few simple rules in life, like a kid needs a father, and a big city is no place for a young girl?

As her belly grew, she had said goodbye to her London flatmates and moved back in with her parents. Her mother cried most of the time. Mainly because this was not what she had wanted for her girl (or herself), also because all the stress with the terrible Italian family could harm the baby. Helen had been paralysed by the thought of being alone with a baby, but staying with her parents had not worked out. If not worrying about the baby and rushing it to the doctor, Mr and Mrs Kings spent their days worrying about Helen's future. Her father was an accountant and her mother an English teacher. Financial security, stability and thorough life-planning were the pillars of their lives. What had happened to their daughter was their worst nightmare come true. The only glimpse of hope was that a guy with a stable job might come along and marry her. Apparently, men married women even though they already had a baby; crazy but true. Buried alive.

An angel came to her rescue, in the shape of her former professor at UCL. On learning about her situation, he helped to organise her a scholarship and a placement in family-student-accommodation, with a crib for Emmy. Her depressed mind had never considered any of that. And in October, she moved back to London into her own tiny place, the bundle of five-months-old Emmy in her arms, and worked it all out from there. Had all this been nothing but a mistake? A stubborn, childish mistake?

She remembered the restroom in the hospital and lay down on her side, knees pulled up, she bit her hand again, and started counting. It helped a bit, but as the panic subsided, a new thought moved to the forefront of her mind. Scenes she had almost forgotten. Luca being so drunk that she had to put *his* arm around her neck to keep him true on the way home. And every night, no matter if they had been out or just made love, he would fumble for a whisky bottle from his nightstand. A nightcap just to sleep. Somehow it always hurt; the smell on his breath when they kissed for the last time before he would doze off. As if her embrace wasn't enough to make him feel safe. What if Emmy took after her father when it came to drinking? What if she was as receptive to that demon as he had been?

And Luca was quiet. "You only ever sneak up on me for a warm and cosy moment, don't you?" she whispered. Coward.

She had to hide the letter; it could not stay here on the kitchen floor. In this house, they did not exist. If she were ever to reveal the full story to Emmy, then certainly this was not a good time. She was much too unstable right now; she would be drawn to this mystical family story like a moth to the light. And get burned the same way. Perhaps when she was older, had a family of her own and would understand. Maybe then, it was much too late anyway.

Helen walked up to her bedroom and knelt in front of her wardrobe. After pushing aside some coats, she pulled out a Clarks shoe box from the deepest spot in its left corner. A shoe box underneath her shoes; nobody would ever suspect a hidden treasure here. The only manifestation of Luca in this house, apart from Emmy herself. Here she kept copies of all the cards and photographs of Emmy she ever sent. Then there were a few little things which reminded her of him. A bee-keychain, as he always called her his busy bee, because she studied so hard; a concert ticket; a pencil sketch he had made of Bains des Pâquis in summer and a handwritten *I love you* note he had once placed on her cushion. They had argued the night before; he had gone out without telling her and then not picked up the phone all night. The closest thing to a love letter she ever got. And the first letter with a black cross, announcing Luca's death, the new envelope hurled right next to it.

Helen leaned against the wardrobe and took a deep breath. Now that the letter was safely locked away, her thoughts began to settle down… The big question was: where to go from here? Be aggressive? Authoritative? What if she then clamped shut like an oyster? Maybe she should be more therapeutic about it, asking questions like, "How did that make you feel?" Or the best-friend-approach: no scolding at all to get information about what went on at that party? Everything seemed right and wrong at the same time.

Helen could have called her parents but they would hardly make her feel any better. Helen would end up comforting them, leaving her even more exhausted afterwards. She could have called any of her university friends, with their perfect lives, but they would neither make her feel better.

"I need to speak to someone. I don't know how to do this on my own," she whispered to herself. And suddenly she knew the person to whom she wanted to talk.

She just had to make sure that another coffee break happened tomorrow, that there were no court hearings or telephone conferences getting in the way. She could then postpone dealing with Emmy to later in the evening, when hopefully her mind had cleared up a bit. That probably made sense anyway. At breakfast, Emmy would still be tired, and nothing good ever came out of that. But how could she ask for a coffee break on a Sunday morning without crossing a line? They never planned their get-togethers; they just happened. She had only ever used his phone number during projects, to coordinate court hearings or meetings.

Helen's eyes fell on the big green plushy paws which were still lying around in the hallway, next to the lonely Cinderella shoe. Suddenly she had an idea. Maybe it was fine to text him if it sounded funny instead of dramatic. Like a text one could show a wife, to share a laugh about a funny colleague. And so she wrote:

Need to tell you all about the dinosaur who saved us from walking barefoot through a winter's night. Coffee break tomorrow! ☺

11

The Cut-Out-Heart

1 February 2017, London

On Monday morning, Emmy looked very pale still and kept her eyes to the ground, hiding behind a veil of blonde hair. Helen's first instinct was to put her arms around her, but that instinct still wrestled with a deep anger. There was nothing here that deserved to be rewarded.

"I've got to rush to a client's meeting, so we'll talk later tonight, okay?" Helen only waited for a brief nod and then rushed out.

On the Tube, she checked her phone every five minutes, or rather seconds. Still nothing from Eric. Babette seemed to raise her grapes in a comforting manner, he will answer, for sure; but Francis' smirk was the same as always. Men! But around ten, she heard steps on the creaking stairs. The noise made her perk up, like a deer hearing a tree branch crack. Her saviour was racing up the stairs of her tower. Not with a sword but with two coffee cups.

Slightly out of breath, even before he sat down, he said: "I want to hear all about this. It did sound kind of worrying, barefoot at night…"

So the joke camouflage had failed. Helen's plan had been to be cool about it and after a short laugh, brainstorm some ideas for a proper talk with Emmy. But when he handed her the teacup and sat down opposite her, looking with honest concern, her guard dropped. Instead of rolling her eyes and starting with a cynical, "You won't believe this!" she burst into tears.

"Hey… is everything all right? Did something happen to Emmy?" He leaned forward with a helpless look.

"No… yes… I mean, she is all right. The weekend was just a nightmare and I don't know what to do. I suck as a mother and she is completely slipping away from me and—"

"Whoa, slow down a bit. Nobody says you suck as a mother. Things happen. Even though I don't really know what happened…"

"We spent Saturday night in the hospital. And Sunday morning. She's fine now. It seems like she drank one too many and I know I shouldn't be making such a big deal out of it but…"

"Okay… so… the most important thing is that she's fine, right?"

"Right, but I mean, not every Saturday night ends in the emergency room."

"It happened at the party of the year?"

"Yes, apparently. I don't know much, actually. They brought her back home because she started *decorating* their bathroom…"

"Oh my, Emmy, way to make your debut in social circles! I thought that rather happens when you have sons…" Eric laughed.

"Really? Never been to an undergrad college party? But it wasn't funny, Eric! She collapsed in my place and I thought, I thought maybe she was gonna die…" It was the first time she had said it out loud and it did not help her to calm down. She pressed her hand against her mouth. There was no need for Gemma or even Albertine to hear her cry.

"Gosh, hey, I didn't know that. The first part sounded funny, but that's certainly not—"

"And I was so fucking alone, in that moment, so fucking alone…" she whispered, trailing off.

"Yes, I think I understand. Listen, try to calm down, okay? Take a deep breath… and then let's go for dinner tonight. We'll take a close look at things and figure out what to do."

Helen stared at him as if he were a ghost. Had he really said that?

"That is, if you can arrange that for tonight? You know, just an idea," he added, getting a bit insecure under her stare.

"No, no," she stammered. "No, I was just wondering, can *you* arrange that?" *With your wife and children at home,* she added in her mind.

"Yes, sure. Why not?" he shrugged, as if they did this all the time.

"Okay," she said, still staring in disbelief over her cup. Then she remembered Emmy waiting for her at home. If she did not want her daughter to run from confrontation, she should probably lead by example. "The only thing is, I can't get home really late. I can't leave Emmy alone right after all this. Even I know that is bad parenting."

"I know a nice little place near Farringdon. When can you get off, like, six thirty? Then you could be home by around eight thirty. That should be early enough, right?"

All Helen could do was nod.

"I'll send you the link for Google Maps. The easiest thing would be to meet up there?" he asked, getting up with a business-like attitude.

"Okay, that works for me." She nodded. The easiest thing would, of course, have been to leave together, given that one was working in the same office.

"Okay, great! Cheer up – if you can – and I guess I will see you later?" Eric got up and walked out of the door backwards, almost stumbling as he turned to close it, and was gone. She took a final sip from her teacup. The hot and sweet tea at the bottom was balm for her soul.

*

Eric had chosen a small Portuguese restaurant, with few tables and slightly dirty tablecloths, a little off the beaten path from Farringdon Station. Hardly a venue the white-collar folks of Holborn frequented. Helen could not help thinking he might have chosen this one only to make sure they did not end up next to any colleagues. A good choice; gossip was not what she wanted, either.

Before leaving, Helen checked in her pocket mirror as to whether she looked a little more civilised than in the morning. She added some lip gloss, but then she wiped it away with toilet paper. It turned out, though, that she had worried in vain. If there was one thing that Bar Lisboa was saving on, apart from a second set of tablecloths for the day, it was electricity. The low light and the unplastered walls gave the place a cave-like note and the candlelit atmosphere was kind to even the palest. It was almost difficult to decipher the menu.

After they had ordered, Eric shifted the candle holder to the side and said: "And now, please, the whole story, from beginning to end."

So she talked him through the entire episode, from the stupid pink *18* sign at the door, the chaperone dropping her baby off, to the tales of Milford in the waiting room, the monster paws, and then her breakdown at home. He just listened and nodded every now and then.

"We have not really spoken since." Helen sighed. "She was so exhausted and I was too confused. I don't even know what exactly happened. And I doubt she really wants to share anything with me, if the past is any reference."

"Maybe she does, that episode may have scared her just as much as you. It must have been so frightening for her to lose control over herself, especially if she got drunk for the first time. Maybe she *wants* to tell you everything."

That made sense, actually. Perhaps it would be less of an uphill battle than she thought? Eric poured her another glass of wine. Helen had emptied hers while talking, in need of something to hold onto. After a short pause, and without taking his eyes off his glass, he said: "Helen, can I ask you something? You don't have to answer but I have been meaning to ask for a while…"

"Please. Anything," she said calmly while her heart started pounding in her throat.

"Who was Emmy's father? Is he still in the picture? I'm just wondering, because it's never come up. You really don't have to tell me …"

"Yes, wow. No, it's fine. That's actually a good question," Helen said, a bit too enthusiastically for a person who had avoided the topic strategically all her life. The entire office could only speculate as to whether she lived with a partner in her Clapham Common mansion or not.

"I mean, are you divorced? Was it an affair? Not judging, of course… I figure you must have been rather young…"

There was something kind in his voice, and there was the Cabernet Sauvignon on an empty stomach.

"We were not married. I was twenty-four when I had Emmy. We met at university in Geneva. But he has never been part of our lives. First, it was family issues. Now, he has a hard time making an appearance – because he is dead. He died when Emmy was about a year old."

The waiter brought their food. *Thank God*, Helen thought, another glass on an empty stomach would have been positively dangerous.

"Wow, I'm so sorry to hear that. So, Emmy does not know her father at all?"

"No, never met. And his family is really a case of good riddance. They paid me a bloody sum to stay away. Bunch of Catholic assholes."

"Were they that religious? And you were something like the Antichrist?"

"Maybe. They are just very Italian and upper-classy. I was not from their circles, a foreigner, so they put pressure on him to stay away from me. And he did."

"Sounds like one hell of a family. But I mean, he was a grown man…?"

"You don't know how these families work. He was totally dependent on them. His job, all his funds, they basically owned his ass. They brainwash their kids. In a way, these Italian dynasties are like sects…"

"I see… I guess I don't know anybody with such a background."

"But you think all this has something to do with Saturday night? I'm so worried that this is all happening because she grew up without a father. Emmy deserves a father, like every other kid. You cannot replace the missing half, no matter how much of an effort you make…"

"Yeah, fathers are pretty great," he said with a wink, and Helen giggled, against her will. "But no, seriously: don't beat yourself up because of that. A father is no guarantee that things run smoothly. A better half can also bring a lot of stress to family life. That never happened in your case…"

"I know, but still. Now she is going way overboard – and it would be really helpful if it were two against one."

That made him smile. "I know exactly what you mean. I so often feel outnumbered with my kids." For a moment, it seemed he would leave it at that and just focus on dissecting his cod. But after he had cut off the head, he asked, "You still hold quite a grudge against them after all these years, don't you? It does not really sound like an old wound to me, if I may say so…"

"There were not many occasions where I could have changed my mind…" *Oh, screw it*, Helen thought, this conversation deserved another glass of wine. It was getting too personal much too fast, but it felt good somehow.

"So without that family, you think he would have stood up for you? You would have lived together like a family?" Eric said, pulling out the poor fish's spine.

"We were very young. None of this was planned… And that is a theoretical question anyway. He was very much under his family's thumb," Helen said evasively.

"It must have hurt badly at the time…"

Helen smiled, grateful for the understanding. "I have thought so often about it… what might have been, without that family, and without that accident. Maybe I am too kind to him… or maybe I am the one who gave up too easily instead of empowering him…"

"And?"

"And I do not come to a conclusion. It is like a drawer that has been blocked for seventeen years now. I would have needed some sort of closure, to understand why he reacted that way. A chance to understand who he was in real life, a few visits for the kid… just anything. Perhaps it would have helped me move on."

Eric nodded. Now there were two fine fish fillets on his plate.

"Do you know how he died?"

"He died from drinking – at least that's what I heard. He might even have killed himself. I don't really know."

Eric paused his fork . "Were you in touch at the time?"

"No. We had not talked for six months by the time Emmy was born. Even when she was born, I heard nothing. He had an accident with his car apparently. He had a problem with drunk driving, actually. It already freaked me out back then."

"How do you know that is what happened?"

"I got an obituary card from their lawyer. The agreement I signed would have allowed me to call the lawyer in principle, but I was too proud to do that. Luca did not have many close friends. He knew a lot of people but they were all rather party acquaintances, buddies. The closest thing to a friend he had in Geneva was Jean-Francois, an investment banker from Paris. I found his office contacts over the internet and they really had stayed in touch. It turned out that Luca got engaged two months after Emmy was born. I even knew the girl. She was some kind of local beauty queen, perfect bride material. Anyway, Jean went to their engagement party. From what he said, Luca's drinking had gotten totally out of hand. In Geneva, he would drink but he was kind of in charge. But Jean said that he was sure that Luca does not remember his own engagement. And that there was something unpleasant to it."

"It is fun up to a certain point, but you notice when it takes a turn to the dark side…"

"That's how Jean described it. He also said he would come over to visit sometime, meet Emmy, but he never has. I still follow him on Instagram. It is full of pictures of him and his Swedish wife and their four blond children. It looks like a commercial basically."

"So, but what happened after his engagement?"

"All I know from Jean is that one night he drove around in his car, no idea why or where to. About two kilometres from his home, he hit a tree full speed and died on the spot."

"Oh my God."

"Jean said, '*They say it was an accident*'. The street was wet or something. Now, you don't expect this kind of family to inform the public about the circumstances of their son's death."

"You don't think it was an accident?"

"Honestly, I don't know. Sometimes I believe I knew him better than anybody, and then again, he might have been a total stranger. There was something depressed about him at times, but it never lasted long. Maybe fate simply sorted things out when he challenged his guardian angels for the hundredth time…"

"That sounds very… *detached*."

Helen sighed.

"Believe me, I have spent many a sleepless night over this. I was angry, I was hurt... and then I was not sure whether I had any right to be. Whether I was actually the one who let him down by striking that deal with his family. Who knows what was going on inside him? How much pressure did they put on him? Should I have reached out to him more? Should I have appeared on their doorstep to claim my rights?"

"Hey... it is simply very tragic: a man dying so young..."

"Yes. It is. I guess part of me had hoped that at some point, down the line, he would reach out to me. And there would be a conversation where everything could be said, understood and resolved. But now this conversation will never come. It was not like him to be so... so radical about anything."

"And then you got stuck with your open drawer..."

"Yes." Helen smiled with a shrug. "I guess that kind of sums it up."

"What does Emmy think about all that?"

"Well, she only knows a short version. She thinks her father died while I was pregnant and that there are no relatives to reach out to. With the mother, I could stick quite to reality. I met her once, the coldest person ever. I did not want her to feel unwanted in any way. I mean, she is smart. She understood pretty quickly that she was a bit of a surprise and for some time she also struggled with that. Kids can be brutal. You know that."

"And she was okay with that? No further questions asked?"

"No, she does not bring it up, that case is closed. She also does not know how loaded they are. It only makes it more hurtful to know how they bought us out."

"But it must be bugging her to find out more about her other half? Spiteful or not?"

"You think? Even if he let her down?"

"I would be like that if I were her. That's all I'm saying. Your parents make you who you are!"

"Yeah," Helen said, moving uncomfortably on her chair, "maybe this is all just too difficult to understand from the outside..."

"Sure, just guessing..." he said then – thank God – returned to his fish.

She tried a seductive and upbeat smile to get things back on track.

"Oh my! I have already bothered you enough with the mess of my life. This all happened a long time ago. It is actually possible to have a nice dinner with me without any problem talk."

"It is really not that there is too much of that, *Elsa*," he smirked. "To be honest, I feel this was the first time I actually made it into the ice palace – although I had tea there many times."

"Who is Elsa? Which ice palace?"

"Oh, maybe your daughter is too old for that," he said, and blushed a little bit. "It's from Disney. I watched that on repeat with Sara, how Princess Elsa cuts off all family ties to live in an ice palace, far up in the mountains…"

"You mean *Frozen*? I know the one! It was on Disney Channel. Gosh, I'm Elsa? Why?" she said, pretending to be scandalised. She could have added how much she loved that he had a nickname for her.

"Just that when I first watched it, it reminded me of you. You also live on your own, high up in a tower. It is also freaking cold up there…" He was obviously a bit embarrassed. He thought of her when watching movies with his kids!

"Yes, absolutely. A very similar situation," she said, a bit cynically, to lighten the mood. "And when I start to sing, the floor gets miraculously shiny and with the very last pirouette, my boobs start to grow, and I find myself in a glittery dress." The bottle of cab sav was almost empty by now.

Eric laughed and leaned back. "That's the one! It is exactly like that! Can't you do that tomorrow at tea time?"

"Not really, you know. ," she said, a bit more harshly than intended. Because there it was: the urge to just lean forward and run her hand through his hair, press her nose into his neck, to inhale that smell and then just say it. Thank God, , Helen thought, there was this massive table between them. It really helped.

What was wrong with her? He was just trying to be a good friend, helping her in a time of need. A married man, a happily married man. No more drama, Helen!

After an awkward pause, Eric said, "Perhaps we should go? It is late and Emmy is waiting for you, right?"

"Yes, sure. It is late. We should leave, absolutely," she said, and got up from her chair to reach for her coat, dynamic and committed to the new plan. Eric looked a bit confused and got up to help her with her coat, but she was too energetic and left him no chance.

"I'll pay at the counter in the front," he said.

How embarrassing, she had entirely forgotten that one usually had to pay in a restaurant before running away from an uncomfortable situation. He paid for both of them as she waited, standing close behind. The waiter probably thought they were a couple, a regular London couple, hard-working, no kids, and in no mood to cook in their fancy flat.

The fresh air sobered her up a bit. It was only a few minutes' walk to Holborn Tube Station. He walked a good two metres apart from her, both hands deep in the pockets of his winter coat. On New Oxford Street, there was the usual excited after-work party crowd, junior associates and paralegals, spilling out of crowded pubs as if it were the last night in Eden. The girls shrieked, exhilarated in their skimpy dresses, eyes wide and with high-pitched voices; the boys, in rolled-up sleeves and loosened ties, were red-faced from drinking and sweating from excitement. Usually, she would have commented with derision on this behaviour, but tonight Helen almost envied them. They were so young; they could throw themselves into life like that. A life of happiness can be made in one night, with no fear of disappointment or regrets. Then, she thought of Emmy. It might have been that exact feeling that had literally kicked Emmy out of her princess shoes. It was not such a bad reason at all.

They walked silently, side by side in their grey and black winter coats, through that nocturnal orgy of the flesh. The next corner would be Holborn Station. They would split up and drive in different directions on the Central Line. Just a few more metres and this nightwalk would be over. Helen suddenly felt as if she would turn into a pumpkin as soon as they were in the station. She had to do something right now. So, in an attempt at bravery, she threw her head towards Eric, pointed with her chin to the screaming girls and asked, "So, is that how you courted Karen?" Drat, what corner of her mind had brought her to that? It was the first time she had ever mentioned his wife. Eric laughed, a little too loudly, a little too nervously, and worst of all, he moved further away from her.

"Yeah, kind of like that. Haha! Thank God she is not a good sprinter."

Oh well. Now the situation was finally completely awkward and they were down to bad jokes. Eric stopped in front of the gate to Holborn Station, definitely more than two metres between them now.

"Thank you for tonight. It really was a pleasure," he said formally, and then did the worst thing. He took one hand out of his coat and stepped forward to give her a tight slap on the shoulder, like one does with a sports buddy. The slap was so hard and unexpected that Helen stumbled a bit to the side but managed to smile somehow, masking her disappointment. He still made no attempt to move into the station. At least they could take the first escalator together.

"I have to thank you. You really put me back together and I appreciate it. Are you not taking the Central Line?"

"No, urm, I think I will catch some more fresh air and walk a few blocks before I go down." *Walk alone*, was what Helen heard, loud and clear.

"Okay then. See you tomorrow, I guess," she said, not sure how to say goodbye.

"Yeah, see you tomorrow," he said, and turned on his heel, eager to get away without turning around one more time.

As she paced towards her home through the dark streets of Clapham Common, she felt her neck growing tense when coming closer to the dark patch where she had met the fox. She slowed down a bit, unsure whether she longed for him or feared his appearance. But he did not come.

The house lay dark; Emmy had gotten to bed early. But Helen was greeted in the hall by a heartbreaking arrangement. A white tablecloth was spread on the floor and resting on it were the Cinderella shoes – both of them! – next to a little flower bouquet, stuffed into one of the green monster-mummy paws. A big heart-shaped note – probably cut out with her kiddy scissors – read, *I'm so sorry, Mum!* Forget about men, Helen thought, her baby was the best.

I love you! Helen wrote at the bottom of the note and pushed it under Emmy's door. Then, she took a piece of paper from the notepad on the kitchen counter, cut out another heart with the kitchen scissors and wrote on it:

PS: We still need to talk! and pushed it under the door as well.

12

The Little Swallow

Mid-March 2017, Vittuone (Milan)

Since the day Flavia had pulled Alma out of bed and sobered her up, things had begun to get better. Gradually and slowly. Every time she woke, it felt impossible to leave the bed or eat a single bite. But somehow she managed to lift herself up and make her way downstairs to the kitchen. She did not want to burden the maids, have them worry about her. The *cornetti* were too dry to chew and she could hardly tell the difference between coffee and water. But the daylight did her good; she had to promise Flavia to stay awake until after lunch. It was those little things that kept her alive.

After breakfast, she would sit in the living room and stare into the park. She refused to sit in the library though and never ventured into the eastern wing of the estate. While her husband was alive, she had hidden in that one room into which he never set foot. Now that he was gone, Alma wanted to sleep on the desk of his office, just to find a trace of his smell. What a ridiculous woman she was.

The Unione ladies kept visiting her, but the intervals grew wider and wider. It surprised Alma they came over at all; it seemed unlikely they would stay in touch, now that she was a widow. No living family member was a member of the Club, no cousin or son; their house was cursed.

Sara especially made surprisingly regular appearances; perhaps she wanted to gain sympathy points with the charity ladies Sofia and Chiara. Alma had never felt close to Sara, and filling her visits with actual conversation was tough. Sara did not seem to mind; she preferred reporting the latest events in her life to having a conversation anyway. Luckily, one of her nieces had gotten married the previous summer, and Sara had prepared an epic photo album, to share the joy as well as the status. Flavia brought in fresh tea twice and rolled her eyes when she saw that Sara was still relentlessly turning page after page. No clichés were spared: the bridesmaids looked great, the mother of the bride cried, the flower girls were cute and ran off in the wrong direction, some guests were impossibly drunk. Alma did not know any of these people. At the end of her visit, Sara gave her some artificial kisses into the air next to her cheek, and said what she always said, "Whatever it is, feel free to call us, darling. We know you don't have anybody."

*

By mid-March, the temperatures started to climb up to the low twenties. Flavia put a deckchair out on the terrace and urged Alma to sit in the sun. At least for a bit, with a blanket over her legs. After a week, Alma got tired of arguing against it and came out to sit as she was told. And for a moment, it was almost pleasant. The sun felt warm on her face, she hadn't noticed that the world outside had moved on to spring. The grass was a fresh green, with violet crocuses mingling about. The trees were putting on new dresses, still modest and not yet the full ballroom of summer.

Alma sat with her eyes closed. The air smelled different in spring. The scent of flowers, soil and sun mingled in its perfume. She turned her head to the right, to rest it more comfortably on the chair. As she opened her eyes, Alma's gaze fell upon the empty aviary flanking the entire northern end of the terrace. It was a beautiful Victorian aviary which had once hosted a swarm of canaries, lending a tropical note to the garden. At least that was what Alma had been told by her mother-in-law. She had never seen a bird chirp in it herself. For decades now, the aviary only played host to pots of dusty artificial flowers. When Luca was a little boy, he had been crazy about the idea of keeping pet birds in there. He painted pictures with trees full of birds and would give them to his parents as strategic gifts. "Only girls want to play with pet birds," her husband had said, and Luca had finally swallowed down his tears. Then, a cloud covered the sun that it was still winter. She felt a chill deep in her bones and walked inside without a second glance.

During the next days, the weather stayed mild but Alma refused to try the terrace again. The chill she had felt, she was sure it was still there. No matter how much Flavia and Maria praised the fresh air and sunlight, Alma refused to sit anywhere but on the sofa in the living room, looking at the world from a safe distance. Until the day the bird died.

It rarely happened. Perhaps because the inside of the house was usually dark or perhaps because there were reflections on the glass that made the windows of the gallery look like a solid wall. They had never put up those awful black bird stickers, thinking they would ruin the front of the house. Alma had been staring into the park, lost in thought, when she caught a tiny shadow in the corner of her eye. Within a split second, something exploded on the glass with a loud bang. A noise so violent amidst the eternal silence. Alma screamed; her heart pounded in her throat as she opened the terrace door and rushed outside. When she bent over the little bird, Alma saw its right wing trembling slightly, but it was nothing more than a final shiver. It looked almost unharmed save for a little stream of blood running from one side of its beak. It was a swallow and it was dying right in front of her. Its day had probably started like any other day; it had woken up a happy swallow full of plans. It was probably a mother and a daughter and a wife, and now it would never return home. Perhaps the sunlight had just blinded it at the wrong moment. It had made one wrong turn and that was the last thing it ever did. Whatever the case, from now on, this swallow could only be remembered.

Life was like that. Life was catastrophe. And despite all the catastrophes around her, it was as if Alma saw it for the first time. Life was not a long sequence of happy events of which only a few cursed and miserable people were deprived. Some people lived a hundred years, others just a few hours. Life owed you nothing. It did not owe the little swallow the joy of flying until old age simply because it was an innocent creature. Weren't all creatures innocent? Nobody was doomed more than another, and none is the master of his own fate.

Maria had been wiping dust in the salon near the terrace and came running, alarmed by Alma's screaming. She found her mistress kneeling on the stone tiles of the terrace, still bending over the little bird and crying, for the bird, for herself, and everyone else.

"A shovel," Alma winced, "we need a shovel to bury the bird. The cat shall not get her."

"It is okay, madame. We will take care of it," said Maria, trying to get hold of the situation.

"No!" exclaimed Alma. "No, I have to do it myself!"

"Okay, madame, okay. No problem. Don't get upset. I will get you a shovel right away," Maria left with an almost inaudible "*Mamma mia.*" It was one thing to look after a mad person with loyalty, but another to become an accomplice in a mad endeavour. But she returned with the shovel and called for Flavia on the way. They found Alma still on her knees, her hands folded in front of her chest. Together they dug a little hole right by the terrace, placed the bird carefully on the shovel and laid it inside. They put some branches from a nearby bush over it so that the mud would not hit the little body so hard, then covered it with earth, and Alma said a little prayer. A little stick in the ground marked the place where they buried it. After the funeral, Flavia and Maria exchanged glances and started to wonder whether they should have consulted the doctor before flushing all those pills. The prayers they said were surely not meant for the passing of the swallow.

But in the following days, Alma got up in the mornings more easily and started to go for walks in the afternoon, surrendering to Flavia's fresh air paradigm. Not long ones, just in the park and then to the main gate and back. She even waved every time she passed by the office building if someone appeared in the window. While the visible Alma was still pale and drifting, her subconscious self had gotten to its feet, willing to hold on to any loose end that would come within reach, determined to not let go.

13

Three Birds

End of March 2017, Vittuone (Milan)

Toward the end of March, Sara Picone called the Carneggio residence to invite Alma for a ladies' lunch. Alma felt obliged to attend. She was no longer in bed and after all their visits, how could she turn them down? She regretted it immediately, though; it had been months since she had been to downtown Milan.

Tramezini's was a popular place, right next to the Scala and Galeria Emilio Vittore. It had a beautiful wooden Art Deco interior and the food was excellent. But the streets were crowded every day; the pavement filled with businessmen in elegant suits, tourists constantly streaming through the Galeria to see the Duomo. The Piazza di Duomo itself was a nightmare. If one stopped for a second, one was either beset by pigeons or an African street vendor would wind a friendship bracelet around your wrist and then demand payment. The mere thought of it exhausted her. But now that Alma had accepted, there was no going back. She did not want to worry anyone, as they were all convinced she was getting better. And she could not forget the little swallow. She should be grateful to be able to go downtown at all, because who knew what would happen next?

Flavia ordered her a taxi and it went well, at first. The taxi was nicely climatised; she almost enjoyed the change of scenery, the spring landscape floating by. With little traffic, they reached Corso Vittore but then the driver stopped about two hundred metres from the Scala and Tramezini's. What had given her comfort was the idea of just stepping from the taxi right into the restaurant, then staying for two hours and then stepping into another taxi which would shuttle her right back to safety. But the gods were not on her side. The road was blocked; there were construction works on the tram tracks. Apparently, for more than two months, but as she never went to town, how could she have known?

"The place is very close, *signora*. Maybe you want to walk? Otherwise, I have to go from the other side, but it is quite a detour," the driver said, and shrugged his shoulders. Of course, it was all no big deal to him, she thought. He was probably in his mid-thirties. What did young men ever know about old women? She left the taxi, too embarrassed to ask for the ridiculous detour. She could walk two hundred metres, why not?

"It is not very hot today, *signora*," the driver shouted after her, still shrugging his shoulders.

Neither heat nor distance was the real problem. She had walked no more than twenty metres down the narrow pavement when a man in a black suit bumped into her when overtaking her. He seemed to be arguing madly with an invisible man. It took Alma a while to spot the earplug and cable as he walked on. She stumbled but managed to regain her balance by putting her hand out against a shop window Then there was a group of Chinese tourists blocking the entire pavement, talking so loudly. Alma could not overtake them, as she was moving too slowly herself, but all the noise made her dizzy. Young, elegant people streamed around her and the Chinese group, as if she were non-existent. The honking of cars, music from the shops, and the shouting and laughter of people turned into an insufferable drone in her head. Everybody was walking with so much purpose at their feet. Didn't they know they were nothing but swallows in the sky? Was everybody so much stronger than her; strong enough to love and make plans knowing they would not last? Or were they all blind? Or did nobody else love?

Her heart started racing quickly; she could not breathe. Her vision blurred and her knees began to feel weak. She knew the feeling; Alma had had severe panic attacks a few times after Luca had died. She slowed down, her right hand reaching out for the mural between two boutiques. If someone were to push her now, she would surely fall. With a few steps more, she managed to take a turn to the right, into one of the smaller side streets, and leaned against the wall. The cool shade helped her calm down and her vision cleared up a bit. She waited, took a few deep breaths, and her heart rate slowed. The few people passing did not take note of her fight to stay on her feet. She longed for a chair and a glass of water, but there was neither. And she knew, as soon as she returned to the main street, the panic would return.

It had clearly been a mistake to come; she was not ready for this. It was less than three months since her husband had died, what was she thinking? But if she turned back around now, they would talk about her; she knew that for sure. They had certainly discussed at great length whether she would really come and had most likely expected her not to. She did not want them to be right, and yet the task felt insurmountable.

The album, she suddenly thought, *what if Sara is showing all those photos again?* It was quite likely that she would feast on it another time. And with that, her decision was clear; she stepped out of the shade and waved for a taxi. She would send the ladies a message that she really had wanted to come but that she felt unwell. Maybe she was coming down with flu. There would be a next time. She would feel better and the album would be history by then.

*

Back at home, Alma went straight to the kitchen. Her stomach directed her there as it had been promised a delicious lunch. She found Flavia polishing up some of the silver spoons. Flavia was worried to see her back so soon, and dead pale at that.

"*Signora* Alma, what's the matter? Are you not feeling well?" she asked, moving a chair next to Alma. She wiped her hand clean on her apron and reached for Alma's forehead. "No, it is not a fever. If anything, you feel a bit cold."

"Yes," Alma said, disheartened. "If anything, I feel a bit cold."

"What happened? They cancelled the lunch?"

"No, I just did not go. I turned around at the last minute. The street, the noise... I think I panicked."

"Perhaps it was just a bit early," Flavia said softly.

"And also their constant chatting, I felt like I could not take it. I was imagining that Sara Picone would show up with her hideous album, and I did not want to go through all the hundreds of pages again," Alma burst out. The sudden anger in her voice surprised both of them.

After a moment of shock, Flavia started to giggle.

"Oh no. That pink album, thick like an encyclopaedia? A second time? Nobody deserves that."

Alma also started to laugh. It felt so liberating that they could not stop and they laughed until they had tears in their eyes.

When she got her breath back, she looked straight at Flavia, her most faithful companion, and asked, "What do I do now?"

"Oh, I don't know, *Signora* Alma. I am in no position to give you advice. Perhaps you eat first and then you take it little by little? Perhaps you think about something that could make you feel happy? I know that this is difficult at the moment, but I mean just a little something to feel a little happy. Like: would you like to visit someone? Or some place? Just nearby, maybe? Or, for starters, think more about what you would like us to cook for you? Just something to keep your mind busy during the day, something to think of—"

"Easier said than done," Alma said. They then sat quiet for a while. Flavia was probably wondering whether the conversation was already over and if she could return to her work.

"You know what," Alma said after a while, "for starters, let's try lunch on the terrace again."

"Very well, *Signora* Alma," Flavia said, happy there was some sort of plan. "I will be right outside with some snacks."

Indeed, this was at least much better than the city. Alma felt a wave of relief at having escaped the lunch. Out here, it was actually a nice day. Food still tasted kind of lame, but for a few days her stomach had tolerated a second espresso after lunch – that was something to look forward to. The park was now a lot greener than when she had last attempted to sit there. The leaves covered the branches. The flowerbeds were blossoming in yellow and blue.

Then, her head turned right again and found the empty aviary; dark and unchanged. She saw the swarm of yellow canaries before her inner eye and her mother-in-law in a summer dress. She had liked to wear those loose ones as she did not take to heat well. Only when there were no guests, of course. Alma imagined her chirping to the birds, maybe holding a piece of apple into the cage for them to snack on.

And suddenly Alma knew what she needed to do. Flavia was right: happiness, at least in the little things, would not fall from the sky. Only unhappiness did. When Flavia came back to clear the table, to her surprise, she found Alma inside the old aviary. Alma could barely stand upright in there and pushed around the flowerpots. Decades-old dust and old spider webs garnished her hair and clothes, but in all her busyness, she did not even realise.

"Flavia," she said, out of breath, "come over here and help me. We have to get these ugly pots out of here."

"It was your idea to put them there. A long time ago," Flavia said, slightly offended and very confused.

"Yes, yes, but it was actually not a good idea." Alma was on a mission; she had no time to assign guilt.

The old girls heaved the china pots out of the aviary one by one so that Alma had more space for her inspection. She carefully jolted the grid and checked the lock of the door.

"It looks fine, doesn't it? And the door also closes perfectly well. It needs a little cleaning but that's really all," she said enthusiastically.

Flavia noticed the rosy cheeks and the unusual active vibe, but she did not trust the situation yet. Was this another sign of madness? Would it lead to a good thing or result in another bird funeral?

"Perhaps you can swing a broom through that thing and get the old leaves out. And I guess we should put some sand on the ground. Isn't that how it is done? The gardener will know. Perhaps you can call him? But first, call a driver. I am going to town again."

Later on, Alma would laugh about this episode whenever she recounted it. How she could not wait a minute after the thought had crossed her mind. It was comical that the most urgent task in years was to buy a pair of pet birds. The bewilderment of the shop assistant in the pet store added to the humour. Alma had stormed into the tiny shop in the heart of Vittuone as if it were the emergency room of a hospital. The bespectacled biology student helping out with the afternoon shift was deeply sunk into a book. He jumped up behind the desk, alarmed by Alma's attitude. There were not many urgent matters in a pet shop on a normal day. Half the day went by with school kids coming into the shop, just to look at the pet of their dreams. Perhaps the lady had a sick pet and wanted her money back? Or she wanted to return a guinea pig because she had found out how boring they were? He looked at them the whole day and was surprised that this did not happen more often.

"I need birds," was all Alma could say when the student asked how he could help.

"Aha, birds. Did you ever own a pet bird, *signora*?"

"No, not at all. But now I need some pretty and cheerful ones for my aviary."

"Pretty and cheerful, aha." For somebody studying biology, that kind of answer was a nightmare, as in that joke where a woman is asked for her favourite car and answers, *"A red one."*

"Maybe you would like to purchase this book first, *signora*?" he suggested, fumbling for a thick book on the shelf. "It is a must-read for everyone who loves *pretty and cheerful birds*."

"Excellent! Put it on the list as well."

"Aha, as well. All right then."

After an hour, the young man had made the deal of the month and had forgiven Alma for all her ignorance when happily swiping her credit card. He had sold a full starter set for the virgin bird owner, including a big cage in case an emergency relocation became necessary. Alma had initially thought of some canaries but then she fell in love straight away with a pair of parrots all snuggled up on a branch, in lovely green with rosy faces. The two were constantly billing and talking to each other. When Alma read on the little label on their cage they were called 'lovebirds', the deal was done.

The young man had to accompany Alma to her taxi. She was incapable of carrying all her stuff because she was holding the carton with the two lovebirds with both hands like it was the most precious and fragile little thing. When they did not move, she was scared that they might have died out of fear. But when they moved and scratched with their little claws over the carton when the taxi went into a curve and Alma could not fully balance out the movement, she got scared that they might scratch and nibble a way out before she reached the terrace. The taxi driver asked her if she had a grandkid that would come to play with the birds and she was so happy that she said, "Yes, that's it."

The three arrived safely, and Flavia and Maria stood in disbelief when the taxi driver carried half the pet shop into the house. But they were curious. Finally *something* was happening. They followed Alma to the terrace where she did exactly as the student had explained to her: "Open the little carton, place it on the ground, and then leave the aviary. Avoid any frightening noises, do not take pictures with flashlight with your phone, and then wait from a distance."

And so, the three women sat by the terrace table, chairs lined up like in a cinema, as excited as children waiting for Father Christmas. When the two little birds finally carefully waddled into their new home, they had already provided so much entertainment. They flew up to a branch and the ladies broke into applause, which scared the birds right back into the box, but fortunately not for very long.

The next morning, Alma woke up early as usual, but she had no time to lie and think. She got up and went straight to the terrace to see if her new flatmates were doing well. They were indeed already awake at dawn, proverbial early birds just like her, and still a bit shy.

Alma went to the library, but this time to study the bird book. To keep her company, she put out the latest photograph from the girl and carefully leaned it between the framed photographs. That beautiful smile. There were a hundred things she needed to know to provide a good home for lovebirds, and she carefully underlined the most important passages with a marker. Around seven, she heard the old Fiat pull over and hastily put the photograph back in the drawer. On the way to the kitchen, she passed by the terrace again, just to check, and found Flavia and Maria in front of the aviary, whistling and chirping to the birds.

From then on, the terrace became her favourite place; it was so enjoyable just to watch and listen. As she sat there and took her meals, Alma began to notice that the place could look a lot better than it did. She had Maria brush up the stone tiles. She called for the gardener to give the rhododendron arrangements opposite the terrace a makeover, and she decided on big pots with lemon trees for the terrace. For some reason, the idea of harvesting her own lemons amazed her.

Suddenly so house-proud, Alma felt eager to show her new favourite place to someone. When Clara called – she called basically every day to check on her, even if only for a few minutes – Alma invited her to stay for a week, to enjoy the garden since the weather was so nice. There was a long silence on the other end.

"You are inviting me?"

"Yes."

"And you do not think it would be too much for you?"

"No!"

"I do not have to invite myself and insist while you keep saying that of course you are not stopping me from coming, but you won't be very entertaining, and so on and so forth?"

Alma bit her tongue. She heard herself all too well in these lines.

"No, no. I actually just think it would be nice. I'm sorry if I've been a bit off-putting lately…"

"That's all right, dear. I'm just surprised…"

"Yes," Alma said. "I guess I am surprised too."

"You sound much better, like your voice is quite different. I haven't heard it like that in years. That's lovely!"

"I am much better indeed."

"So what happened? Did you see one of those 'people' your friends recommended?"

"No, I did not. It is not my thing really."
"I know, dear, I know…What was it then?"
"I guess it was… I guess it was three birds."
"Three birds?"
"Yes. A dead swallow and two lovebirds."

14

Drinking Games

February to March, 2017, London

When Emmy came down for breakfast the next morning, she broke into tears before she had even unscrewed the Nutella jar.

Helen gave her a handkerchief and she trumpeted into it like a little elephant. When the sobbing had calmed down a bit, she pulled her daughter close and was not pushed away. Emmy had to leave for school, but they agreed to order pizza that night, to talk things through. And then Emmy looked a bit happier.

On the Tube, she got her phone out to text Eric. Perhaps she had overinterpreted the goodbye fiasco. And he had been right about Emmy being eager to talk; he deserved some credit for that. But halfway through the drafting process, a message from him popped up:

Hope things got sorted out! Have a big hearing on Friday, will be underwater for the rest of the week. Tc!

What it actually said was: *Let's keep a distance to cool down.* Helen deleted her draft. Perhaps it was for the best. Clearly they were not headed towards a good place last night. Being in the same office, the most important thing probably was to keep that from happening again.

*

That night, as soon as the pizzas were heaved out of the box, Emmy started talking like a little waterfall. Eric had been right about another thing: the reason why Emmy had been super excited about the party was a guy: Ali-Saa's brother Amir, the non-chivalrous knight. In a way, that was great news. From the way he had *returned* Emmy, she was on absolutely safe territory. Helen also learned that Emmy had gotten those red nails at Ali-Saa's house, with the prospect of impressing Amir with the new look.

To the excitement of the gang, Amir and some of his friends had been ordered to chaperone his little sister's birthday party. To avoid any resemblance to a homemade kiddie birthday, the girls had put some effort into setting up a real cocktail bar, like adults have it. How that had escaped the host-parents' attention was a miracle to Helen. Ali-Saa knew a place where no one asked for ID, so the kids had scraped some money together to equip a full-sized downtown cocktail bar.

When Emmy got to the scene on Saturday night, Ali-Saa and Sadie were already on a mission. Their entire plan was in danger as Amir & friends did not so much consider themselves as guests at the elusive party (surprise, surprise) but had settled around a DVD player in a room upstairs, just checking every now and then on the pimped-up minors. To get the guys' attention, the girls came up with a drinking game – a great way to prove how wild and grown-up they actually were. Although *game* was a bit of an overstatement. The whole idea was to put on some songs and whenever the lyrics said 'Fuck', they would gulp down a shot. Emmy was particularly determined to get it right. Looking back, Emmy suspected that Ali-Saa and Sadie were giggling so much that they missed more than half of the Fucks. Life is hard on those playing by the rules. Helen reconstructed that her sweet little daughter had probably emptied a bottle of vodka on her own within four to five songs, roughly twenty minutes. Then they started dancing wildly, which was probably when she lost the Cinderella shoe. After this, things got vague. Emmy could not tell whether other guests had arrived in the meantime or who said what to whom. Somebody handed her another Coke-sized glass of Bailey's (yikes) and that finally tipped her over. Emmy's biggest concern seemed to be that someone had taken a video of her, but there was little that could be done about it now.

After finishing the pizza, they curled up on the sofa, almost like when Emmy was little and came running into the living room from a bad dream.

"Saturday night was my worst nightmare, you know that, right?" Helen finally admitted. "You could have died. I never want to have to go through something like this again." Emmy shook her head. "What I really want is for you to be content with yourself, not caring so much what others think or expect you to do. I know that is easier said than done and also not true for most adults. But it is the only way to steer away from all kinds of mess." Helen had planned quite a speech on self-control and self-respect, but she was too emotional herself to get it together.

"Didn't you go to a lot of parties or want to be friends with people when you were my age?" Emmy asked into her pause.

"I did. The point is: it may look so important at the time but it is not..."

"How do you know?" Emmy sat up straight now. "If you would have been out and about more with people, maybe you would have met a really cool guy in high school and you would have married him and..." and then she caught her mother's gaze and bit on her tongue.

Helen forced herself to smile. "I *am* perfectly happy, and then I would not have you." That was how she usually closed that topic. With a line so impersonal that it could be from one of those cheesy movies where J-Lo plays the tough single mum that is rewarded with a guy who looks like Ralph Fiennes.

"You know, the best party nights of my life, I actually had with your dad. It is a good thing to feel lighter than air, but one has to know where one belongs and where one is headed. Or other people will decide this for you – and you might not like the outcome." She had not planned to say that but there it was.

Emmy just sat and stared at her for a moment. "You have never said anything like that before..."

"I know," she said. "And I'm sorry. It is hard to find the right measure of things sometimes..." Perhaps it was the most powerful lesson she could use, right? The story of her own father.

"There must be stories, right, stories about him you haven't told me yet? Even though you were not together for long?" My God. There was so much tension buried inside her little girl and now it was close to bursting out. Red spots appeared on her face like lava surfacing for an eruption. There was no going back now, and actually, what was the harm in talking a bit more about him? Helen could still make sure Emmy did not get hurt by keeping this godforsaken family out of it…

"Yes, there are, but I will stay very clear on one thing: we never needed him. Who knows how things would have turned out had he been around."

"Okay." She nodded vigorously. "Mum, I promise, I won't love him too much." And that one made her heart flinch.

"Was he a good student? Like one of those who can go out all the time and still get good grades?" Emmy had immediately found the weak spot.

"Actually, no. He hated economics, and given how popular he was, he always found someone he could copy the assignments from… It drove me mad sometimes," she added for educational reasons.

"Why did he study it then?"

"Hard to say… I think he had not yet found his passion in life. He was under a lot of pressure from home. His father had high expectations and his mother was pulling quite a guilt-trip on him. He tried to reduce contact to a minimum, therefore…"

A big fat lie. It was obvious that he blossomed more the further he was away from home. And yet, he called Mummy and Daddy every day. The five-star son he could not stop trying to be, while messing up all of his grades. Once in bed, he had even whispered that he missed his dad, like a little boy. Every woman likes a soft-hearted man…

"So you think he died before he found out what he wanted to do with his life? But that is so sad," Emmy said, and her eyes filled with tears.

"In a way, yes…That is why it is so important to me that you do in life what you really want to!" That somehow brightened Emmy's mood instantly.

"No matter what? As long as it makes me happy?"

"Yes, of course…" although that to me was truly unsettling. So Helen added: "And, honey, don't worry. It takes time to find the right thing. Something you like, that pays your bills, all those things. How about this? In the next few weeks, we will sit here together every Wednesday for a pizza-night. You will tell me about your thoughts, what you are interested in and I will tell you an anecdote about your dad.…"

Emmy was smart enough to sense that she was entering into a deal here, but she agreed.

When Helen brushed her teeth later that night, bent over to spit out the foam and came up again, she saw Luca in the mirror. He leaned on the bathroom door, his arms crossed in front of his chest, and he looked very satisfied with himself. "Thank you," Helen whispered, "for helping me keep the foot in this door."

"You did that all on your own, Dulcinea," he smirked, and left. She would meet him again later tonight.

*

During the next week, Eric still kept his distance while officially running out of excuses. Helen spent entire mornings listening for the creak of the stairs and went to the watering hole three times a day. Sometimes, he wrote her a short email saying he was awfully busy, but most of the time there was nothing. She always responded with a question or a little teaser to invite him to ask about Emmy, but he never picked it up. Perhaps he was right and this was the only way to keep them out of trouble.

Helen's mind would probably not have stopped obsessing about Eric if there were not so many good things going on at home. On their first Wednesday's pizza-night, Emmy had reported in a jubilant tone that all the guys from Saturday's party had added her on Facebook. Perhaps they just wanted to follow her future disasters, but the more likely explanation was that Emmy now counted as cool. As annoyed as this Amir guy had seemed, in terms of social media, she somehow had made the cut. Emmy showed Helen Amir's Facebook pages and clearly, everything this guy did was 'cute'. Her face was glowing as if she had gotten access to a treasure box. Most pictures were harmless, just him and the same guys hanging out for movie nights, some stuff on a baseball team, and that was basically it. Hopefully admiring someone digitally would get old after a while, then she would meet someone her age. Emmy was so taken by all this that she did not even push for a story about her dad. Instead, she took her mum for a tour in her virtual world. A tour which made Helen truly feel old. She learned about influencers and fashion bloggers, all keywords she had heard in passing, mostly from Albertine. And to her surprise, there was a bit more science behind the shoe frenzy than a teenager dressing up for a party. Had she never listened or had Emmy held back so much? Her daughter knew all the big fashion shows in the world, who was presenting where with what theme, who was the designer behind which brand, etc. She had favourite bloggers and could give sophisticated explanations for her preferences. She would say things like, "Chiara Ferragni is super-popular, but to my taste she is too much concerned with her own brand nowadays than with actual fashion." And that also explained the bond with Ali-Saa; they shared a common interest here. Lots of the things she showed Helen had been sent to her or commented on by Ali-Saa, with no less expertise. Helen could not quite grasp the fascination behind all that; most clothes looked weird to her, and the people wearing them no less. But everyone was entitled to a hobby, and after this pizza, she felt she knew her daughter a lot better. Also, the forwarding and commenting on all those posts was a good explanation for typing on that little phone the whole day.

*

The third week after the Farringdon dinner brought no change on the Eric front. She missed him and his conversations. Sometimes she wondered whether she should tell him that she was not interested in any further dinners and would never overstep any line. But this could also turn into a huge embarrassment. If he had simply lost interest, she would look like an idiot. If he wanted to keep his distance, it was better not to run after him.

The second pizza-night was even more revealing. Helen had told Emmy a story about a night out in Geneva, always emphasising Luca's independent soul and cheerful nature, leaving out the drinking habit, not to give her ideas. That night they had run into a group of young fashion designers who had come to the city for a contest. Emmy's eyes lit up with the words 'fashion designer', as expected. She asked many questions on what they looked like and whether they became famous.

"So you want to be a designer?" Helen enquired. She had mentally prepared herself for that after all the blogs and influencers she got to see last time.

"Not exactly... I don't really have ideas for new clothes, and I am not interested in tailoring or anything like that." That was true, actually; Emmy had never been a fan of any kind of craftsmanship; tasks involving glue and scissors had always ended with tears.

"Do you want to write about it then? Have your own blog or something?" Journalism, that could be a thing.

Emmy made a face. "Gee, writing, I don't really know. I wouldn't know a funny thing to say about an outfit..."

That was also true; she was rather the quiet type. "So what is it then, what would you like to do?" Helen got a growing sense that Emmy actually knew but was holding back.

Emmy took a deep breath. "I want to be a stylist for clothes and make-up. For fashion shows or VIPs."

"What?? Is that even a job?"

"Of course it is! My idol is the stylist of Kate Middleton. Or that of Lady Gaga, although that one is different..."

"Yes yes, quite different... I mean, I know people pay others to pick out their clothes, but still, is that a *profession*?"

"It is not just picking out clothes, Mum! You really need to have an eye for it. Fashion is a language. And sometimes politics!"

"Well, I, like most people, have to pick out my clothes on my own and it works just fine!"

"Yeah, right." Emmy rolled her eyes.

"Now what does that mean?"

"The question is, do you think you could dress Kate Middleton, let's say, for a state visit to Australia? Because if my childhood outfits are your reference, you can't!"

"Hey!"

"What I mean is that it is a special talent which not everybody has. But I think I could be really good at it." Emmy was awfully calm. There was nothing of that hysterical teenager; she absolutely stood behind her word here. Helen took a deep breath.

"My point is that I really think women should stop putting all their energy into their looks or, even worse, their clothes. All that effort just to please men. Orbiting around them like a decorated planet. Doesn't that ring a bit superficial to you? And also kind of backward? Women can study everything today…"

"I don't think that Kate Middleton is *orbiting* around Prince William. She just gives a kick-ass performance and her outfit is a vital part of that. Every piece shows how much she is in charge. And I would like to learn that and be good at it."

"Kate Middleton does not have *a job* apart from being married. She is like the worst example here…" Helen began to lose her cool, unlike her Zen daughter.

"Okay, then let's say Lady Gaga. Clearly no men there…"

"Right, one never hears of Lord Gaga." Helen tried to be funny, but Emmy did not even twitch an eye. "Is that the one with the fillet steak dress?"

"Yes, but that is, like, the most extreme example, she is an icon…"

"Okay, okay, I still haven't understood how far this is an actual *profession*. Like, what would you study?"

Emmy leaned back a bit on the sofa, as if she wanted to preemptively gain some distance: "I would not study at all…"

"What? But you have got good grades!"

"It is not that I would not *learn* anything, I would train as a *visagiste* or stylist. Some universities do have bachelor programmes like 'fashion communication and styling' or 'fashion styling and creative direction', but academic stuff is not so relevant. It is really much more about connections and experience in this field. I have read a lot about it, the most important thing is to get hold of all sorts of internships, and so on, real-life experience…"

Helen felt slightly dizzy. Emmy not studying was something she had never even considered. What was all the college blood money saved from Italy for then?

"Mu-um, you said whatever makes me happy. I really don't think I am the academic type. Like, I am not exactly a bookworm… and also, I think I have a different idea of feminism. It should not mean that women have turned away from fashion and make-up. It is rather that they should be allowed to really do whatever they want. If they want just babies, or are into fashion, there should be no lecture. Whatever is fun!"

"You don't have to be a bookworm…" Helen said faintly. "And what would you earn? I mean Kate Middleton's girl probably has a decent salary, but otherwise…"

"Obviously, that varies a lot," Emmy said wisely. Helen was asking the childish questions here. It made no sense to keep arguing with her tonight, she had made up her mind.

"I'll think about it, honey," she said to conclude the topic, painting a triumphant smile on her daughter's face. Helen felt more exhausted than after the longest working day.

*

For the rest of the week, Emmy would let the topic rest; she knew she had won Round 1. And Helen was surprised herself at how much her daughter's announcement terrified her. She did want her to be happy and do whatever she wanted to do, she had meant that. But for the first time, she experienced that one can totally wish one's baby happiness and yet at the same time wish to block its very path. Because it is scary if they want to sail off into a world you know nothing about. Struggling with university exams, she could have coached her through that. But internships in the world of fashion? There was no chance she could protect her baby in that kind of jungle! Wasn't that where all those #metoo incidents happened? And whenever her mind travelled back to their discussion, her resolute daughter, enlightening her about her motives like a little Buddha, she could not help thinking of Luca.

Would it have changed things if he had talked to his parents like that? Perhaps, his parents had also wanted to protect him, in their own narrow-minded way. Protect him rather than destroy him for sure, no parent wants that. And yet it was not so easy.

*

On a Monday, four weeks after their Farringdon dinner, she finally ran into Eric. Unfortunately, he was not alone. It was six in the evening, and Helen had made it down the staircase to take the Tube home. The man who was 'too busy' for tea breaks stood in front of the office, in a group together with Henry Reynolds, a senior partner from Real Estate. With them were two of the newbies of the firm: Matt Macen, an impertinent Oxbridge graduate and Nicole Perkins, a sweet and perfectly dressed new associate in the firm.

Henry Reynolds was a big rainmaker in the firm so it was by no means surprising that Mr Oxbridge and someone who wanted to combine femininity with a steep career would trail behind him. But why did Eric have to join this trifecta? The group was obviously ready to go for an after-work drink. Eric's tie was pulled down a bit, his jacket slung casually over his arm, and his hair was dishevelled as always, from all the hard thinking.

He looked at her as if he were a boy caught with his hand in the cookie jar.

"Oh, hi," he said, and Helen slowed down.

The group knew they were acquainted. Everybody knew. It was impossible for him to not say anything and impossible for her not to stop.

"Heading home already? Come with us for drinks. It's going to be good fun!" he said, as if Helen was one of his drinking buddies – she almost felt that slap on the shoulder again.

Taken by surprise, a *blitzkrieg* was happening inside her. One voice strongly argued for joining them no matter what. This would give her the chance to figure out what the hell was going on with him – and to check on that blonde woman. Another voice told her to just raise her chin and walk past him.

"Oh yes, that would be so lovely. We haven't seen you around in ages!" Nicole added, sweet as sugar as long as men were watching. Meet her alone in the hallway and she would just be the stressed-out weirdo she actually was. The 'we' did of course not really make things better. As the war in her head could not be decided on at such short notice, Helen flashed the group a professional smile, a smile that could have been for everyone.

"Thanks, guys, some other time!"

Henry Reynolds did not even look up from his phone, as if he had not expected the cold fish from the labour law department to join them anyway. Damn it, Eric could go for drinks with whomever he wanted. She was the idiot that did not join in and still fought for attention. Was it maybe now her turn for some drinking games with the boys? Ten metres away, she stopped short and turned on her heel.

"Actually," she said, turning around, "actually, it was one hell of a day, and I think I do deserve a drink!"

That line sounded awfully rehearsed. Henry Reynolds looked up from his phone, to check whether she was really *that* Helen, and then kept typing. Eric smiled at her, for the first time in a month. Helen had to look away to not blush and so she gave Nicole a radiant smile instead. That one knew the rules of sisterhood and let out an enthusiastic scream.

"That's great, Helen, so I won't be all alone with these boys!" she shouted, and slid her hand under Helen's elbow. This exaggerated affection made it all too clear how much Nicole disliked having competition tonight, but none of the boys would ever pick up on that. Matt clearly seemed to have spent too much time in Oxbridge. He found her joining them just "Splendid!"

"Henry, could you just text Thomas? We are going to the Swan's Inn in Lambs Conduit. Maybe he got held up on his call," Eric said, suddenly eager to get the group moving. Henry nodded without taking his eyes from the screen.

Lamb's Conduit was a picturesque little street in the middle of hectic London, lined with Victorian pubs, little craft shops and cafés serving organic and gluten-free muffins. It was refreshing to be able to walk a few hundred metres without bumping into a Pret a Manger or Boots. It was a mild evening in early March, some people were standing outside the pubs with their beers, their ties loosened up.

Nicole was no longer holding on to her elbow – why would she? – but was talking to Eric instead – and he was laughing! Come on! Nicole's mission was to convince everybody that family and career do go together nowadays. Heartwarming, and good news for all chauvinists. If Nicole was right, men would not have to change a bit. Her demonstration involved a lot of truly annoying activity. In one meeting, Nicole kept putting her hair behind her ear so that everyone would see the diamond engagement ring. "It is a tradition in my husband's family that a proper engagement ring has to be worth three times the groom's monthly salary. And we are *very* traditional people. So in that sense, you make a mistake if you marry so young, because the wages are still so low! Haha! Just kidding, of course!" And with such a tight blouse, even British men who usually run from everything feminine suddenly enjoy listening to such cultural hokum.

"Oh really?" Helen had felt like saying. "That is so interesting. In my family, we just put the bride on some scales and the groom's family has to fill up three times her weight in pure gold. In that sense, you are better off marrying when you get old and fat – and that is my plan, haha!" Instead, Helen just smiled with her jaw clenched. It would only have come across as bitter – because it *was*.

Matt was on the heels of Henry, making sure he got his latest insight into Brexit's impact on business. Helen trailed behind the four of them like the proverbial fifth wheel. For a moment, she wondered whether she should fake a phone call and make an exit, but it was kind of too late for that.

The Swan's Inn was an old pub, popular among locals of Bloomsbury as well as among the commuters. They had a burger special on Mondays and, apparently, these four had made it a habit to reserve a table. How come she had never heard of that at their tea breaks? The inside was crowded and noisy; without the reservation, they clearly would have had to stand. When pushing their way through the crowd and hearing all the people laughing and talking to each other, Helen felt she deserved to loosen up a bit, especially after the events of the past weeks. Independent of who said what to whom, and who cared about the blonde woman! Perhaps she really should do that more often!

But as soon as they sat down, the evening turned into more of a struggle than a delightful time out. Nicole apparently used burger night to showcase what a good buddy she was, not one of those boring girls who went vegan and never drank. If Helen did not want to come across as the buzzkill everybody expected her to be, she had no choice but pretend to be entertained by stories like the one about a friend of hers who had gotten her boyfriend to grill tofu. (Oh no, what a nightmare!)

Helen did her best to laugh at the right moments and catch Eric's gaze whenever she could. And, despite the distance he had kept in the past weeks, she could surprisingly often. Most of the time, when she turned to him, Helen looked straight into his eyes. She had to look away immediately to not blush. It was tough, to pretend to be at ease while at the same time closely observing the interaction between Eric and Nicole. That girl clearly had a focus on him.

A smart choice from her perspective. Bonding with another junior associate like Matt was pointless. Panting after a senior partner like Henry would give off a sugar daddy vibe. But Eric, the middle-management, that made perfect sense. One could only hope it was that and not something else.

But Helen slowly gained ground. She got some cheers, at least, when she finished her massive burger (she would not have dared to give up). The situation further improved when the topic shifted to *Last Week Tonight* with John Oliver. Helen was a fanatic of that show –"He is the last man I see before I go to sleep," got her a few laughs. She could also recommend some episodes the others had not seen yet. Henry Reynolds even saved the list on YouTube.

A downer came when Nicole asked Eric to finish her beer because she did not like that type of lager, and he just drank it, like couples do when they go out.

After two beers, Helen began to feel a little light-headed. If she rejected a third pint, she might look like a party pooper, but if she drank more, she might start to say stupid things or finally start to smile at Eric like a little girl who saw a unicorn. God, her own daughter would probably handle a date more smoothly by now. But before she could devise her exit strategy, things changed really quickly. Henry suddenly got up and said he wanted to see how his associate was doing with a draft. He put a twenty-pound note on the table and left to head back. Then, a minute later, Matt got a call and with a stupid grin and the even stupider phrase, "My government is calling," he left the pub to take it. Nicole simultaneously took this opportunity to go to the ladies. All of a sudden it was just the two of them.

"Huh, *the government*," Helen said, "do they really still say that, I mean, this generation?"

Helen expected a laugh and a snarky comment but Eric just leaned forward, squeezed her hand and said, "Listen, these two will leave soon. They always do. Please stay behind with me. Stay longer," he said, and there was an urgency in his eyes she had never seen before.

"What?" Helen said in bewilderment, as if she were hard of hearing.

"Just do it. Get another drink, say you are in the mood to stay out, whatever. Please?" he said.

Before she could answer, Matt returned. He said something like, "Sorry, guys, my government is calling the troops home." He put down a twenty-pound note and left. Nicole stayed a polite fifteen minutes for chit-chat while every single second Helen secretly begged her to leave. Either she got the vibe or she really was no longer interested in an evening with such a small audience. Soon she began to fumble with her purse in a complicated manner, giving Eric enough time to notice.

"That's fine, it's on me," Eric said. Perhaps an appropriate gesture, in view of the difference in salary. Now that he had not squeezed Nicole's hand and begged her to stay behind with him, it was easy to be generous.

They both followed her with their eyes when she got up and made it through the crowd and to the door. Helen then looked at Eric, with a tense smile and almost clenched teeth. But he just grabbed the salad of pound notes on the table and said, "I'll just pay and we'll get out of here," and with that he made his way to the counter, leaving the confused Helen at the table.

"Why? Where are we going?" she asked when he came back with the bill.

"Come on," he said, taking her coat from her chair. "I need to show you something."

"What? Where?" she said while slipping obediently into the coat. Eric pushed his way through the crowd and Helen trailed behind. Outside, he was walking quickly, so quickly that she almost had trouble keeping up with him.

"If you want to show me something, you'd better make sure I can keep up," she said, half joking, half complaining. She had hoped that he wanted to have a private moment with her, maybe go somewhere for another drink where it was a bit quieter. Instead, things had turned hectic and now they were running through the cold.

"I'm sorry," he said, and then did the most unthinkable thing: he turned and reached for her hand, as if to make sure that he would not lose her. Out here in the crowded street, for everyone to see. Helen was so stunned that she did not say another word. This street was close to the office and there might be people or colleagues around that knew both of them. She did not mind being dragged behind anymore.

At the corner of The Perseverance, another popular pub with the firm, Eric suddenly turned right into a cul-de-sac.

"What the heck…?" she started again, but then they suddenly stopped. So abruptly that she almost bumped into him.

"We are here," he said.

"We are where?"

"This is what I need to show you, Helen," he said, and pointed to the door right next to him. The street was full of cute little brick houses that were leaning and snuggling into each other. They stood in front of a wooden door, nice woodwork with a lion's head door knocker, repainted in royal blue.

"Yes, *wow*. It is a nice door, but I don't really get it…"

"It is *my* door," he said, his eyes fixed on her. "This is where I live."

"What?"

"It is where I live. For more than a month now, basically since after Christmas."

"What?" Helen had heard him but she was incapable of processing. It just made no sense.

"I moved out. I just... I did not tell anyone, did not know how to bring it up, I guess."

"But... why? Why do you live here?" Helen said, still with the same disbelieving stare. In Helen's universe, the most likely answer was at the same time the most unlikely, the most difficult to reconcile with all she knew about Eric.

He paused, searching for words. "Things have not been going so well. And I have moved here. It is practical for work, you see, and then I just stay longer in the office. I... I tell people I want to walk a bit on... I..." He paused again. "Bottom line is: nobody noticed."

Helen still stood and stared in turn at the blue door and then back at him. This changed everything. When she continued to say nothing, Eric just typed the code in the little silver box next to the door, and with a humming sound, it sprung open, losing a bit of its antique charm.

His apartment was at the back, at ground level, a one-room apartment with an empty smell. There was a small kitchen unit in the windowless aisle and a bedroom towards the back. There was hardly any furniture, just a few boxes on the ground, and a light bulb hanging from the ceiling.

Helen was trying to take in where she was for a moment when she felt his hand on her back. She turned around and before she could say another word, Eric pulled her close and pressed her body against his. She felt his racing heart through her coat.

15

Shards

Early April, 2017, Vittuone (Milan)

Clara walked up and down the terrace, inspecting the new space. She frowned at the birds, then slowly circled the new ceramic pots one by one. Alma carefully observed her sister. She used to keep her hair in the same Sophia Loren perm, but for a few years, it had to be one of those modern haircuts, short and silver-grey. And the skirt and blouse with pumps had been replaced by slippers and a white linen… well, kaftan. Alma had mentioned neither the birds nor the terrace work to Clara. She had not consciously concealed any of it, but now that Clara stood there, with her full authority and energy, she knew why she had acted in secret. And quickly, before Clara could say what she was going to say now.

Her sister stopped next to the lemon tree closest to Alma's chair, took one of the leaves between her fingers as if checking its quality, and then it came: "This all looks very nice, but I don't quite understand what this is all about. The trees, flowers and… *birds*? Does it really make sense to do all this when you will move out of here anyway? I thought we all agreed that you cannot live alone in this huge place, after all."

"No, no, you make perfect sense, of course. What do I do all day alone here in the house, right?" Alma tried to end the conversation by letting her sister win from the start; sometimes it worked.

"Exactly. Therefore, I don't quite understand what this is all about…

You do look better, though, I must say." She let go of the lemon leaf and put her hands on her hips. "Doesn't she look much better, Flavia?"

Flavia had come to the terrace with a tea tray.

"Yes, absolutely, *Signora* Clara. Everybody says so."

"So, I think I will not move before next year," Alma suddenly heard herself say, firmly, as if this could possibly be the last word in this discussion.

"Next year?" Clara gasped. "What are you gonna do all these months?"

Alma had no idea. All she knew was she could not leave. Clara leaned forward and took her hand, as if to make sure that her words would reach her sister, like one does with a little kid. Then she spoke extra slowly: "We are just all a little worried that it will be too much for you here, all alone and buried by memories. Perhaps it is time to let go."

"Why would the memories bury me?" Alma said with resilience.

"What?" Clara looked more puzzled than ever.

God, Alma thought, *I really should have prepared myself for this kind of conversation.* She twisted the cup in her hand, again the Ginori cup with the orange fake Chinese temple. It had lived in this house before she came. It had been on the coffee table in the first days of her life in the house, when she sat on this terrace as a young nervous girl, listening anxiously to everything her new in-laws said or did.

You don't have to worry about anything. The nest is already built. You just have to hatch the eggs, her mother used to say.

"What will we do with all these things?" Alma finally said, just to end the silence, raising the cup high in the air. "We cannot put everything in your place. Where will it all go?"

That kind of anxious comment sounded more familiar to Clara. "Ah. If that is what you are worried about, there are people to take care of this. Di Marco will take care of everything."

"And… for example, what will happen to Flavia and Maria?"

"You will write them a good reference and they will find a new position."

Now this sounded like the most absurd plan ever. Alma looked at the birds. Romeo was cleaning the feathers on the back of Juliet's head, and she was enjoying it with her eyes closed. Alma had really tried to convince Flavia and Maria to choose other names for the birds, but they had insisted on those absolute clichés for two lovebirds.

"I will stay for another year. It is better at this point. There is so much to do," Alma said. It was all she could come up with.

"*To do*? What are you doing in here? I am glad to find you dressed, actually! Alma, perhaps we should really take it step by step? This whole idea of moving seems to confuse you an awful lot," Clara said, switching back to her kindergarten voice.

Alma said nothing. *Was* she just confused? Was it really the only thing that made sense, to leave here, as everybody told her? She felt trapped suddenly, trapped in a conversation she could neither handle nor steer. She pushed back her chair, so abruptly it made a screeching noise on the terrace tiles and scared off the birds. They went to hide in the darkest corner of their cage.

"What is it now?" Clara was obviously annoyed.

"If I am so *confused*, perhaps I should lie down for a bit," Alma snapped.

"Alma, good lord!" Clara rolled her eyes. "I only meant well, no need to get upset…" Having said that, Clara leaned back and looked over the park, as if it was now simply Alma's task to get back to her senses, and all Clara would have to do was wait. There she was again, the older sister, who always knew better, whom Alma could never keep up with and who got away with everything.

But instead of leaving as announced, Alma stopped in the frame of the terrace door. She looked at her sister, her self-sufficient sister, who was looking over the park as if Alma were not even there – as if it were her park, actually. And she still held that stupid Ginori cup in her hand. Out of impulse, Alma rushed towards her. She grabbed the cup out of her sister's hand and threw it on the ground.

"You lied to me! You *all* lied to me!" she yelled at her sister. Clara screamed and jumped from her chair, looking at her sister in terror.

"What did that cup ever do to you?" Clara yelled back at her little sister.

"Forget the cup! The house is full of those cups! I am talking about *you*! You lied to me!"

"When? Where?"

"All my life! You all did!"

"Alma, are you taking pills? Or perhaps I should ask: Are you *not* taking your pills?"

"This is not about pills!"

"I'm sorry," Clara said, putting her hands on her hips again. "I get the feeling I should apologise for something, but I have not yet been told what it is…"

"I have always done everything, you know. Everything I have ever been told. Because it was the *right thing*. Always trying to do the right thing. The good wife, the good mother – and now what? You just change with the wind! 'Make-up is for cheap girls' you were telling me when we were sixteen. Or maybe you were just parroting it back from our mother? Until you met your husband. Then, one had to scrape colour from the wall to make sure it was you! 'All people that do not go to church on Sundays are to be mistrusted and misguided by the modern lifestyle.' How often did I have to hear that from you? Until your husband stopped driving you there, because he was dead, and now, Sunday mornings, Pilates class is as good a church as any. 'Modern tourism is only for shallow people that search for meaning in life' – and now I can stop any stupid tour bus in the country and you will be sitting in it with a sponsored cap on your head!"

"So, let me get this straight. You are angry with me because I changed my attitude to make-up between the ages of, say, sixteen and twenty-five, and my attitude to church in my sixties?" Clara asked, in mockery, but Alma was no longer in the mood to be the fool in this conversation.

"No! I am sick and tired of being told what to do! I know myself what to do. Or at least, you people *also* don't know what to do! You just make stuff up as long as it floats your boat."

"Are you now trying to hold me responsible for how you lived your life until you were sixty-five? Or can you just not handle the fact that I am happy and you are not?"

Her older sister twisting the knife in her wound like only an older sister could, Alma was left speechless. In her helpless fury, she reached for her own cup and also smashed it on the ground.

"Alma! Stop it!" Clara screamed.

"There are too many cups in this house!" Alma screamed, and then stormed off the terrace inside the house.

Halfway into the living room, she almost collided with Maria coming along with another tray. Maria's bewilderment made Alma stop for a moment and think of whether she could explain the situation or at least have some orders to give. "I threw around some cups," was all she came up with, and then ran off.

*

The rest of the day she hid in the library, pretending to read. In her fury, she suddenly felt the urge to go back to her old hiding spot. Where else could she go? She had expected Clara to leave after her outburst but she never heard the engine of her car. Perhaps her sister was in the guest room or still sitting on the terrace? Or discussing with Flavia and Maria whether they should call for the doctor?

Alma pulled a book on British countryside manors from the shelf, but she did not really look at it. She was so angry she could hardly think. Then she began to go back and forth between feeling remorse and being proud of herself. She had never talked to her sister like that, perhaps not to anybody. Clara had been as she always was and, of course, she could not understand Alma's outburst. And Alma knew Clara meant well – who else could she count on? Wasn't yelling at her like biting the hand that feeds you, like something only idiots do? Though as she searched for some part of her speech she would take back, she found none. The liberation of throwing those cups still felt so real, it made her chuckle.

When the sun began to set and the shadows of the trees grew longer, Alma switched on the little desk lamp and started to wonder what would happen next. Sooner or later, she would have to come out of her cave. Would they have dinner together? Would she apologise, just to restore everything to good order and get the visit over with? Would they start fighting again if Clara started acting smart as always?

Would her sister perhaps try to talk her into some new pills? This was the first time in a while that Alma found herself in a situation that had no protocol.

Before her thoughts could come to any conclusion, there was a knock on the door.

"Is it safe to bring some porcelain in here?" she heard Clara's muffled voice through the door.

Alma giggled.

"Yes, but keep a safe distance!" she shouted through the door.

She heard Clara giggle back and the door handle was pushed down. Clara came in backwards, pushing the door open with her butt and carrying a tray. Apparently, Flavia and Maria had prepared some sort of takeaway dinner. She moved a few metres into the room and then stopped, uncertain what to do. Obviously, Clara was also out of protocol.

Alma looked at her from the armchair. A purple cardigan was now draped elegantly over Clara's shoulders against the evening chill. Her sister was beautiful. And when she was feeling insecure, there was a softness to her face that made her look even younger.

"I hear this is where you usually hide," Clara finally said.

"Yes," Alma said, looking straight at her, "my favourite place."

"Is there somewhere we can put this?" Clara lifted the tray shyly.

Alma looked around. The library was not a place to host a dinner. There was a long rectangular coffee table by the window, though just for decoration, home to a Chinese vase. And between the bookshelves was a small footstool, hosting the taller sister of the window vase.

"If we pull this armchair over and put the two vases down, we can get a nice dinner table together," Alma said, pointing with one hand to the window and to the gap between the shelves with the other.

"All right then," Clara said, and parked the tray on the floor.

Carefully, they moved the big vase to the floor and the smaller one was temporarily placed on the secretary desk. Then, they pulled the table and stool to the middle of the room and Alma put an old newspaper on top as a makeshift tablecloth. Clara arranged the dinner while Alma pulled over the armchair.

The food was simple: parmesan cheese, dried tomatoes, bread, olives and a jug of red wine. Alma felt terribly hungry; her outburst had cut her lunch break short. For the first few minutes, they just sat and ate. Alma wondered if Clara was also hungry or if neither of them knew how to start.

"It is like we are having a picnic inside the house," Alma said after a while, and smiled.

"Yes," Clara said, obviously relieved. "With food we stole from the kitchen." This was followed by a slightly tense giggle. Then, they continued eating quietly.

"I'm sorry," Clara suddenly said, in such an open and serene way that it moved Alma deeply.

"I'm sorry too," was all she could say.

"I should have listened more to what you want, I guess. I just did not understand."

"I know, I know. It is not as though I made a good point of what I want, either. I have never been good at that."

Clara nodded. "So tell me: what is it that makes you want to stay here? These past few weeks, public opinion is that you hate this place and are going insane in here…"

"I'm not even sure myself," Alma said. "It is true, everything connected to this place went wrong in every possible way. But I have to find out why. And I can only find out while I am here."

"*Everything* is perhaps a little harsh," Clara said, reaching for her sister's hand. "And you cannot change the past, Clara… these things happen…"

Alma shook her head. "I just want to understand it, I guess. It is like I have been in a fog for years."

Clara turned pale and looked at her plate. Maybe you'd better give these old stories a rest? It was an accident, we all know that…"

"What if we don't? We will never know for sure, but I am not sure we ever really wanted to know…"

"Whatever is haunting you, you are forgiven! God forgave you a long time ago."

"Oh? Did he blame me in the first place? I did not know."

"I did not mean that…"

"Then his generosity seems a bit of an empty gesture to me."

Clara returned to eating, taken aback by this wave of sarcasm.

"Why do you even think like that? Luca had everything here. A perfect home, parents that loved him, a beautiful fiancée, a great job too…"

"People talk."

"Who does? I will give them a talking-to that will make them stop theirs!"

That was also Clara. She might be a bully at times, but she was also a lioness, biting away everyone coming close to her little sister.

"Nobody said it straight to my face, of course. It is just a feeling. I could tell from how people looked at me back then."

"Ah, this is all happening in your head. Nobody thinks like that. He had everything and people know that. He was pure sunshine in our hearts. It is a tragedy, nothing but a tragedy."

"Perhaps it is never right to say to anybody: *you have everything*. That's where it all goes wrong. All you can say is: *you have what many people would like to have*. At the most, we can say that."

"Maybe… I never thought of it that way. So, you really think he was unhappy? Always charming, always laughing. He was like the most charismatic young man I knew." Clara stopped. A sob had escaped Alma's throat, like an animal that had been stuck there for a long time.

"I'm sorry, amore, but you started it… I did not mean to upset you."

But this time, Alma quickly regained control over herself. "No, it is all right. I've wanted to talk about all this for so long. "

"Then why didn't you? I was always there if you needed me," Clara said, and she meant it.

"I guess I wasn't ready. And to be honest, I don't think it is quite fair to say that *everybody* was waiting to have that conversation with me. Giacomo never tolerated the thought that his son was unhappy – certainly not *that* unhappy. He would have been very upset if he heard me speak about it to someone. And we had stopped speaking altogether."

"Don't be too harsh on him. It was so hard for him to lose his only son."

Alma paused and looked out of the window. "It was as if we had climbed in the tomb with him. We certainly did every night."

"Oh, what a terrible thing to say!" Clara exclaimed, not used to her sister making such statements.

"I find it hard to say a not-so-terrible thing about my son's death."

"You have to find a way to make peace with it – as terrible as it may be – or it will be a tomb indeed." Alma had heard that a thousand times before.

"So the thing is, I don't think he was happy. We could have seen it, but we failed him."

"How?"

"Did you think he was the type to run a company, like an executive director?"

"Yes, dear, absolutely. He was so enthusiastic about working side by side with his father. He was just a bit of an eternal bachelor type. You know, like some grapes take a bit longer until they give a good vine. Some men are like that."

"Really? They always run away from what they want? I don't know about that."

"But he got engaged, Alma. He was about to start a family. That's a reason to live even if you don't like your job – especially if it is a job that pays well."

"Aah, that *fiancée*. I still get a Christmas card from her but that is it. The whole thing never struck you as weird?"

"What do you mean *weird*?"

"I thought about it a lot lately. He never had a stable girlfriend and then, out of the blue, after that English affair and a few months of dating, he wants to marry the Pizzutelli daughter – whom he always knew and, I guess, who had always been more than available to him."

"She was the prettiest girl in town – and probably his type!"

"That's what I'm saying. She had always been the prettiest girl in town but apparently until then *not* his type... all the time he was out and about, hanging out with friends none of us knew."

"Alma, nobody forced him to marry her. He probably just wanted to do what was right and start a family..."

"But the question still is: was he happy? Not everyone is happy because they have a spouse, although we *like* to believe that."

Clara shifted in her chair. "They were not the most affectionate couple, I do remember that. You know, my theory was that, you know, that after the other issue was finally settled, he was so relieved and – I don't know how to say – kind of *chastened*. I thought he had learned a lesson from it and wanted to start a solid life, settle down and all. Aren't these young men all like that, afraid of responsibility? The time where the babies do nothing but cry? It is not their thing, really."

"There was no baby yet. And seriously, drinking in your room instead of being with your girl? Is that a common sport for a young man? Flavia cleared out the bottles from his room every week."

Clara took a deep breath. "So, you believe he loved that other girl? Is that what you are trying to say?"

Alma looked at her hands. She wasn't sure what to tell Clara. Nobody knew about the letters. Nobody knew that she knew; neither what the girl looked like nor where she lived. If she looked at Clara now, her sister would be able to read in her face that she was hiding something.

"Good question. I have been thinking about that too."

"Oh Jesus. I really don't think so, Alma! The poor thing was so stressed when he ran into that sgualdrina's trap – and so relieved when it was all sorted out. He never brought it up again, never said he loved her or wanted to marry her, right?"

"No, he never said that. Not that there had been a serious conversation about it." Alma got up to get a shawl. With the sun fading, a bit of a chill crept through the library walls. Clara busied herself with mushing the dried tomatoes and the olives into some sort of purée, giving Alma a little space to think.

That wedding party was the only occasion she had seen them together. Had Luca been more happy than usual next to the English girl? It was hard to say. When he finally confessed to them that the girl was expecting, all Alma could see was guilt, not a man standing up to his family – but to which one anyway?

His head was hanging low and Giacomo was so silent, it had scared her. If only he had shouted at the boy, but his disappointment rendered him speechless. Only when they had retreated to their bedroom, did he finally explode: "We should never have let him bring that girl to the wedding, Alma! We should have stopped him there and then!" It was clear that with 'we', he meant her. It would have been a mother's duty, and she had failed him.

"At the time it seemed so harmless…" She tried her usual manoeuvre: to agree with him and defend herself at the same time.

"Well, for a man like our son, games with foreign girls are never harmless. Didn't I make that abundantly clear?" And that he had. Ever so often, Giacomo had brought up the story of a Swiss business partner, a vastly wealthy man with most of his fortune held by the family. He had convinced his son to undergo a vasectomy at the age of nineteen, to be in full control of the family's fate. When his time would come to father a child, this could be done in-vitro, consciously and with a pre-nuptial agreement in place. Of course, Giacomo had laughed about this crazy man at the time, castrating his own son. But the message had been more than clear.

"And I can tell you exactly what will happen next," he went on, his face red and out of breath at the mere thought of it. "That girl will come over here, with a bunch of lawyers in tow, and try to sue the living daylights out of us! We have to put an end to it right away! First thing in the morning, I will send di Marco. That guy can lead a bull to the shambles and the bull would thank him for it."

Feeling so guilty for the wedding conundrum, she had promised herself to not let him down a second time. The thought of that woman disturbing her family's peace for good was deeply unsettling. And she would do everything to keep her out of her realm.

The plan was broken to Luca during breakfast, and again, he only sat there with his head hanging low. When Luca stayed silent, his father got up and coldly patted his shoulder: "We all make mistakes." But he did not mean it. She never saw him look at his son the way he had before.

"She was after his money, we all know that," Clara mumbled. Her mouth was so full of bread and olives she had to cover it with one hand. "Nobody gets pregnant by accident nowadays, and that one was not a stupid girl," she said with her usual confidence.

Alma filled their glasses again; they had almost emptied the entire jug together.

"He never said a bad word about her."

"Well, that was very decent of him. This was all such a long time ago, Alma… and these things happen."

"There was no discussion at all. Get it out of the way and life carries on. But it is a big deal, no? A baby? My son, becoming a father? Me becoming a grandmother?"

"What it was *not* supposed to be was also a big deal. She was *not* part of this family. And when she saw this fancy wedding, she probably thought she had struck gold, saw herself parading around in a white dress already, that meagre little thing. You did not want him to run into that kind of trap. Of course, it must have been tempting for her. Families are the heart of Italian society, and where she comes from, everybody divorces just like that." Clara snipped with two fingers. "She saw what a life he had and knew she was no fit. So, she needed a plan to force her way in!"

"I'm not so sure, Clara. She had not completed her studies and her entire family lived in England. Wasn't it more of a catastrophe for her as well? What you describe sounds more like, I don't know, women hanging out on a beach in Thailand, hitting on white tourists to get a better passport. Or something like that, I don't know. There was a documentary on TV."

"Women all over the world are the same."

"Oh God, Clara. Where do you get all this 'wisdom' from? Do you inhale it with your morning coffee?"

"I just know. Everybody knows that…"

"How? We know absolutely nothing about this woman. Everybody pretended to know exactly what had been going on in her mind but we, as a matter of fact, knew nothing about that."

"So, what do you want? This is coming really late now. We don't even know where she is. And who knows, do not even think of opening this Pandora's box! If she is in financial trouble, she might still try to drain some money out of you – what if she starts some litigation?" There was now some honest panic in Clara's face.

"I'm just saying it is bothering me. And also, she might *know*."

"Know what?"

"Know whether he was happy…"

"How can that woman know our family better than we do? Now that is ridiculous!" Clara looked scandalised.

"Because we failed him, Clara! Ever since he died, I realise we had no idea what really moved him, what drove him, what he wanted from life. I was his mother. I lived with him in the same house, but I had no idea. He might have told her things he never told us!"

"They had an affair, Alma. A pretty little something on the side, as they all have when they go to study abroad… These girls mean nothing and they *know* nothing." Clara's face had hardened with her last words.

"Maybe it is the other way round. Maybe they are the only ones that know everything. Maybe the affair is the one place where men can be really honest, like a safe place that is not part of their real life…"

Something in Clara's gaze stopped Alma. Clara's pain was her pain, after all, and Clara's heart had turned into a battlefield. For once, she had no control over her smiles and charms. They went back to eating bread and olives for a while.

"So, you want to search for her on TV or something? I'm telling you, she might not be in the mood for a sentimental chat over the good old times…"

"Maybe after all these years, she would want to talk." Alma jumped up from her armchair, too agitated to sit.

"Sounds pretty naïve to me. That is not the kind of situation that you can just resolve with a friendly *kaffeeklatsch*. That ship sailed a long time ago."

To Clara, apparently, all Alma would ever say would sound naïve. Her tone had become so unbearable that Alma could not resist throwing her biggest trump card in the game.

"You know *nothing* about all this. *In fact*, she has been writing to me."

That bomb had landed well. Clara sat frozen for more than ten seconds at least, her mouth wide open in disbelief.

"There. You did not expect *that*, did you?" Alma said, and sat back down in her throne.

After more than a minute, Clara finally found her words again. "Did you write back? Can I see the letter?"

"No, no, no. What I mean is, I do have the address. I *could* write to her, that is what I mean…"

Alma had not thought this through. She had betrayed her husband by storing this tiny box in his house like a treasure. It was her own private revolution sleeping in that box. Alma walked a half-circle around her armchair, standing now between the chair and the secretary desk as if she wanted to fend off intruders. It felt so good to hold this trump card, and once played, it would be gone.

"Of course, I would never write to her. I know this would be so disrespectful to Giacomo and our family, it wouldn't be right…" she said, and made a pathetic gesture with her arm, as if she were on the stage of some theatre.

"Alma!" Clara screamed – but it was too late. Alma had thrown her shawl off her shoulder. Upon falling off, it landed on the tip of the Chinese vase that had just been parked on the secretary desk. Alma had not remembered the precious thing standing right behind her. The heavy wool was enough to tip over the vase and, after a dramatic pause, it hit the parquet. Alma turned right in time to see the artefact – which had survived centuries and travelled from China to Europe in a silk road caravan – disappear into a hundred pieces.

Alma stood in shock for a second, then looked over at Clara who still stared in disbelief at all the pieces on the ground.

"I actually kind of liked that one," Alma said after a while.

"You know, whatever you do, please don't break this house into pieces, okay?" Clara finally said.

"No, I won't," Alma said. "Although I must say, I like the noise."

"God, this brings me back to my pill question," Clara said, but this time she giggled. Not condescendingly, but more like the kind of giggle she had when they were children sharing a secret.

"I know!" Alma whispered with a mad voice, and then they both burst out laughing.

"We have to clean this up or somebody might get hurt," Clara said when she could breathe again, returning to more pragmatic thoughts.

"Yes. Also, I don't want Flavia and Maria to notice. They have been worrying so much about me lately, they will think who-knows-what when they find the library in such a state," Alma added.

"Now that is a difficult one. Is it actually possible to hide anything that happens in here from those two? Even if we put the shards in the bin, they will know…"

"Yes, the bin in the kitchen would not do the trick. We have to put this in a plastic bag and carry it over to the office. There are containers behind the office building which nobody checks."

"Goodness, what a wicked plan. Will they not notice that the vase is missing?"

"The house is full of stuff. I doubt it. We will just put the other one in the window and a flowerpot between the shelves. Even I would not notice."

Alma found a dustpan and brush after rummaging around in the kitchen for half an hour. Clara could not help making a few remarks about how she herself likes to stay ahead of things in her own household – another way of expressing her good old envy for Alma's regal lifestyle.

Clara's husband had always done well. She used to have a cleaning lady and a nanny, but she could not just ring a bell and have somebody rush to her feet. At least Clara had forgotten about the letters for a while. Alma was too happy for having caught a break and played along, pretending to be a little embarrassed over her disorientation in her own kitchen, opening a few more cabinet doors saying, "Oh, pans! Who would have thought?"

Then, the ladies crawled over the library floor and did their best to catch all the shards that were scattered over the parquet. It would take a vacuum cleaner to catch them all, but Alma really did not know where that beast was hidden.

Then, they sneaked through the kitchen door toward the containers at the back of the office, like two children trying to hide the traces of a prank. The night was quite chilly and the moon hung so full and bright in the sky. Their two clear-cut shadows fell upon the gravel as they walked across the yard. Clara held the lid open so that Alma could lift a few of the shredded papers to cover the plastic bag. With her free hand, Clara grabbed a handful of the paper salad and held it up to Alma's face.

"Actually, do you have any idea how the company is doing? Or what is going on there right now?"

"I have absolutely no idea. It all seems to be taken care of…"

"Hmm," Clara said, and dropped the papers back in the bin. Alma's total ignorance of the family's financial matters was apparently absolutely fine, while no knowledge of the location of a dustpan gave rise to mockery.

"Apparently, they are thinking about moving the office closer to the factory," Alma added. "This place was really only here because it was so comfortable for Giacomo, and his father before him. It is not really practical for the other staff to come out here where they have no canteen or anything."

"Oh my, Alma. It will be even more lonely here then."

The only strategy Alma could think of was making a quick exit before Clara could fixate again on either moving out of the house or the English woman.

"My dear, it has been a really long day for me and I have taken to the habit of going to bed really early. Perhaps we should call it a day now?" she said to her sister, perhaps a bit too formally, like an actor rehearsing a line.

Clara looked at her in surprise but then let her off the leash. Even more surprisingly, Clara turned and wrapped both arms around her younger sister, for a tight hug.

*

But instead of going to bed, Alma walked back to the library. It still bore the remains of their picnic and Alma pushed the armchair back to the desk for a place to think. She took the wooden box out again and went through the pictures one by one. What was she afraid of now? Of course, it would be nice to share all this with someone she trusted. As children, they had never told on one another, not to parents, not to teachers. The thing was that Alma herself was not sure where to go from here. If she told Clara, within a minute her sister would have a plan that sounded oh-so-convincing and would tell Alma exactly what to do. And she would feel obliged to obey. Alma sighed. Wasn't it terrible that somehow one never truly grew up?

Alma looked at the last photograph. With the backpack and her hair put up, it seemed to Alma as if the girl was about to embark on the journey of her life. Following an inner impulse, Alma grabbed a pen and started writing. Some thoughts had just worked their way up and wanted to come out on paper.

Dear Ms Kings, she started her letter, and then immediately got stuck. It wasn't easy to write a letter to someone who presumably hated you, especially when the extent of that disdain was unknown. She wrote a sentence and crossed it out, started over again, and then threw that one away. It would be better to address it to the girl, as the mother might not be too keen to talk to her at all. In the end, all she wrote was:

> *Dear Emilia,*
> *We have much appreciated receiving all the pictures of your life. We would like to let you know that, as a young woman now, you are more than welcome to visit the Carneggio estate. Maybe you wish to learn about the place where your father grew up.*
> *Best regards,*
> *Alma Carneggio*

Alma found an envelope and carried the letter down to the basket where her private mail was collected. With trembling hands, she placed it between two trivial letters she had written in response to some well-wishing cards from relatives. Flavia would take the mail over to the office during the day. No one checked the boring letters she wrote and no one would recognise the address. It was already one thirty in the morning when she made her way upstairs to her new bedroom. As soon as Alma's head touched the pillow she fell into a deep dreamless sleep.

16

Behind the Blue Door

Early March 2017, London

Helen and Eric's first encounter behind the blue door had ended abruptly. She had imagined kissing him so many times, but when it finally happened, she had panicked.

With a "What are we doing here?" she had wrestled out of his arms and rushed towards the door. Eric seemed overwhelmed too, but he caught her hand on her way out.

"Let me explain this to you tomorrow, okay?"

"Okay!" she shouted back, already on the run before he could undercut her flight distance once more.

She spent the entire Tube ride texting; they assured each other that everything was really fine and that they would speak tomorrow. On the way from the Tube station, she slowed down again at the dark patch to see the fox. And indeed she heard something rustle and she thought she vaguely saw a red bushy tail disappear between the rubbish bins. Maybe next time.

Emmy was still up and they briefly discussed the next day's geography paper, and Helen managed to sound astoundingly normal and seriously interested in offshore energy parks. But that feeling of panic stayed with her all night. It was not like she had met some random guy online and was now smitten by his kiss. In that case, she could have just fooled around for a few weeks and lived in the moment, to see where it took them. But *this* was different. This could have serious consequences for her job, her reputation (an affair on top of an illegitimate child, that clearly meant social death) – and last but not least, her heart.

Thank God her brain apparently had an override switch and forced her legs to run. Was there even the slightest chance that this would end well for her? He had always sounded like the perfect family man. A bit exhausted and annoyed sometimes, but happy. And now, nothing was what it seemed. Was there even going to be a divorce? An apartment close to the office had its merits in any case, especially if one wanted to sleep around a bit.

Helen had heard so many stories about men starting and ending meaningless affairs at the workplace, without giving it a second thought. Hitting on random girls in bars would certainly be more practical – but who had the time? Was he that kind of guy?

When the alarm showed four o'clock, Helen was still wide awake, and the same thought kept going round in her mind: The most important thing was NOT TO RUSH INTO THIS. Helen had to keep her brain in charge from now on. Before she had figured him out, she would not get pulled behind that blue door again. If he was serious about this – and if *she* was serious about this, that also needed to be figured out! The kissing and touching could wait. With this resolution, her mind finally calmed down. It had felt so good to be held by him, as if he had kissed her body awake after decades of sleeping. It was already getting bright outside when she fell into a light sleep.

*

The next day, Helen climbed the stairs to her office like any other day. Only that Babette shouted, "You rock, girl!" after her, using those grapes like a cheerleader its pom-poms, and Francis whistled. Albertine messed up a dictation as she never learned the difference between *quiet* and *quite* and again confused some addresses. And a partner from Real Estate had gotten lost on the staircase and ended up at Albertine's desk. "May I ask, Albertine, that is such an unusual name for your generation ..." And Almond Eyes giggled as desired and told the story of her great-grand-aunt on the *Titanic* – for the hundredth time.

And then she would shriek: "Nooo, I am British through and through..." Helen rolled her eyes. But as always, she did look stunning in her light yellow shift dress, as if it were summer already. Everything was a flirt with this one, except for the grammar.

Helen tried to focus on her client letter, but when she heard the stairs creak, her heart did not skip the usual beat; it stopped entirely. Part of her had been afraid that Eric would withdraw again. Another part of her was hoping for that – she had escaped for a reason. But there he was, with a shy smile and two teacups, as if he had come to stay.

"I'm sorry if that was a bit of an ambush yesterday," Eric began.

"Yes," Helen said, blushing like a schoolgirl. "At least now I know why your suits look like you have slept in them for the last few weeks."

"That bad? But yeah, the household is not quite up and running yet." Her comment seemed to embarrass him a bit and he stared into his teacup. That was the last thing she had wanted.

"No, I don't think anybody else has noticed. I'm sure that it's not so easy with work and everything..." she offered.

"No, it is actually not..." he said, still focussed on the teacup. When he stayed quiet, she could no longer hold back.

"What happened, Eric? A few weeks ago, we were talking about Christmas and your perfect family, and now you have your own place?"

"Yes, I know... In the end, it all happened kind of fast. I mean, things had been rough for a while, but it all finally blew up after Christmas. That's a classic, I guess. I felt that for the sake of the children, it would be better if I moved out. All the years before, it had been the opposite. I was convinced I had to stay because of them, but I was just fooling myself..."

"Oh, Eric, I am so sorry..." Seeing him so lost was heartbreaking.

"Anyway, a good friend of mine is in real estate and he found me that place. It was pure coincidence. Initially, I wanted something close to the kids but it was either expensive houses or really shitty places. Then, I thought this place was also an option – I gotta go to work anyway... And if people ask, I could tell them we bought it as an investment and before it gets renovated, I use it if I work long hours, something like that." Obviously, he was much more comfortable talking about the practicalities of his new situation.

"So, you haven't told anyone?"

"No. Nobody knows apart from you. I feel I have to figure this out a bit by myself before I roll it out to the public."

Helen felt a strong urge to wrap her arms around him, despite that shrill voice inside her head, yelling: *See, he has not figured it out yet! Watch out for yourself!*

"I really did not plan that, last night. I would certainly have gone for a better setting than that awkward burger restaurant But suddenly I did not want you to leave without telling you... I already hated that after our Farringdon dinner."

The voice kept yelling: *It was just a spur-of-the-moment thing. He does not have a plan!* But it was drowning in a jubilant choir. She had not been the only one longing to kiss him that night!

"I was thinking, what about dinner on Saturday? We cannot really talk here, in the office." And that was an official date!

"Dinner sounds nice," Helen said, as calmly as possible. "Emmy has a sleepover with some girls from her arts club on Saturday." Nonsense. It was just dinner, she would be back home on the last Tube. Why had she said that?

"Perfect... I just have to warn you... the next morning, it is my turn to take Jameson to hockey class." And damn it, he had understood.

"The next day... well, that should be no problem."

"Great. I think I will get back to work, try my best to focus," Eric added with a boyish smile, much happier than when he had entered with the cups. "I will be out for a meeting tomorrow, so... I guess I will see you Saturday?"

"Right," Helen said, trying her best to wipe the stupid grin off her face. But when she carried a file back to the girls, Albertine's first comment was: "Ooh, Ms Kings, have you just met a unicorn!"

Back in her office, she briefly wondered whether unicorn was actually a euphemism for something else. And she wondered whether going to that dinner was the best or worst decision of her life.

*

For the rest of the week, everything went as it should. Eric texted late in the evenings for a goodnight kiss. He texted Friday at teatime, saying he was thinking of her. He called Friday night and they talked for about half an hour; a bit about work, and a bit about how much they were looking forward to their dinner. Came Saturday, Helen decided to stop all those negative thoughts and to just try to have a good time.

She had also confessed to her daughter that someone she really liked had asked her out. With a few minor amendments, of course. She turned Eric into a 'friend of a friend', who was divorced but worked in a different firm. She tried to make it sound casual. "I don't really need a relationship right now," but she could not mislead Emmy that much. Her daughter was a smart girl and could tell that her mum was excited like a teenager. And she took great pleasure in preparing her mum for a date. This nightmare in the A&E really had a silver lining – it had been years since Emmy had suggested an outing.

On Saturday, they walked up and down Oxford Street together with the crowds, pushing through the racks at H&M, which as always stood ridiculously close, and waited in an endless queue at Zara's changing rooms. Emmy knew all the designers behind the brands and which celebrity was spotted wearing them. As expected, the result was window shopping for Helen but a new top for Emmy – surprisingly in sparkly pink, which was really not the colour of the season. That would have been all shades of nude. She looked like Barbie but happy.

They stopped for lunch at Pizza Express, a restaurant Emmy found cool and Helen 'not too loud'. Over a milkshake for dessert, Emmy generously announced that her mum could stay out all night if she wanted to and that made Helen laugh. It was so nice to be out together like this – and not just because it distracted her from all the worrying about her scandalous date.

"Where do you think you are going to wear the pink top? Just wondering, because it is not *high fashion*."

"That is true. I liked the pink colour for some reason... and I thought Amir might like it. It looks a bit Indian with all the beads."

Helen would have choked on her cappuccino had she taken a sip at that very moment.

"Wow! Amir again? Are you guys going out now?" She tried to sound as casual as possible.

"Not really. He drives me and Ali-Saa to places and sometimes we all hang out. But we chat a lot. I think we are like friends with a special interest by now."

Emmy was beaming with happiness. Perhaps it would be wise to gather more information on these people, Helen thought. Apparently, they were not going away.

"That sounds nice. You never really told me – where do Ali-Saa and Amir get their caramel complexion from?"

"From their parents," Emmy said with a grin.

"*Funny!*"

"Mu-um, that is a *very* racist question to ask," Emmy rolled her eyes.

"Oh, come on. That is a very obvious thing to ask! Where are his parents from? You said India?"

"Yes, from nearby Delhi," Emmy said, stirring her milkshake with great focus.

"What do you mean 'nearby'? Like a suburb?"

"I mean Pakistan."

"*Pakistan?*" Helen said, much louder than she had intended. Some people turned their heads.

"See! 'Nearby Delhi' was better."

"You should go into marketing. Or politics!" Helen said with honest admiration.

"Is that a problem now? They have lived here forever and their house is bigger than ours and you know Ali-Saa. She doesn't wear a burqa or anything."

"I know, honey. It is just sometimes—"

"*Sometimes*, what?"

"Sometimes dating people from different cultures can be complicated, even if they seem to live the same way we do."

"We are NOT dating. And again, that *does* sound racist!"

"I don't think 'complicated' is racist. Anyway, I am just a little worried here."

Emmy slurped the remaining milk from between the ice cubes Apparently, she had nothing to add here but Helen would not give up so easily.

"For example, he's in college, at SOAS, right? There are certainly all kinds of groups and events held by women's rights activists. Is he supporting any of these?"

"Oh, Mum. No man *actively* supports those groups. Even if he is not 'caramel'." At 'caramel', Emmy raised her hands, making quotation marks in the air and Helen had to laugh.

"You've got a point there!"

"He is into movies and football. Pretty much like anybody else. They also lived in the US for some time, and he really liked it there."

"Sure, sure. Does he have any plans to go back?"

"Mum!"

"Sorry! Movies and football sounds fine… I think my point is that we sometimes underestimate these things. Italians are European but still very different in my experience. That is all I mean…"

"Yes, I know that is what you mean. But not even all Italians are the same. Not all men are the same." Emmy said this very calmly, not to hurt anybody's feelings, and yet with determination. She was a good daughter. No idiot should ever be mean to her.

"Fair enough. I also don't want you to think that I am evil and eager to ruin your happiness. Just be a little smart, okay?"

"Okay," Emmy said, followed by a bright smile. Somebody was already head over heels. It was even more important then to keep a cool head over all this Eric-business; better set an example for the hormone-driven teenager.

*

"I'm happy," was the first thing Eric said in the morning. Still half asleep, he spooned her, stretched one leg over hers, so that their feet touched gently. Helen pressed her cheek against his face. For a moment, they just stayed like that, like two matching pieces of a puzzle. Helen went to pick him up at his place; it had seemed like a good idea as the last time she didn't really get to see his new home. But they never made it out of the apartment. Things moved on from where they had left them on Monday, and were unstoppable from there. Right now she was having a hard time regretting any of it.

Their bodies were so entangled and yet deeply comfortable, as only new loves can be. No arm squeezed too hard, no bone too sharp, no skin too sweaty. *I could lie like this forever*, she thought, because it felt so damn good, when suddenly he pulled his arm back so that Helen's head bounced onto the mattress.

"Oh God! It is already 8am," he said with terror in his eyes.

"So?" Helen was confused.

Eric rolled to the edge of the bed, swung his legs out, and started to pick up his boxers from the floor.

Without turning, he said, more to his jeans than to her, "Jameson's hockey! I totally forgot! I better get going. I really can't be late. That boy is so upside down with how things are already."

"Sure. I understand," Helen said, putting on a brave face. "They need their dad more than ever now." She could not have come up with a better platitude to hide her disappointment. Helen sat up and pulled the blanket over her chest while Eric ran around frantically, looking for the car keys. Now that Eric was dressed, she felt naked and decided to stay where she was. At least he knelt on the bed and crawled over to her for a goodbye kiss.

"Help yourself to some coffee," he shouted while running out.

As the door slammed shut, Helen stayed on the bed for a few more minutes. Her entire body seemed to refuse to leave lover's land. He had told her before, hadn't he? It was fine he had to leave; he just could have broken it a bit more gently to her. She walked around his tiny apartment like a Roman lady, wearing the blanket like a toga. The small kitchen counter indeed had a coffee machine, and in the upper cupboard she found two cups with the company logo. Eric the thief. Helen smiled. Staying alone in this bachelor cave was not tempting; but neither was going back to her empty house. Helen decided to get dressed and hunt for coffee, maybe walk down to the Thames if it wasn't too cold.

*

For a day in March, the weather was incredibly mild and the streets were empty. Helen could not remember the last time she had walked through the city on Sunday morning in last night's outfit. Actually, the answer was *never*. Walking down High Holborn in high heels, a small black dress, wrapped in a big shawl, and with messy hair – Kate Moss would have been so proud. She kept walking for a while, just for the heck of it, feeling so out and about. The Starbucks near Leicester Square was open, and one of the armchairs in the window was free. It was free because it was her lucky day. She sipped on her cappuccino, watched the people passing by, convinced that their days had not started half as spectacular as hers. After the coffee was almost halfway down, she took her phone out. There was one message from Emmy. She would be dropped off at about three in the afternoon. Three big smileys and one pink heart – life was good, wasn't it?

On the way back, Helen got some food from Tesco City at Holborn, to cook a healthy dinner for Emmy. At the checkout, she was reminded that this was insanely expensive, but she was not in the mood for the ugly Clapham Sainsbury's today. When she stepped off the Tube at Clapham Common, the sun had disappeared. By the time Helen reached home, she was shivering in her little dress. She put the bags down in the hallway and rubbed her hands where the plastic had been cutting into her palms. When she looked up again, there he was. He was leaning against the kitchen counter and there was something sad in his smile.

"You think this one is going to save you, Dulcinea?"

"Don't look at me like that," she mumbled, and bent over the bags again. When she looked up to carry them over, he was gone.

17

Half the Story

April 2017, Vittuone (Milan)

Clara left the morning right after the big confession. She had signed up for a bus tour to the Netherlands; this was the best time to see the tulips blossom. No array of good advice and wisdom had accompanied her goodbye this time. After the taxi had disappeared out of sight and the main gate closed again, Alma stepped out on the terrace to take a deep breath. Their night talk had obviously taken Clara aback – though it was only a matter of time and she would be her old *wisenheimer* self. And she knew that tomorrow morning, she would miss her. Clara might be bossy, but she did bring life into a house. Apart from the distant humming of a vacuum cleaner, the house was silent.

The swallows had returned from their winter retreat and now they flew across the park, carrying straw and little branches to build the matrimonial home for the season. Even the birds are busy, she thought. Had she been too bold to insist on staying here on her own? Childish even? What could she do, simply to fill her days and not go mad? Deprived of its instigator, her rebellious attitude immediately vanished. Staying posted for an unknown grandchild who might never come was hardly an occupation. So better pack up and drive right after Clara?

Amidst all these dark thoughts, the phone rang inside. Where was

Maria? The vacuum couldn't possibly be that loud. By the third ring, she had turned back inside. The caller was persistent; Alma reached the phone at what might have been the eighth or tenth ring.

"Carneggio residence."

"*Signora* Alma, is that you?" an energetic young voice came from the other end. It had been a while, but Alma recognised it immediately. The last time she had heard it in a different life, of a different house, but such an impertinence one does not easily forget.

"It is me, Ana! From the Trustees Board of Amici di Brera?"

Alma took a deep breath. The Amici di Brera had for sure received a card as well, hadn't they? Otherwise, that would be something to point out to di Marco…

"First of all, please let me express my most sincere condolences. My husband passed away many years ago. He was my everything. So I know how difficult these times must be for you."

Oh God, another expert on grief. How to keep this short?

"You know," Ana continued, "at first, I hesitated to contact you. But then I thought, that is not quite right. Especially at times like this, I remember, one needs nothing more than a little distraction. The silent phone is the worst in those times. Silence in general, I would say. And if I am wrong, there is always the option to hang up on me." There was that laugh again, a slightly mad chuckle but coming from the heart.

This was so unexpectedly honest that it took Alma aback. To gain time, she repeated what she had just heard: "Yes, very difficult times indeed, true, true…"

"And, well, the only distraction I have to offer," Ana said, "is supporting young artists for the summer academy… For myself, I can say, it gives me great satisfaction to support young artists and then watch over the years how they build their careers." Her tone reminded Alma of a TV commercial. There was only one young man she had wanted to watch prosper and grow, she thought bitterly. But as she said nothing, Ana went on with her spiel.

"I know this is all a bit abstract at this point. But if it would not mean any trouble for you, I could give you a bit of an introduction to the programme and the candidates we have selected for this year's summer events. I could pay you a visit, to spare you the trouble of coming downtown. I have it all on my laptop!" The last sentence came out triumphantly, as if she had only recently mastered this beast.

That was a shameless self-invitation and Alma's first impulse was to respond with a detached *I will think about it*. But something stopped her. Hadn't she just complained that the house was so empty? Silence was the worst, the museum woman had so rightly said. Now there was a potential guest and what was there to lose? She would have to hold on to her purse a little but that should be possible; Miss Ana's persuasive skills seemed rather pedestrian. So to her own surprise she said in a business-like manner, "When are you available this week? I would prefer afternoons but otherwise I am quite flexible…"

And what a good decision this was. As a next step, she would inform Flavia and think about what to serve and what to wear. She could also enquire with di Marco as to the scope of their past sponsoring. Perhaps this was the way forward for the next weeks? Just take life day by day and trust that something would come up to keep her busy.

Two days later, Ana stood in the foyer. Her appearance was exactly as ungraceful as Alma had remembered. She was wearing a tight knee-long dress in screaming turquoise with red owls and cats printed on it. Again, it was a size too small; hips and breasts pushed heavily against the garment, as if her clothes were a prison her body wanted to escape. Alma had become anxious the day before; she had never before managed such a situation all on her own. But when she walked down the stairs and saw Ana, with red spots on her face and cleavage despite the modest temperatures, her confidence returned. She should not forget who she was, after all. When she shook Ana's hand, she saw a drop of sweat roll down her sternum and disappear in the slit of her bosom, all visible because of this daringly *décolleté* dress. She could at least cover up with a scarf. Nobody wanted to see an old woman's skin.

Ana was obviously impressed by the entry hall, marvelled at the fireplace and probably also at Alma's elegant appearance. Alma was used to this reaction; it had been her favourite moment when mothers of Luca's friends came for the first time to a play-date and their jaws dropped. When Alma led her towards the terrace, Ana trailed behind, stopped every now and then to sniff at the roses, and praised the park in a voice more than a tad too loud.

Flavia had prepared tea and some snacks. Ana placed the teacup next to the saucer and giggled when she couldn't find her cup the next time she reached for it. Really, Alma could not believe she had been nervous about this. After a bit of chit-chat, Ana heaved a small computer out of her bulky handbag and suggested starting with the presentation. In terms of etiquette, this was nothing but rude, yet Alma was grateful. They were about to officially run out of topics any moment.

Alma expected the presentation to be as dilettante as her guest's attire, but to her surprise it wasn't. Ms Ana moved her glasses too often and took a very long time to find the right file on her laptop, but she obviously knew what she was talking about. The Pinacoteca traditionally hosted exhibitions of classic artists such as da Vinci or Vermeer; in other words, one had to be dead for quite a while to hang in there. The summer events, however, were all about giving 'newcomers' to the art scene a chance. Ana had compiled photographs of the artists and their works and, for each one, she could tell why he or she deserved recognition. Alma was at a loss when Ana explained that *this one brings the art of painting back to figuration* or how that one demonstrates how a sculptor could *champion the divergent trends of materialism and virtuality*, but she threw in "Ahs" and "Oh reallys" whenever it seemed appropriate. And the spark did come across. Alma couldn't help but feel a tad of admiration for her strange guest. Ana had obviously been very nervous, but she had stood her ground and pulled through. At the end, Alma did as previously rehearsed with di Marco and said: "I will think about it and then revert to you in a few days." And Ana was professional enough to be completely fine with that.

To honour Ana's bravery, Alma felt it would be impolite to see her to the door right after the presentation. So she asked for another round of tea, and since Ana had liked the flowers so much, she took her on a small tour through the park so they could stretch their legs a bit. It took longer than expected as Ana had to bend down to stick her nose in every flower, and shrieked in amazement when a squirrel ran up the tree next to them, and then stood for a minute to find out where it lived. Back on the terrace, Ana wrung her hands together in admiration: "*Signora* Alma, you are so blessed living in such an amazing house! Waking up in so much beauty every day!"

"Yes, well," Alma said hesitantly, "I will probably move by the end of the year. This place is no longer appropriate for me…"

"What?" Ana sat down as if her knees had suddenly weakened. "Why would one ever leave such a place?" she shouted, throwing her arms up in the air.

Again, no distance whatsoever. This woman was a stranger and this was none of her business. Nonetheless, Alma heard herself say: "I will move in with my sister. The house is nice but I have no family here. All these dinners and receptions, I cannot really attend them alone. I would be the odd one out among the couples. And anyway, I am a family person. I don't care much for meeting friends for a *kaffeeklatsch*." That was what she suspected an odd woman like Ana spent her days doing.

"Maybe. Or maybe you just need something to do! Even the greatest *kaffeeklatsch* does not give your life purpose," Ana said.

"I am very traditional in that sense. I live for my family," Alma said, slightly annoyed, and trying to sound determined. "And now, as God has willed, my only family is Clara."

"Aha." Ana paused for a moment, unimpressed by Alma's clerical tone. "And what does that entail? Living for Clara? Will you be some sort of housekeeper for her?"

"Of course not!" Where had this come from now?

"I mean, is she ailing, or sick? Does she need some kind of help?"

"Not really." All these people who had their spoonful of wisdom for breakfast, Alma thought. Had this woman even tried to stand in her shoes for a second? "I am not entirely sure where you are going with this. It is simply that I have no other place to go. I cannot live on my own in such a huge house."

"Who says that?"

"Everybody."

"Aha." Ana said, folding her arms in front of her chest, anything but convinced. "I think you need a plan. A plan for something to do."

Next Ana would suggest Pilates or Senior Yoga. "A plan, my God, that is so easy to say. Let us be realistic for a moment. What kind of plan can a woman of my constitution and at my age make?"

Ana widened her eyes: "You mean, what plan can a healthy, rich woman living in a palace make? My gut feeling is there are a bunch of options…"

"There is no need to be sarcastic," Alma snapped. "I am certainly not in good health."

"Oh my God, I am so sorry!" Ana shout-whispered, clutching her hands to her cheeks. Finally, this woman looked as embarrassed as she should be.

"I have a bad hip and my blood pressure is always too low," Alma continued triumphantly.

Ana laughed and clapped her hands together: "Everybody without a plan has a bad hip and low blood pressure! Come on, this is a great house! To me, moving out of here does not sound like a plan, it sounds like defeat!"

Defeat. That was exactly what it felt like, but still.

"I believe you simply don't understand what this is like for me," Alma said.

"I lost my second husband to cancer more than ten years ago. He was the love of my life. I have no children because my first husband left me for another woman, at just the wrong age."

Now it was Alma's turn to be embarrassed. "I'm sorry to hear that. It is just that no other mother lost my son. With that grief, I am always alone."

Ana nodded and they sat together quietly for a while. Actually, it was nice talking to Ana. There was a lot of truth hidden in all that chattiness. And unlike the rotary ladies, she did know when to keep quiet. There was something truly kind about her.

The sun was about to set and Maria brought out some blankets.

They watched the early evening sun bathing the trees in a golden glow and the swallows began to fly their evening laps to get ready for the night. The chirping of Romeo and Juliet slowed down as soon as the sunlight faded.

"This really is a paradise," Alma said, her head leaning against the end of the deckchair. "The problem is inside."

"Why?"

"Because of all the things in there. The place is stuffed with things up to the ceiling, and every single one comes with a painful memory. Already after my in-laws died, the house was too big, even for three people. In the eastern wing where my in-laws lived, we left most of the things in cupboards and boxes. We always planned to clear it up, but never did. I guess Giacomo was more sentimental about his parents than he ever cared to admit. He did not like guests in the house, not more than social convention required, so we never used the space. And when my son died, I never had the heart to go through his belongings. And we did not need that part of the house, either. At some point, I believe Giacomo had it all boxed up. He said it was unhealthy to keep the room as if Luca would return any minute. He could not bear the thought of it. So basically half the house is a museum; it would take years to go through everything. And now... all the things my husband left behind... I cannot just throw away all those memories. These are the last traces on earth of my family. Nothing else survives; nobody to tell our stories."

Ana nodded and thought about all this for a while. "I remember that part. Dealing with a loved one's belongings is incredibly difficult. You need to move on, but when getting rid of things, it feels as if you are causing that person to die once again."

"Yes, exactly, as if you are finally erasing them! What did you do with the things of your husband back then? His clothes, all the things he loved?"

Ana took a deep breath. "For years, nothing... so take your time. The clothes were the worst. He was a banker, you know. Every time I opened his wardrobe, I was determined this time at least to put away some stuff, but couldn't. The suits, the ties, I saw him so clearly in front of me, knotting his tie in front of the mirror. He really loved his job. Each time, I closed the cupboard and was miserable for several days. I was afraid of losing that connection."

"See! And I have, like, a whole chateau full! It is an avalanche of stuff that will wash me away over and over."

"One day, I asked myself what my husband would have to say about all this, if he could see me. Are you religious?"

"Well, my mother..." Alma began.

"Me neither. And I realised he would feel nothing but pity. And perhaps he would even feel helpless on his cloud. And guilty because I was in such bad shape. I did not want him to feel bad, up there. I wanted him to be proud of his kick-ass Ana! And with that image in mind, I could do it. I cleared the cupboard and had the whole apartment renovated." She put on a brave smile. "I never found anyone that compares to him, though... but maybe that's all right."

"I never looked at it that way..." Alma said, holding back her tears. It was ridiculous to cry in front of someone she only met that day.

"What do you think your son would have wanted you to do? Would he want you to move?" Ana was relentless.

"I... well, I guess, he would surely want me to be happy... but the thing is, the thing is..." and then finally the tears came, as if a dam had broken right behind her eyes.

"What is the thing?" Ana said patiently, reaching for Alma's hand, not disturbed at all by this outbreak.

"The thing is, I feel I did not really know my son," Alma said. "And now I cannot ask him anymore. I do not know what he would want me to do... not really... So, I guess, your theory is unfortunately of no use to me."

"I would not say that, we all have to make peace with that too."

"Like that art class... not only did I not know about the class, but I never would have guessed that he was even interested in such a thing... not remotely. I am still not sure I can believe that." Alma pulled the blanket up to her chest; the cold evening air began to settle under her skin.

Ana tilted her head. "Young people like to have secrets from their parents. That does not mean that you did not know him at all. And maybe you still have the wrong impression of this. He did not take it very seriously. He laughed throughout and kept joking with the ladies. Nobody got much done…"

Alma had to laugh through her tears. "Was he talented?"

"I thought so… but even back then I had the feeling he was not going to invest in this."

"You know, that was the thing with him. Always enthusiastic, but it would never last… soon it would be something else. Like, one summer, he found an old Dutch bike somewhere. He repaired it with a friend for weeks, drove everywhere on it for a month, and then it ended up in the garage and was never looked at again. In fall, he bought a scooter."

"Some people are like that. They do not have one passion guiding them through life. At the time," Ana said, "I remember him saying that he was particularly drawn to da Vinci as a character, and that he had read a lot about him."

"Da Vinci?"

"Yes, he said he admired him because he was good at everything – he was a technician, an artist, a philosopher… while Luca felt that he was good at nothing."

Alma felt a pain in her chest. "Oh my God, why did you have to say that?"

"Why? He laughed at that too!"

"There was a clear expectation to take over the family business. For my husband, the trust his own father had placed in him had been the greatest honour. But no matter how often he handed his son the Economy & Finance section of the newspaper at breakfast, he would never give it more than a cursory reading. That would come, we always thought, and since Luca was his only son, my husband was so patient. Strong dynastic bonds are the backbone of this country, he used to say."

"Well, yes, it is a nice tradition… but I guess that stems from a time when people had a dozen children, and then one of them would be a good fit for the family business."

Alma had never considered that; it had just been a rule in their house. "I guess Giacomo never thought much about it because it worked out so well for him and his father. My husband was an only child too."

"Well, everybody is different," Ana said carefully, and turned her gaze back to the park. As if, in case she stirred some emotions, she would not embarrass Alma by looking at her. And suddenly Alma felt as if she could tell this woman everything.

"Actually, what keeps me up at night is that it could be more than just that… there might have been something wrong with him and we did not want to see it, like, I mean…" and here her voice turned into a whisper, "I mean, mentally!"

"Ha? Why would you think that?" Ana shout-whispered back. She did not seem nervous at all about considering this.

"Because he was so all over the place. He would retreat into his room and not come out for days. Then there was the drinking, and he would not pick a girl…"

"But had there ever been some kind of diagnosis?"

"No, of course not!"

"You were worried that your child was sick and did not take him to a therapist?"

"It only occurred to me later, when he was older and there was no taking him anywhere. Also, I doubt Giacomo would have accepted that…"

"Oh my, your husband really seemed to run the show here, with all due respect. After my husband died, I went to therapy for *three years*, what's the big deal?"

Alma had no answer to this; all she knew was that *it was a big deal*!

"Anyway, from what you are saying, I would not be so sure. Just because a young man is acting like a rock star, apart from the girls thing, that does not mean he is mentally ill… we would need more evidence than that!"

We. Somehow they had formed a team over the last half-hour. For a moment, she even considered telling her about the English girl, the drinking and the fiancée, but then decided against it. Ana would never fully understand what their life was like. Sending Luca to a therapist, what if anybody found out the future head of the company went to a shrink?

*

Flavia and Maria had already left when she finally saw Ana to the door. The house fell quiet again. The sun had set over the garden, the small lanterns on the terrace came on; di Marco had them programmed to stay on all night, so the house would never fall too dark. There was something so rich about the mingling of evening blue with the warm lights of night, and if her legs were not ice cold by now, she would have sat outside a little longer. She got herself another tea and walked over to the library. She took out one of Emmy's photos; she particularly liked the 15th in school uniform and placed it between the frames. She tried to read a bit, but her mind constantly wandered off. She tried to imagine the artwork Luca must have created as a young man. She imagined colourful and bright paintings, abstract and yet so lively. Like those of Franz Marc perhaps, and then it grieved her that he had never shown them to her. With the fading of daylight, her thoughts turned darker as well. How cruel God sometimes is, she thought. Why couldn't she have died first? Why was she left alone with all these questions and all this guilt?

She started walking alongside the edge of the carpet. Her eyes fell on the high shelves where catalogues from art exhibitions or photo collections were stored. She was almost sure there was one labelled *Leonardo da Vinci*, but she could not find it. She tried to imagine Luca, all alone in his room, sunk into his drawings, forgetting the world around him. Perhaps that had been the thing that gave him inner peace? These two, father and son, had loved each other so much, had lived in the same house and yet in different worlds, it was almost as if they never really got the chance to meet.

After his funeral, Luca's fiancée had come back once, together with her mother, to take the few belongings she had kept in their house. From then on, there had been only a few courtesy visits, although Vittuone was a small town and the families had been acquainted before. She had never called Alma 'mother'. The visits stopped entirely when Monica married another man and moved to Rome. Officially, she had put this down to the Pizzutellis being materialist and selfish. Once the prince was dead and there was no money to inherit, they lost all interest.

But deep down, Alma feared that the Pizzutellis also believed there had been problems, that they were glad that their daughter got out in time, as if this were a haunted house.

We need more evidence than that... she heard Ana say.

And suddenly she knew; there was one thing she could do. She passed the gallery and the living room, switching on all the lights, leaving a trail of light behind her. Her husband's private study was at the end of the Northern wing, extending from the living room. He mostly used it to keep some private documents or to make an undisturbed phone call. With a deep breath, she entered; in his room, a ghost might step out from between the shelves at any time.

She did not have to search for long. Between the folders Insurance Como I/2 and Insurance Como I/3, there was a folder with a black label. Giacomo had told her years ago that this was where he kept all the certificates about Luca, in case she needed them. And she had immediately understood. It would have been too painful to see his name standing on the shelf, like a case closed.

She pulled out the file and started to flip through, not stopping at his birth certificate or at graduation papers out of fear she would then not make it any further. The police report she was looking for came last; it was four pages long. Page 1 of 4 began with some general information, the name of the victim, Luca Carneggio, and the location of the accident. On page 2 of 4, the report from the laboratory under *Tasso Alcolemico* said 1.2 blood alcohol level. And then it ended. There were two small paper ears still stuck in the staple in the upper-left corner. Somebody had torn out pages 3 and 4. And Alma knew the culprit. Her husband had been too good a citizen to simply suppress the entire report. Only the part that broke his heart, he had thrown away.

Part III

18

Penises

April 2017, Vittuone (Milan)

After having found half of the police report, Alma went through a roller coaster of emotions. Despair mixed with anger, and when her energy faded it all went back to that numb feeling of sadness. Why had everybody lied to her? As if she were a child who needed to be shielded from the ugly truth. And mostly she was angry with herself. Why had she never asked to see the report? Why had she been so satisfied with everybody telling her lies, when this was about her son? How could she have been a good mother when everybody treated her as a child? In the end, she deserved to be eaten up by her guilty conscience.

In principle, she could still try to recover the lost pages; she also thought about that. Maybe there was a record at the police station? But after all these years? Or she could ask di Marco? But it was embarrassing to reveal that it had taken her more than twenty years to find the courage to look for the cause of her son's death. And if anybody saw her going into the police station, that would also be suspicious…

And in any case, Giacomo would not have appreciated her enquiries at all. And after the first anger vanished, she wondered whether he was right. What would all this change now? Why not let it rest, respecting her husband's wishes? Or in other words, how could she ever find peace, if she disrespected him. After all, it was his son too. And he deserved to find peace on his cloud.

Despite all this emotional turmoil, Alma's health slowly improved with the weather. The days grew long and bright in May and she extended her walks from the park to short outings circling the house. Afterwards, she felt incredibly tired, as if she had been running a marathon. She therefore stayed close to the house at all times, worried that this fatigue would hit her when she was without shelter. Every time she returned, she checked the basket containing the post by the kitchen. And with every day, it seemed less likely that there would ever be a letter from London. What had she been thinking anyway? Hastily drafting up a letter to undo the past, how ridiculous… and when she thought about Giacomo on his cloud, she felt eternally grateful for there being no response. Though she never went to church, she actually thought about confessing this one.

One fine morning, Ana called her up with a plan. She had a day off and wanted to take Alma to an exhibition at the Triennale Museum of Modern Art in Milan. Alma tried to lament herself out of it: modern art was too abstract for her; she couldn't stand that long because of her hip, etc. But Ana was simply having none of it so Alma ended up with a date.

At 2pm, she stood in front of the Triennale in the centre of Milan, dressed in comfy pants, flat shoes and a handbag strapped over her shoulder, as if she were going on one of Clara's bus tours. She had been complaining in the kitchen about how she would certainly return with a sore back and aching feet. Flavia had rolled her eyes and told her to simply wear comfortable shoes, as if she were going for a walk in the countryside. When Alma protested that that was not a feasible outfit in which to go downtown, Flavia had said that there were actually people downtown that only had one pair of shoes. "*The 'People'* will not think anything," she said, throwing up air quotes for 'people'. That was a new tone coming from Flavia, but her point was not all bad.

*

She recognised Ana already from afar, this time in a bright green jumpsuit with a jungle print – of course a size too small. But the exhibition Ana had chosen for them was interesting indeed. It was about young female artists from Mexico City, no abstract cubicles or naked body parts in sight. It was mostly photographs, capturing the people's poverty, often with a little object standing *pars pro toto*: an old plastic comb with only a few teeth left, bearing a bundle of hairs ranging from grey to black, one comb for the entire family. At least they had a family, Alma thought. After the photographs, it was sculptures. Some artists had taken up themes from the indigenous culture and fused them with contemporary symbolism like mother earth carrying a gun or injecting heroin.

The third room seemed to be empty and Alma was about to joke that this was the real artistic expression of poverty when she noticed the other visitors standing in the middle of the room, looking up to the ceiling. Alma moved towards them and did the same – and there it was. A massive papier-mâché penis in a light pink. The viewer looked at the testicles, physiognomically accurate, but as big as a small car. The penis rose from between the testicles, slightly tilted to the side, so one could see it even if one stood directly beneath the artefact. The entire piece was held by a wire from the ceiling, painfully pierced through the papier-mâché foreskin. The other visitors stood in intellectual awe, as if this were not at all inappropriate and much too private. Alma glanced over to Ana for help but she had tilted her head back and had that same look on her face. God, what if Ana asked for her opinion or even expected her to make a dirty joke? Alma panicked, there was only one solution: get the hell out of there as quickly as possible.

Before leaving the room, she managed to scan the little note on the wall: the artist was a woman of thirty-five who lived with her husband and their three sons in Mexico City. While experiencing the machismo culture in public life, she experienced the male as extremely vulnerable in private, symbolised by the male private parts being exposed, open to hurt and ridicule and in permanent need of protection. Alma realised she didn't feel any more comfortable reading about penises in public. Following her flight instinct, she left the room and waited as casually as possible by the next exhibit, a harmless bronze statue of some indigenous Incan, without genitalia, and pretended to be completely absorbed by it. And thank God, when Ana caught up with her, she did not say a word about the penis hovering over their heads.

After one more room, they were back in the foyer. Ana had promised Alma a short tour and now she clapped her hands. "That was lovely," she exclaimed. "Let's have some lunch – but in comfortable chairs."

"Wonderful, where do we go?" Alma said, not without dramatically putting a hand to her lower back and bending a bit backwards against it, as if she had been weeding potato fields all day.

It turned out that Ana knew all the good places, giving Alma a long list of potential cafés. But when she caught the blank look on Alma's face, signalling neither recognition nor preference, she stormed ahead.

"Let's go to Brera. I will show you my favourite restaurant. It's, like, right under my apartment, my second home, so to speak," and with a glance at Alma's posture, she added, "and let's take a taxi."

It turned out Alma needed a few cushions for the chairs of Osteria di Brera, but otherwise it was a great choice. The decor of the place was tasteful; the clientele made her feel neither too young nor too old, and it was not too noisy. And indeed, the *second home* was not an exaggeration. It turned out that Ana was good friends with everyone in the restaurant, and she and Alma were treated like family. Everybody seemed to adore Ana, despite her blunt and direct talk. But then again, Alma thought, that is probably the life of a widow. You must learn to converse with whomever you come across if you don't want to live in utter silence.

When Ana got into a longer conversation with one of the waiters on their recent difficulty with a drunk guest, Alma's mind travelled back to the penis. Half the population had one, but the ones she had seen in her life could be counted on one hand. On one occasion, her father had come out of the bathroom and had been a bit careless with the towel. When she was sixteen, she had crossed a park and a man opened his coat to flash his genitals at her. She had only ever told her sister, and she had hardly seen anything anyway. Then there was Giacomo, of course – and her son, but that again was different.

She was not willing to accept that monster penis as art. And she would tell Ana that if it ever came up. But still, she had never thought about it that way, the vulnerability of the penetrator…

"You look so absent-minded all of a sudden. What is tripping you up?" Ana said. The waiter had served the soup without Alma even noticing.

"How many penises have you seen in your life?" Alma blurted out.

"What?" Ana almost spat the tomato soup over the table but managed to press her napkin in front of her mouth right on time. Alma blushed. This might actually have been the first time she had said that word aloud, not using a synonym to handle the toilet business with a little boy.

"That is what I call an original topic for conversation." Ana smacked her flat hand on the table, so hard that it shook the glasses and cutlery a bit.

"Ssh, not that loud." Alma already regretted her outburst and looked around. Nobody was really taking any notice of them, though.

"No, no, I like the question, but I'm afraid we have to travel back in time a bit for that one…" Ana even raised one hand and started to count with her fingers; so embarrassing.

"No, not literally. I was just thinking because of that exhibit." Alma tried to save herself.

"Oh, I see, absolutely!" When the topic was art, Ana caught fire. "So impressive and so true; we always think of men as strong, the decision-makers, the rocks we can trust, the ones we look to for shelter. But they are very vulnerable – perhaps even more so than us girls!"

"Really?" Alma was more than relieved that the conversation was shifting from her own awkwardness to general psychology. "Why would you think that?"

"Take my own husband! I was twenty-eight when we met, and he was fifteen years my senior. Before we fell in love, he had only had one serious relationship. He met her in the first year at university and they were together for more than ten years. Then she left him for another man, a colleague from work. It took him another eight years to recover. He had random affairs but he lived in a very reclusive way. Men are like clams, you know. If something hurtful happens, they slam shut and it is really hard work to knock them open again... Did you never observe that?" Ana said, tilting her head curiously to one side. She looked very young all of a sudden, like one could see the clam-charmer she had once been.

"Hmm." Alma tried to give the impression she was thinking hard. "Well, I never gave it much thought... my husband did not have any serious relationships before me..."

"How old were you when you met?"

"I was eighteen and he was twenty-three... the perfect age to meet your husband," she added in an attempt to impress Ana. She was used to envious looks and some impressed 'oohs' and 'aahs' for finding love so early in life.

But Ana shrugged her shoulders. "My mother used to say there is no perfect age to meet your husband," she replied. Alma tried to picture a mother saying such a thing, but came up with nothing. The topic still made her uncomfortable. "I have to admit I love good soups," she said in a serious tone, the best diversion she could come up with for the moment.

Ana giggled as if Alma had made a great joke. "I will join you in that confession booth. So do I, sister!" she said, and raised her spoon in the air.

In all her quirkiness, Ana had a rare talent. She never made you feel stupid, no matter what terribly blunt thing you might have just said. She always made the best out of every piece of conversation. Probably the reason why everybody loved to talk to her.

"The soup was out of this world," Alma said to the waiter when he picked up her plate. Like a woman drawn to worldly pleasures. Such as soup.

The rest of the lunch passed with pleasant and harmless topics: the good memories Ana had with this restaurant, some of the cafés Alma had been to with the Unione ladies. They both agreed that this place was simply the best. When they left, the waiter pointed to a candy bar, set up on a small table next to the counter. Not the decent bowl of mints you usually find, but a kid's paradise of gummy bears in all shades and colours. One of those quirks restaurants adopt these days, to stand out from the crowd. If one already had some golden hips right there, a regretful smile should be as good as it gets for the candy bar. But Ana squealed with joy: "And here comes the best part!" And the waiter, knowing Ana, already had a small paper bag at the ready which Ana filled up to the brim. When she saw Alma's hesitation, she did not stop for a second but simply shouted, "Giovanni, bring me another bag. I have to fill it for my shy friend here!"

*

When Alma got home, for once she felt almost happy, inspired by all the things she had seen and heard. Clara called at 7pm; Alma saw her number on the display but did not pick up. She would call her in the morning so her sister would not have to worry. She made herself a strong tea and installed herself on the sofa, chewing slowly on a pink heart-shaped wine gum.

The park was bathed in the golden glow of the evening sun. Perhaps one could rent the place to a movie company? It did look a bit like one of those houses in romantic comedies which aired on a Sunday evening, usually involving some confusion about identical twin sisters. Well, probably renting it out was not a good idea; the guests would break all sorts of things and never come back for a second time. "What nonsense," Alma chuckled. But there must be a way to put these old walls to use.

By sunset, the candy bag was empty. It had been a long day, and now the fatigue came, pressing Alma into the cushions like a blanket of stones. She closed her eyes for a moment, but she knew her back would punish her if she fell asleep in this position. With a deep breath, she heaved herself up, planning to go to bed without brushing her teeth, so tired she felt.

She only realised her mistake when standing in the door frame. The place she had walked up to was the bedroom she had shared with Giacomo. The bed was made; Flavia and Maria had put on the duvet cover with the large pink magnolia on a white background. The only smell in the air was that of fabric softener. It could have been a room in a hotel, so neat and untouched it was. She leaned against the wall, then slowly slid down it until she safely reached the ground. She took a deep breath and waited, waited for the strength to return so she could lift herself up and walk out of here. The image of the exhibition returned to her mind, the large flesh-coloured penis, pierced at its softest spot. Vulnerable.

"Giacomo," she whispered. "Were you vulnerable?" The question was so naive; one could only ever ask a dead person like that. A faint laugh escaped her throat and she bit her tongue to make it stop. There was nothing more depressing than listening to your own laughter in an empty house.

She sat down on the bed. With her fingers, she tenderly followed the embroidery lines, as if she was painting the magnolias on the duvet. This was the very place where they could have licked each other's wounds, shared their worries and sorrows without being afraid that insult would be added to injury. She had always imagined a marriage like that. She had even believed, as a young girl, that apart from having children and a great house, this was the very purpose of getting married. Creating a safe space, having one person in your life whom you could trust blindly.

But Ana was absolutely right with her clam comparison. Giacomo had been like that. When they got married, they had to learn to be intimate with each other. Their wedding night was romantic, the first real night she had ever shared with a man. And for the first few months everything was great; it was exciting to discover each other despite being so shy. But they hardly spoke during those nights, and she felt that Giacomo was – not unhappy, not at all – but tense, even after weeks. She quickly learned that she had to tread carefully; the faintest sign of disrespect – or something that could be interpreted as disrespect – could bring their intimacy to an abrupt end. She remembered one night when Giacomo was having difficulty putting a condom on. Being a Catholic girl, Alma did not want to get a prescription for the pill as people might see her walking in and out of the gynaecologist's and she might either have to confess or to lie, both of which scenarios gave her stomach cramps. His erection was simply not hard enough yet, but he did not want to wait. It took more than two attempts and when he threw the second condom away with a frustrated moan, Alma laughed. Not at his fumbling or because she found him ridiculous but at that moan; so deeply desperate, as if this were a humanitarian crisis and not a passing softness. He tossed the third condom on the ground and turned his back to her. At first, she was confused, then she felt guilty. It took her half an hour of stroking his back and whispering sweet words into his ear to get him to turn around. And she promised herself never to laugh again in bed.

The more time passed, the more she felt that their intimacy was like moving on a field of landmines. Ironically, although she was apparently the one laying the landmines out, she had no idea as to when one would go off. The most innocent acts or conversations had the potential to leave everybody wounded. Giacomo got more and more involved in the company; he worked late hours and was often somewhere else with his thoughts. During the few intimate encounters they still had, he always made sure they stayed under the blanket. Although he was her husband, she rarely saw him naked. Only when he was satisfied with his erection would he throw off the blanket in a triumphant gesture before sinking into her. But when his erections stopped being an automatism, she did not know how to bring them back. Sometimes she tried, but he would swat her hand away and give her a goodnight kiss.

The second baby never came. When Alma was thirty-one, the doctor discovered cysts in her ovaries and she had them removed. Luca was already eight years old. She had wanted a second baby so much; the thought that she had escaped cancer meant nothing to her. But she also wondered if she would have had that baby anyway.

Should she have tried to listen more? Ask Giacomo more often what upset him? Whatever she did to open him up, it seemed she locked the door even more, pushed him away even further. He had never been one for talking.

"Giacomo, where are you now?" she whispered in the dark. How could she ever sleep with all these questions unanswered?

She lay down on the duvet. She did not dare to throw it back and slip under it; it felt as if she would tear open a crusted wound. He, who had always made her feel weak and small, he might have been the loneliest of all. Obeying all his commands, without questioning them, was the easiest option. But it was also a way of leaving him in his solitude. Being raised by his parents, he might never have accepted any other way. But only because he did not know any better...

And over these thoughts, she fell asleep amidst the magnolias.

19

Not in this Life

March 2017, London

While the days before had a million tasks and chores, Helen's life now seemed to happen within 20 square metres, on an IKEA bed under a light bulb. And it was more than enough; there was a whole new world to discover. Eric had opened a door inside her; she had even forgotten it was there. There was so much to discover about him. How his skin tasted so good, and how it was so surprisingly soft for a man, especially the tops of his feet. She finally could run her hands through his hair after they made love. And it was even more incredible to be discovered like that by him.

He indulged every inch of her body; there was no part he did not seem drawn to, from her bony shoulders to her tiny bird-like toes. Only in the eyes of a lover do we truly come to life. When she now walked in the street, she was conscious of her hips and felt her breasts resting in the cups of her bra. As if she had come into a new physical existence. She suddenly could not stand her outfits anymore. The harsh feel of her blouse limited her movements; she needed something more flowing. Dresses with cardigans worked much better. And she kept her hair down most of the time, because it reminded her how much Eric liked to run his hands through it.

"You seem so hungry…" he had said after their first night, but without judging her for that poverty that is behind every hunger.

Nonetheless, she felt forced to give a number. "Well, it has been, what, boy, I think two years, can you believe it?" But the truth was, she had never made love like that. She remembered loving Luca vividly, but the body she had inhabited back then, the body of her nightly fantasies, was actually lost. It owned a different story now, and it wasn't a bad thing. She was even more acutely aware of all the sensations running through it, enjoyed the passion and tenderness towards it even more. Back then, her young confident self had believed that, naturally, a life filled with good sex lay ahead of her.

And yet, in moments when her brain had dibs on her blood supply, she found herself observing him anxiously. He had shared a bed with the same woman for so many years. What if his wife was still living under his skin? What if he was following a certain routine he had grown accustomed to with another woman? But it never felt like that. It all seemed to be as new for Eric as it was for her. As if he also had to learn again to be tender, to let go and lose himself in the other.

When two people fall in love, there should be nothing but butterflies, a pink sky and the desire to see each other every moment of the day. But in an adult world, it is not quite like that. To be fair, as long as they were together, it basically was. After making love, they lay together for an hour or two and talked about everything and nothing. Helen loved listening to all his theories, no matter whether they were about a second Brexit referendum or the life of trees.

But two nights a week were enough for him. "I cannot realistically manage more than that with my schedule," he told her. *Realistically*. Weekends were only an option if he did not have to take care of the kids, and those were rare. The fact that they could see each other every day at work could have compensated for this scarcity, but Eric put a halt to that too. He refused to continue their coffee-break tradition.

"It will only start rumours, and people gossiping will take the fun out of it…"

"But we have taken that risk in the past," she tried to argue. It seemed ironic that now that they were a couple, they should see less of each other.

But Eric was adamant. "Even more important that we stop this now. People will notice the looks on our faces, especially your assistants. They are the queens of corridor gossips…"

In fact, Albertine had already made a snide comment when the tea breaks stopped, along the lines of, "Can I take Mr Thomson out of your personal calendar?" and it had annoyed her to no end. She longed to see him during the day even more than she used to, but there was no talking him out of it. Of course, it was too early to roll this out to the public. She had to be reasonable too and could not jeopardise her job. It was important to stay ahead of this.

Sometimes they made plans to go for a nice dinner or a drink, but they hardly ever left the room. It was also the safest place for a secret affair. And every night at 23:15, Helen pulled herself up and got dressed to catch the last Tube. For all Emmy knew, she and Eric had extensive dinners and were getting to know each other better. Because that was how adults went about a new relationship. Whether or not Emmy believed this was, a different story. Helen did not want to learn from neighbours about a young, caramel-skinned chaperone leaving her house after breakfast. And perhaps it would help to keep the brain in charge, keep some distance as it was all so new.

Ironically, the return of lovemaking into her life also brought back Luca with a new intensity. He came back just when she seemed to overwrite him. One morning, after she had spent the evening at Eric's, she turned on her stomach, just to stay one minute longer in bed. And without warning, in the warmth of the blanket, she could suddenly smell Luca so clearly, could feel his body pressed against hers. His aftershave, his chest hair tickling her back while he hardened against her. She jumped out of bed, whispering, "I am sorry," not even sure to whom she was apologising. She walked straight down to the kitchen, in just a T-shirt and her hair a mess.

"Have you seen a ghost?" Emmy asked her pale mother. Helen felt tempted to simply say yes, but blamed menstrual problems instead.

Sometimes she also dreamt of Luca's mother, always the same dream in slight variations. She shook Alma's hand at what appeared to be Luca's wedding reception, but Alma looked a hundred years old.

Then she heard Emmy call for her from somewhere, but when she wanted to move, she found that their hands had grown together.

*

The best distractions were still the Wednesday night talks with Emmy. After a short update on what the week had been like for them – Helen had learned that it was helpful to not just run an inquisition but to also share some of her own thoughts – Emmy usually asked for anecdotes of her life with Luca in Geneva. She was truly intrigued by Helen's description of Geneva in summer. The Mediterranean summer nights, people swimming at midnight, while sheiks paraded with their wives along the promenade, passing a group of hippies smoking pot, sitting next to an African delegation visiting the United Nations. Also, to her, it had seemed like a fantasy land where the usual rules of society didn't apply.

It was nice to share the joy of those days with someone. And Helen suddenly remembered episodes she had almost forgotten. Actually, it was more than just remembering. Telling them to Emmy showed Luca in a new light.

One night, she told Emmy the story of their trip to Chamonix. In contrast to summer, winters in Geneva were so bleak and boring that everyone tried to escape them. The sheiks and their families left Switzerland in late autumn, internships with the United Nations were scheduled to end in October, so the population was easily halved from November to February. Those who stayed behind went to the French Alps for skiing as often as they could; the resorts were booked out every weekend. One Friday afternoon, they were lying in bed and thinking about where to go that night when Luca said, "Let's drive down to Chamonix. We'll have a good weekend there!"

She told him that this was insane. They would arrive late in the night and where would they sleep – in the car at minus temperatures?

"Those trips are the best, Dulcinea. Good things will come our way!" he had said.

Emmy clapped her hands, enjoying the idea of her daredevil father shaking up her boring and constantly worried mother.

As the first houses of the Chamonix valley came into view, it was already 22:00 and pitch dark. They had called tourist information on the way and every room was booked, the weather forecast predicting amazing skiing conditions. Then Luca hit the brakes at a green *vacant* sign dangling on a wooden fence, the house behind it not as bad as Bates Motel, but almost. An old lady opened the door, hunched and dressed as if she were waiting for Hänsel and Gretel. The room she showed them had an orange tapestry from the sixties, and it smelled like no windows had been opened since. Helen dreaded the thought of sleeping in those dusty sheets.

"The place is perfect!" Luca was so enthusiastic that it still made Helen laugh when thinking of it. All he had seen was a small balcony attached to one of the rooms, so they put out a mattress and gathered all the blankets and sheets they could find. They stayed half the night out there all snuggled up, singing and laughing after emptying two bottles of wine together. This far from the city lights, the silver snow reflected the bright moon, and Helen had never seen the Milky Way like that. And Luca held her so tight all night, as if she were the most precious thing on earth. It was one of the nights which left her eternally grateful for having known this man.

The next morning, the old woman greeted them with a face as if she were going to eat them for breakfast. They had disturbed her night's sleep. But Luca knew how to charm old ladies. He got her to have breakfast with them, poured her coffee and complimented her on her house. She ended up telling them the story of how she fell in love with her husband, the best skier in Chamonix, and Luca promised they would stay at her place again next time. The woman would have adopted him if she could.

"And did you? Spend more nights under the stars?" Emmy was caught in a romantic fever now. But they had never gone back and Helen had planned to end her story here, but then she remembered a little detail. Back in Geneva, Luca found the keys in his pants.

"Let's call Amélie so she does not have to worry about the keys; maybe she'll want us to send them," Helen had said. It was not the key card of a Hilton; the old lady might only have the one key rarely left the house.

"It's just a key, Dulcinea," was all Luca had said, as if it was a stupid idea, and threw the key in the bin. And that was certainly also Luca, the eternally spoilt son. Always living in the moment, and amazing at creating unforgettable ones, but also never thinking about any consequences of what he did to others.

After emptying her cup of Ben & Jerry's, Emmy said: "Maybe people loved him too much from the outset. Then he had to disappoint them in the end."

Her wise daughter sometimes did that, dropping a piece of wisdom without any further explanation. This was so well put. It was as if his good looks and his generous nature gave away a promise his heart could never keep. People thought they had found a new best friend in him, and then he did not return their calls. His family thought he would be the perfect son, and then he ran off. She had thought he would mean eternal happiness, and then he disappeared.

*

The next Friday, she spent the evening at Eric's again. From the way he embraced her behind the door, holding her tight and measuring the entire length of her back with both hands, she could tell that it was one of those nights when they would make love slowly and only once. She could decipher his body so well by now, with all its moods and energies. For the entire game of love, he did not stop kissing her, kept his body close, their lips never parted even when he thrust against her hips. He came with a long, deep shiver and stayed inside her until their breath had calmed down, so much in need of affection and shelter.

After he had gotten up to carry the condom to the bathroom and had returned with two glasses of water, she curled into him and told him the same story she had told Emmy. Without mentioning her fears about Chamonix being booked out, to make her younger self sound fun, and with more emphasis on the stars and snow than on her lover. As she finished, she rested her head against his shoulder, waiting for his reaction.

"What a stargazer," was the only dry comment she got.

"Hey, what's that supposed to mean?"

"No, nothing, it is a nice story…"

"You don't sound entertained though."

"No… I mean, I find it a bit weird how you idolise the guy. Sometimes I think this is a bit like that James Dean and Marlon Brando thing."

"Like what?"

"Well, because James Dean died young, he will forever be cool and sexy. There are still posters today of him balancing that ridiculous cigarette on his lips. Marlon Brando started off the same, but because we all saw him get old and fat, nobody dreams of him at night."

"I was just telling you a story…" Helen said defensively, and pulled a bit away from him.

"I just think you give him an awful lot of credit for things that… well… I can see that this was all really cool when you were twenty-something."

"Okay, okay, it was just a story. And we *were* twenty-three…"

Usually, it was hard to leave the warm bed right before they were about to doze off. Tonight was definitely easier. At the age of twenty-three, Eric had already made solid future plans with Karen, so day trips to watch the night sky might seem childish to Mr Perfect. But was it fair to rub that in? Or maybe he was jealous because his adolescence had kind of ended before it began.

And although she was fine with their arrangement, it wouldn't hurt him to ask her to stay over every now and then. When she started making a move, he waited for her to be dressed and then walked her to the door for the goodnight kiss.

*

That night, from afar, she saw the fox stepping out of the shadow and crossing the street, but he quickly disappeared into one of the hedges. No chance to catch his piercing yellow eyes.

In the hallway, Emmy's trainers lay scattered across the floor amidst the day's post. The usual mosaic that welcomed her home. She bent down to gather the envelopes, advertisements mostly, when something stopped her short. There it was again, that same feeling. The same thick white paper, with a handwritten address. Helen leaned against the door frame and let herself slide down until she was sitting on the carpet. Although she thought so much about him and his fancy Milanese family, it was a shock whenever they materialised. If she wasn't careful enough, they could still mess with her life. She took a closer look at the envelope. There was no black cross this time, and no sender. The real difference, however, Helen only spotted on second glance – and it turned her ghostly shiver into raging fury. The letter was addressed to Ms Emilia Kings.

Bypassing her, marching on straight to her daughter! Out of nowhere! How dare they? First, they ban her before she was even born, and then, seventeen years later, they have a change of heart? The anger rising in her was almost painful. She got up and walked towards the kitchen bin. It was still possible to pretend this had never happened. Just throw away the letter and then empty out the bins so that Emmy would not find it. This was a power she still held. She could deny their existence as much as they denied hers. But somehow she hesitated, weighing the letter in her hand over the open bin. And then she could not do it. What if they mentioned the photos? It would be fun to know whether the family ever got the photos. With one harsh pull, she thrust her thumb into the envelope and tore it open. Just to check for that, no other reason.

It was not even a proper letter, just a few hasty lines. And it was all too easy to see what was going on over there. That old woman was feeling alone in her ridiculously big house with all her stupid paintings and jewellery. Suddenly it would be fun if a well-raised granddaughter showed up to spent some quality time with Granny. In their world, forgiveness could certainly be bought, same as it had only taken a petty sum to dispose of her. Leading with an apology, a big fat one, was the least one could expect! Alma was a mother too; she of all people should have known what their rejection had meant to her. Being alone with every little worry of the day, going through labour and giving birth, without your man by your side. If these people believed they could bend the world to their liking, on every single day, Helen would prove them wrong. She stuffed the letter back in the envelope.

Her phone hummed and the screen sprang to life. A message from

Eric. *Goodnight kiss, sorry for being a bit of a grump tonight, felt burnt out from work. Will make up for it next time. Kiss your shoulder, left one.* The silky white paper in her hand seemed to weigh a ton. If he was still awake, perhaps she should call him? Read the letter to him, pour out her heart to feel lighter?

But she did not. It was all too clear what anybody would tell her. This was Emmy's letter. But nobody stood in her shoes; sometimes things were not that simple. This letter would create nothing but false hope. Hope for another, better, family out there, perfectly rich and making great promises which they would not keep. The feeling of despair and loneliness would pass; Emmy would soon be forgotten, on a beach on St Barths or during a decadent shopping tour in Milan. They would lose interest and forget about her entirely. She walked upstairs, clenching the envelope with both hands against her chest, as if it were a wild animal that needed to be carried to its cage. Then it disappeared in the shoe box in her cupboard.

"I'll make sure you won't get to see my girl, not in this life!" she whispered.

20

Morning Glory

April 2017, Vittuone (Milan)

Alma woke in the same position in which she remembered falling asleep. The first thing that caught her eye was a landscape of huge pink magnolia, and her first guess was another bad dream involving carnivorous flowers. Then she remembered the nocturnal encounter with her husband. Her left shoulder was squeezed by her body weight; her neck was bent in an unnatural position: punishment for not having pulled out any pillows from under the duvet. The alarm on the nightstand showed 5:45. A pulsating pain hammered against her temples, and a visit to the adjacent bathroom showed a wild woman with red eyes with duvet embroidery patterns imprinted on her left cheek. All kinds of painkillers were still safely stored away; the caring Flavia had not even left her an aspirin.

 She decided to try some fresh air against the headache and went downstairs. The lovebirds were awake but still blinking sleepily on their favourite night-time branch. They were used to Alma's early morning visits; her cooing no longer stirred them. Morning dew shimmered in the grass, the air fresh and full of promise. Alma stepped out of her slippers; the green grass looked so tempting. Her naked feet were wet within seconds. She walked up and down alongside the terrace, and the coldness together with the bright light chased away the heavy thoughts of the night.

Maybe, she thought, maybe I just have to accept that I have turned into an early bird. Better get used to it, instead of hiding like a madwoman until there is breakfast in the kitchen. But the question remained: what to do with the mornings? *Yoga*, she heard Clara say. Apparently, in many *ashrams* in India, the first round of yoga took place at something like 4am. Clara started before breakfast. But Alma wanted something that would make her feel more needed than a sun salutation. She paced once more up and down the terrace and then she had it. So surprised by her own epiphany, she let out a little scream which led to some fluttering in the aviary.

It would have been unthinkable when Giacomo was still alive. He would have said that this finally upsets the order of the house and disrupts everything. Staff need to be treated with respect but also shown their place at all times. Her sitting with them in the kitchen was bad enough.

But then again... who knows? Maybe he would have liked the idea when he saw that it gave her pleasure and restored a good spirit to the house. He was not infallible; wasn't that the revelation of last night? Flavia and Maria had been with them for thirty years; they would not start a revolution right away. No, the idea was great: from now on, Alma would be in charge of breakfast! She would walk down to the bakery every morning, set the little table, make coffee, and everything would be ready when they arrived. It was one little thing she could do for them, after all they had done for her and her family. And she was sure about one thing: Luca would have loved it!

She rushed back into the house and got dressed. In her walking shoes, she headed through the front gate and onto the road. Their estate was the last of a spread-out assortment of villas with big gardens. The further she walked, the closer the houses stood together. After some minutes, the streets were lined with parked cars and the gardens no more than a patch of green in front of the houses. At this early hour, there was nobody on the road. Only a cat crossed the street from left to right and then jumped onto the pillar of a garden wall, to watch this unusual sight passing by.

When Alma reached the little *panetteria*, she was out of breath and had red cheeks. It felt like having reached an oasis. The *panetteria* looked exactly like she remembered it. The last time she had come was with little Luca holding her hand. Taking him for a walk to buy an ice cream was one of the strategies to handle an afternoon when his energy was too much for the house and the *panetteria* was the only destination in reach of children's feet. How well she remembered all the details of a place, though she had not thought of it in more than twenty years. There was the same street sign which was carried outside and folded up every day, with a steaming cup of coffee held by a smiling donkey. When little Luca told his father about the donkey, he provoked a whole lecture on good and bad marketing strategies. Putting a donkey on a street sign when you are not selling donkeys and the name of the place was not 'Donkey House', was apparently very bad. Luca kept saying 'Donkey House' and laughed so hard that he ended up rolling on the floor.

Inside the *panetteria* they had the same shop counter, and there were still the usual three to five wasps trapped under the glass. And it smelled so good, of butter and honey. The maids usually had a *cornetto* each for breakfast, but to start the new breakfast routine, Alma felt they needed something more festive – and bought a *panettone* as well.

She made it back just in time and even managed to pick some flowers from the garden before the old Fiat parked in the front yard. And when Flavia and Maria entered the kitchen, they did not disappoint. Flavia's jaw dropped and Maria put her hands together and said, "*Madonna!*"

This special occasion deserved a celebration, and it was somehow clear that nobody would have to leave the table for work before noon. Flavia brewed a second round of coffee and Alma opened the papers. These days, she tried to make them laugh and not read out all the dramas of the world. "Did you know that Michelle Hunziker used to be brainwashed by a sect? Called *Guerrieror della Luce* or something like that?"

"Ah yes," Flavia nodded. "There was something about this girl on TV yesterday…"

"Mind you, she looks like a girl, but she must be over forty by now…" Alma said, inspecting her picture more closely.

"Forty? I thought twenty-eight!" Maria shouted.

"Maria, you've watched her stupid shows for twenty years. How can she be so young!"

"Apparently, the sect is also responsible for her divorce from Eros Ramazzotti! Ha, now I understand. That divorce always puzzled me!" Frowning upon divorced women had become a common sport for them.

"Yes, he is such a handsome man!" Maria said, and when they saw her dreamy look, Alma and Flavia burst into laughter.

Of course, they could not finish all the cake and the *cornetti* which Maria and Flavia had brought. When Alma started to wonder what to do with the remaining patisserie, Flavia suggested inviting di Marco over from the office. It was Wednesday and *Signor* di Marco would be there. That was such an obvious idea that Alma almost felt embarrassed they had never invited him before. It seemed unlikely, though, that he would be interested in spending his mornings with women folk.

She expected the usual impeccable di Marco to come through the door, in a dark designer suit, a decent tie and a matching handkerchief. As usual, he greeted her formally and complimented her on her appearance, but Alma could barely follow. So much did his appearance take her by surprise. His hair had grown an inch, and he used some kind of gel to keep it up in spikes. His shirt was a bright yellow, and the sleeves rolled up! And although the tie radiated the elegance of a Hermès piece, upon closer inspection, wasn't that this cartoon dog, Snoopy, who wandered across it in a geometrical pattern?

But, of course, he could wear whatever he wanted these days. When he worked from the family office, hardly anybody saw him all day; he could have sat there without his pants and nobody would have taken offence. They chatted a bit about the weather, he assured her that everything was going well in the firm and thanked her exuberantly for the cake. Unlike the first months after the funeral, he seemed unbent, younger somehow.

He had been Giacomo's closest companion, Alma thought. It must have been hard on him, to lose him and then still come to work on the estate. Probably he heard Giacomo's voice and expected him to come round the corner as often as she did. Having been so close to him, di Marco probably knew what she had only understood last night: that her husband was not infallible. That his mistrusting nature and his craving for formality were at times a bit exaggerated. Why else would he have brought her the letters?

In the most sensitive family matter, he had decided to be disloyal and connected her with her grandchild. She was eternally grateful for this gesture, and yet her sense of obedience had not even allowed her to thank him properly. "You should join us more often for breakfast, before you leave this beautiful building in a few months," Alma said with her most charming smile, heaving another piece of *panettone* onto di Marco's plate. He reached for the plate and politely said, "Of course, I would love to," and Alma for a moment believed she saw his eyes getting a bit watery. Alma watched him chew the cake, laughing about Maria's "*Madonna!*" when the old lady had finally identified the dog on his tie through her thick glasses. Perhaps she could share her thoughts with him, tell him about the letter she had sent. But being sentimental was one thing; if she really had got them into some kind of legal trouble, di Marco would be the last person to take it lightly. Snoopy or no Snoopy on his tie. Even if Giacomo from his cloud, with a better view, would understand.

She needed an ally; she needed to get Clara on her side, before she could take on di Marco.

21
A Man Like My Dad

Easter Weekend, April 2017, London/Kent

Although it was officially spring in London, winter kept making appearances. Sunny patches wildly disrupted cold and gloomy days, rain could suddenly turn into snow but none of it ever lasted. Nobody was ever wearing the right coat. The weather was the dominating topic at the watering hole. Helen had made it a habit to at least once a day climb down the stairs for a coffee break. Lately, she received compliments on her new look. She had not only let her hair down, but also done a lot of shopping on her free weekends Emmy had found all shades of red actually suited her very well. She could tell her female colleagues were dying to ask whether she was seeing someone, but she wasn't close enough to any of them. The main purpose of these coffee excursions was of course to innocently meet Eric, but it wasn't easy to catch him on a busy day.

The colleagues with little children worried about the weather during the upcoming Easter holidays. Rachel Simmons from Criminal Law entertained them all quite well with horror stories of last year's rainy seaside trip: An impromptu stage-diving party by her sons from the sofa quickly ended in hospital. She laughed with the others and deeply hoped that no one would ask her for her plans. So one thing had not changed.

Eric would take a week off to leave with Jameson and Sara and grandparents for Tenerife. The better she got to know him, the more she got a faint idea of what might have challenged his marriage. Amidst all the stresses of life, he sometimes had a hard time being a team player. He made plans and then only later noticed that he should have discussed them first. Easter holidays probably belonged to the kids anyway, but a little chat about it would have been nice.

And he truly loved his job. Being with him was always a fight against all the clients requesting his attention. But she had known that from the start.

She had spent the last night before the holidays at his place. After long and tender lovemaking, she curled into him and he kissed her on her forehead. His heart rate had just calmed down when he said: "Is it okay with you if I just write an email? Then it is done and off my mind. Otherwise, I'll keep thinking about it…" Helen's mind was nowhere near an inbox. Warm waves were still radiating from her pelvis through her body, and all she could sense was the moist and warm feeling where their bodies touched. But she knew by now that he needed less time than her after making love, to return to the world. And once he was back, with a deadline in mind, he wouldn't be able to rest.

"Go ahead, as long as you stay here in bed…" she said, leaned into him and kissed his shoulder. He got his laptop and sat naked on the blanket, with a cushion in his back, his penis resting against his leg, soft but still a bit larger in size. He held one arm around her and she just watched him type, choosing the right words, deleting them, shaking his head, typing again and forgetting the world around him. *I'm falling in love with him*, she thought, *and there is nothing I can do about it. I can run for the last Tube, but it won't save me from that.*

It was not only the holidays. Jameson and Sara were children from a high-profile home and training every day for a successful life. Their piano, ballet, karate and football lessons often led to performances and tournaments at weekends, and Eric was needed to chauffeur one of them, to attend and to applaud. The children's calendar had barely been manageable when the family was still intact, and now it was even more complicated. Time was always scarce. Eric expressed regret every now and then that they had not enough time to go out and see places, all the things lovers usually do. But neither did he make an effort to change it.

To Helen, it began to feel as if they behaved like a couple being together for years and only meeting up to maintain the bond, otherwise happy to have lives of their own. But this wasn't really their case, was it? They needed to build something here, get to know each other better and conquer some space in each other's life. Sometimes, she thought it might be that because he had been married for so long, he had actually forgotten how to build a relationship.

"But I know you already. I've known you for more than a year, that is not the case for most fresh couples," was all he would say whenever she suggested they should see each other more often, get to know each other better.

"But, actually, I would like to see your home. Can't we meet at your place sometime?" was the only advance he ever made in her direction. But Helen kept making excuses. She felt this would only unbalance them further, make her feel even more vulnerable. Why should he meet Emmy, when her meeting Sara and Jameson was never discussed?

*

On the morning of Good Friday, a few snowflakes danced by the kitchen window and instead of feeling gloomy for days, Helen decided to drive up to Kent with Emmy, to see her parents. There was little protest as most of Emmy's friends, including Amir, had left for the Easter holidays, and she could play on her phone just as well in Kent.

To her own surprise, Helen found her hometown quite charming this time. It was drizzling most days and her childhood bedroom and the nosy neighbours were unchanged. Yet she found it almost relaxing to be there, in its own comical way. Of course, it only took two meals until her mother picked up her old mission: to get Helen's legs into compression stockings for good.

"Maybe you are protesting because you are thinking of the old ones," was her line of argument this time. "But modern compression stockings are really comfortable! John has to help me put them on in the morning, but then there is basically no difference to regular stockings, right, John?"

"Muum, please," was all she came up with, sounding a lot like Emmy. Usually, whenever she was in Kent and felt annoyed or pressurised by her parents, Luca would appear to stand by her side. He knew a thing or two about family pressure, and his voice saying *You've got this, Dulcinea*, had always helped her to be with her family and yet be herself. It was funny, though, if she thought about it now. Would he ever have actually said that? For the first time on this rainy Easter weekend, she felt so clearly the impossibility of it all. Not once, not even just for a short encounter, would she have sat with Emmy and Luca as a happy family on this very sofa. Not once for a short visit. They would never have been able to create a new haven and build bridges to their different worlds. He was supportive and kind, yes, but he was not the rock on which you build a new life with this eternal desire to please at every moment. Luca did not appear to contradict.

Now her father lowered the Sunday paper to join the stocking discussion: "Indeed, your mother is right! The textile industry has made great advances in this field. Apparently, they are using the same material on astronauts on the international space station." Her mum nodded vigorously. This was a clear invitation for a snarky comment on her mum and space travel, but Helen said nothing. It was somehow adorable, wasn't it? Being able to make compression stockings a staple piece of fashion in the house, without having to fear that your husband would run out of the back door, to pantsy after a girl below compression-stocking age? Wasn't that the essence of what we all want from life?

Maybe Emmy had gotten a similar vibe, because she suddenly looked up from her phone and said: "Grandma, what made you fall in love with Grandpa?" An awfully personal question for a household where emotions were only expressed via cookies, Sunday roasts or stockings. Helen's mother blushed for a moment, but then she parked the cookie tray and sat down. Grandpa kept the paper down and looked at her in expectation.

"His looks, of course. And he was the only one in our class driving a scooter. There were not many of those at the time..." Helen remembered a photo of her young parents on a scooter, although it was hard to imagine her mother doing something so dangerous.

"And were your parents happy that you married Grandpa?"

"Not at first ... you know, my dad was a farmer and your grandpa an accountant. I guess girls in those days were always expected to marry a guy like their dad..." Grandpa smiled and raised the paper again. The role of the rebel groom on a scooter still pleased him an awful lot.

*

On Easter Monday, when they were packing up to drive home, her mother pulled out another old classic. She insisted Helen take the rubber tree, which was currently taking up half of her old bedroom, to London. It was getting too big for their house and Helen needed more green in the big city apparently – so it was perfect! Helen figured she could either take it today or keep fighting against it for another year, and then take it. She took a selfie with the poor tree strapped to the passenger seat, from an angle and with a filter that made her look like a blonde elf in a magical forest taxi. *Checking out the hidden life of trees, hoping my co-passenger is as much a conversationalist as Attenborough promised*, she texted to Eric. *My God, when did I turn so mild?* Helen thought. The answer was obvious, though, even to her. Falling in love was the biggest act of emancipation. No wonder cultures all over the world went to great lengths to control their children's lovers.

On the back seat, Emmy was again transfixed to her phone. Helen had to smile. She remembered the countless times she had looked at her sleeping baby in the rear-view mirror. Almost every weekend she had driven up to Kent, to offer her baby a bit of family life at least at the weekend. On the drive home, she had always felt as if she were returning from the bottom of a deep ocean. She would leave at night, to make sure Emmy would be fast asleep in her Maxi-Cosi. When taking the exit from the M1, housing areas were still interrupted by patches of green or a canal. The car would dive in and out of the intervals of light from the street lanterns, reminding Helen of a very slow pulse, like that of a big sea mammal. Only when the gaps disappeared and turned into bright city lights, she had felt like she had broken through the surface to breathe again.

"Do you want me to marry a man like my dad?" Emmy suddenly interrupted her nostalgia.

Damn, she had hoped to ditch that bullet. Helen played for time: "Do you think Amir is like your dad?" she asked.

"I don't really know. I still find it hard to tell what my dad was like…" and thinking of Amir, Emmy smiled so happily that it was impossible for Helen not to melt. Eric was right; this was the age to fall in love. And why should Helen be the only one in this house with butterflies in her stomach? Perhaps this Amir guy was not as bad as he seemed at first glance. He looked after his sisters, he delivered the girls back home on time all the time. And the messages Emmy showed her were always pretty decent.

"In any case, please tell me when or where you are going. There is no need to do any of this behind my back, okay? You can tell me everything…" Helen was not even sure whether she wanted an update on her daughter's intimate life. You hear about those modern mums who practise putting condoms on cucumbers with their daughters, but Helen could not see how anybody enjoyed this family moment. And at home, the letters from Italy burned a hole through the box.

Helen focussed her attention back on the traffic. Emmy was back to texting. As painful as this was to admit and as much as she cherished the memory of Luca, the answer was No. She wished for someone who would take better care of her girl. With nicer in-laws, but still, the problem did start with the guy. There were quite a few stories she did not like to share with Emmy, situations she would not like to see her daughter in. Actually, she would be pretty mad at the guy if Emmy told her those kinds of stories.

Sometimes they got invited to parties in those decadent lakeside villas, because Luca had bonded with the adolescent children of some UN diplomat. The grudges these kids held for being dragged across the world turned them into amazing hosts. They invited absolutely everyone, hoping that the crowd would bring the roof down. Luca usually found some guys to drink with while Helen got bored by the girls who tagged along. Often, she simply wasn't drunk enough. There was one party she remembered in particular; it must have been the end of the summer term, towards the end of their Geneva year. The poolside was crowded with Eastern European girls, going after every man with grey hair.

"First prize in this party's raffle is a Western passport," Helen whispered in Luca's ear, but socio-economics with a gender perspective were never his thing.

"Maybe it is in their culture to like old men," was all he said.

Helen went to the bar looking for a drink, stepping past a glass table with stashed white lines on it, and two guys ready to snort them, and over a topless girl whose breasts had obviously been painted by someone but who now only giggled hysterically on the floor. Fascinated by all that, she overlooked the old man sitting on the sofa as she passed by. She did not see the hand reaching out for her. But the firm grip on her wrist almost made her trip over and fall onto the sofa. As a good middle-class girl, she had never before been in a physical confrontation. The man's breath reeked of booze and garlic. He was too drunk to hold her down when she finally fought back. Luca's reaction when she told him what had happened had been more than disappointing.

"Come on, everybody is having a good time..." he had said. Maybe she did not explain it well, maybe it was too dark for him to see the fury in her eyes, or maybe he was too drunk at this point. But the worst part came when they were finally about to leave and she asked the staggering Luca for the car keys.

"Hee hee, no, Dulcinea, you don't drive my car!" He said that with a heavy tongue but the ease of a man whose life had taught him that women do not tell him off. Only Daddy does.

"Really? And why is that?" Luca really was a lousy driver; the entire car was covered in dents.

"No, no, baby. A woman does not drive my car. You know, my father is worse than me. Once, we were on a business trip, already sitting in the plane, and it turns out the captain was a woman! You should have seen my dad's face! Grey and green, and he had already unfastened his seatbelt..."

In the end, he left her no choice. There were no cell phones at the time, and nothing would make her go back into that house. They drove home in silence, at 30 km/h through the empty streets of Geneva.

Before switching off the light, he reached for his nightcap and she could smell the whisky. She remembered she turned away from him, pretending to be asleep, but really to hide her tears. Perhaps her shoulders were shaking or her sobs somehow changed her rhythm of breathing. He was never good at asking for forgiveness, but he moved close to her and started to kiss her, from her shoulder to her neck until she turned around and offered her lips, giving him permission to go further. She did not want to reward this evening with passionate lovemaking; rather, she felt such an urgent need to be loved. And things were always good when they were alone. Their year could just have been a love story, to remember for the rest of their lives, had they not made a baby.

"Emmy," she said, her eyes on the rear-view mirror, "if he were more responsible and more mature than your father, then that would be good." From the way she spoke, Emmy understood that it was better to not ask any further questions now.

22

Monkey Theories

After Easter, April 2017, London

To make up for his Easter absence, Eric invited Helen to a nice little restaurant in Notting Hill. He chose the place because it had received good reviews in *Time Out* magazine. Eric might have a reputation for partying hard in the office, but for the last decade, he had also been limited to after-work drinks around the corner and the occasional office party. He had to Google fun places, the same as her. Whether or not the twenty-something Eric would have run in disgust from a lakeside party with prostitutes, it was hard to tell. But there was something to Eric's James Dean comment. Maybe the dates with Eric were not spectacular, no spontaneous midnight road trips or glamorous parties at strangers' houses, but she returned happy from them. And he deserved to know that, rather than being told stargazing stories from Chamonix.

As she walked along Kenwyn Road in her short black dress and high heels, all the worrying and obsessing over wife and children were forgotten. She was just a happy girl on the way to a date.

*

Eric waved at her from a table in the corner. Upon looking around, Helen noted that a hip crowd had taken over, which was what usually happened when *Time Out* recommended a place. Everyone seemed to be either in the fashion or creative industry – or at least desperately trying to look like that. Nobody was the least bit heavy around the hips or followed last year's sense of style. Eric caught her gaze.

"I'm sorry I did not bring my tight green pants," he said with a grin.

"Even though *Vogue Men* clearly recommended it," she said with a serious face.

"*Vogue Men*? That's a thing?"

"It's been around for a while," Helen laughed.

"It is strange, though, isn't it?" He suddenly had this spark in his eyes he always got when something intrigued him.

"What? That men are starting to care more about their looks?"

"No, rather the opposite. How can this be a recent thing? Because the saying goes, for men, it is all about sex. If that is the case, the strategies we apply are somewhat surprising. Women care a lot whether a man is well dressed and all that. Women going for the unshaved, smelly drunkard… that only ever happened out of lack of other options."

"I guess so." Helen had to smile at his scientific analysis.

"And still, for centuries, men did not get that…"

"Actually, it is puzzling," Helen said, "how most women find attractive what for many men passes as gay…"

"And it isn't just the clothes, it's all the, let's call it, behavioural patterns of young men at social events. I mean, for the first few years, these Oxford college parties start in a tuxedo, but after a few hours, someone's naked buttocks are on the pool table… or minutes, rather."

"And that one would not necessarily be the loser who does not get a girl…" Helen chuckled.

"Exactly!" Eric said with true enthusiasm. "Come to think of it, most of these tactics are really only to impress the other guys, not the girls."

"I think that's true."

Eric looked more than pleased. "And here comes my theory. I started to think about this when I was watching a documentary about apes…"

"Oh my God, that sounds about right," Helen laughed.

"No, wait." He squeezed her hand. "So they live in the forest, right, like in a group or a large family. But, they are not a group of couples, as in a human family. There is only one alpha-male that gets all the mating rights. Like, he can have all the females he wants and the others get to sit and watch…"

"Really? That's so sad!"

"It is! But it also means, there is no point fighting for the girls' attention and pleasing them in any way. You only have to win against the other males. Drink harder, look more scary, whatever – and then the girls are yours anyway!" He looked triumphant.

"That does explain a lot of jackass behaviour." But Helen couldn't get one image out of her head. "Did you sit naked on the pool table?"

Eric laughed. "Umm, no, I was never one to take my clothes off when drunk. But still, I am afraid I did help make my own point…" He blushed a little, and the boyish look on his face made her think of the Lakeside party. Maybe at all those college parties, Eric had not been a saint, either. But afterwards, back home or the next day, they would have talked: about the Ukrainian woman, the old man, the drinking and simply everything. Eric was still on fire:

"This also leads me to another interesting point: what do women fight for? Women are known to be competitive. Following my apes theorem, you would have to fight for the attention of the one ape that enters the ring. That explains the frenzy over shoes and make-up, because there is never enough for everyone…"

Their aperitifs arrived and she took a big sip. She loved listening to his theories, but at this point she felt that his construct fell a bit short.

"Yes, we are competitive…" she said, "…but there is a different angle to it. Other than the girls, the guys really sort it out among themselves. The fastest runner is a winner, the toughest drinker gets the respect of the group and so on… Effectively, you don't even need the girls to crown your king, right? For girls, it is different. You can be pretty and all, but you only ever win if you get the guy, if you are the chosen one. Everybody wants to be loved, but among women, being loved is really all that counts. No substitutes. Very stressful."

Helen got a little more agitated than she intended. The scientific curiosity gave way to the memory of countless office or kids' birthday parties, sitting between couples or women with a golden ring. These days, you didn't have to be married; but at the same time, being single meant there was something wrong with you.

"Interesting point... although I must say that this does not sound very romantic to me."

"Well," Helen tilted her head, "that is in my opinion the biggest misconception, that women are the romantic half. When something is needed so badly for survival and social status as women need relationships, then they can hardly afford to be romantic about it. In a way, climbing a mountain out of sheer love for nature might be more romantic than getting married. Although there are, of course, relationships which go beyond monkey theory..." she added when she caught Eric's scornful gaze.

"I should hope so," he said, pulling both her hands over to his side of the table. Perhaps this was a good moment to tell him.

"And you know... to be really honest, I think that is the reason why I have such a hard time giving up these Luca stories. Or even building them up more in my mind. I wanted to claim that, at least once upon a time, I was the chosen one. Having lost him was hard, so I tried to build up what we had. You were right, though, the other night; you should not have to listen to all these heroic tales as if we were still teenagers..."

"That's all right," he said, feeling her distress. "To me, you are doing pretty well with this game of life. Being left alone is hard on everyone." Their hands lay on the table, entangled in a public space for everyone to see. There was a long pause, their fingers moving against each other's, caressing and learning every detail. It felt so good to talk openly. *Perhaps I can also tell him about the Italian letters*, she thought. Nothing was heavier to carry than a secret, and nothing separates you more from your lover. But before she could speak, Eric looked up. The emotion in his eyes showed that he also felt that this was a special moment. A good one for saying something meaningful.

"Yesterday, we went to see a marriage counsellor."

"What?" Helen pulled back her hand. The couple next to them

turned their heads.

"No, no, I mean, more of a divorce counsellor. Because of the kids… I would just like to get through this without a lot of court hearings."

"That makes sense…" She did her best to sound composed. It all made sense, and yet, it was the most painful thought. "And… how did it go?"

"Hey, come back," he said, and reached over to her side to recapture her hands. "We had the first session this Thursday. There was a lot of yelling and a lot of guilt, but I think in the end we made some progress. At least there will be another meeting."

"Good, good…" Helen looked at their hands again, the same hands she had admired a moment ago. There was no ring on his hands now, but the ring finger was still thinner than the others, from years of golden restraint.

It would fit back on at any time.

23

Seventeen Pictures

May 2017, Vittuone (Milan)

Clara did not come back until early May. Her trip to the Netherlands was followed by a cruise on the River Nile, because after April it would get too hot to travel there.

When the first shades of dim morning light peeked through the curtain, Alma slipped into her bathrobe and rushed straight down to the library. She did not need to switch on the little Tiffany lamp this time; the moving sun already filled the room. For a moment, she watched two rabbits hopping over the grass, so peacefully, and even through the closed door she could hear the birds sing their morning song. She pulled out the wooden box from the drawer.

What would be the worst case scenario with that foreign Englishwoman? She could get back at Alma with some hateful speech? Sue her? Di Marco would handle it – what was all the money for anyway?

Two blackbirds landed next to the rabbits, picking for food. Even if they found nothing, they always rose in the air again after seconds, afraid of a predator waiting behind the bush.

All of those options were scary, and enough to make her heart beat in her throat. Up and down the birds went, too hasty to find anything and seemingly unnoticed by the grazing bunnies. She could not take her eyes off them. The most frightening option was that there might never be an answer, no matter how many letters she wrote.

By seven, Alma heard Flavia and Maria's car pull over. The tiny wooden box was still in her hands and the urge to hastily push it back in its cave was gone. She suddenly felt like dressing up and doing her hair. Her granddaughter should have her big day today.

When she passed by Clara's room to get dressed, Alma heard some spiritual music coming through the door, featuring a gong, little bells and a woman chanting in a high-pitched voice. If someone had described her that scene three years ago, Alma would simply not have believed it. But, apparently, one was allowed to do whatever was needed to be happy. And at this point of their lives, who was left to care?

She found a white silk blouse and a matching skirt. From all the grieving, Alma had lost weight and many old pieces surprisingly fitted her again. She sat down at the dressing table to gather herself. The skin of her face was grey at best, and her hair needed a perm so badly. She held it in shape with hair needles, like some farmer's wife. Clearly, no one would compare her to a film star today. She felt tears rise up but fought them down. Today was not a day to be sad. And with a bit of make-up, this would be good enough to give the breakfast an official air. Perhaps Flavia could take a picture of the four of them, so they could always remember this morning.

In the dining room, Clara was already reading the papers, dressed from head to toe in a pink batik-coloured suit. Not quite the family album outfit, but Alma could hardly ask her to change at such short notice.

When Clara saw Alma enter, she raised her eyebrows and lowered the paper.

"Oh amore, what is happening here? I thought I would ease up a bit on the protocol in this house, after seeing you in those stretchy pants for the very old for weeks now. For once, I thought, 'I will have breakfast as if I were at home'– *and now this*! Is somebody coming to join us?" Clara asked, checking the plates on the table as if she had overlooked something.

"No, not really. I just felt like it... I did not even know you owned such a thing," Alma replied, gesturing at the jumpsuit, "and I was fine *not* knowing, to be honest…"

"It is a bit of a screaming colour, I know, but it is super comfortable to move around in. As if you're not wearing anything," Clara said, and got up from her chair to demonstrate the garment's flexibility with a downward-facing dog pose on the Persian carpet.

"Yes, yes, thanks. I can totally see what you mean."

This was now getting a bit too casual for what Alma had in mind. She sat down, placing the wooden box next to her. Clara was on all fours for a few seconds and then struggled to collect herself for half a minute. God, Alma thought, she's about to turn seventy, too late to turn into an agile dog. Then there was a bit of a rumble, Clara's butt collided with the coffee table when she got off the ground with an energetic push.

"Too much furniture in this house," her sister complained with a red face as she stumbled back to the breakfast table. Alma felt tempted to comment but then bit her tongue. She had an agenda for today and did not want to risk a fight.

Flavia came in to serve coffee and Alma pushed the tiny box aside. Clara had not yet taken any notice of it, too busy reaching for a croissant and the butter, then putting sugar in her coffee. Always making sure she got everything she needed while Alma waited for her turn, hoping there would be enough butter and sugar left for her. While watching Clara munch and stir in her cup at the same time, Alma realised that the truth she wanted to break to her sister needed to be offered with a lot of care as well. It would be confusing for her to learn all this now. Clara might feel hurt because Alma had not trusted her enough, despite all her efforts. After all, there was a heart of gold resting under that pink Ms-Know-It-All jumpsuit.

Alma waited for Clara to finish the croissant and a second cup of coffee. This conversation was not for an empty stomach. When Clara was about to reach for the papers again, it was now or never. Clara could pick up the topic of 'that woman' any time, then get a head start and direct the conversation the way she wanted.

"*Clara*," Alma began, and the seriousness of her voice made Clara look up from an article on the alarming increase in lactose intolerance in the Italian population. "Remember when we had that library picnic and I told you about the letter from the Englishwoman? Before I hit the vase?"

Clara immediately changed into a posture which meant business, putting the paper aside and leaning forward, all eyes and ears.

"Of course I remember. I was thinking of asking you about it again—"

"I thought so," Alma interrupted. "I just needed some time to think about how to break this to you."

"Oh, Alma. *Now* you are worrying me…"

Alma smiled nervously. "No, you don't need to worry. It is just that there is something I need to tell you, something that I have kept to myself all these years. Believe me, it was neither easy to keep it a secret *nor* is it now easy to share. I have had a really rough time over all this." Alma pushed her plate aside and placed the wooden box right in front of her. Clara's eyes widened.

"It is not quite correct to say that this woman has written me letters," Alma said. "I know absolutely nothing about her apart from her name and address."

Clara stared at the treasure case but said nothing. Alma opened the box and heaved out all seventeen rosé envelopes. She had never looked at them anywhere else than in the library and never in daylight. She took a deep breath.

"She has been sending me these photographs, every year around Christmas. Not to me even, but to di Marco. As I understand it, she signed something saying that she will never address the family directly. Yet, every year, she sends a picture of the child. I have never answered. Giacomo would have killed me. At least that is what I thought."

"He did not know about this?"

"No, nothing. I am not sure why, but I guess di Marco somehow thought it would be better this way. It was an incredible act of disloyalty, if you come to think about it, so unlike him. I don't know this girl, Clara, but somehow, I have seen her growing up. There have been seventeen pictures up to now. The girl is seventeen. Actually, she is your niece," Alma said, her voice trembling, her hands shaking. She was amazed, listening to herself say all this out loud in her own house.

Clara still stared at the envelopes and said nothing.

"Here, see?" Alma said and got up.

The table was built to host a big family feast. Clara and Alma only occupied the left corner, and the rest of the white tablecloth lay empty. Alma took the photos out of the envelopes and, beginning in the upper-right corner, she laid them out, like a game of memory. Alma knew their order by heart, so she knew exactly how much space she had to leave between them. The first one she pulled out was from year three, so she left two gaps above. The next was from year ten so Alma placed it further apart. When she had finished and all seventeen pictures were out on the table, she looked at Clara.

Her sister sat still on her chair, stared from a distance and said nothing. Then, Alma took one of the cards from its envelope.

"They always come with this card, but it says nothing much. See?"

Clara took the card, turned it over, and went back to staring at the photographs. Alma waited. After a while, Clara got up and came to stand next to her. She touched the tablecloth and let her hand run down alongside the timeline. At year twelve, she stopped and picked up the photo. Alma saw tears running down her face.

"The smile, Alma. The smile," she whispered.

"I know, I know," Alma said. "It moves me every time I look at the pictures. It starts at about year ten and then it is clearly there, in every picture."

"And nobody knows about this?"

"No."

"Oh Cara, how could you keep this all to yourself?"

Alma sighed. "In the first year, I did not care so much and I did not want to upset my son's engagement. Luca was about to start his own family, right? Then, in the following years, I think I was so deeply grief-stricken, that I could not handle it. I just locked them away. Plus, there was no way of breaking this to Giacomo without telling him it had been going on for years, I knew he would not want to hear a word about this. He had not cleaned things up only to have me carry the dirt into the house through the back door. That is what he would have said. Also, I was tired, Clara. Just *tired,* all the time."

"I know, I know," Clara mumbled They stood together for a while, saying nothing, just looking at the pictures.

"Why do you think she did this?" Clara asked after a while. And indeed, that was a really good question.

"I really don't know." Alma shrugged. "To make us feel guilty? First, I thought she was counting on these being forwarded to Luca, to provoke a reaction from him, maybe make him change his mind. But she kept sending the cards even after he passed away."

"Did she know about that?"

"I guess so. I don't know for sure…"

"You think the girl knows about all this?" Clara said, gesturing at the photographs.

"I know nothing more than you see laid out here. The girl is a woman now, Clara. That is what keeps me awake at night – among other things. She could find out things, you know? She could even come here…"

"Jesus Christ," Clara reached for a chair to sit down. She suddenly looked very much her age, and the jumpsuit like a carnival costume.

"Is everything all right in here?" Flavia's head peered round the door. They had been so absorbed that they had not heard her coming. "*Mamma mia, signora* Clara. You look like you have seen a ghost," Flavia said, opening the door wider to step in.

"No, no. Thank you. I… I just did a bit too much exercise this morning," Clara stammered, leaving Flavia confused and waiting for further instructions.

"Yes, it is fine, Flavia. She does not need anything, but perhaps you can call for Maria? We have something to discuss, I think," Alma added.

"Is there a problem, *signora* Alma? We just did as we always do…"

"No, of course not. It is more something that concerns the entire household."

"Very well," Flavia said, and her head disappeared behind the door.

"You think it is a good idea to tell them?" Clara whispered, eyes wide in shock. Good old Clara, always willing to sweep a scandal under the carpet if needed.

"I don't know. I just think if the girl shows up here, they'd better know," Alma said. She had not planned for this, but now Alma wanted the existence of her granddaughter to be a known fact in this house. *Her* house, *her* granddaughter.

Flavia came back in with Maria in tow, both looking like children about to be grounded. Hadn't she explained to Maria that they were just discussing a general matter?

"Just come in and take a seat," Alma said, in the most cheerful tone she could muster.

Maria, with her thick glasses, always looking a bit sad, sat down with her eyes fixed on the ground. Flavia sat next to her, looking anxiously up to her mistress. Neither of them noticed the photos on the table.

"So," Alma started, a bit confused by the pathetic posture of her maids, "I will not beat around the bush and will make this short."

"*Madonna*," said Maria and her eyes rose from the tablecloth up to the Almighty. Now, even Clara gave Alma a confused look.

"I know this news will certainly come as a bit of a surprise, to say the least."

Now Maria folded her hands together and kept her gaze transfixed on an invisible deity. That was a little too much then for Alma's patience.

"Maria, what is wrong with you?" she asked slightly annoyed.

"*Signora*, we know what you are going to say. We have been expecting it for a while."

"What?" Now it was Alma who turned pale. "Did you look into the drawers of my secretary desk?"

"No! Of course not, madame! Why would we do that?" Flavia said, and looked insulted as much as confused. "We just know because everybody is talking about it. We know that the office will shift to the factory, then you will move out, and the house will not need our help anymore," Flavia explained as calmly as she could.

"*Madonna!*" Maria interjected once again.

"Oh my God! *No, no, no,* that is *absolutely* not it! Why didn't you say something if you were worried about this? Every day, we have breakfast together and you've never said a word?" Alma exclaimed. But what else could they have thought? Talk had indeed been all over the place in the last months. *Every* guest brought it up, with Clara being the absolute front-runner.

"Jesus!" Alma said, finally responding to all the *Madonnas*. "I can see that I myself should have addressed this sooner. As you know, I have not been in the best state of mind and needed time to gather my thoughts. But for now, I will stay here. That is decided. And so will the two of you – don't give it a second thought unless I tell you to."

"*Madonna!*" Maria said again, but this time combined with a deep sigh of relief.

"Oh madame, this is such good news!" Flavia said. Unlike her usually controlled manner, the maid jumped from her chair and wrapped her arms around Alma. The gesture and her happiness made Alma laugh. It was so nice to feel that there was a real bond between them; they did not just want to bring anyone breakfast, but stay here with her. Maria also got up from her chair and wiped some tears from beneath her glasses. When Flavia took a step back, she finally saw the pictures.

"Madame, what is all this? Photos laid out like a card game?" she said. Maria came closer and put her glasses back on.

"Yes," Alma said, getting a bit nervous again. "That is what I originally wanted to talk about. The announcement I have to make." She made a dramatic pause to gather her thoughts. "I want you to be aware of a few things, although they, of course, do not directly affect our daily life."

Flavia and Maria looked at her in blank confusion.

"What looks like a card game are actually pictures of Luca's daughter. She lives in England and is now seventeen years old."

There, she had said it.

A little scream escaped Flavia's lips before she covered her mouth with her hands. "*Madonna!*" Maria said again, also covering her mouth with her hands. This was better than any *telenovela,* but Alma could see it was not that. They had both known Luca as a child, had helped to raise him. His death had broken their hearts too.

"Very pretty girl!" Maria said after a while, with an approving nod.

"Yes," Flavia added, "and she takes after her father very much! But, *signora,* may I ask, where do all these pictures come from?"

"Yes," Maria said with big eyes. "How can we know now, after all this time?"

"Her mother sent them. Just like that, nothing more. I don't even know her name. And I don't know if she knows mine."

"Will we meet her?" Maria asked.

"Maria!" Flavia hushed her. "Nobody said that!"

Indeed, that question made Clara uncomfortable enough to intervene.

"Yes, *nobody* said that. That is not what this is about. *Signora* Alma just felt that you should be aware in case the issue comes up in the future. Of course, it is understood that this was all discussed in private and should be kept confidential, only among us. Nobody else knows about it and we are trusting you both to keep it like that."

With that last sentence, Clara's voice had gotten a little loud. Despite being moved, she was obviously uncomfortable with this revelation. Although it should have been Alma's task to give that order, she let it slide. It was too late anyway: the letter was sent out. She would have to bear the consequences on her own if she had to.

Alma could see in her maids' faces the strong urge to pick up the pictures, to look at them more closely, and speculate about the girl's life, her character, and certainly also her mother's, that blonde girl they had only seen once from afar. Thankfully, they felt that any further inquisition would be out of place. When Maria still stood dumbstruck in front of the pictures, Flavia pulled her sleeve towards the door.

"Is there anything we could bring you?" she asked, bringing the conversation back to familiar terrain.

"I definitely need another coffee," Clara said, still looking a bit pale around the nose.

"Coming right up, *signora*," Flavia said, and closed the door behind her.

For a moment, Clara and Alma just stood there and said nothing, looking at the photos, then out of the windows, and back to the photos.

After a while, Clara sat up straight and looked at her sister. "Cara don't be naïve about this. We don't know these people. I don't want to sound mean, but little girls *always* look sweet. This can really open up a lot of old wounds and do no good. Even if the mother signed something, that does not keep her from putting on pressure, you know?"

"I know," Alma said, but she knew Clara only meant well.

Flavia brought the coffee and then left the room as quickly as possible. Alma reached for another croissant and Clara poured the steaming coffee for them both.

The world in which they had their second breakfast was different from the one of the first. You cannot say that of many days.

24

Running in Circles

May & June 2017, London

In May, spring finally pushed through. The weather grew mild and people began to sit outside in the cafés and restaurants around Clapham Common. Apart from that, nothing much seemed to change. Eric and Helen still rarely left the IKEA bed. Almost every weekend belonged to the kids – the family he still lived with somehow. Emmy was hardly around, spending all her free time with Amir, and in the evening, she returned with that glow which only young lovers have. What Helen admittedly liked about Amir was that he seemed to take it slowly. There were no demands for sleepovers or any kind of crazy outings to night clubs. Emmy was still a minor – without feeling like one, of course.

The weekends were beginning to be worse than entire holidays. At least on holidays, the ex-wife was clearly out of the picture. But on weekends they sometimes took the kids out together. Watching the very children you made together playing in the sand – how could this not be a bonding moment? "Don't worry, Elsa, we are really just there for the kids," was all he had to say on the topic. But to really feel better, Helen needed more. Could emotions really disappear like that?

And not a day went by without Emmy showing her a blog or an Instagram post with some superficial person in stylish clothes. Helen did not dare to speak against this without jeopardising their newly formed bond. And now that the Pandora was out of the box, Emmy herself changed more and more. Her clothes became more fashionable; she was developing *her own style*. Many of them were second-hand now, to keep things affordable. And Helen could not help finding that this was also a good thing. She had always wanted her to be a strong, individual personality and to stand out from the mainstream was exactly that, wasn't it? She had thought of more intellectual achievements, for sure, but what can you do? The latest thing was bleaching her blonde hair, to get the tips coloured in a light rosé. This was apparently a harmless version of what Emmy called *unicorn hair*. She matched them with a long-cut blazer over her jeans, which perfectly picked up the hair colour.

"How do you think people will take you seriously with pink hair?" Helen had asked her.

"I don't plan on impressing people with my looks, Mum," had been the wise answer. And there was something so confident about her lately that she might even have a point. If you can only feel your true self with hair tips in rosé, then this might be the best way to stand your ground.

Helen really tried to see things positively. Some months ago, she had no sex life and her daughter would not talk to her. So things were improving, right? Her job was exhausting and these weekends alone were a chance to do all the things she had not been doing in a while. She booked herself a spa day, got a manicure, or did the tax declaration way before the deadline. But as soon as she had filled out the last form or stepped out of that overly expensive Mandarin Spa in Chelsea, she would think of Eric. And the visions of Eric and Karen patching up their marriage in some playground returned and she couldn't help checking her phone obsessively. On rare occasions, Luca still made an appearance. After her Wednesday talks with Emmy or on lazy Sunday mornings, she saw him leaning in the door frame or lying on the carpet, but there was something vague about him. Like a layer of fog, and it never felt as if she could touch him. Nor did she want to.

On Mondays, they would meet at Eric's place or at least talk longer on the phone. He would always have some stories to tell, funny comments the children had made or some anecdote. Last Sunday, a mother had called the coach an asshole across the green of a fancy private London school. Helen remembered those first school years with Emmy. Parenting was at times quite an awkward occupation. But it was a real one; it gave you purpose, no matter how.

By the end of May, it dawned on her: if this relationship was supposed to go on in that mode, at least for a while, she had to find something to do. And what was most surprising was that she had such a hard time coming up with an idea. What had she been doing or wanting to do all these years, apart from work, fussing over Emmy, flirting with visions of Luca and ranting at Alma Carneggio? The latter especially seemed, more and more, like an awful waste of time...

When Emmy was little, there had been no time. Later on, not engaging in sports had been one of Helen's ways of holding their money together – no fee to join a club, no equipment and whatnot. She was not the type to put on weight, but lately she compared herself with other women on the Tube. Sometimes, she wound up happy; sometimes, she disliked the thought that Eric also took the Tube.

When Helen came home with a bag full of running gear the next Saturday, Emmy turned out to be equally enthusiastic about the idea. She had also been thinking about getting in shape and art club would not do the trick. Helen pushed away the obvious conclusion that Emmy was also planning to take her clothes off somewhere. Anyway, exercise was to be encouraged, and without Emmy, Helen might just have given up after two weekends. Emmy put her heart and soul into it. She got Helen a fitness app and made them watch all sorts of YouTube tutorials on how to get started and what to eat when.

Twice a week, Helen and Emmy walked over to Clapham Common and started running laps. To no one's surprise, their fitness levels were very different and they quickly agreed that, to enjoy this, it was best for them if each ran according to their own pace. Clapham Common was just one plain meadow with a *mandala* of footpaths for people to walk their dog or do sports. Whenever she stopped, Helen could see where Emmy was running her track, sometimes only by the colour of her shirt, and soon again she would pass her and wave. It occurred to Helen that this was perhaps exactly what it was like, a parent's relationship with an adult child. You would never fully lose them but you had to let them run free, focus on your own pace instead, and just enjoy the occasional get-together. You were no longer entitled to more than that.

Afterwards, she and Emmy sometimes sat for a moment at the Artisanal Café at The Pavement, outside if the weather allowed it. Emmy checked their latest progress on the fitness app – she won all the time – and usually she was talkative in these moments, sharing things on her phone and talking about the events of the week. The rolling of eyes and shrugging of shoulders had diminished. Helen every now and then threw in bits and pieces about suicide rates and low income in the fashion industry, but Zen-Emmy would not pick up on it.

Over the weeks filled with work, lovemaking and running their circles, spring turned to summer. The nights in May and June were the longest of the year, and the Clapham Common meadows were crowded until late. One Thursday in late June, they sat on the plastic chairs of the Artisanal Café, the air still so mild, they could have been sitting in Italy, the sky a faint blue at 9pm. Helen was listening to Emmy's story about an invalid maths test which had to be repeated, an event which almost caused a riot among her classmates, when a woman's voice said, "Hello, ladies. I haven't seen you in a while!"

Helen looked up and had to search her mind for a moment before she could place the woman her age, in leggings and carrying a yoga mat. It was one of the mothers she knew from Emmy's elementary school but had then lost sight of. They chatted for a bit and before she left, she threw Helen a glance and said, "This really looks like a fine mother-daughter day. Enjoy, you two!".

And yes, somebody passing by might indeed think she had it all, no trace of an unwanted pregnancy or a secret affair.

If only that Milanese witch could see her like this, only this once.

25

Summer Solstice

June to mid-July 2017, Vittuone (Milan)

The summer reached Milan in early June this year. The rhododendron bushes stood in full bloom and Ana had visited to take some pictures of the pink, purple and mauve explosion. Apparently, she was also a hobby photographer. Then the temperatures began to rise to a point where being on the terrace was no longer pleasant. By July, the Italian heat had attained its usual peak. All the flowers were gone, and the green grass showed brown patches despite the constant watering. The Milanese who could afford it left for the seaside – or somewhere more exotic these days.

Alma kept up her new habit and left the house at dawn to walk down to the panetteria, but the streets were now deserted. Nobody dragged schoolchildren into cars or ran to bus stops to go to work. The rest of the day she stayed inside, her only company being Flavia and Maria, with occasionally di Marco joining them for breakfast. Clara had asked Alma to visit her at her house in Como. Her husband's family had a house by the lake and Clara usually spent the summer there. But although she felt closer to Clara since her confession, Alma was in no mood to join her.

She had given herself a year to figure out what to do with the house. The summer solstice had passed. All that had grown and prospered in spring was about to get burnt, and still, she was none the wiser.

What would Luca want her to do with this place? What would make him smile on his cloud? Ana's question kept going round in her head. The most painful questions her inner voice rarely spelled out, but they meandered in the subtext of her mind, constantly and mercilessly.

The hottest time of the day she spent in the salon next to the foyer. Even in late July, the thick walls only heated up slowly. Flavia had put a fan near the big sofa in the corner; it scanned the room from left to right, as relentless as her thoughts. And as often as the gentle breeze touched her sweaty scalp, she changed her mind. Luca had been happy here, the happiest a son could be. She remembered his laughter filling the rooms, being greeted with a kiss on her cheek every morning. She saw him waiting on this very sofa, in a suit and fine coat, ready to leave for a business trip with his father. He had loved his parents, so it must have been an accident. *Breeze.*

Other images appeared. The days when he would not come down for breakfast, would barely answer when she knocked at his door. The distant look on his face when his father talked about the company. Who knows where his mind went in these moments? Him being so drunk at his engagement party that he owed people an apology. A happy man would not have behaved like that. He hated his life, so it was not an accident. *Breeze.*

Or maybe he wanted to be happy but suffered from clinical depression, of a type which went unnoticed most of the time? She had read about that. Perhaps he had needed medication and everything would have been fine. Was it their stigma against psychotherapy which ultimately killed him? *Breeze.*

And with every change of heart, the English woman kept crossing her mind. She imagined her in a fancy London apartment that another rich man had bought her by now (if one was to believe Clara), having breakfast with Alma's beautiful granddaughter, who did not even speak Italian. She might have answers. There had been no letter from London and Alma did not have the courage to write another one. After some days of vegetating on the sofa, she felt that she might just sit there forever and go insane.

The Pinacoteca di Brera came to her mind; Ana had called Luca *a familiar face* around there. Alma thought about searching for people there he might have known, but it seemed unlikely to lead anywhere. The old ladies from Ana's workshop had certainly never been in touch with him; besides, they might even be dead by now. And the young people he had hung out with on the patio of the Pinacoteca, they could be anywhere in the world now. Alma had thought about putting leaflets at the pillars of the patio. *Did you know Luca Carneggio? Please call...* And then a photograph next to it. But she still feared the scandal if anyone from Unione would see the note; a few of the ladies were sponsors with *Amici di Brera*. And the chances of getting valuable information that way were basically zero. Ana had recalled nothing more than seeing him with a random group of people. What could these people really know about his life?

She also thought about his friends from school times, but he seemed to have abandoned almost all of them when he started working. Except for one. The Oliegas still lived in the same house in Vittuone. When she finally found the heart to call, his mother was happy to pass her David's new phone number, without asking too many questions. David Oliega's heavy voice with hoarse laughter did not match her memory of the sluggish boy her son had departed with to Geneva. David lived in Rome now, with four daughters, a belly, and an untimely addiction to cigarettes. His mother's words. The alien voice was clearly moved to hear hers.

"I should have called from time to time, *signora* Carneggio. I thought so often, but then you know how it is," he said at least five times, like a grandson with a guilty conscience. But although he was generally talkative, the call was a disappointment.

"Did you feel he was happy with his life," Alma finally asked, "working in the family business? Did he say anything during that Geneva year?" It took all her strength to ask a stranger so openly, to hand him the knife to stab through her heart.

"I am so sorry, but I don't know what to tell you, *signora* Carneggio," he said. "We left together for Geneva, but I hardly saw him over there. At the time, he wanted a break from everything – home, friends, maybe even himself..."

The fan's cold breeze ran through her hair. "So… you would say he *did* want to leave us behind and live somewhere else, outside Italy?"

"No, no, that I also cannot say. Whenever I saw him, in class or ran into him in the hallway, he would say that he missed home, especially the food…"

Breeze. So he was happy. All that getting away was just a bachelor's attitude.

"Do you remember anyone he was particularly close with during that year?"

"I hardly saw him… but I know there was a girl he was seeing. Blonde girl, British, I think, but I don't remember the name." The only possible clue and it couldn't be more foreclosed.

"*Signora* Carneggio," he said in a softer register, "may I ask why you are making these enquiries now? He was a great man. It is a shame he left us so early."

"Thanks," she said. "You are very kind to say so."

"You should not worry too much, *signora*… Sometimes, there is no reason for these things."

These things? *Breeze.*

*

In the second week of July, she asked di Marco to install a parasol for the aviary. The two lovebirds had been sitting all apathetic on their branch, no pecking or flirting. But when Alma called the vet, alarmed, he rightly pointed out that they were probably boiling up in there. The day it was delivered, di Marco joined them for breakfast. Not only to oversee the installation but, as it turned out, also to ask her whether she could possibly spare some time in the afternoon. Although this probably meant a business talk involving lots of confusing figures, it was a welcome change from all that pointless brooding in summer heat. And since in the past weeks he had joined them regularly for breakfast, his presence had become less intimidating for her. Their conversations were still reduced to an exchange of pleasantries, and the ladies still chose more formal topics for their morning chat as soon as he entered, but she no longer sat up straight as soon as he spoke.

At 3pm, she tried to fit her feet into her pumps, to look official for once, but her feet were too bloated, so flip-flops it was. Anyway, it was impossible to look appropriate with a puffy red face. The few metres over the courtyard in plain sun were enough to make sweat run down her back, droplets heavy as mercury.

He was sitting behind his mahogany desk when she entered, though he promptly jumped to his feet to greet her. She still expected him to wear a dark blue suit, a tie with silver clip and a matching handkerchief. Today, he was even wearing a shirt with short sleeves, white with a pink and orange paisley pattern. In the well-designed office space, which he always kept in perfect order, no paperwork trailing around, he almost looked like a parrot, his appearance mirrored by the Japanese lacquer vase behind him.

He offered her a coffee and she kindly rejected. A bucket of ice water for her feet was what she wanted, although the office building was surprisingly cool. The thick stone walls held off the heat almost as much as the hall did. The old sycamore tree in the yard also offered some shade; its branches sheltered the window so perfectly that there was no need to draw the curtains. Di Marco then started off in his usual tone, explaining the current financial situation to her. He pushed printouts over to her side of the table, leaning over it in a twist as if to take her perspective, but she barely listened. The management of the company and their assets seemed to function well; she could die in a coffin of pure gold if she intended to, was all she understood.

She watched di Marco, so dutifully pointing with his Mont Blanc pen to an aspect of the chart, as if her husband was standing right behind him. And still, seemed so different from the di Marco who she had met every year on a winter's night in early January by the kitchen door. Hunched and with the haste of a traitor.

He had met the English woman when she was pregnant was all Alma could think about. He might know what she was like, whether there was any chance Alma would get an answer to her letters. Or whether a team of British lawyers was already lining up to go after her. Alma looked out of the window; the branches of the tree moved lightly in the wind, and every now and then, a sparrow landed on the windowsill, before it flew up again into the tree. Di Marco paused and the sudden silence made her look up. Obviously, he was done with his presentation and it was her turn to say something. Quickly, she pulled out the one phrase she always used on these occasions: "Oh, *Signor* di Marco, when I hear all these figures, sometimes I wish I were poor! What would I do without you!"

He smiled mildly, used to her tendency to avoid a conversation of any kind of substance. But instead of switching to small talk, he suddenly leaned forward, one hand moving across the table and into her sphere.

"There is another issue, *signora* Carneggio, I would like to address. I never even discussed it with your husband, simply because I did not know how." And with that line, he had her fullest attention. He took a deep breath: "You know, the pictures of the little girl I always give you, a few days after New Year…"

Her heart skipped a beat. Could he read her mind? "Did she contact you?" she burst out.

Di Marco pulled back in surprise. "No, why? All I ever received, I gave to you. Don't worry, everything is in good order. It is just that our payment obligations are going to expire this year. You are aware of the deal, aren't you?"

She nodded, too embarrassed to admit that she had nothing more than a vague idea. "But if you could summarise it from your perspective, that would be helpful."

"Very well. In a nutshell, we agreed on a monthly payment of 1,000 pounds sterling until the girl, your granddaughter, turns eighteen. In exchange, there would be absolutely no contact with the family, and the girl would not be considered an heiress to the Carneggio family."

When Alma said nothing, di Marco continued: "This is the point I wanted to raise with you. It is nothing you have to worry about right now, but according to Italian law, that last point is not legally valid. The mother cannot sign an agreement on behalf of the daughter and waive her claim to any kind of heritage. The daughter could only do that herself or, while she is still a minor, via a proxy to represent the daughter's interest."

"I see... Did my husband not know that?"

"Well, *signora*, of course I tried to alert him to it, but in this affair, frankly speaking, he seemed not quite rational. All he wanted was to find a way out, to make it all look as if it never happened." Di Marco crouched a little bit, as if he had a stomach cramp. He was a loyal man, but it was easy to see that this one time his superior had overstretched his spine.

"You know," Alma started in a soft voice, "I sometimes think we were all so used to trusting his decisions, that it hit us unarmed when he made some that were, let's say, difficult to understand. At least in hindsight..."

"Yes, and he loved his son very much," di Marco said, his left eye reflecting the light, as though a tear was building up. "His son's reputation being shattered – or even worse, Luca moving out, perhaps to another country – it was more than he could handle..."

Alma nodded. Who, if not di Marco, could be her ally in this? "I have to ask," she said, "you have met the English woman – what was she like?"

"The woman, well, it is hard to tell what she is really like," he said, suddenly sitting up straight, his eyes fixating on a point on the far horizon. The encounter obviously still moved him, after seventeen long years. "She came with her father and a lawyer and she did not say much. Her lawyer was an idiot; he had obviously no clue what he could have asked for, and what on the other hand we could not claim. Perhaps she knew – she is a lawyer herself. But she clearly did not want to push for it, either. It was almost as if she wanted to discard us just as urgently."

"We did discard her, didn't we...?"

Di Marco sighed. "In a way, yes... but we did offer compensation and she was more than willing to accept it. She asked for a payment of 1,000 pounds sterling per month until the girl was eighteen, and nothing more. The only condition was that the money would have to be transferred monthly. She was adamant on that..." *Signor* di Marco paused, as if seeing the scene again before his inner eye.

"So you don't think she was after his money?"

"I doubt it... But my initial point was, you see, the girl is what by now? Eighteen? Seventeen?"

"Turned seventeen last April..." Alma said, and now she could no longer hold back. "You know, it may sound a bit naive, but I have been thinking that I would be curious to meet her – the daughter, my granddaughter, and perhaps her mother too. Do you think that is an idiotic thing to even think?"

Di Marco held his breath. For now, it was perhaps better to leave her letters out of the story. If di Marco would not take her side, she might still get away with her stupid letter writing since no answer came anyway.

"Well," he frowned, and then exhaled slowly like an overflowing pressure cooker. "Giacomo would surely not have appreciated that..."

"*Not appreciated* is putting it mildly," Alma had to smile at this diplomatic language, "... but still I wonder. When he now sits on his cloud, you know, I wonder if he would not rethink some of his decisions."

"In this case, I have sometimes wondered about that too," he admitted, and for a moment his looks softened as if he was about to squeeze her hand. Then he straightened his back. "Personally, I always believe in being prepared. My point is, although we have no indication whether this is a realistic concern, the girl could sue us to be acknowledged as an heir. We should think through all the claims she could raise against us and how we would like to react."

And we are back on the legal track, Alma thought, somewhat disappointed but not surprised. "And I guess you already did that years ago?"

"Well, I never discussed it with Giacomo, but I did my homework," he said, not without pride. "Right now, there is not too much to worry about. At the time Luca died, he did not own much. No share of the company was registered under his name; no assets really belonged to him at that time. Giacomo had taken care of that."

"What does that mean?"

"Well, if she should come with a lawyer one day, we would not have to pay that much right away. The only thing would be... well, *signora*, how do I put it...?"

But it dawned on her before he found a way. "She is the only survivor. One day, she would be my heir too."

"Yes, that's right. Of course that is far-future thinking," he was quick to add.

"Well, we have just seen how quickly things change…" she added, tilting her head, as if this could take the edge off her words.

"I'm glad you can see it that way. Now, there are a number of things we can do at this stage. For example, if we reallocate some of our assets to, let's say, a foundation …"

Alma looked out of the window. Another sparrow landed on the windowsill. He seemed to be enjoying the shade of the sycamore tree and the cool stone. Instead of flying up again, the tiny bird settled down and puffed up its feathers, turning into a furry little ball. Somehow she did not like where this conversation was going; it felt like discarding the girl for a second time. And what was the point of that? Who cared about all the money when she died, apart from some greedy relatives?

"Technically, the money would then not belong to you but to the foundation. Giacomo was already considering something like this for tax reasons, but we did not really solidify this plan, before he…"

"I see," she said. "In any case, whatever we do with all this money when I'm dead, I would like it to be something that would honour my son, our son. Other than donating to *Alcolisti Anonimi*…" she added in a tone that was more bitter than intended. But yes, for God's sake, part of her was disappointed in Luca. Drinking his life away; how could he? "The thing that is on my mind is the house, the future of this estate," Alma went on.

"In principle, the house could go to the foundation as well," said di Marco, skipping over her sarcastic remark.

That was an interesting point indeed. "You think a foundation might be able to put the house to good use?"

"Why not? It of course depends on the type of foundation and its purpose. Is there something you have in mind?"

Alma sank into her chair. "I wish I did. To my embarrassment, I have to admit that I have no idea what my son was truly interested in; my feeling is the family business was not really it."

"That was my impression as well, to be honest..." di Marco said in a low voice.

"Exactly." Alma nodded vigorously. "I tried to find some of his old friends, but it wasn't helpful at all..." The image of the torn police report came to mind. "And I searched for the police report, but Giacomo threw away the last two pages. Do you know what I should not see? Or do you have the full report?"

Di Marco moved in his chair like a tired serpent; the question obviously caused him pain. "I don't have the report, but I know why he did that. The last pages said that the sky was clear, the streets were dry and that there were no traces of skid marks on the road. For a while, he argued with the officers not to write the report that way, but they were adamant. Luca fell asleep while driving, *Signora* Alma, we are sure of that. Giacomo was concerned that this wording sounded as if... well, as if..."

"As if he took his own life..." Alma completed his sentence.

"Yes... it is hard to say something so absurd. And please, *Signora* Alma, maybe it is also important to let the past rest at some point. You deserve it. And I know that *Signor* Giacomo would have wanted the same. That was why he wanted to move all of Luca's belongings out of the house..."

"But they are still here, right?" A thought began to form in Alma's mind.

"Yes, stored in the basement, not a piece is missing, of course. It was hard for Giacomo to move on as well, if he ever did..." Actually, *letting the past rest* had helped neither of them to move on.

The room seemed to get even hotter. Alma felt a fresh layer of sweat form in her neck.

"*Signora* Alma, are you all right? Shall I get you something?" His face showed regret for even having touched upon the subject.

"Some cold water would be nice, actually."

Instead of calling the assistant, di Marco left the room to get it himself. If he knew one thing, it was when to retreat in discretion, no further questions asked.

When the door opened, she had regained control; the grief-stricken mother and widow putting on a brave face. Di Marco entered, followed by his assistant who carried the glass of water.

"So," di Marco sat behind the desk again, rubbing his hands energetically to return to the safe ground of all his figures and charts, "we were basically done here anyway. Let me see, how can we wrap things up?" Alma nodded; di Marco always ended their meetings with a professional high-level summary.

The glass felt cool in Alma's hand. She barely listened to anything he said, though. Instead, Ana's voice kept going round in her head: *As long as we do not find a letter or something, we will never know.* Before she could think any further about the foundation or anything that could arguably be a legacy of her son, she needed to confront that one question. As much as she had avoided thinking about it, neither could she rest without knowing whether he took his own life. And there was no better way of gaining certainty than searching, turning everything upside down; only then was there a chance of finding peace.

For so many years, she had preferred to travel with hope rather than to arrive. Now it was time to arrive – or at least to try.

"Actually, I would like to have his belongings carried over to my house. It would be uncomfortable to go through them in the basement," she interrupted his speech.

*

The next day, ten moving boxes were lined up in the living room. Luca was moving back in.

26

Boxes

July, 2017, Vittuone (Milan)

"But they cannot stay here for too long! What if we have guests?" Flavia eyed the boxes nervously whenever she passed by the living room.

"*Madonna!*" Maria said whenever she passed by.

This was not the reaction Alma had hoped for. At times, she felt like an inspector insisting on the exhumation of a murdered body while the family was begging for peace. Only that she was at the same time the murder suspect and the inspector. She longed to call Ana, but whenever she began to dial her number, she put the phone down again. She had opened up more than enough already to her new acquaintance. This was something she had to do alone.

Luca had not owned much; he was never interested in the world of things. Perhaps because he always had in abundance. And only a marginal amount of his possessions was paperwork. She had asked di Marco to pre-check the boxes and sort out the ones with clothes, electronic devices, etc. There was no point putting herself through all that again. The only comfort was that the search for a letter, an invoice from a therapist or whatever clue she could find, would not take long. And he was safe in her heart anyway, right? So what could it change to look at these things?

In the first box, there were his notebooks from elementary school, his first maths test and an essay on his summer holidays. *My mother likes sun lotion and my father always pays in the restaurant.* She and Giacomo had laughed so much about this. It was incredibly painful to look at his childish handwriting. How close you are to your child at that age. There was not a single piece in this box she did not know or could not remember. Nothing happens without Mummy; it is almost as if you are one person.

She did not expect to find any personal notes from him between these kid's papers. He had probably never looked at them again. However, despite trying to skim through them as briefly as possible, she needed a break of several days after the first box. It would get easier by time, she told herself.

*

The second box was children's books, from the time when parents read bedtime stories. Every night, she had read endless stories but he would not get tired. And like all kids, he wanted to hear the same stories again and again, complaining instantly if she skipped a line. The Disney's *Pinocchio* book she still knew by heart; the pages were worn out and creased from all the love. Afterwards, he would still come downstairs and stand in the door frame in his pyjamas, always afraid to miss out, until his father got angry.

Alma picked up book after book and let the pages flip over her thumb. To be absolutely sure that no letter was hidden between the pages, she held them by the cover and turned them upside down, like a helpless bird held by its wings. Then she shook them two to three times to see if something fell out. Twice, a receipt from a cashier fell to the floor; twice, it was meaningless.

*

After the second box, she only took a short break. As hard as it was to relive the happy days of his childhood, neither could she wait to get it over with. The third box contained notebooks and documents from his high school years. The handwriting was so terrible that one could hardly decipher anything. The pages were often loose, like one would expect from a boy's notebook. He had never taken schoolwork to heart, always just sitting through it. *Luca shows great reluctance in making more effort than is absolutely necessary to pass a test,* a teacher had written in red ink on one of his mid-term tests. Little drawings were scribbled on the covers of the notebooks; the kids had obviously played hangman during class. Some girls had written their names in pink, and if their name contained an *i*, it was topped with a little heart.

In the fourth box, there were a few books from his teenage years, mostly on detectives and espionage, things like that. Like his father, he was not much of a reader. All the books she found looked familiar. She remembered either buying them or him unwrapping them and thanking an aunt or uncle with a hug. She flipped thoroughly through every single one and shook them – but nothing fell out.

The fifth box contained the first surprise. She found a whole pile of journals on design and architecture. Going by the publication dates, he had collected them between the ages of nineteen and twenty-three. Many of them were in French, maybe bought in Geneva. No wonder she had never seen those. She remembered that he had left for Geneva with only one suitcase – feeling extremely cool because of that – but bringing back loads of stuff. His father had teased him for having been shopping like a girl. She could see he had studied them intensively. Pages had earmarks and Post-its; some were torn. She tried to picture her son reading one of these – him, who had always needed persuasion to wear a clean shirt and get a haircut. Wasn't art and design rather something for men that liked to wear pink and a lot of perfume? At the bottom of the box, she found catalogues of art exhibitions. They had taken place in New York, San Francisco, Sydney and London and all over the course of 2003 to 2005. He had been to Geneva in 2004. He could not have been to all of these exhibitions, even if some might have, in theory, coincided with business trips. Perhaps the girl had something to do with this; perhaps they were actually hers.

In the sixth box, she finally found the drawings Ana had been talking about, a whole pile of them. Studies on the Vitruvian Man by Da Vinci, a few photocopies with explanations which Ana had apparently handed out as class material. The class had really left an impression on him. There was an entire folder containing more sheets of fine paper with sketches and variations – and then something that at first glance looked like a huge mess of torn paper. The sheets had been folded and torn in two or four pieces. Obviously, Luca wanted to destroy them but then did not have the heart to throw them away. Alma spread out all the pieces on the carpet like a giant puzzle. It was not hard to fit them together. They were all different versions of the Vitruvian Man. The wheel that da Vinci had drawn around the body to define the proportions, in Luca's drawings had become an actual wheel. The man was tied to it, limbs outspread, naked, but the worst were the faces. Old, young, crying and laughing. A disturbing flood of men on what looked like a wheel of torture.

The most disturbing ones were those where he had not focussed on the faces but on the Vitruvian Man's best piece. In about half of them, the man had an erection; in some he looked down on it, as if he was scared of it or had discovered it for the first time. Alma blushed and put them down. Thank God Luca had had the good sense to destroy them and had never shown these to anybody. But that alone was not soothing; the pain in these pictures came straight from Luca's soul.

She reached for a blanket and wrapped it around her feet, they felt ice cold. Summer or winter, her heart did not pump blood into her feet. For the first time in hours, she looked up from the boxes and realised that she had missed the sunset. The blue hour had started already and the pine trees stood black against a sapphire sky. There were a few more drawings at the bottom of the box, studies on shapes and objects, but he never drew any people. No portraits of a lover to flatter her. The drawings were all dated; they all seemed to stem from the pre-Geneva days and then they stopped. Nothing else was hidden in between them. Her eyes felt tired and her heart so empty. As if it was overwhelmed by the task of consoling all these men spread out on her carpet.

Her back hurt from bending over the boxes and there was so much she did not understand. What if there would be no answers, but only more questions she had to live with? What if it only got darker instead of lighter, and there was nothing she could do about it?

But she would not be able to rest ever again before she had gone through all the boxes. She got up to switch on the big lights in the ceiling. Their brightness blinded out the world outside. When she looked at the terrace door, all she could see was the mirror image of herself sitting amidst boxes.

The seventh box contained photographs. A loose pile, of course, it was not like him to organise them in an album. Some were in bad shape, as if some liquid had been spilled over them or as if they had been lying in the sun for too long. Some girls, Daniela and Romina according to the heart-dotted signatures (vague faces from schooldays came to mind), had put together a little collage from a school trip to Rome. It had not helped them much, in retrospect. Most pictures were full of random faces. Some she believed to be from the Geneva year, judging from his age and clothes; a few had dates imprinted on the back. All these pictures had been taken by other people, as he was in all of them. They were mostly group pictures, to commemorate a happy day or moment. In one of them, she thought she recognised the English woman, but she stood in a crowd and they were all jumping on the command of the photographer, to make it look as if they were weightless. On many pictures were fingerprints as if he had looked through them with greasy fingers, and she caressed each of them gently.

It took hours to go through all the pictures. The air in the living room felt damp, the heat of the day still lingering between the walls. But with the big lights on, she could not open the terrace door; the mosquitoes would come in, drawn to the light and eat her alive. Her back and hip started to hurt again, but somehow, she could not stop; she was drawn to something too.

The eighth box contained study material from Geneva. Handouts from class, notes and exam papers, all carelessly put together in a few ring binders. The papers had been punched anywhere, not necessarily in the middle. They were hanging out on all sides of the ring binder. Some had not been punched at all and fell out when Alma lifted the binder. She would have smiled about her naughty son if it were not so sad. Clearly, he had not cared at all about his studies. All he wanted was a year to get away from it all, and yet he had gotten nowhere.

The ninth box was again magazines. A few rather unsurprising this time, about cars and some about music, all from his early twenties or before. The kind of stuff a young man might have shared with his mates. But then at the bottom again were rather exotic ones, about seemingly random topics. Many existed just in a single edition, like the ones on molecular cooking, deep-sea diving or extraterrestrial appearances. He had hardly followed up on anything, it seemed. There was only one journal which he had bought over the course of one year. *East European Politics* had been read thoroughly, with a particular interest on articles about Azerbaijan; text passages were underlined, pages were earmarked. Alma could not even guess why. In any case, it seemed he had lost interest after a few months. She shook them all, one by one. Nothing.

The tenth box was books; these must have been gifts he received in his early twenties. The kind a bookstore recommends for a young man: *The Firm* by John Grisham, Umberto Eco's *Il nome della rosa*. It looked like he had never touched most of them; none of them looked familiar. And again she performed the same ritual. She flipped through them, shook them, but nothing. It must have been about the twelfth book when she suddenly stopped in her routine. She had seen this one before; it was the Disney *Pinocchio* book she had held in her hands when going through the first box. Not exactly, though, it was only its dust jacket, showing the same image as the hardcover. She remembered the illustration with the wooden puppet held by its master before it turned human. But this time it did not quite fit. The book it was wrapped around was of a different format; top and bottom of the yellow hard cover of another book peeked out of the worn-out wrapping. And now she also remembered that when reading *Pinocchio* to him for the hundredth time, the paper cover had unnerved her and she had finally removed it and put it empty on the shelf, the book being on the nightstand all the time anyway. Her hands were shaking as she unveiled the hidden book – and there it was. The front cover showed a smiling pregnant woman and a young man standing next to her, holding up a teddy bear. *A Parent's Guide to Baby's First Years* it said. Almost mechanically, she turned it around, held it up like a bird by its wings – and a card and a photograph fell out. The photograph fell to the carpet face up, so she did not even have to gather the courage to reach for it. Looking at her was a portrait of a young woman in her best years, the evening sun painting a golden glow on her summer face. She did not look straight at her but off to the side, showing the line of her nose and chin. There was no doubt; Alma immediately recognised the hawk nose and thin lips of the English woman. The card was pink with little white sheep on it, jumping around a baby in a basket, and on top, the line, *It's a girl*.

Alma stared at the find for minutes. Shaking all over, she reached down to pick up the card. Upon opening, it made a screeching sound and she dropped it again out of shock. It took her a while to realise that it was one of those cards that play a little music when you open them. It still worked after all these years. This one played a simplified version of Mozart's *Evening Serenade*. Through the silence of the night, the metallic melody of the musical clock, its slight delays and creaking tunes, filled the hall, as if a dead man was slowly playing the piano. There was a small note inside the card and it was clearly Luca's terrible handwriting; the date was a few days after the birth of his daughter. And what the card had never got to say was:

> *I guess you will just throw this away and I understand that. Anyway, here it is and I hope you are both doing well, please let me know if you need anything.*
> *I'm so sorry, but this is all I can do.*
> *Luca*
> *PS: Perhaps you can send a picture some time.*

She could almost hear his voice when reading the lavish text. So childish, and yet it was them who had not taught him any better. She sat there as if in a trance, just opening and closing the card, and every time the serenade seemed to get louder while everything else around her disappeared. The pain he must have felt. So many words unspoken; and now it was too late. And if he had come to her, talked to her in all honesty, had shown her the book and the card – what would she have done?

That was the worst part. In the darkness of this night, she could not even tell if she would have supported him. Maybe, if he had pleaded strongly, if she could have seen the pain in his eyes. Maybe. But in all likelihood, she would just have feared the upheaval this would cause to her home. She would just have told him that these feelings were a passing thing. That he should not feel guilty, because the English woman tricked him and they paid her, and he would get over it. That everything was good as his father had arranged it, would have asked him to trust them. She would only have cared about holding her own world together. And that was why he had not come to her. Because there was no hope in reaching out to her. That this card had never been sent was as much her failure as it was his.

She stared at the card then looked around the living room, the entire floor covered with books, journals and a scattered array of Vitruvian Men. Manifestations of a life she had brought into existence. It had happened right next to her and yet in a galaxy completely unknown. She switched off the light, unable to run and yet not wanting to see any of this anymore. She lay down on the carpet and that was where Flavia and Maria found her the next morning.

27

Betrayal

July 2017, London

In July, a heatwave struck the city. The temperatures climbed up to almost forty degrees. Sometimes, the early evening began with lightning, but it never turned into thunder or brought any coolness. On the Underground, temperatures soared over forty degrees, bringing the entire system to the verge of collapse. The news was filled with incidents – a woman had reportedly died from heatstroke at Tower Hill, a beggar from dehydration at Mile End. Helen's office under the roof had turned into an oven, baking lawyers instead of bread. Helen changed her office dresses to loose linen blouses with a skirt and sandals. Albertine could not help commenting that this was probably a lawyer's beach outfit. In contrast to the lax attire, the hair went back into a bun to crown her head. To keep her neck free in case there was a cool draft. Gemma breathed so heavily when walking the few metres from her desk to Helen's that Helen sent her home early whenever possible. Albertine's skirts kept getting shorter, but although she kept lamenting over the heat, that girl never seemed to sweat.

Only Emmy's mood was impeccable. Things with Amir were going great; they were now officially dating – but taking things slowly. This guy's inertia had a bright side; he was still living with his parents. They might have been lousy party supervisors, but they did not allow boyfriend/girlfriend sleepovers. Modern Muslim culture came in handy here.

While Emmy's cheeks seemed to get more rosy every day, Helen had to fight to keep up her smile. "Everything's great," she told Emmy whenever her daughter asked her about her mysterious date. They were also taking it slowly, but Helen was running out of reasons as to why.

Eric's apartment had been pleasantly cool for the longest time as it was on the ground floor and hardly got any sun. But after two weeks, the inside temperature finally matched the outside and the air did not move. The heat numbed their conversations and sometimes their hunger for each other. On top of that, the question as to where they were going from here was hanging between them and making it even harder to breathe. Helen caught herself thinking that the heat might kill their love, like a small flower burnt into the ground.

Sometimes, when there was a pause in their conversation, he dozed off. He didn't snore, but breathed with his mouth half open. He looked old in these moments; she felt the tender need to touch the bags under his eyes, as if she could wipe them away. More grey hair mingled between the black than it had around Christmas. His private wars were weighing him down. What if it all came to an end, simply because his priorities were always family and work – and at some point he would run out of energy to keep seeing her? If it was simply too tiring? Or was she overreacting? The heat made everyone and everything unbearable. Perhaps it was nothing more than that.

One night, by the end of the second week of merciless heat, they made love like two lazy animals. Briefly and in a position that kept body friction at a minimum, with the windows wide open. Afterwards, they lay motionless and without a blanket, their bodies covered in sweat. And then he told her casually:

"I think I might look for another apartment." As if this was something you could just mumble before you finally fall asleep. Helen felt her body getting tense, like a sleepy lioness hearing another predator rustle in the grass.

"This one is good for work, you know," he added, realising that this required at least a bit of explanation, "but it would be nice if the kids could come over with their little bikes, get the feel that their dad is still around. Somewhere near Acton Town would be nice."

Helen just nodded. *Good for work*. Work and kids, those were the parameters of his life, determined where he lived and where he went. She was last on the list, if she was on it at all.

"It will be difficult to meet during the week then, you know, given that I would have to commute to the other end of the city," she carefully added, trying to sound as casual as he did.

"I know, I haven't decided yet." Case closed, no kiss, no embrace, no *We will figure it out. Together.*

That night, when rushing home on the hot and sticky night train, she could still feel Eric's erection thrusting between her legs and his pulse in her soft flesh. The back of her hair was still crushed from being pressed against the mattress. People might easily recognise her for what she was: a lover in exile. Many women had stopped wearing a bra in this heat, nipples pressing through thin, sweaty garments. She stood next to a young woman in a fluttery silk dress. In the intimacy of public transport, the left strap slipped from her shoulder, and a pink, delicately soft nipple was revealed. Helen could not decide whether to leave her innocently exposed or to point it out and embarrass her. But then the woman stepped off at the next station and carelessly corrected the strap.

*

In the third week of July, the weather forecast announced a new peak of 39 degrees. People were no longer allowed to water their lawns. The Tube filled with posters encouraging people not to flush after a 'yellow moment' in the toilet. Thursday was usually date night, but around noon, Eric surprised her, suggesting they leave for Hampstead Heath to escape the damp air in his place. It was the first time he'd suggested going out in a while and it filled her with joy. While packing an imaginary picnic basket, she started thinking she might have been worried for nothing. Maybe he was all in on their relationship and had just been tired from work, the heat and getting divorced. Who could blame him?

They both closed their files early and met on Hampstead High Street, arriving on separate Tubes, of course. Eric was carrying a big towel as an improvised picnic blanket under his arm and Helen had stopped at Pret a Manger for snacks. Half of London was forming a caravan to set up camp in the green hills of Hampstead. Countless young couples, eager to snuggle up on their blankets. Actually, it was like summer nights by Lake Geneva, but better. They lived in the same city and worked together, which meant this did not have to end after a few months. They could build something; there was no reason to be so negative. He held her hand as they walked down the street, pulling her close at every traffic light to plant a kiss on her forehead or her lips. Once, they even missed the green light entirely and had to start kissing for another turn. Maybe it would be a good night to bring up the apartment issue again, since he seemed to be in such a good mood. For starters, she could tell him how much he had scared her. Perhaps he was not even fully aware of that.

But they never got that far. Before they turned to walk down towards the meadows, Helen spotted a small Starbucks on Hampstead High Street. "I'd like to get a *chai* tea for the picnic," she said. Those sweet foamy teas were her favourite treat lately; it was somehow too hot for coffee. She was already through the door when Eric suddenly grabbed her arm and pulled her back. His eyes were fixated on the counter as if he had seen a monster. Despite being dragged out violently, she managed to look over her shoulder, and then she saw her too. A perfect bob and a petite figure in a pink T-shirt dress: it was unmistakably Albertine. Outside, Eric kept racing down the street, his eyes wide with terror.

"Do you think she has seen us?" he asked Helen without even looking back.

"Since she had her back turned to us, that seems kind of unlikely," she said, but he would not slow down. After a first moment of shock, she could not help feeling annoyed. It was one thing to be discreet. Being paralysed by the mere thought of being seen was insulting. When they were a good hundred metres down the road, Helen pulled back her arm.

"Why are you so freaked out?" she hissed defensively.

"She might come out there any minute, do you want to bump into her then? She may be headed to the park with some new squeeze of hers." She let herself fall behind a bit, holding back the tears swelling up behind her eyes. Eric did not even notice; he was still deeply into the practicalities of mitigating this alleged disaster.

"I think it is best if we take separate Tubes. You can take the High Street one and I'll walk down to the next stop, it is just a couple of minutes. See you at my apartment in fifteen."

He gave her a hasty kiss on the cheek and all she could do was watch him race down Hampstead High Street without turning around. She walked back to the Tube station. Of course, Albertine was nowhere to be seen.

*

When she opened the door to his apartment, he immediately pulled her close, some guilty conscience showing in his face.

"I'm sorry I dragged you along like that. I think I overreacted a bit," he mumbled into her ear, but it was no longer enough. The tears had finally come out on the Tube and everybody had been staring at her. That scene had been the last droplet it took for her emotions to overflow. She deserved better than feeling embarrassed like that on date night.

"What the hell is going on here, Eric?" She freed herself from his embrace and sat down on the edge of the bed. Droplets of sweat were drying on her skin, Eric had bought a ventilation fan; it stood in the middle of the room, turning its head from left to right. Like a child between arguing parents.

"Why? Do you think this was a good moment to roll it out to the public?" He still sounded agitated.

"My goodness, we did not have to tell her anything. We might have bumped into each other by coincidence. And a few rumours wouldn't kill us, would they?" she said while she searched for a Pret a Manger napkin to touch her neck dry.

"Sorry, maybe I did not come up with the best of plans on the spot. But I wanted to protect us."

"Did you? I feel there is something very wrong here. And we don't talk about it, although we used to talk about... anything."

He sighed, as if Helen was exhausting to him. "Why is it always about talking for you girls?" he said and then he stepped forward and really tried to tickle her to end the conversation, but she caught his hand.

"I'm not stupid, Eric. This is starting to feel like some sort of cheap affair." Helen pointed at the room around her. "The kind that takes place in a dirty motel bed. If this were an American movie..."

"Oh, come on, the past few months have been amazing. Why do you have to make it sound so bad, now?"

"I know they were amazing. But we cannot go on like this forever. There is a distance between us, and I don't know why..."

"Maybe 'cause it's nothing," he said defensively, and walked over to the kitchen counter, putting the sandwiches she had bought into the fridge. But this time she did not give up so easily. She had been patient for far too long.

"For example, I never understood why we can't do tea breaks anymore. The rumours, I somehow don't buy this. You never cared much what other people think."

"So what? Do we have to spend the days *and* the nights together? With all I'm going through at home, I also need some time to breathe, you know. I have tried to explain that many times." He said it in a strange tone, something between playful and annoyed. This was not at all the conversation she had hoped for, and a sudden rush of anger made her bold.

"Are you sure you have really broken up with your wife? Because there is still only one *home* and a makeshift place for having sex."

"I told you a hundred times not to worry..." Now he even wiped the kitchen counter clean. So housewifey; only to avoid looking at her.

"Then, what is *our* plan...? If you are that freaked out when meeting a colleague, I have to wonder whether there is maybe no need for a plan. How can this turn into a real relationship, when it can't even be a rumour?"

He did not respond. No response? Really? Helen sat motionless for another minute. She had only been so bold because part of her had been sure that he would rush towards her and hold her, tell her that of course there would be a future. How could he be so in love all the time and then this silence?

He sighed as though he had not been breathing out for a while and turned around. "Maybe there is something I need to tell you…" His lips had turned into a tense line and his gaze still avoided hers. "There is a reason why it is especially bad if Albertine sees us together." He walked over and sat down on the other end of the mattress. "I should have told you this a long time ago… and if you have to hear it, you'd better hear it from me." Then he paused, as if searching for words. "Look, it was never a big deal, and it ended before we got together…"

Helen felt her hands getting cold. Despite the heat, she wanted to get up and switch off that stupid fan, but she did not dare move.

"The thing is, my marriage did not break down overnight; there have been some rough years, you know. Things with Karen have been going downhill basically since Sara was born…"

And I never would have guessed it from all those happy home stories, Helen thought. If the Honourable *Signora* Carneggio could see her now, sitting with a married man in a secret hideaway. Exactly the scene to prove that woman right.

"Okay," he took a deep breath, "this is not getting better so I may as well say it now. You know I stayed out late at the Christmas party…"

"You always do, I believe…"

"Yes, I was pretty frustrated at the time…"

That was the Christmas party when they had sat at the bar together, when their tea conversations had started.

"I was not keen on going back home. It was late and that always meant a fight with Karen. So I stayed. It is always the same crowd that stays behind…"

And I am never part of that crowd, Helen thought.

"Somehow we moved on to the 101 in Leicester Square. Ewan Sheffield from Real Estate, two paralegals and Albertine, the rest I can't remember. We lost some more people on the way and I started talking to Albertine. I swear to God I had never even looked at her before. I remember I said something stupid like: *Albertine! That is such a strange name. Where does it come from?* And then she told me a story about her family and I was really drunk, and so was she. I don't know, she had a way of listening to me which made me feel so good in that moment. I guess then one thing led to another..."

Helen's heart beat in her throat, but still she could not run. This was way worse than anything she had imagined.

"So the thing is, I... I had an affair with Albertine. And... the only important thing for you to know is that it is completely over. It was just two or three weeks, a few dates. It is not like I still think about it or anything. But that is why I was so freaked out when I saw her at Starbucks. She was quite mad when I broke it off with her. Helen, look at me..."

Thoughts in her mind came whirling out of the fog. Slowly, she began to grasp what that revelation meant to her, though her mind still refused to process the information. The first thing she said was: "Was she in here too?"

"No, no! It happened before I moved here. It was nothing more than two or three times in a hotel... and it ended before New Years"

"How old is she?"

"Twenty-five," he said, defenceless.

Nothing really was what it seemed. She had always taken comfort in the thought that he risked office rumours, his good reputation – in short, his career which meant so much to him – to have an affair with her. He *must* be somewhat serious with her because of that, she had thought. But apparently this was simply the way he usually handled his affairs. This was much more than a fact he had concealed. It felt like he had lied to her every single day in everything he did. From one second to the other, she did not know the man sitting two metres away from her.

"So, whenever you came up for that stupid tea break, you were actually looking for an excuse to say hi to *her*? I thought *we* met at that damn Christmas party, Eric!" Her voice had gotten more shrill than she wanted it to be.

"No! I mean, yes! We did! You know it was not like that! Maybe, in the beginning, I had a bit of a double-purpose walking up those stairs..."

"And I always thought that was so polite of you, how you exchanged a few words with the assistants."

"I *did* come to see you. And I wanted to be polite. Albertine was always super jealous of you; she kept asking me why I spent time with such an old…"

"Stop it, Eric."

"*She* said that. I never thought you were old…"

"You'd better not because you are three years my senior… What the hell were you thinking, Eric? Fucking around in the office? Because, you know, *rumours*! You were either really seriously into her – or a complete idiot!"

"I wasn't thinking much. It just happened… If she saw us, she might have said something; you never know with her. And that was the last thing I wanted."

"How noble of you. And nothing *just happens*!" Helen hissed.

"That's not fair and also not true," he said defensively.

"So how do you *happen to sleep with someone*? That's bullshit!"

"Oh, come on. Most things in my life just happened… and I think the same is true for yours…" That was not the smartest thing to say to Helen. But the returning anger helped; she found the strength to lift herself up to her feet.

"So what is this here, a rush of hormones or an irresistible force of nature?" She finally sounded furious.

Eric looked desperate; he was trying hard to figure out the right answer: "I think I'd go with force of nature?"

"You knew that I am not interested in being one of many office affairs!"

"I never said you were!"

"No, not explicitly. But what else is this here? It is your own place, okay, but apart from that, how is it different from meeting twice a week in a hotel?"

"It is very different…"

"How? If we don't make plans to go any further than this, do not make any effort to become part of the other person's life, how is that any different from having a random affair?"

Eric looked hurt, but his voice was angry. "Well, if you really think this was a cheap affair, then I am sorry for you. But you know how my life is at the moment... this is all I can do for now. I am sorry if it is not enough."

"Your last word?" The fan turned from one to the other in silent expectation.

"Yes." He sounded tired and defeated, but he looked her straight in the eye. He really meant it. There was a long pause. A part of Helen still tried to unhear what he had said. He had been nothing but fooling around with her. She had feared it all along, and finally he had admitted it. Slowly, she began to move towards the door.

"You know what, thanks for telling me. I feel extremely ridiculous right now, but of course, it's better I know now than later. I have no idea who you are and I don't want to be here," and with that, she grabbed her handbag and stormed past him. She heard him shout something after her but she kept going.

On the street, she tried to focus on walking up Holborn High Street without people thinking she was mad. The shop windows she passed made her look surprisingly normal. Upset, yes, but no more than if she had lost a battle in court.

Her heart was still beating in her throat when she got off the train at Clapham and marched towards her house. The few people moving in slow summer mode on the main street stepped to the side, afraid she would run them over in her stampede. She was still racing when she got off the main road. There were fewer people now, but she just wanted to hide, from all of them. Eric's words kept going round and round in her head; she barely paid attention to the world around her, so she screamed when a small creature moved out of the hedge right in front of her. It was the fox. He took a leap when she shrieked, but in the middle of the road, he stopped and turned. They locked eyes again, the same yellow eyes, piercing despite the twilight. But something was different. He made a few more hasty steps, but when he then turned his head towards her again, she saw it: he carried a dead swallow in his mouth.

After he disappeared into the garden on the opposite site, Helen stood motionless for a moment. Something she could not name had deeply frightened her. She felt as if she needed to hold her world together and she almost ran for shelter. When her home came in sight, the TV lights were flickering behind the curtain, taking quick turns in pink, purple and blue. Even in her panic, it reminded Helen of Disney's Sleeping Beauty's house, when the fairies used their long-suppressed magic to make the dress and birthday cake. The thought soothed the fear in her chest. She stopped for a minute to catch her breath; otherwise, Emmy would think she had gone mad. The good fairies were like mums for Sleeping Beauty, protecting her from evil. That is exactly what she should be concerned with, she thought, instead of getting her heart broken by a liar. And she had been much too lenient with Emmy and that dubious WhatsApp-hero.

"I'm home," she shouted as she unlocked the door. She saw the man-sized trainers in the hallway next to her daughter's Adidas in the same second she heard her daughter scream. With one leap, she reached the living room. On the sofa, her daughter was struggling to get her t-shirt back on, while an equally bare young man sitting next to her was stuck with his head in his, his forearms pedalling in the air. She knew who it was before his head finally appeared.

"I'm sorry, Mum, I meant to tell you…" Emmy winced, her eyes begging.

But Helen did not even look at her daughter. All she saw was another one of those sleazebags messing with young girls' lives.

"You know what? You should be ashamed of yourself. A man your age going after a minor…" she yelled at Amir, tempted to grab him by the neck and drag him to the door if he were not two feet taller than her.

"Mum!"

"Emmy, shut up and go to your room! And you, you leave my house, right now! I don't want to hear another word from you!"

"I haven't said anything so far," Amir remarked calmly.

"OUT!"

"I'll call you later," he said to Emmy over his shoulder, while fumbling into his trainers, as if absolutely nothing exciting was happening around him. The door fell shut.

"Mum!" Somewhere between embarrassment and outrage, Emmy was having trouble finding her words, but Helen was not willing to wait.

"Forget about *Mum*! I trusted you! And now I have to come home to *this*!"

"This is MY LIFE," Emmy yelled, raced up the stairs and banged the door behind her.

And only yesterday, she and Emmy had been running in the park as if they were friends. This might easily count as the worst day of her life. Thank God she had not come home any later. And in that vein, thank God she had learned the truth about Eric before making a fool of herself. So in the end, it was all not that bad, right?

She thought about eating, but she wasn't hungry. The day was more than lost, so she decided just to go to her bedroom and hide in there. Out of pure exhaustion, she immediately fell into a light sleep. She found herself in that room in Chamonix, where everything was dark but the orange tapestry was still screaming brightly. But the girl Luca was entangled with on the bed was not her; it was a petite girl with dark almond eyes. She woke with a scream, but now the images would not leave her. Eric and Albertine, in the white linen of a hotel room, doing all the same things that he'd done with her when making love. She saw her legs wrapped around his hips, him moving slowly inside her, kissing her face as if he had all the time in the world for this. She saw the soft flesh of Albertine's full breasts shaking in their rhythm. Whether it was over or not, it hurt so badly.

Part IV

28

Belated Wishes

End of July 2017, Vittuone (Milan)

When Flavia and Maria found Alma on the carpet, they helped her to her feet and guided her to her bedroom upstairs. She mumbled something incoherent about a birthday and kept a pink piece of paper pressed to her chest. They did not need to look at it in detail to understand.

The boxes disappeared from the living room, but Alma did not notice. She did not leave her bed again.

They brought her food on a tray but she rarely ate. Flavia and Maria took turns again to sleep in the guest room, but although they told her this every time after dinner, she hardly realised it. Company was not something she was longing for. This time it was not grief but defeat that locked her in. She had failed, so badly, at the one thing at which she had never wanted to fail. Her own child, her family. She had gone through the private belongings of a stranger. All she knew was he had been sad, at the end of his life, very sad. Whether he had steered his car on purpose against that tree or not, in the end, it did not even matter. His will to live had not been strong in the end, and that was all she needed to know. And the nightmares returned. But this time it was not only Giacomo or Luca looking down on her. As soon as she closed her eyes, a jury gathered on the *baldachin;* she could see their bodies pressing through the white linen, their heads hanging over the frame upside down, to look at her. Always different ones; often her mother, her mother-in-law, then random ones like the principal of Luca's school, a girl she had known as a child, and when she least expected them, Giacomo and Luca. Sometimes, they looked young; sometimes, their skin was yellow and their heads deformed.

What else could one do than loathe her for the life she lived? She found no other way to look at her own self. It pulled her down as if her entire body was covered in lead. She was the one who ultimately did not deserve to live.

*

On day seven, the door swung open around noon with the expected lunch tray. She had already mentally prepared for refusing it against Flavia's lamenting about her bedrest, but this time it was Ana carrying the tray, followed by an apologetic looking Flavia.

"I told her you are not feeling well, *Signora* Alma, and that visitors would at the moment not be appropriate—" Flavia began to excuse herself pre-emptively.

"Yes, that's what she said." Ana cut into Flavia's speech. "I immediately told her that that is some twisted logic right there! The more you feel unwell, the more you need a visitor. Isn't that right, dear? You tell her that!" Ana was not behaving at all as if she had invaded someone's privacy. With confidence and too much energy, she placed the tray on the nightstand, making the cutlery and platter jump. The noise made Alma shriek; she almost made it to a sitting position. In the presence of Ana's energy, Alma felt even more tired, but she merely waved Flavia out: "It's okay this time," and Flavia immediately left for the door, not interested in fighting this battle if she did not have to.

If I just keep lying here like this, she will leave sooner or later, Alma thought. Ana inspected the guest bedroom. "My my," she said, "I've never seen much of the interior of your palace. Quite regal, I must say. Lucky you!" and saying that, she knocked against the dark wood framing the canopy bed. "You should add a red and gold curtain, and you would rest like a queen, hee-hee!" she added, now testing the stability of the bare frame for this endeavour.

"Certainly not, that would be a bit too kitsch," Alma mumbled. In all her misery, she could not help wondering where Ana always got those atrocious clothes from. Today, she was wearing a gigantic tunic out of white chiffon, held together by a golden belt with turquoise fake stones. When she sat down at her bedside, she needed to organise all the cloth around her so as not to crumple her outfit. The Romans were back, at least fashion-wise. It seemed a little intrusive to sit on an adult person's bed, who was neither your husband nor your mother or father. Alma braced herself for all sorts of chit-chat, but she had forgotten what Ana was like. She never wore velvet gloves when facing a patient. She was more of a surgeon, cutting right through the crap.

"So, you tell me: what made you stumble backwards again?"

"Backwards?"

"Yes, backwards! You know what I mean! When I met you, you would not leave the house. You were just hiding in here and feeling miserable. And just when you started to get out and about, suddenly you run back into the cave. Worse than before, actually – before I was allowed to visit at least! So, what's changed?" The last words were spoken softly. As always, Ana had a way of looking at her as though she really wanted to know.

"There is just no point going any further from here…" Alma began.

"But what happened?"

"I should have never looked into those boxes; now I can no longer pretend!"

"Boxes? What are you talking about?"

And so Alma told her everything, not stopping for a full hour. How she had not recognised most of the things she had pulled out of the boxes, as if she were discovering the secret life of a stranger, the journals, the photographs and, worst of all, the torn-up drawings. Finally, she also told her the story in full about the London girl. The daughter, the hidden book on parenting, and the card that was never sent.

"Can I see?" was all that Ana said after she had finished.

"Don't open it more than once, please…" Alma added, pressing her hands over her ears when the metallic piano started to play. Ana slammed the card shut right away.

"God, that noise is monstrous indeed," Ana murmured. They sat in silence for a while, Ana holding the card in one hand and reaching for Alma's hand with the other.

"Did you find anything apart from this and the drawings? A goodbye letter, invoices from a therapist?"

"No." Alma shook her head. "Nothing. But he must have felt so alone… and he actually was!" At that, Alma burst into tears, sobbing uncontrollably, the tears streaming like waterfalls out of her eyes and dropping from her chin. Ana said nothing, just sat there and waited.

"We wanted to keep it all together, so much so that we lost everything…" Alma finally said, after she found time to breathe between her sobs.

"That happens," Ana said, and nodded. "And indeed that story with the granddaughter is like from a *telenovela* – and nothing to be proud of!"

"That does not cheer me up!" Alma said in a nasal voice before she trumpeted into her handkerchief.

"Oh, you want me to cheer you up? That's good news!" Ana said, and pinched Alma's arm. "Remember our conversation on the terrace? When I first came here? Don't you think he has forgiven you already, sitting up there on his fancy cloud? This all happened more than seventeen years ago. Do you think he wants you to lie in bed and cry all the time? I think it just freaks him out! See… Your son was still young when he died, you know, and not necessarily… the most mature."

"I think it is fair to say that he was eternally immature."

"Yes, let's go with that. It just took him a bit longer to figure it all out and then he ran out of time."

"Figure what out?"

"What he wanted from life. And how to get it. It seems to me that until he was twenty-three, he was just skating by. Trying to please everyone, get the most possible enjoyment out of every day. He could have talked to his father about what he wanted, what he really thought, could have taken up a job elsewhere – then perhaps returned to change a part of the business to something he liked."

"Clearly, you did not know my husband."

"Oh mamma mia, what could he have done? He just had the one son, right?"

"That is also true," Alma admitted.

"At that age, many adolescents go through a depressed phase, struggling to give life a purpose. And they seek distance from their parents to resolve that."

"A distance, a space we would not give him…"

"What I mean is, if he had lived longer, probably by the age of thirty or so, he would have taken a flight to London and sorted things out. His way. Then he could still have met a woman that really suited his way of life…"

"You think the London woman was not the one?"

"I kind of doubt it," Ana said, tilting her head. "He seemed to be so much all over the place. Why should it have been any different in the love department? Also, he wrote nothing about that in the note. Nothing about trying to get her back."

"He was just so light-headed all the time," Alma said, pulling herself up to a sitting position. "What did we do for him to become like that? Did I raise him too softly, too much like the girl I wanted? Giacomo used to say that nobody in the family was like him!"

"Yes, that made it harder for him, a bit like a cuckoo in the nest. But a kid is not a clot of clay that can be shaped into just anything, and not everybody is made for family ties. Some people need to live free as a bird, and Luca had to figure that out by himself. Everybody has to. And he would have, if he had not fallen asleep behind the wheel…"

They sat in silence for a moment, both lost in their thoughts. Ana was right. Since it was impossible to know for sure, didn't she deserve mercy herself? Shouldn't she allow herself to simply believe in that version of the story? As much as this thought was balm for her nerves, it only lifted some of the weight from her heavy heart.

"You know, what weighs me down is, that even if I forgive myself, set aside all the guilt, the grief for having lost the chance to really know him and accept the lost grandchild," Alma said, looking down at her hands in her lap, "what weighs me down is that he died before his life could get... could get any meaning. Before people got the chance to see who he was, before he himself knew who he really wanted to be. Because then at least, we could all now remember him as he really was – and talk about him. But even in our memories, we kind of deny him his existence..." She had stopped crying and looked at Ana with a stern expression.

"I think I understand what you mean," Ana said. "But maybe there is something you can do about that. Now that you know, maybe there is something that can be done to, how can I put this, to make his footprints seen...."

"Like what? A special Mass at church?"

"Was he religious?"

"No!"

"Then let's keep thinking... but not in here! The weather is great this time of the day. Come on, get on your feet!"

Alma was not sure whether after days of bed rest, her legs would be strong enough for a walk, but she obeyed the command.

"Let me just freshen up," Alma said. She had been in the same pyjamas for a week. She felt smelly all of a sudden, and her eyes were red and swollen.

When she came down the stairs, a bit shaky but in fresh clothes and a cloud of perfume, she saw Ana waiting in the foyer; the sunlight of a summer afternoon falling through the big windows from the park. She almost looked like an angel in that floating white tunic dress with the golden belt. This friend had saved her more than once. It seemed like a miracle to her that this cheerful and good-natured person kept putting up with her, and now she had to ask: "Ana, why do you want to be my friend?"

"Hmm... I don't think anybody has ever asked me that," Ana said, and looked aside for a moment to think. "But I think the answer would always be the same. You know you have found a friend when you can go through the worst times and turn them into an afternoon that you like to remember. For me, it is like that with you."

Alma's knees got a bit weaker, but she made it down the stairs safely.

When they returned, the fresh air had indeed helped to organise Alma's thoughts. It was late already and as Ana had no immediate plans for the next day, she asked the maids to set up a guest room. She felt much better, but she was still afraid of the dark. What if the jury returned and eyed her from high above? Would she have a good answer? Maybe this was a good time to move back into the matrimonial bedroom…

*

Apparently, it was Ana's fixed habit to watch some murder mystery after dinner. Alma agreed to that, although she did not care for crime shows on TV. They settled on the sofa with a bowl of popcorn between them, but somehow Alma could not focus on the story. Her mind kept wandering off. There was another crime scene, a real one, she needed to tend to. She excused herself while the FBI agent was still examining the body in the opening scene.

She walked over to the library to have a moment for herself and gather her thoughts. All the windows in the lounge and the library were wide open now. It had been Flavia's idea to invite the cool air of the evening and she would close them before she went to bed. It was nice actually to feel a bit of a breeze in this part of the building too.

There were still so many things unresolved, and despite Ana's optimism, she doubted whether she would ever make peace with the past. She was a different character to Ana, more nostalgic, heavier in her thoughts somehow. But there was one thing she knew she had to do, a puddle of blood she could clean up herself. It was late, but not too late. She had kept the birthday card with her all day. It was in her handbag when they went for a walk and rested in the pocket of her cardigan when they had dinner. She sat down by the secretary desk and switched on the Tiffany lamp. The light attracted first a cicada and then a ladybird. Alma watched them bump into the light with a whizzing sound and then, to recover from the shock, crawl across the lampstand with its fake art deco flowers and leaves. *We just have to make sure they find the way out again in the morning*, she thought.

Then she pulled out a fresh envelope and a blank sheet and wrote:

Dear Emilia,

I believe this belongs to you and I want you to have it. I know this comes very late in life, too late. I can only hope you believe me when I say that I only found it last week in my house.

I still hope to meet you someday in person. From the card, I know that it would mean a lot to Luca as well.

With all my heart,
Alma

So the card finally started its journey to London, a much-belated wish from a dead man.

29

Gone Girl

End of July 2017, London

The next morning, Helen felt as if she were going through a terrible hangover. Her muscles were aching, someone seemed to be hammering against her skull, and her mouth felt dry and tasted strange. She had experienced this before; strong emotional reactions had this effect on her. When Luca let her down, she had woken up like that for days. Why would it be any different this time?

Stay in bed, her inner voice begged her; never go to that office again. She turned on her belly and pressed her nose deep into the cushion. With smart timing and abstinence from the coffee machine, she might be able to avoid Eric for a few days. But Almond Eyes was sitting right in front of her door. Perhaps this was what modern fairy tales were like? The prince, getting off his horse, pulling out his sword to free the princess in the tower – but then on the stairs, halfway up, he just stops short for a quick snack. She tried to laugh at her own joke, but it wasn't really funny. Fuck you, Eric. Why did it have to end so badly? Losing against a well-established wife was one thing. But this… besides, who knows, he might still return to Karen on top of everything else.

She heard the shower being turned off – her baby was up even earlier than usual. Right, her baby. How could she even think of not getting out of bed? After all the ground she had gained in the past few months, last night's fight could not be the final word in this matter. It would probably take a serious apology and some time to cool things down. But also Emmy hadn't been fair. She had promised to tell Helen in advance, and instead this sleepover happened behind her back. When Helen came down to the kitchen, Emmy stormed out without a single word.

*

When Helen stepped outside her house, she put her sunglasses down in surprise and looked up to the sky. It was still hot, but the brightness of the past days was gone. A thick layer of grey clouds pressed the heat down onto the city, adding a new moist quality to the heat. Helen had not found the energy to put her hair up and now she regretted it. On the Tube, she held it up in a bun with her hands, to catch a cool draft, but all the air coming in was as hot as a hairdryer. She would look as if she had not showered for days when she got to the office.

Luckily, she made it up into her tower without having to say, "Good Morning" once. Francis' and Babette's looks were supportive and kind this morning: *We never liked this guy!* And the door to her assistants' room was closed, so she did not have to see Almond Eyes' fresh and shiny face. Her lucky streak ended, however, when Eric showed up with two cups around 11am. Of course. Now that a serious relationship was off the table, the tea breaks were back. So ridiculous of him to believe that things could be mended like that. She was so done with this; she was not going to make a fool of herself, not now, not ever.

"Sorry, I really have to work today, I'm very busy." She hid her face behind a veil of hair, then she remembered how messy it looked today and pushed it back behind her ears, without looking up.

He kept standing in the door for a while, but then the door fell shut. *If he stops now to chat with Albertine, I will explode here, right over this file*, she thought. But he walked straight back down. For the entire morning, every one of Albertine's stupid giggles travelling through the walls hiked up Helen's blood pressure. She asked Gemma to get her a coffee from downstairs, pretending to wait for an important call. She felt a bit sorry when Gemma appeared with her tea, out of breath and red-faced, but there was no way she was walking down there today. Or asking Albertine for a favour.

Surprisingly, she did get a few things done. The dictations were flowing easily, perhaps fuelled by her anger, and she voraciously typed one email after the other. Yes, she was angry and incredibly disappointed, but she did not even want to give him that. Wishful thinking clearly had gotten the better of her. She should have known this was a bad idea when Eric started flirting with her out of the blue. There would have been time for all that once the separation was official; and a good man would have told her everything from the start. But Eric only did when he feared Almond Eyes might blow his cover. So how could the affair with Albertine not have meant something to him, if it freaked him out so much after all this time?

She forced her mind back to the subject of Emmy. First, she needed to apologise for her outburst. Emmy was too old to be scolded like that, and it wasn't her fault that Eric turned out to be a complete ass. Her rage would only get Emmy and her lover into a Romeo and Juliet mood. Maybe it was even better to do it right away, before they could bond further over despising her.

Really sorry for last night, she texted. *It took me by surprise, but my reaction was inappropriate. Can we talk about it tonight over a pizza? 8pm? Xx Mum*

She did not have to stare at her phone for too long. Two minutes later, a message from Emmy appeared on the screen: *Ok. Will be there.*

Helen felt lighter; she smiled for the first time that day. So the new bond was not so easily destroyed. They would work it out and then go for a run the next day. The phone rang; the screen showed Eric's extension. It rang six times; then it stopped.

*

When Helen finally left the office at about 7pm, with an exasperated sigh, she found there was reason to be proud. Despite the occasional fighting-back of tears and the permanent lump in her throat, she had hung in there. Things would be more difficult when one of their joint projects came back around, but one thing at a time.

When she climbed up the stairs from the Tube station, it felt like hitting a wall. The humidity had increased so much over the day, it felt like stepping out of a plane in Bangkok. The sky looked the same grey as it had that morning. The air seemed to stand still.

Despite the draining climate, Helen walked home as quickly as she could. There was no fox this time and no magic colours were dancing behind the curtains when she approached her home. When she entered, only Emmy's shoes were lying in the middle of the hallway, no letters. No music or TV was running, nobody speaking on the phone. Maybe she had gone downstairs to take a nap?

"Hi, I'm home!" Helen shouted, and made her way towards the kitchen to get a glass of water. But when she passed through the living room, she bounced back and shrieked.

Emmy was sitting in the semi-dark on the sofa, her legs crossed. She sat there, as if she had been waiting for hours. She did not look up; her eyes were fixed on the table in front of her. It took Helen a split second to understand what she was staring at. And when she did, her heart stood still for some beats, before it started racing in her throat. The Clarks' shoe box stood on the right side of the table. All seventeen photographs were spread out, as if it were a memory game. Only the pink card standing on the left corner of the table did not look familiar.

Helen felt betrayed and caught red-handed at the same time. "You searched my things!" she began, but when Emmy looked up, the fury in her eyes stopped her short.

"That is all you have to say? This time, I found the letter first. The third one this year! And they were all addressed to me! They were *my* letters from *my* family."

Helen felt cold sweat form on the back of her neck. Her knees felt weak all of a sudden and she reached for the armchair to sit down. What the hell had that woman written this time?

But Emmy was far from done. "And even worse: *you* wrote letters to them, all those years! You guys are like pen pals. You even sent them pictures of me!" The sentences came out in a tense staccato; Emmy hardly opened her jaws when speaking. Her entire body was trembling with anger. This was not a teenager's temper tantrum; it was a deep and righteous anger.

"Well... these people concern me as well, and I can... write letters... to whomever I want." Helen's voice almost faded out. There was nothing to say in her defence; she knew she had made a terrible mistake.

"You were lying to me all these last months. All this, *Oooh, Emmy, we are a team. I'll tell you everything.* That was all bullshit!"

"I wasn't lying to you," Helen said defensively. "And pen pal is really a strong word for what it was. You really have everything on the table there. I kept copies of what I sent. They did not write back once... those bastards, you see?" The last words came out almost begging.

"Why would I believe you? They wrote back three times and I did not know. They invited me. The letter was addressed to *me*! Yes, they were mean, nobody wanted to marry you – that does not give you any right to fuck with my life. With *my life*, do you get that?"

Tears were running down Helen's face now, but Emmy was unstoppable.

"You thanked them for something, every year, every fucking year of my life. For what?"

"There is not much to tell, Emmy. I just did not want you to get hurt, that's all."

"Great job! By lying to me!"

"I did not lie to you... I..."

Emmy picked up one of those white cards, walked three steps towards the armchair her mother was sitting in, and held it right into her face. "WHAT DID YOU THANK THEM FOR?"

"Look," Helen tried to look at Emmy past the card. "Can I make a cup of tea and we talk it through?"

But her offer only enraged Emmy more. "For fuck's sake, you've had your sit-downs for the last couple of months and you blew it! Why can't you answer me?" Emmy's free hand was clenched in a fist at her side, the knuckles white.

"I thanked them for money. Just money. They agreed to transfer a thousand pounds every month until you were eighteen. And that is really all they ever did. And I have never spent a penny, it is all there, saved up for emergencies, for you... apart from the money I took for the shoes in January..."

Emmy's body relaxed slightly, but her eyes were no less hostile.

"So they did care for me," she said in a cold voice. Her anger had been wiped away by cold contempt.

"Oh, Emmy... *care*." A dry laugh escaped Helen's throat. "I don't know if that deserves to be called *care*. *I* cared for you!"

But putting it that way was another big mistake. "*You* wanted me all to yourself," Emmy said, "that is *not* caring. They did not want you so they can't have me – that is all the logic that there is. And now with Amir – that is just the same thing! He loves me and it has nothing to do with you, and that is why you hate it."

"Emmy, calm down. That is not how it is..."

"That is *exactly* how it is! And also you can't handle the fact that other people *do* have relationships that make them happy. It does happen in this world – can you understand that?"

"Emmy, I don't think that is very fair now," Helen said, wishing to disappear into a hole in the ground. "I did not *keep* you from them, Emmy. For God's sake, I would never have done that. They did not want us anywhere near. This money is blood money. They made me sign a contract to make you disappear from their lives, and the money is only because I drove a hard bargain. I never got any answer when sending those photos of you. I don't even know if that lawyer handed them over. These letters only started coming in this year! Out of nowhere, after seventeen years, they start to fuck with our lives again. What the hell!"

Emmy was breathing rapidly, though she stood perfectly still.

"You fucked with my life too." Then she turned without a second glance and walked into her room.

"Emmy, stay here..." but all Helen heard was the door to her room falling shut with a bang. A second later, the key turned in the lock. Helen sat in the living room and could not move. There was a pain in her chest and it found nowhere to go. After a moment, she walked over to the coffee table and reached for that alien pink card standing on the corner. Damn it, this one time she had been too late. Why did Emmy have to take an interest in the post today?

As Helen turned over the card, and as she understood what it really was, her knees gave in and she came to kneel on the carpet. She held the card in her hand and then pressed her forehead to the ground, as if in prayer. Of course her baby was out of her mind, receiving a card from her father, after seventeen years.

"What could they have done to you, Luca, just for sending one card?" she whispered into the ground.

She wanted to be mad at him, for seriously thinking of sending such a ridiculous card, and then not even doing it. But instead she lifted her head, lay down on her tummy and then placed the card in front of her. She followed the writing with her fingertips, caressing each letter. It was barely legible; he had always scribbled like a first-grader. On inspecting the card more closely, she found that it had probably played some music at the time. It felt thick on the back and there were some notes dancing around the sheep. But no matter how far, or quickly, or slowly one flipped it open, it stayed silent. The battery must have died after all these years, before the card had its grand debut. Her hands started shivering and her shoulders hurt. She had to put the card down. She sat up and wrapped her arms around her to gently rock herself from side to side. Perhaps one could put a new battery in; was this even possible with these cards made in China? If Emmy could hear the music her father had chosen for her, would it soothe her?

Then Helen noticed the letter which had been resting next to the card and she leaned forward to pick it up. The third letter was undoubtedly the best one the old witch had sent. Quite close to a real apology – and at least addressed to both of them.

She knew it was a futile effort right now, but she walked downstairs and knocked on Emmy's door:

"Emmy! Please talk to me!"

Silence.

"You have to believe me, this card I would have given to you."

Silence.

"Emmy, please…! I am so, so sorry you had to find this card like that… I am so sorry for everything…" It was the saddest thing in the world. This card after all those years, and no chance to write back. But it was no use. Emmy was probably wearing headphones and could not even hear. Maybe she was even crying herself and there was no way to get through to her.

As if in a trance, she started to prepare sandwiches, though she did not feel hungry. Then she left the plate to the side of Emmy's door, so that she would not trip over them. No sound was coming from the inside.

She went back into the living room, the photographs still spread out on the table. She knelt in front of them and touched every single one. That was the life Luca had missed. From the first steps to the first day at school, up to this beautiful young woman. It was a life Helen had always tried to make as wonderful as possible. As a young mum, she had spent many a sleepless night, just like all parents probably do, pondering whether she did the right thing here, whether she reacted in a good way there. Never had she doubted that it was right to keep all of this from her. But having seen Emmy so out of her mind…

She remembered so clearly the day she had struck a deal with them. Every month, her bank account reminded her, and she had wanted it that way. The Carneggios' lawyer had called for a meeting when she was four months pregnant. A strategic choice; the chances of a miscarriage drop significantly after the fourth month. Of course, she had tried to talk to Luca before. They had not exactly broken up when she left Geneva. They were still texting almost every day and there was talk about a holiday in Sardinia, when her exams were done. But the messages kept getting shorter, the plans more vague. His world claimed him back and he was too weak to resist. Without his family's approval, he was spineless.

When she finally found the courage to tell him about the baby, their phone call ended after only a few minutes and with a lot of stammering in the sense of "That's lovely," "We'll manage" and "I can't talk much now." He did call again in the evening, basically repeating the same excuses in the same trembling voice. She wrote emails for days, always finding new ways to express her low expectations, not to frighten him or his peers. She just wanted to talk. But there was no way to reach through. He loved children; she had seen him play with his cousins' children at that wedding. In a parallel universe, he would have made the best father.

Weeks later, she got an invitation to a meeting at a law firm, probably involved in the Carneggios' UK business. Helen still remembered the smell of the place. A heavy room perfume, something between cinnamon and old books. Being pregnant, it almost made her throw up. The place was dead quiet; a thick carpet swallowed all the noise. Apart from the elegant woman in a Prada costume at the reception, there was nobody to be seen. Once you got money, you probably just have to keep quiet and sit on it.

The lawyer her father had brought along looked terribly out of place in his Regular Joe suit, with a receding hairline and a worn-out leather bag. The futile attempt of a servant to appear regal in front of a king. Apparently, he had done a great job in a divorce at her dad's tennis club.

It was almost thirty minutes before diMarco appeared, in a perfect designer suit, the thick black hair well trimmed, right out of a Mont Blanc commercial. Until the last minute, she had hoped Luca would come through that door. The meeting only lasted an hour and the deal was simple: for a 'generous compensation', she had to stay away, not get in touch with anyone from the family nor request anything beyond what would be agreed today. No recognition, no inheritance, no father, no daughter.

In the end, they offered her 250,000 pounds, a ridiculous sum for them. They clearly counted on this being a lot of money for a girl like her. Her father's lawyer was useless; it was a lot of money for him too. Either that or he was too embarrassed about his HSBC give-away pen.

As they were about to rise from their chairs, Helen spoke up. Out of mere intuition, she had not planned for any of this. She was too proud to fight for more money, but she wanted to send a reminder, one to which she was entitled. Once a month, every fucking month, on a bank statement, there would be a sign of their existence. There was a bit of protest regarding the administrative burden, but finally Mr

Mont Blanc agreed. She tried so hard to read that man's face during the meeting. Was this just a job for him? Did he often buy out girls for the family men? But his face was a flawless mask, loyal to the bone. Back home, it struck her how idiotic this move had been. Those people were not like Mum and Dad, checking their bank statement every Sunday evening together, to keep track of their expenses. Their lawyer would organise for the transfer and the family would not know a thing about it. It was then that she came up with the idea of the cards...

And she had made it! She had raised a great girl all by herself, and she had not taken a penny off those people. Or from anyone else. But if Luca would have sent a card back then, she would have responded. Until he died, she had been hoping for such a sign, had felt her pulse rise whenever there was a mysterious letter or a dubious email in her inbox. But it always turned out to be nothing.

Luca's voice had not called her *Dulcinea* for the longest time and he was silent now. He never had anything to say for himself. She lay down on the sofa and buried her face in a cushion.

The painful question was: had she really been motivated by the noble desire to protect her daughter, seventeen years ago? She always thought that they had not left her much choice. And yes, no choice to be anything but a single mum. But she could have fought, dragged them to court and had it out in the open, for her daughter. Her daughter had not made that shady deal at some mahogany desk. At the time, she felt she had to look after herself; she did not have the strength to stand up in court. But in the end, she had protected her own broken heart more than her daughter. And even if she had, Helen could have been more honest with her when Emmy was old enough to understand. She could have told her the whole story instead of making her part of her crusade. What was she so afraid of, even today? Was it really so likely that after all these years, Emmy would run over to them, as smart and considerate as she was?

Lying there, on the carpet of her living room, curled up like a baby, deep down inside, Helen knew that there was another reason – and it was nothing to be proud of: jealousy. Those people had dumped her, left her alone, treated her as if she were nothing but a disgrace. Her true fear was that, despite all that, Emmy would be accepted. Old age turns people mild, sometimes even wise. And they had lost their only son. What if they changed their minds when they saw cute little Emmy and fell for her? Who wouldn't? And what if Emmy also really liked them, maybe started to go on holidays with them and who knows what else? It was Italy, after all, and they were rich; they could offer her a lot. The thought of herself sitting alone in London in front of a pile of bills while Emmy was sunbathing on a yacht near Capri with Grandma made Helen's stomach turn, even now. They did not deserve Emmy. It would have made things more unfair; the balance of justice would have been disturbed for good. But that was selfish, wasn't it? It came pretty close to what Emmy had thrown right in her face.

It was 3am when Helen finally went downstairs to her bed. She could not tell whether she had slept at all, but the next time she looked at the alarm, it showed 5am. She felt as if she had been woken by a noise. She listened for a few moments but it was all quiet. She reached for her phone; there was another message from Eric, sent at 4.50am. Maybe that had been it. She deleted it without reading.

By 6.30 she gave up on sleeping. The house was still quiet; the sandwiches were untouched in front of Emmy's door. She carried them down, threw them in the bin and placed the plate into the sink. Her head felt heavy like a stone and she set up the coffee machine, watching the water drop through the filter and the carafe fill, too tired to move. Only when she turned to the table with the cup in her hand did she see the note:

Dear Mum,
I have to see for myself, you would not understand.
Please don't come after me.
Emmy

30

Helen Calls

End of July 2017, Vittuone (Milan)

To make sure that Alma would not retreat in her cave again, Ana decided to stay for some days. She was certainly a caring soul, but Alma suspected she also preferred cool stone walls and the park to her cramped and overheated apartment downtown. After Alma had understood that Ana could do most of her work on that portable computer thing, she simply invited her to make this place her summer house. As Ana was not the type to worry about imposing, she packed a suitcase and moved in.

In these last days of July, a light wind came up making the summer's heat more bearable. Ana refused to spent the day indoors in the dark salon, and so together with Flavia and Maria, they moved the deckchairs away from the terrace and into the shade of the trees. After breakfast, the ladies crossed the meadow with a pile of cushions and the newspaper and set up camp for the next few hours. It was nice to be outside, but it was still hot. Whenever they lifted the papers, it was only to put them back down after a minute and stare up into the leaves, watching the dance of blue and white light. Alma was more than grateful for Ana's presence. It had been a bold move to send the birth card and she did not want to be alone when the answer finally came. And especially not when no answer came. It would be a different silence to that following the previous two letters. Nothing she could ever write to them would hold as much power as a card from Luca. If they did not answer now, she had to make peace with the idea of never meeting her granddaughter.

Ana did not have much work to do over the summer; her fundraising activities did not make any sense when the rich people left the city. Usually, she disappeared to her room for one to two hours in the afternoon, checking her emails and making a few calls. Alma used this time to freshen up. Sometimes, she pretended to have some paperwork too and sat down in the library to write a card, and then it was almost time for dinner.

"We are living like the people in Hemingway's *Fiesta*, just without all the sex and the drugs," Ana said, and when Alma did not know the novel, Ana immediately ordered it via Amazon. According to Ana's nutshell summary, it was about rich young people wasting their lives away in sweet nothingness. But Alma could not help it, to her these were exciting days. A friend staying after a sleepover and now a package with a book arriving on her doorstep! They had just set up their camp under the trees and Alma was about to dive into the section called '*feuilleton*', when Ana's mobile buzzed.

"Sorry," she said, rolling her eyes. "There is a problem with a sponsor's name on the board in the entry hall. I've got to make a few calls." And with that, she put her sunhat back on and waded all the way back over the sunny meadow and disappeared into the shade of the house. Alma stayed on her deckchair, immediately feeling kind of lost when there was nobody sitting beside her. She tried to read an article on a Spanish sculptor rebuilding the Easter Islands in the middle of Madrid, but it wasn't really interesting. Even reading seemed easier when someone was reading next to her.

A squirrel came down a tree and started hopping over the meadows. Alma wondered whether it would accept a cookie from her hand one day and began spreading some cookie crumble into the grass for future reference, when she heard the telephone ring inside. After one more ring, she heard Flavia's muffled voice say, "*Pronto*."

A few seconds later, the terrace door opened. With a sigh, she swung her legs off her deckchair. "Who is it?" she asked as she reached the terrace, but the look on Flavia's face stopped her short. Flavia was dead pale and tense. She did not say anything but pressed a finger to her lips and kept waving her inside. There was none of her usual resolute demeanour; her hand was flapping like a fish on land. Following an instinct, Alma also kept quiet and followed her into the living room. As soon as she was close enough, Flavia grabbed her by the arm so that she would move more quickly. That lack of decorum was so unlike her, and a feeling of panic rose inside Alma. There had been too much bad news in this life. Flavia pulled her through the living room and into the hallway. The phone was still lying next to the cradle. Flavia picked it up and held her hand over the speaker. Still pale and with wide eyes, she shout-whispered:

"It is the *signora* from London!"

Alma's heart jumped, she had to swallow hard before she could speak. "Which one?" she said with a trembling voice.

"Mother, I believe! Very upset! Crying maybe!"

"I see..." Alma said, her heart beating in her throat. For a second, she thought of calling for Ana, to get moral support for whatever would come next. But this phone call was only for her.

"Tell her to wait a second, I'll take it in the library," she said, and turned on her heels to hurry through the foyer and the gallery over into the eastern wing.

Please don't hang up, was all she could think.

31

Like a Fox to a Swallow

End of July 2017, London/Dover

Not for a second did Helen think that Emmy was joking. Upon quickly checking her room, it seemed that Emmy hadn't packed much. A sports bag was missing and her toothbrush and some other bathroom items. There was no thought of going to work. Helen called Ali-Saa's mum; she had their number from the party but did not have the mobile number of that Amir guy. But there was no need; Amir was hanging out in his room, watching DVDs. Maybe it was technically impossible to run away with that guy. Other than that, they knew nothing, or Amir did not tell them at least. She called two mothers she knew via Emmy's art club but nobody picked up. And that was all the numbers she had. Anyway, on a Thursday in the middle of the school term, Emmy was probably alone in this. In a way, this Amir guy on tour with her would have been a relief. She called Emmy's phone every five minutes, but it always went straight to voicemail.

Without thinking, Helen sent a text to Eric: "I'm home. My baby ran away! I don't know what to do!" It simply felt like the most natural thing.

It was obvious, though, where Emmy was headed. The letters from Alma had the sender's address on the back of the envelope. The most likely scenario was that she had boarded a plane to see the place and her grandmother with her own eyes. The thought of her daughter running over to them hurt so much. In all her despair, she could not help but imagine the smirk on that old woman's face, thinking of that English hussy who could not even control her own daughter.

Everybody ran from her, sooner or later.

But this was idle thinking; the worst would be if they told Emmy off. Then her baby might roam the streets of Milan, in tears, without a place to stay. It was only a matter of time then until someone took advantage of her.

Clearly, there was one thing Helen had to do. Nonetheless, she waited until noon in the faint hope that Emmy had just been upset and was sitting in some Starbucks in town, her phone switched off to punish her mother. She must have been out of her mind, to run away like that. Despite being seventeen, she was pretty innocent for her age. Apart from a few school trips, she had not been out and about much. It had felt safest to keep her little girl around her. God, clearly, that had been a mistake too.

The little paper note was trembling between Helen's shaking hands. It had been given to her eighteen years ago, one of the relics sleeping in the shoe box. Luca had scribbled his parents' landline on the back of a till receipt from the Migros supermarket at Plainpalais. He was about to leave Geneva for a week of holidays at his parents' and she was supposed to join him for this cousin's wedding. The number was for her to call him if she or the taxi got lost.

Emmy must have seen the receipt in the box but had probably not been able to make any sense of it. It was highly unlikely that she had called them up beforehand. Thank God mobile phones had not really been around at the time; there was hope that their residence might not change its landline until everybody was dead. She remembered that the mother spoke English. Luca had told her that his mother had a teacher coming to the house, to be better suited for hosting international guests. Helen would scrape together the few Italian words she had learned back then; she had to make it work somehow!

She took a deep breath and began to type the number into her phone, pacing up and down the living room, like a tiger in a cage. It rang once, twice... it was a big house... then, on the fifth ring, someone picked up.

"*Residencia Carneggio,*" an old woman said. The voice sounded totally alien to her.

"*Urm, buongiorno, signora… este la signora Alma Carneggio en casa? Eso Helen Kings, di London, es molto importante!*" She wasn't even sure if this was rather Spanish. There was a pause on the line.

"*Un momento, signora,*" the voice said, without any audible emotion, and then it fell silent again. Perhaps she was the housekeeper. Then there were voices in the background. "*Signora!*" the voice was shouting, and a distant voice answered. She heard the voice say her name, say her name in that house. Suddenly there was another woman's voice at the other end, and she recognised it immediately. Out of a million voices she would have known that voice, so much it was imprinted in her brain. It had grown a little weaker, it sounded older, but it was clearly Alma Carneggio.

"Please do not-te hang up," the other voice said to Helen with a strong accent.

A minute passed and it felt like an hour. Then there was a click and the voice was back.

"Yes?" Alma Carneggio said, a bit out of breath.

"Ms Carneggio?"

"Yes?"

"So, urm… this is Helen Kings, *signora*. I am very sorry to disturb you…"

"Yes?" God, the familiar voice seemed to be more nervous than she was herself; it almost had a bit of a high pitch. A thousand things were running through Helen's head while she gathered courage to speak. Did that woman ever get her cards? Would she care? Would she know what her daughter looked like or would she have to describe her, maybe send a fax with her photo? To that lawyer perhaps? Or should she give up on this and call the police in Milan straight away? She had to start somewhere, though.

"*Signora* Carneggio, I am calling you because this is very important!" Helen spoke slowly and loudly, to an almost insulting degree. "This is about my daughter, Emilia. Have you seen her photos?" There, she had said it.

There was a gasping breath at the other end. Fury? A panic attack? Would she just hang up? But then the familiar voice said:

"Yes, all the letters are here in my desk."

Helen stood speechless with her mouth open for a while. This was so much more than she had hoped for.

"Missus?" the familiar voice now asked, reminding her of the purpose of her call.

"Sorry, yes... I mean, good. You see, this morning, my daughter ran away from home," and with that sentence, maternal instincts pushed away all other sensations and thoughts. When there was no answer, she repeated the sentence slowly, almost yelling every word.

"*Madonna!*" said an equally shocked voice. That was a good sign, wasn't it?

"Yes, and I believe she is on her way to Milan! To your house! To find out about her father." Helen's knees felt suddenly weak and she let herself drop on the sofa behind her.

"Oh!" was all she got as an answer, but it sounded kind.

"And... and I am very worried because she is only seventeen and she has never travelled alone..." Helen spoke in a calmer register now.

"Yes, yes, no good for a girl to travel alone," the voice said.

" Yes! So, if she comes to your place, please call me. I will give you my phone number."

"Shall we call *polizia*?" The voice sounded agitated now.

"Maybe later, in the evening, too soon now..."

"Okay," the voice said. Helen had to push back tears. Partly because it was such a relief that they would look out for her, partly because it still hurt to ask them for help. Helen dictated her mobile number through the phone and Mrs Carneggio had to repeat it several times. Numbers were not her strong suit, but in the end she got it right. The call ended after several helpless exchanges of "Thank you" and "No, no, thank you!"

After she hung up, Helen felt a bit dizzy. She stumbled over to the sofa and buried her face in her hands. Now it was done, what else could she do but wait? When she looked up, she saw Luca leaning in the door towards the kitchen. He did not look up this time, his head hanging low. She waited for him to say something, but he didn't. Then her phone rang and he was gone.

Her first thought was that it might be Eric; she already regretted that she had reached out to him in a moment of weakness. But the screen on her phone said 'Emmy'.

"Baby, where are you?" she screamed into the speaker. And it really was her baby on the other end, and she was sobbing into her phone from a McDonalds in Dover. Helen did not fully understand the situation. Emmy was stammering something about really wanting to go but then she could not and all the time she said she was sorry. And most importantly: she wanted her mum to come and pick her up. The only question Helen had for now was the precise address. There was a bit of toing and froing then as Emmy tried to argue that a McDonalds never has an address, but is just McDonalds, but Helen Googled it and they figured it out.

"Do not move for the next two hours!" Helen said in the end, and Emmy, sobbing a little less, promised she would not.

Frantically, Helen gathered a few things for the drive: a bottle of water – would she need a sweater? Nonsense, a shawl would do in this heat, if it ever got cold – driver's licence, purse, phone. She was still rummaging in her handbag when she bumped into him on the doorstep. For the first time ever, he stood in front of her house. One hand raised to ring the bell, his phone with Google Maps Directory in the other. Eric was out of breath and his shirt was stained with sweat. Damn it, she had been so strong and then this crisis had made her weak.

"I came straight away," was all he said, a bit taken aback as she did not smile, not even a bit. But he gathered some courage, made a step forward and put his arms around her. Despite the sweat, it felt amazing, the smell, the warmth, the solace, but she managed to pull back. One warm embrace for months of lying? What a stupid bargain that was.

"You didn't have to come, with all your work piling up. I can manage…" She tried to find a way out.

"No, I really wanted to."

"It's okay, really. I should not have texted and made you come here," she said as firmly as she could. But he would not turn on his heels like that.

"Stop it, Elsa! I made a mistake, all right? I should have told you earlier but I did not know how!"

"Damn right, you should have told me a lot of things – but I really don't have time for this now…" And she stepped forward to close the door behind her.

"Helen, I meant everything I said to you. Please don't shut me out of this!"

Helen's eyes started to fill with tears; the voices in her head were still fighting. "I guess if I did shut you out, a lot of people would understand," she said.

"People never understand what goes on with a couple, what to forgive and what not to forgive. But *you* know what we had. And I know it meant a lot to you as well, perhaps as much as it meant to me. Please let me explain, Elsa…" He paused and looked straight at her as if he could see right through her eyes to a much deeper place.

And with that, longing so much for comfort after all she had been through, Helen gave up. She stepped forward to bury her face in his shoulder, enjoying the best feeling in the world: the feeling of being held.

"Can you drive with me?" she mumbled against his shoulder.

"Drive to where?" he mumbled back, his face buried in her neck.

"Dover, she is in Dover."

"Emmy? How do you know?"

"She called, some minutes ago. I was just about to get in the car. She wanted to take the ferry and then gave up…"

"Elsa, that is so great!" he interrupted her, and his joy was real. He had truly worried about her child. "Then, let's go! I will drive you."

*

It was a two-hour ride from London to Dover. When they left, it was 2pm, still before the rush hour. While Eric steered the car through city traffic and the AC cooled them down to a normal temperature, Helen briefly filled him in on the last two days. How she had found Amir and how Emmy had then received the card. He mostly listened; only when she described the birth card did he speak: "Oh my God, that poor, poor thing!" Then Helen did not have the heart to tell him about the other letters. They moved on in silence for a while. Helen watched Eric changing gears and lanes, manoeuvring them slowly and safely from one red light to the next.

After a fight, couples should always go on a car ride together, Helen thought. There was something so healing about sitting in the intimate space of the car together, heading towards the same destination. It was a sweet act of nothingness, and no silence had to be awkward. At every other traffic light, he would reach for her leg or her hand and she took his hand, before he had to shift gears and focus on the road again. She asked him about his day at work and they talked a bit about that, then fell silent for some minutes before he asked something casually back.

As they reached the highway, the driving did not require all of his attention anymore.

"I want to explain this affair thing to you..." he said, both hands now tensely pressed against the steering wheel.

"Do I want to hear it?"

"Please let me at least try... I can see how this must look to you."

I already got into the car with him, so what's the harm? Helen thought.

"It started two years ago. I met a woman while waiting for Laura's Saturday ballet class to finish. One of the mothers. I had a foot in the door from the start, simply because I was picking up my daughter, which her husband never did. You won't believe how much frustration there is among young parents."

"Oh... I do know that, perhaps better than you do, you married man..."

"Sorry, of course you do."

"Were you in love with her?"

"No. It was just for the sex. At the time it felt like taking a drug. As if it cured everything I was suffering from in a minute. It ended after a few weeks, but it was long enough for me to notice how much Karen and I had fallen apart. If I smelled like rose perfume and came home with lipstick on my collar, she would not have cared."

"Are you complaining now about not getting caught?"

"No... it just made me realise how bad things really were. After it ended, things stayed the same from the outside but actually it all kept getting worse. Work-home, work-home, again there was not much time to think about anything. I guess it is no surprise it then happened in the office. These things always happen at work... Helen?" he added, begging for her understanding.

"What are you trying to tell me with this?"

"That there was a final stretch when my marriage broke down, when I took up a bad habit. It is nothing I have done before or I plan to do again. And Albertine was unfortunately a part of that time, but there was never anything special between us..."

"Okay..." Helen thought about this for a moment. "How do I know this *crisis* is over now? If things with you and Karen were bad for so long, how did it end all of a sudden?"

"I know. I should have talked more about this..."

"Yes, why didn't you?"

"I don't know. I think I just wanted a happy place. The time with you, I wanted to keep it clean from all those things that were troubling me. Even I can hear that that sounds a little selfish..."

"It clearly does. And even before that, during our tea breaks, I never had the faintest clue that something was wrong. Why were you lying all the time?" Helen was suddenly too tired from the events of the day to be angry at him.

"I also lied to myself because I liked people seeing me the way you did! The successful husband and father of two, the man who has it all! And day in, day out, we were covering it all up because of the kids, because it is never their fault. You get so good at it that you start to believe it yourself. That maybe things are not perfect but worth it for all those family moments you create, that you can hold it all together. But you can't, not without going insane."

"So this year, after Christmas, you got into a big fight?"

"Not exactly. The day after Christmas, we went for a walk in Boston Manor Park with the kids, to get some fresh air after all the food. Jameson found a small turtle on the pavement I guess it was someone's pet which had escaped. He picked it up to show it to us. It was dripping strangely and when he lifted it up to my face, I saw that rats had eaten all of its limbs hollow, the legs were bleeding. It was dying probably. I've read somewhere, when they get stiff from the cold, they can no longer defend themselves against rodents. That's why you have to take them inside in winter."

"That is terrible, the poor kid…" The image sent a shiver up her spine.

"It looked like a perfect turtle from the outset, but it was actually a hollow, bloody corpse. I took it out of his hand before he could turn it and see for himself. I said the turtle needs rest and put it deep in a bush at the side. I was expecting protest for taking a toy out of his hands but none of the kids said a word. We finished the walk and at home I suddenly felt really unwell. I went up into my study to sit down for a moment and suddenly I started to cry. Like a baby, for more than an hour and I could not stop. I guess I had a kind of nervous breakdown. I could not stop thinking that our family was in every way like that turtle and it brought me down. Karen found me up there before dinner. First, she only said that I was probably working too much… but then she admitted that she had been seeing someone for about a year. And we agreed that we needed to find a different arrangement. Until now, that is basically all we've agreed on."

"Eric, I am so sorry," she said, and she meant it. His face now showed all the weight she had observed in it over the last months.

"And at first, I wasn't even angry. I knew she had hung in there for a long time. I had had affairs as well, and I was constantly thinking about you. So I thought, well, maybe everything is just falling into place now."

"Okay… and now you don't think that anymore?"

"I do… but I totally underestimated how hard it would be to start over. When I took you to my place, I thought now my life simply takes a turn for the better. But once we started seeing each other, and it felt so good, it became complicated. I was happy like I had not been in years and it threw me back to my heyday with Karen. I'm not saying I was thinking of her when we were together. But in my head, so many things were happening at the same time. The grief over the loss, the joy over the new life, and then the fear that this might not work out, either... I failed once, who's to say it won't happen again?"

"I think I know what you mean."

"Every time you came over, I was happy – and terrified. Terrified you would say that this sex-always-in-the-same-room arrangement would not be enough. Then I would not know what to do and you would break up with me."

"You really thought I would do that?" Amidst her own fear, she had never considered that.

"Yes! Actually, I believe I brought up that stupid Albertine story as a kind of sabotage. Because it really wasn't important and besides, what could she ever say to you? But if I brought it up and made a fuss about it, then you would walk out on me and it would be terrible. But at least the wait for you leaving me would be over. Stupid, I know..."

"Stupid, yes. Actually, I never made that claim, because I was afraid if I became more demanding, you would break up with *me*."

"Oh God, it sounds like we both had a terrible time of it!"

Helen shook her head. "Time with you is time well spent, Eric. I always thought so. We simply should have talked more."

"Yes, we need to be more honest with each other, even if it is scary..."

"If I have learned one thing in the last few days, then it is that honesty is not my strong suit – so good luck with that!"

This made Eric laugh. At some point, she really had to tell him about the letters. He seemed more relaxed now, his back resting against the seat and his fists no longer clutching the wheel, steering the car one-handed.

"With Luca, I never pushed for honesty. If I asked the uncomfortable questions – such as Where are we going with this when the year is over? Did you sleep with that Azerbaijani woman last night? – I might have had a much better sense of what I was getting into. But I feared the answers, so I took the liberty of seeing whatever I needed to see in him. In the end, I also used *him*."

"I actually have a theory on this. Wanna hear it, Elsa?"

"Sure." Against her own will, Helen smiled. These conversations felt like home, more than any apartment ever would.

"We tend to use our lovers to fulfil all our hopes and dreams. I mean *we* as in *everybody*. It is part of Disney's *get married and live happily ever after cure*. The two become hopelessly intertwined, although actually, love and life plans are two separate matters."

"Well… yes, but there is no relationship that is not tied to the fulfilment of people's hopes and dreams," Helen said. "That is the whole point of living life together."

"Sure, we need to pursue our hopes and dreams in life. But everyone deserves to be loved for her or his own sake. Romantic love can mean many things for different people. But the social norm requires that it always means the desire to live together, build a house and have children as soon as possible. Those who need other things, can they be loved?"

"Oh, Eric, that relationship model you are suggesting there requires a lot of talking and negotiating. You are not really a fan of that…"

Eric chuckled. "Not lately, I know. But generally I love talking to you… and to get back to my initial point; at least in theory, honesty about the hopes and dreams in the room is key." He paused. "Love is such a fragile thing. One needs to protect it. Otherwise, all the demands of daily life will eat it up. Life can be to love, like… like…"

"Like a fox to a swallow," Helen said, the image of the fox suddenly returning to her mind.

"I could not have said it better." Eric smiled.

Helen remembered the elegant flight of the swallows as they circled over Lake Geneva. Luca had loved watching them when lying on his back. They reminded him of home, he had said. Outside, a motorway sign was flying by: 35 miles to Dover.

"I believe there is a lot of truth in what you just said," she said after a while, "but it isn't exactly a solution to our problems. You want to move back to be near your family and I deserve a partner that wants to be with me."

"For now, I'm not moving anywhere. I have also grown fond of my apartment. Elsa, I really want what we have. But you're right, things won't change overnight. I'm afraid you will have to be patient with me."

Helen nodded and turned her gaze back to the window. This had been a lot of information within an hour – and objectively, the affairs had rather multiplied. She wasn't ready yet to twirl her arms around his neck and end this conversation with a kiss. But in the car, she didn't have to.

*

By the time they left the highway, the light had dimmed. The thick grey layer of clouds had changed; now it was a wild landscape piling up, in all shades of grey to dark blue. As the first buildings of the port came in sight, Helen grew tense again. A tiny part of her was still afraid that Emmy might have changed her mind and they would find the McDonalds empty. Or, even if she was there, Helen was afraid that after a short moment of relief, the old hostility would return to Emmy's eyes, and she would never get back the girl she had lost. Eric noticed her tension and took a hand off the wheel to hold hers. "It will be fine, you will see," he said. All she could do was nod.

The McDonalds at Dover Ferry Port was easy to find; the golden M was visible from a mile away. When they stepped out of the car in the car park, the suffocating heat had vanished. A warm wind had come up and it whirled through her hair. It was still humid, but the air was filled with the scent of soil, a metallic note mingling with it.

The first thing Helen noticed was that clearly this McDonalds was the dirtiest she had ever seen. Rubbish was piling up on every table and the floor. Ferry guests stopped by, in a hurry, certain they would not become regular customers. In all this chaos, it took her a moment to spot pale little Emmy in the back corner, sitting behind a tray full of empty boxes and cups. Her entertainment for the past few hours. Her shoulders were drooping and her grey hoodie suddenly seemed too big for her. Helen ran across the place, almost slipping on a ketchup package, and held her for minutes. Emmy did not push her away.

After a bit of hugging and crying, Emmy wanted to go home immediately. Eric went into the queue to get them a snack to eat on the road; Helen was too happy to ask the big questions. "You're sure you are not hungry?" was all she could say, although it was unlikely that after being stuck for hours in a McDonalds, Emmy would be craving a Happy Meal.

The moment they stepped outside, it started to rain. Heavy single droplets fell on the tarmac and the cars, making a tapping sound on the aluminium roofs. The tapping grew faster and stronger with every second, the overture to a big spectacle. The three of them had to run across the car park, Emmy squeaking with delight, like a little child running from a garden hose. The few metres to the car were enough, though, to get them wet. "Monsoon season," Eric said when he fastened his seat belt.

The single droplets turned into a steady rain, drumming heavily on the car roof. Eric had to switch the wipers to the fastest mode, the sky was finally willing to pour down what it had withheld during the past weeks of summer heat. The road seemed to turn into a river and the heavy rain tore leaves off the trees, getting caught in the wipers. The water was streaming around the car and slowed down the traffic. As if they were sitting in a boat, Eric slowly shuttled them towards the highway. Right on time as they reached the ramp, the rainfall got lighter. Eric could turn the wipers down a bit and his shoulders relaxed. Only then did Helen remember that at least for educative reasons, she had to get angry with her daughter. For bunking school and for making her worry so much.

"So, young lady," she began, "now you tell me, what the hell were you thinking? What was the plan here? And where did the money for that trip come from?"

"There was not much money and not much of a plan," Emmy admitted in a low voice. "I was so angry, so I bought a ticket online for the bus and the ferry. From Calais, I wanted to make it with BlaBlaCar from one place to the other up to Milan."

"What car?"

"BlaBlaCar. It is very practical. You sign up and then you can see which people are going in the direction you want and whether they have a free space and then ..." but she got no further than that.

"You were thinking of *hitchhiking*?" Helen screamed so that her voice almost broke.

"Helen!" Eric said, in a calm voice, putting one hand on her leg.

"What *Helen*? That is insane! What did we watch all those horror movies for?"

"But Mum, it is an app...."

"Oh right, they don't let just anybody use an app these days!" Helen snapped back.

"She did not do it in the end, Elsa," Eric said. And that was true; it was a good point which got her a bit out of her combat mode.

"And who is that by the way?" Emmy shouted, pointing at Eric. It was an obvious attempt to change the subject, but in all the hugging and crying in McDonalds, Helen had indeed forgotten to introduce him.

"Oh, that is just a guy who picked me up while I held out my thumb, you know, it seemed to be the safest option." Helen was still shouting a bit, but with less momentum.

Eric suppressed a laugh. "Sorry," he said, "the thought is just so funny." And this made them all laugh; Helen's anger vanished a bit. For a while, they just drove in silence. The only noise was that of the rustling brown paper bag whenever Eric or Helen reached into it, and the wooshing sound of car tyres in the rain. The smell of McDonald's fries filled the car.

"Mum, can't you understand why I did that?" Emmy said after a while from the back seat.

"Yes, I can," Helen said, turning around to the young woman who was her daughter. "I do know it is my fault. I handled this whole thing very badly and I am really sorry. I should have been more honest." They looked at each other for a moment, then Emmy turned her gaze to the window.

"You know," Helen said, "I spoke to them on the phone."

"Who?" Emmy stared at her in disbelief.

"The Carneggios. Your grandmother, to be more precise. Because

I thought you might end up there and I wanted them to look out for you."

Emmy covered her mouth with both hands.

"And?" she finally said, a bit muffled through her hands.

"Well, we only spoke very briefly, and then I called her again to say it was all good, that we were picking you up. She sounded fine, actually, and in the second call, she said she would write us another letter. Now, I don't know if she will really do that, and I don't want you to expect too much… but of course you can write to her or call her if you want to." Her last words were drowned in a squeeze as Emmy flung her arms around her mum's neck from the back seat.

"Thank you, thank you, thank you, Mummy!" and she sounded truly happy.

'I'm proud of you,' Eric mouthed to her, and it felt damn good. Who would have thought that this day would end like this?

"The hitchhiker's name is Eric, by the way," Helen said, after having been released.

"Hello, hitchhiker Eric," Emmy giggled. She was in too good a mood now. And Eric smiled; he looked more than pleased with himself.

Emmy kept talking for a while about what they could write; she wanted all the details of the phone call and Helen gave her a word-by-word report. Emmy fantasised a bit about the three of them driving to Italy, then she changed the subject to her two hours at McDonalds, all the things she had eaten and all the information she had uncovered with her smartphone on self-experiments with McDonalds food and their harmful effects. Helen only added a, "Yeah, why not…" or "Aha…" Every now and then, Emmy suddenly fell quiet. Another look in the rear-view mirror showed that her head was tilted to the side, resting against the window, slightly bobbing with the motion of the car. Sound asleep, like the baby she used to drive home from Kent — only that this time she was not driving and had time to look at her in the back.

"You know what the weird thing about this age is?" she said to Eric after a while.

"Tell me," he said, eyes fixed on the road.

"In one moment, they seem so smart, wise almost, maybe wiser than you and you wonder where it comes from. And in the next moment, they are a baby again, someone with no clue, who needs all the protection in the world."

"Yeah," Eric said, looking briefly into the rear-view mirror too. "But I wonder sometimes if that is not true for all of us."

"Hmm," Helen said, "yeah,." She leaned back and made herself comfortable in her seat, the drumming sound of the rain you might be right almost hypnotic.

*

She woke when someone gently touched her cheek and she then heard a car door slam shut. The car had stopped; they were home. When she turned her head, she saw Emmy running to the front door, the jacket held over her head. Eric gently touched Helen's neck and massaged it a bit, then pulled her over for a kiss.

"You slept for more than an hour," he whispered in her ear.

"Did I really?" Helen said, turning towards him. "I didn't know I was so tired."

"You look beautiful when you are asleep, just like another Disney princess... except for the drooling part..."

"What?" Helen rose from the seat with panic in her face.

"Just kidding," he said, and kissed her, laughing.

"Gee, now I'm awake," she said, kissing him back.

They stayed entangled over the console, all lips and tongues, apologising and forgiving.

"What do we do now?" Helen said when they came to a break, and it really was a pragmatic question. "You want to stay here? It is late already, no?" It was 7pm but it felt much later to her.

"Maybe I'll just leave the two of you alone for now. It has been a long day, don't you think?"

"Hmm, maybe you are right," she said, and leaned over to kiss him again.

"I could come over here for dinner tomorrow? I'd still like to see your place," he said through the kisses.

"Sounds perfect," she said with a bright smile. He started the engine and she had already opened the door with one foot on the pavement when she leaned back in.

"Eric?"

"Yes?"

"You are a good man."

32

Legacy

August 2017, Vittuone (Milan)

Helen's phone call left Alma exhilarated for days. Alma had felt relieved as well as disappointed. She had already been discussing with Flavia what kind of dinner a seventeen-year-old would like, while Ana had suggested patrolling the town in her car, in case the girl had got lost. Her adrenaline levels only marginally receded when Helen called again two hours later, informing her that Emmy had been found in Dover. The phone call had stopped their commotion short. But the mere fact that her granddaughter had been on the run, towards her, massively increased her chances of meeting her in this life.

When the phone remained silent the next day, she finally opened up to di Marco. To her surprise, after this episode, he was all for being proactive and helped her to write a formal invitation letter. When they had sat together for more than an hour choosing the words carefully, having a hard time deciding between 'it would be a pleasure' and 'it would be *our* pleasure', she realised how much the other two letters had been written in haste. And with more than ambiguous feelings, which the woman had probably sensed between the lines. It felt to Alma as though she was truly inviting them for the first time. When the letter was sealed and out with the post, again, all she could do was wait.

To take her mind off things, Alma accompanied Ana on a trip

downtown. Ana had decided to stay longer in Vittuone and was running out of clothes. To Ana's surprise, it was Alma who suggested stopping by the Triennale di Milan for a cappuccino in the museum's café. It had occurred to Alma that if she wanted to figure out a way to have Luca remembered in a way he himself would have liked, she would not find it in his bedroom, but rather in places he had visited. In places where he felt free.

Ana had seen him in the Pinacoteca, so maybe he had also liked the café in the museum's modern entry hall with its geometric white walls. There was something clinical about these modern buildings, which Alma usually criticised as inhuman, no improvement on the elegance of ancient architecture. But because of the café at the end of the entry hall, the smell of freshly brewed coffee lingered in the air, and the beehive humming of voices made it almost pleasant. The English woman, Ms. Kings, would probably like it here. There were many pale and skinny women walking around or typing something in a phone or laptop.

But she could not imagine Luca in this place at all, engaging in intellectual talk on fancy chairs; that was so not him. They must have had something in common, right? She carefully observed all the young people around her. If they were not talking to someone, they were focussed on their phones or iPads, some of them drawing on them; some had big portfolios placed next to them to transport their work. Maybe they were from the nearby art academy, looking for inspiration over coffee. Alma had thought of funding the art school. But somehow the idea did not bring real satisfaction. It wasn't the answer she was looking for; she could clearly feel that. Luca had been drawn to art, but even after going through the boxes, she did not feel he had actually wanted to go through the hardships of art school. Rather, it had been a phase – a way to find a space for himself, but not a strong desire, one of many things he was enthusiastic about.

Their coffees arrived and Ana twirled her spoon in the milk foam of her latte, reminding Alma of a toddler splashing around in a bubble bath.

"You know," Alma finally said, "I was just thinking… where do young artists go, if they do not find the space to work at home? I mean, that must happen a lot, right? Parents do not approve of their choice or simply do not have enough space at home. Where can they work, where can they breathe? Do they all get their own *atelier* at the art academy?"

"Hmm, good question." Ana stopped plunging her spoon into the foam and put it in her mouth for better thinking. "Artists always have that trouble, you know, finding a good workspace and support for their passion. It never ends, unless you get super famous while you are still alive."

Alma felt a hot needle run up her spine.

"There are many options," Ana said, now looking to the ceiling as if the options were all listed there. "I know of some friends forming a group of artists, like an association, and renting a place together. Or they apply for scholarships for retreats and residencies to get some time and space for their work. I would say these stays are vital in the sense that creative periods can often be traced back to certain residencies."

"How would that work? I mean, where exactly do they find such residencies?"

"I went to one when I was younger and was still painting more and giving classes, and so on. There are different types. Sometimes, there are foundations running them, trusts set up in the name of famous artists, or by some patron of the arts. For example, the 'Civitella Ranieri Foundation' by a rich Italian lady from New York. She owns a castle in Umbria and opens its doors for all kinds of artists to spend their time there and work together, like an oasis for creativity. It is actually really great, you know, that there are people committed to all this. Otherwise, art would probably not exist!" Then she focussed on the little wrapped cookie next to her coffee cup; her long explanations apparently called for some sugar.

But Alma was too excited to think about coffee or cookies. Something big was about to emerge from the fog. That was what had kept her up in the last two weeks. More than her hip, her spine, or a headache. The feeling that there was a solution. As if you wake up from a dream and you know it is there because you can still feel all the emotion running through you but you can't see the images anymore. And now Ana had spelled it out for her.

"What's with you now?" Ana said, looking curiously at Alma through her big glasses. "You look like you have seen a ghost."

"Almost, almost," Alma stammered. "I just need to wash up, I'll be back." Alma got up, but on her way to the bathroom she passed the stairs leading down to the outdoor area in the back. She quickly changed her mind and walked down until she was standing on the meadows. A bar to her right was playing soft music, and beds with white linen were spread all over the area, in between the sculptures and installations. She did not recognise any of the artists; only that the fountain in the back was clearly by Niki de Saint Phalle. All the beds were occupied by people, sometimes sitting in a circle and chatting, holding a drink or simply staring at the sky. There was something weird about beds in a garden, as if these were for people who had lost their homes. Or who travelled between worlds and needed a place to rest. And if she closed her eyes, she could easily see Luca and the blonde girl sitting on one of them, could imagine them smiling at each other, lost in a conversation. In a space which was everything and nothing and would just let them be. That was the idea. Not because Luca would have made a great artist, but to give that space.

No such spaces would exist without people committed to them, Ana had said. She took another deep breath, then turned on her heel and went back to their table.

"Ah, there you are!" Ana said with honest relief. "I was about to go after you. You looked so pale but you look so much better. Almost rosy, look at you!"

"Yes, yes, the thing is, I think I have got the solution!"

"Solution? What solution?"

"The solution for everything!" And then they changed roles. Ana sat quietly and stared while Alma talked for five minutes without breathing, making excited gestures while she talked.

The puzzle as she laid it out for Ana was this:

First, Alma lived alone in a big house with too much space for her and an aura of past unhappiness and unfulfilled dreams – and yet she did not want to leave such an amazing place.

Second, she wanted to give her son's past life an expression in the here and now.

And third, di Marco wanted to set up a trust and she had to think about a name and purpose for it.

All these problems would be solved if she converted the entire estate into an artist residency. She did not need much space for herself; the rest of the house and the office building too could be devoted to young artists. This plan also ensured that Flavia and Maria could stay. Maybe they would even have to hire more staff – but Ana with all her knowledge and connections could certainly help a bit with that, no?

After a moment of shock, Ana jumped from her chair and swung her arms around Alma.

"My lovely friend, that is such a brilliant idea! Of course it can be done, of course! And Luca would so love it, darling, he would so love it! They would all be really proud of you! You are putting the estate to such good use!"

When Ana sat back down, she had tears in her eyes. She had been a little too loud as usual and people were looking at them. But Alma did not care this time; she had tears in her eyes too. She felt dizzy, her pulse beating in her throat.

"We have to celebrate this, Alma. Coffee and cake is not enough for this news, let's go!"

And so the two old ladies left the museum, giggling, painting future scenarios in the sky. Alma had hooked into Ana's arm as her legs were still a bit shaky. Without discussing it, it was clear that there was only one place to celebrate: the Osteria di Brera. Before they sat down, Ana had already shared the good news, which in turn prompted Paolo to offer a bottle of champagne on the house. Alma was a bit shocked first at this lack of discretion but she was getting more and more convinced that being indiscreet was more fun. Come dinnertime, more friends of Ana stopped by the restaurant. Her neighbours Isabella and Guillermo, who always took care of her plants when she went on holiday, Guiseppe, a painter she knew from the museum and who also lived in the area. He was so well mannered that Alma could never believe he was unmarried. They joined tables and in the end they were a loud, joyful table of five. Alma had not been to a real party for the longest time, if ever, and she was not sure whether Guiseppe was smiling at her a second too long. Many bottles of champagne later, the two ladies walked out. Alma hooked into Ana's arm again, but now for a totally different reason.

"You cannot drive home now," Ana slurred. "I insiss you ssay over a my pace!" she added, with a finger raised theatrically in the air. Ana's apartment was on the third floor right above the osteria, and on the staircase, between all the puffing and giggling, it became clear they would never have made it much further. Being too tired and tipsy to have an opinion, Alma crashed on a friend's sofa for the first time in her life. Also for the first time in her life, she had to put one foot down on the ground to make it stop turning as she lay down.

*

At 7am, Alma woke from the ringing of her mobile phone. Her head was aching and her phone sounded unusually shrill. Flavia was worried sick when she found that her mistress had not come home, and Alma had to apologise many times and promise to come right away.

"Ana!" she shouted from the sofa. "Wake up, you have to drive me, we have to break the news to Flavia and Maria also…"

Ana only answered something like "Ooouuh," and looked a bit destroyed when she emerged from her bedroom. "Not before I throw a round of aspirin," she moaned.

"Looks like there are many reasons to start the day with a painkiller," Alma remarked sarcastically, and Ana laughed.

"See, see," she winced, holding her head, "sometimes, there is such a dry sense of humour about you."

Flavia and Maria forgot all about being angry when they saw the two hungover ladies in yesterday's clothes, leaning into each other when waddling through the courtyard, sheltering their eyes with one hand from the harsh daylight. They started laughing and could not stop. After decades of elegance and self-control, this sight was simply too much. "*Signora*, look at you!" Maria shouted, and had to hold on to the kitchen worktop, so hard she was laughing. Alma felt a bit offended for a second but then she had to laugh as well; it was simply contagious. When she got her breath back, she raised her hands:

"Ladies, calm down and take a seat, we have an announcement to make. Maybe I should also get di Marco," she said, and waddled back towards the terrace door.

"Oh, what is it?" Flavia giggled. "Are the two of you getting married?"

That joke almost killed Maria. She could only shout "*Madonna!*" and almost sank to her knees.

"Oh, my head, laughing still hurts so much," Ana said, wiping her eyes.

"Stupid girls," Alma muttered, in an attempt to regain authority, but she was laughing as well.

33
Officially Invited

August 2017, London

The invitation letter had come a week after Emmy's safe return. It was a different paper this time; the letterhead was that of the family lawyer. It basically said that they were glad to hear that the whole affair (Emmy's escape, they meant; it was typical of them to never call things by their name) had ended happily. On another note, they were planning to restructure the estate and Emilia and her mother would be welcome to visit the place before, to see it the way it was when her father lived in it. It was signed by Alma Carneggio herself – for the personal touch. Helen had put it on Emmy's bed and when she came home she had come over to open it together with her mum. They were sitting in their small back yard, decorated only by a pot with a fern struggling for survival and two tarnished plastic chairs, the stone tiles still warm from the sun. Decorating the back yard was a plan every year, before it fell victim to budgetary restraints or a rainy summer. Despite their wobbliness, Emmy managed to sit with folded legs, her eyes resting on the letterhead.

"That is weird," even Emmy noted. "Now is this a formal invitation from the office or does it come from her?"

Helen felt like saying, *This is a letter from a very rich housewife who will always have a man speak on her behalf, especially when it is about taking some responsibility.* But for the sake of peace, she said:

"Urmm, when we go there, you can form your own opinion," and forced herself to smile.

"She will eternally piss you off, right?" Emmy said, putting that wise Zen face on again.

Helen sighed. "I know it is ridiculous after such a long time, but it is difficult to totally give up on the idea of a sincere apology. I still feel she owes me one."

"Yea, I guess she does… Will you push for one when we go there?"

"Actually, I've thought about it. And the answer is no."

"No? Really?" Emmy shouted in disbelief and finally almost toppled over with her chair. Helen managed to grab the back of it at the last moment.

"Let's see if I can go through with it. But actually, Luca is the one who owed me an apology, and that will never happen. And also, what does the mother know? *That* kind of woman knows nothing about my life."

Emmy looked puzzled. Perhaps she got this from her dad, Helen thought. Emmy did not have that thing for analysing and observing people, was never interested in discussing women's role in society. Or maybe this generation of young women could do without all that. This would be a good thing, so Helen left it at that.

But there was one thing left to say; it had kind of drowned in all the excitement but needed to be said. "I'm sorry for having been rude to Amir. Do you think he wants to come to Milan with us?" Helen was not really keen on that but she felt she had to ask.

Emmy smiled a little sourly. "For starters, it would be good if he were allowed to sit on our couch."

"He is not allowed to sit *naked* on our couch…"

"Mum!"

"I just want him to treat you well. That's all. You figure it out," Helen said and passed her hand over her daughter's golden hair while heading to the kitchen to get more tea.

When she came back, Emmy looked at her straight. "You know, I think for this trip, I would want to go by myself. I can take pictures and tell him later. Otherwise, I will have to make sure he is fine, *and* that you guys get along – it will all be too much."

Helen had to chuckle; her daughter sounded like a mum considering whether she wanted to take her two toddlers to the supermarket or whether this would finally make her brain explode.

"Would it then be fine with you if Eric comes along? Just be honest, it is okay if not…"

"No, that's fine. He keeps you busy," Emmy added with a grin.

*

And so they planned their first trip together for mid-October, the three of them on the road again. Things with Eric were still not as they should be for a picture-postcard couple. The affair was still a secret and most weekends he spent with another family, with a woman with whom he had two children. Some weekends, Helen could not help staring at her phone, then observing him anxiously on Monday. Was he more distant than usual, the embrace shorter or the kiss less passionate? Part of her still feared he might want his family back and would break up with her. But she got used to the idea that this anxiety would stay with her for a while. Once bitten, twice shy. He needed time to transition from one life into another, and she had to take a leap of faith. He was worth it and that was all she needed to know.

And in all fairness, things were moving. He came to her house every other week and stayed overnight. This way, they could be together and she could still monitor (or block if necessary) Emmy's amorous activities. And having breakfast together became her new favourite part of the week. She still hated going to the office and meeting Almond Eyes, but the tea breaks were back and even more fun than they used to be, as their intimacy was real now.

And last but not least, it meant the world to her that he was taking some days off to accompany her to Milan. It was childish, but he was one reason why she could so easily agree to go there now. With Eric by her side – he could have been her partner for the last fifteen years, who knew – and a beautiful daughter, it would seem as if the Carneggios were nothing but an episode which had left her unharmed. With her pride so well protected, perhaps she could even do without an apology.

34

Serenity

Late August, Vittuone (Milan)

In late August, Clara returned from her Alaska trip and announced she was staying for a week. Ana had moved back into town as she had work to catch up on. The maids set the table on the terrace for a welcome dinner; it looked festive with a white tablecloth and a candelabra in the middle. The nights were still warm; they could stay out here as long as they needed to.

Alma had dreaded the idea of her sister visiting at this stage of her project. Right now it was nothing but an ambitious castle in the air, still easy to shake its foundations. The architect had already provided them with plans to tear down walls and pull up new ones, renovate rooms for the artists in residence for their *ateliers*, classes and events. A colony of craftsmen was supposed to take over the residence next year, but what if Clara's comments made her lose courage, convince her that it was all nonsense? Clara would have endless questions and whenever Alma imagined their conversation, she never had an answer on the spot. But, to her own surprise, she pulled through every time. She always found someone to ask and came up with a solution. In the end, it was the cross-examination by an imaginary Clara which helped her to make real progress.

"How will you protect all your valuable possessions? What if a poor artist decides to rob you?" A viable question. She had a sleepless night over this and then discussed it with di Marco. They came to the conclusion that the security system needed to be adapted. Cameras were needed as the entire house would basically turn into a public space, at least for some months of the year. When thinking about it further, she realised it would also be most liberating to get rid of a large part of their possessions – for the benefit of the foundation. Only a few personal items she would keep: gifts from her husband, teacups she liked. Big furniture and paintings which were hard to remove could also stay. Di Marco hired an agency to sort and evaluate all those carpets, vases and paintings to set up an auction.

"Amore, how will you decide who actually has talent and deserves to be funded? What do you know about selecting promising artists?" Indeed, she knew nothing about that. And if she was being honest, her interest in art would forever remain marginal. But when discussing this with Ana, it turned out that the Amici di Brera was interested in getting acting as a casting committee. One idea was to make the selection an annual event in the context of the summer events which would at the same time be a good promotion for the residency. In the back of her mind, Alma toyed with the idea of hiring Ana, but it was too early to bring that up.

"How will you handle all the paperwork? You have never even touched a computer!" A graphic designer had sent first drafts for a website and brochure – Alma had refused to look at them on the screen and asked for a paper version – which led them all to the inevitable conclusion that an assistant was urgently needed to handle the office work. *Signor* di Marco's assistant promised to help them hire one – and also to help out in the meantime.

"How will you be comfortable around all these strangers in your house?" That was a crucial one. In past years, when Flavia and Maria asked for a few days of leave, they had to undergo some tearful lamenting. Some woman from their village would replace them and Alma could barely put up with one stranger in her house. How would she share the house with a whole legion of young, creative people she did not know and had nothing in common with? Even sleeping next door to them was not a comforting thought. Neither would tiptoeing around a grandmother be the ambiance to spur creativity. The house needed to be remodelled, but how? Finally, she dialled Chiara Marchesa's number and asked for the architect Chiara used for all her renovation efforts. (He did not only pick new curtains for their *loggia* but had also converted their various holiday houses into luxury homes.) Chiara was absolutely delighted to hear her voice after such a long time – and even more delighted that there was some remodelling on the way. They might not exactly be soulmates, but somehow it was nice to chat with her and hear how excited she was. Ana was right; it was easier to talk to people if one had a plan.

The architect's suggestion, after having reviewed the property, was so simple that she could not believe she had never thought of it herself. Alma would move to the upper floor of the office building. This way, she would have her own cosy, private space and would neither feel lost nor be in anybody's way. Neither would she have to live among all those painful memories, and yet she could take care of the family estate. The office downstairs could then be used for the administration of the foundation and as some kind of reception for the residents.

A gentle evening breeze came up, making the tablecloth flare and then sink down again gently. A flock of swallows glided in low circles over the park. Maybe there was a change of weather ahead. Clara nonetheless entered the terrace fanning herself. She went on and on about all the heat being due to climate change. She did not get tired of mentioning how the Alaskan summer was so much more suited to people her age and that they should all move there. When parading around in Anchorage, she surely had been proclaiming the opposite to her co-travellers.

Alma glanced to the side, over the meadow to the trees at the back of the park, over the small fountain and back to the terrace, when a vision caught her eyes. Luca had not appeared since she had sent off the birth card. But now he sat on the edge of the terrace, facing the pine trees. A young man in his early twenties, in a fresh white shirt, ready for dinner. She had often seen him like this – it was one of his favourite spots around the house – but had forgotten about it. It had not seemed important. Sometimes, when they had guests or after she had called for dinner, she would find him there. Cutting out a few minutes for himself, to breathe the air on an evening like this one, before he returned to the table. When he looked out into the green, he seemed so serene and calm.

And seeing him like this, Alma knew, nothing would stop her now.

35

A Walk in the Park

Mid-October 2017, Vittuone (Milan)

"You never mentioned that we were off to see a bunch of hippies," Eric whispered in her ear as they walked across the white gravel towards their welcoming committee.

"'Cause I only ever knew the hippie in beige Chanel," she whispered back, and tensely squeezed his hand.

Helen had played the moment of her return over and over again in her mind. It felt almost surreal now that it was finally here. In her endless versions of a final confrontation, one detail never changed: she had always imagined them greeting her like a black wall, dripping with morality, their noses high up in the air. And Helen had dressed herself accordingly; like the heroine of a movie, she was trying to set herself aside in a white summer blouse. She kept her blonde-silver hair hanging loose over her shoulders, like an innocent girl would wear it, sweet but serious. Alma Carneggio was the only one who did not disappoint entirely in terms of clothing. Her Chanel outfit made her look stiff, but it was a beige dress with a cream-coloured jacket. The woman next to her was introduced as her sister Clara, and she looked as if she had just escaped from an ashram, sponsored by Prada. The expensive shoes and handbag contrasted nicely with a batik kaftan in all colours of the rainbow. Next to Clara stood a woman who was introduced as a friend. Obviously, she was not part of the family; her clothes were off-brand and ill fitting. She was bursting out of a burgundy jumpsuit matched with a yellow silk scarf. Di Marco was only recognisable to her because of his flawless Clooney-esque face. He wore a linen suit in a light mint, matched with a tie in pink, which went nicely with the sister's outfit. Two older women stood in the background, in simple skirts and blouses. She remembered pictures from home Luca had shown her. Family dinners were served by maids in black dresses with white aprons. The dress code had loosened up over here. It spoke volumes that these two were not introduced, but it was no surprise.

"They look kind of fun," Emmy whispered.

"Who knew...?" was all Helen could respond.

But other than that, the location did not fail to impress. The mansion, the front yard with a small fountain in the middle and the majestic sycamore tree, shielded behind a stone wall, was as regal as she had remembered. Emmy looked as stunned as she had when arriving for the wedding, eighteen years ago, with her jaw dropping and counting the windows to guess the size of the place. There was a brief commotion as nobody knew exactly how to greet the other. Alma made an uncertain step forward as if she wanted to shake a hand but then stepped back again. In the end, they bowed strangely to each other.

The afternoon started with a tour around the estate. Showing off came first on the agenda, of course. The whole affair had the atmosphere of a state visit. Di Marco, the host's ambassador, was leading the tour, followed by the two heads of state, Alma and Emmy. The guest entourage, Helen and Eric and Clara and the friend, followed at a respectful distance. Alma avoided Helen's gaze. She seemed much shorter than Helen remembered, even against Emmy. Her Sophia-Loren attire was gone. The shoulders hung a bit like those of a sad person, and there was not much make-up on that face. Her hair was simply grey; perhaps it was even her natural colour. And yet, life might have torn some masks off her face, but she was still the same woman, hiding behind her etiquette, and the only topic she knew was her possessions. The one time she interrupted di Marco, it was to point out that the garden had already been designed in the seventeenth century, and not in the eighteenth. As if she knew the difference. And the only personal question she directed at Emmy throughout the whole tour was triggered when they stepped through the terrace door into the library. She came close enough to notice her watch and complimented her on it. When it turned out it was only a Swatch, there was no follow-up.

But as soon as they walked into the garden, Helen forgot about observing Alma. It was over eighteen years ago that she had set foot on these grounds, but it felt as though it had only been yesterday. The sensation grew strongest when they crossed the wide green meadow. Helen clearly saw the scenery right in front of her – the white tents set up for the buffet, the elegant people standing together in groups, and the violin quartet by the terrace, its sound flowing gently around the conversations. She had been so embarrassed for her pale legs, even in summer. All these Italian women in their coral and royal blue mermaid dresses radiated a confidence, seeming to know where they belonged in a way she probably never would. The light yellow of her dress made her look even more like a helpless chicklet among the peacocks. She saw Luca, so absorbed with greeting and talking to everyone, and then turning to her, whispering, "We won't stay too long, Dulcinea, don't worry…" only to then move on to the next group of people.

She looked over to Emmy, and she knew she had worried in vain. She walked next to the old lady, her long red summer dress flowing around her. She was a walking flame next to that ashen woman. But it was not the dress, but the way she walked that made her a queen. With a straight back and her head held high, she listened to all the explanations, asking a question every now and then. If she felt Alma Carneggio owed her, she overlooked it gracefully. None of what they saw today would uproot this girl; she knew who she was and she did not pick sides. Her mother's heart burst with pride. Emmy took endless pictures and ignored the light dismay in *Signora* Carneggio's face whenever she raised her phone. Maybe she did not even notice; she needed these photos for her inner peace. Certainly, it would have been polite to ask before taking pictures of a private property, but Helen felt no need to remind her.

She was only half-listening to all of di Marco's explanations, most of which were things Luca had already told her back then. While he explained the origins of the fountain, the sculptor had been a family friend and now he correctly dated it back to the seventeenth century, his voice mixed in her mind with that of Luca's, and the tension in her body diffused. Part of her had been afraid that the place her imagination had built up so much did not in the end even exist. But it did, and it was exactly as she had seen it in her inner eye. Standing in the middle of it, she could recall this feeling of terrible insecurity, but it did not return. Her life had actually gravitated away from all this. She had outgrown the need to prove her worth to these people, even if it had taken half a lifetime.

After the tour through the park, they were invited to a light snack on the terrace. Emmy admired the parrots and Helen also thought they were the best feature of the place so far. Helen sat as far as possible from Alma, feeling safest between Emmy and Eric. Di Marco was still the one talking all the time; the harem clearly seemed to run under this guidance, now that the patriarch was no longer there. He explained the plan for remodelling the house, and Alma's pink sister never grew tired of praising the future success they would have. It seemed to have been mostly her idea. The role of the burgundy woman never became quite clear to Helen; she seemed a little funny, but also kind of sweet. She threw Helen an encouraging smile whenever she peered in her direction, and on two occasions she saw her squeeze Alma's arm.

*

In her answering letter, Helen had mentioned that she would like to visit Luca's grave on her own. Emmy would then get to see it separately, on the next day probably. She had discussed with Eric what she could do to find some sort of closure. "Maybe do what all grieving people do, even if you are twenty years late..." he had said. Luca's grave had appeared in her dreams countless times. Sometimes, it was a big cross in the shade of trees; sometimes, it was like the inside of a chapel, lit up with candles, and it always felt like he wanted to tell her something important, and then she woke before he did.

So, at the end of the day, Alma and Helen walked down the narrow paths of the cemetery of Vittuone. It was an old cemetery, just a few minutes' drive from the Carneggio residence. Death was by no means an equaliser; the status of people was well perpetuated. To the right was a field with graves, small ones as wide as the gravestones standing on them, decorated with flowers and battery-powered grave candles. To the left, they walked alongside a high wall of white marble, divided into small caskets, a bit like lockers in the gym. Just large enough to host the urns and have the names with the dates. The sun was already standing low on this day in mid-October. Its last rays painted the entire wall of lockers in a heavy gold, as if it was trying to melt it, reflecting in the small vases attached to them, bleaching the poor plastic flowers. She and Alma walked a good two metres apart from each other, Alma in the lead. An unlikely pair, living a moment they never expected to happen, while at the same time having waited for it half their lives. Despite the golden light, there was already a cold nip in the air. Alma had brought a cashmere pashmina and pulled it closer around her. Of course, the Italian lady knew what the evenings here were like. Helen had just gotten up from the coffee table in her blouse. In Italy, she had thought it would be warm, a common mistake. Helen folded her arms in front of her chest against the cold. The birds were singing their evening song, a voluptuous crescendo to conclude the day.

Without speaking a word, they kept walking towards the west end of the cemetery. Where the graves of the commoners ended, the cemetery was framed by a row of what looked like small marble temples, each with a glass front. Those were the graves of the well-off families of Vittuone; even after death, they did not have to mingle with the plebs. Alma steered towards one in dark grey marble in the middle of the row. It looked a bit like a Roman temple with its pillars next to the entrance, but it had none of the mystical charms of the chapel in Helen's dreams. The marble was as polished as a kitchen worktop and the glass door added to the sterile ambiance. They walked up a few stairs and then Alma pulled a key out of her handbag. Inside, there was barely space for more than two people. It was somewhat unpleasant to feel Alma so close behind her, but she did not have the courage to ask her to leave, not in this place. To the right stood a massive vase holding an artificial bouquet of plastic flowers. The three walls of the little temple were covered in caskets of dark marble, hosting the urns of the deceased. Same as on the wall, only more grand and exclusive. Helen recognised the names of Luca's grandfather and father. And in the backside wall, in the lower-right casket, there he was. Luca Carneggio. She looked at the engraved name, the date and then the name again. For a moment, it felt as if the whole world closed in on these letters, tears swelling up in her eyes. She had known that this place existed, that this gravestone was somewhere in the world even if she had not exactly known what it looked like. Yet seeing it right in front of her was a totally different matter. The man that she could not put to rest was resting here, and this was all that was left of him. And despite the sudden wave of grief, not having to imagine this place anymore, not being haunted by it, but being able to come to it and leave it again, meant imminent peace.

And when standing there, in this very spot, she felt it so clearly. You never know where life takes you, who leaves a trace, who will be the one we can never forget. It can take a moment to see your life in someone, and it will change you forever. They had shared no more than a few months of their lives, a lifetime ago. Six months, eighteen years ago, to be precise. Yet, being close to someone, knowing someone in a way you can never forget, is not a matter of time. Such moments can stretch out to an eternity. The deep connection, the intensity of the emotions – she had often wondered whether it was more a result of her loneliness than a lived reality. But standing there, in front of his grave, next to his mother, she knew it with certainty. It had all been real. There are all kinds of love stories, and theirs had been real despite its ending. She had known a side to this man like nobody else had. In that brief period, he had been able to be a different version of himself, one his family never knew. That was a truth of their lives, not a fantasy to soothe her pain.

And there was never a chance it could have ended well, not for her and not for him. Being here it was so easy to see. Why part of him had loved this place and this family so much. Why a childish heart like his had to love such a place so much, a place to make you believe life is a fairy tale. Where you will always have abundance and be looked after, where you are safe from all evil, where you can do nothing all day but run in the park and talk to the animals. And where your fate is carved in stone, like the name of a dead man. If you stay a child in your heart, you can never leave such a place, never pull a sword and make your way out in the world. A heart like his also had to love this sweet, innocent mother, and would never have it in him to start a rebellion. And at the same time, a place so heavy with tradition and values, a light soul like that of young Luca was bound to suffocate. The responsibility, the expectations, covered his wings with lead and pushed him to the ground where he was easy prey for the foxes.

Standing here, she could once again feel his despair, him being so torn between the child he was and the young man he yearned to be. Acknowledging his struggle, she finally found peace with the way he had retreated from her. She could forgive at last because she also knew with certainty that he had not returned and forgotten her, entirely, to live happily ever after. She was a missing element, the promise of a different life, and it had been missing forever after. He had not been entirely happy here, but he could never have been happy anywhere – not with her, not with anyone else. He had just made another desperate attempt to fit in, to please, marry, work – and lost his life over it. One way or another, he always would have.

Helen was pulled out of her thoughts by a rustling noise; *Signora* Carneggio was looking for a tissue. Tears were running silently over her face. Helen had forgotten she was even there and now her feeling of discomfort returned. She felt she had to say something, but she did not know what.

"I'm sorry for your loss," she said after a while, the only staple comment she could think of.

"*Grazie*," Alma mumbled before she trumpeted into her handkerchief.

It was also my loss, Helen thought, *how about a little word about that? You did not come here to ask for an apology.* She took a deep breath and closed her eyes, repeating this like a mantra.

"I think he happy to see you stand here," Alma suddenly said.

Helen opened her eyes and turned to her in surprise.

"Yes, maybe," she said hesitantly, not sure if she could trust in the open kindness of this remark. She tried to imagine Luca standing between them, trying to facilitate a conversation, but the picture would not come up. What words could he possibly say? He had probably never thought about how he could reconcile the two.

Helen was still overwhelmed by feeling so close to Luca, and all she could do was think of a harmless way to phrase Luca's dilemma:

"He was so full of life. It is hard to believe that such a person can die and never come back."

"Yes!" Alma's face lit up for a moment. "Yes, that is very true."

Standing there by his graveside in the cold air of the evening, Helen's anger was suddenly gone. From the corner of her eye, she could see that the golden light only touched the outer edge of the cemetery; the sky was about to fire up in purple. She felt so light it was almost hard to believe all this weight had been with her for all those years. And with all the sense of guilt and drama stripped from her, she felt the need to say something that would console the woman, if there was anything that could. No one was to blame. He had been lighter than air, loving them all and going nowhere with this love. "Some people are like birds in the sky, not meant to grow and build roots," she finally said.

Now Alma looked at her, obviously astounded. For a moment, Helen feared that she had offended her. But it was the essence of what Helen so strongly felt in this place. Alma just turned her gaze back to the grave and said nothing.

They fell quiet again and after a while Helen started to wonder how this scene would be resolved. Would they stand here for another eternity because neither of them dared to make a move? But Alma made her thoughts obsolete by suddenly coming to life. She turned to Helen and in the same movement took the pashmina off her shoulders and swung it in front of her like a cape. Helen almost ducked away, as she had not seen this coming. With another swing, she draped it around Helen's shoulders.

"You must be cold, Miss Helen," the old woman said in a maternal tone and with a shy smile. "You stay alone for a moment." And with that, she turned on her heels, determined to make her departure for the car. But after two steps, she abruptly stopped. Helen could tell from her face that it took her guts to ask what she asked now:

"Did you think he marry you?" Her poor English made the question come out a bit more harshly than intended. But what did it matter now? Helen could just as well answer honestly.

"I guess the answer is no. But we loved each other."

Alma nodded, and then turned around to continue her way. Between the gravestones, she was covered in the dim pink light of the sunset, glowing almost, but as she reached the gate to the car park, she was no more than a shadowy figure in the twilight.

Helen stood motionless for a while. Probably that was as close as she would ever get to reproach someone in this family for her broken heart. It did not really matter anymore.

She looked around her, the high walls of dark marble of the family grave surrounding her, such a monument. Even dead, this place was unsuitable for him. So regal; better designed for burying a king or a general. She thought of something meaningful to say, some famous last words of *gravitas*. But she felt like she had already talked so much to him, all her life, that now there was nothing really left to say. Finally, she made a few steps forward, until she was standing so close to the stone plate that she could feel the cold that radiated from the marble towards her skin. She pressed her palms against it, the last bit of tension leaving her body and her shoulders sinking. She leaned forward and also rested her forehead against the white stone.

"There would have been ways to handle all this so much better, you know that," she whispered. "But it is all forgiven. Thank you. Thank you for everything. Most of all, thank you for your love."

Then she was simply done. She lifted herself up, gave the plate a little knock as if to say goodbye. "Your daughter will also come to visit you," she said over her shoulder, and then walked off to join Alma in the car.

36

Like A Bird in the Sky

Mid-October 2017, Vittuone (Milan)

Emilia and Ms Kings left after they returned from the cemetery. They would stay in the area for a few days. Emmy would come back to see the grave of her father on their way home; it had gotten too late to see it in daylight. And that was a good thing, actually; maybe they would even have a moment alone together, and talk a bit more. In the presence of her mother, Alma had barely dared to address her, as if she had no right to. Who knew if they would meet again after that day? But she could keep writing to her, and if she invited her over to spend some more time, also after the remodelling, perhaps she would accept it. From how she had taken in the place, she seemed to like it, and she had asked.

Ana had left after Alma had assured her that she was fine and needed some time for herself. Clara went upstairs to lie down. She had not even asked for her usual glass of wine before going to bed.

Although Alma felt exhausted too, she could not even sit down for dinner. She ate some bread and cheese standing in the kitchen, swaying from one foot to the other. What a beautiful young girl her granddaughter was, and she took after Luca so much. Unbelievable, how things are passed on, although they had never met. From the pictures, one might think it was only the smile, but it was also the gestures, like the way she ran her hand through her hair. Can those things be genetic? She would ask Flavia and Maria tomorrow if they had noticed it too. A fine girl she seemed to be, not one of these light-hearted and spoilt teenagers. And when she had asked her about her watch, the carelessness when she said "It is not an expensive one, I just like it," was so much like Luca. He had never cared for brands; it was only ever whether he liked it. She was well dressed, though, a good sense of what suited her. She did play an awful lot with her phone, and her taking pictures everywhere had been a little disturbing. But Clara said all teenagers did that these days. And why shouldn't she have some pictures to take home?

Nobody had asked Alma any uncomfortable questions, or been hostile to her. She would not even have needed Ana, Clara or di Marco as her entourage, but who knew, better safe than sorry. There might not be another opportunity to speak to the mother though. Standing next to her, Alma had not dared to ask her any private questions about Luca. Somehow she had the feeling that there were some questions one could simply not ask twenty years later. Perhaps she knew enough.

The lanterns in the courtyard flickered to life. The little yellow islands of light formed all over the property. She had done what she had longed to do for years, met the one person she had been thinking about day in, day out, for more than a decade. And yet, that wave of inner peace which she had so clearly expected would not come. Relieved, yes. But deep inside, it felt as if there was something really important which still needed to be done.

She put her plate in the sink and walked over to the library. It was completely dark now and the smell of dust and old books embraced her before she switched on the light. Sitting by her secretary desk, in the light of the small Tiffany lamp, was still the most soothing thing she could think of, an island for her thoughts. Maybe this was as good as it gets, she thought – maybe she was just not capable of real inner peace anymore. She looked at the stacks of paper, piling up on her desk where before there had been nothing but Christmas cards.

She had to review the proposal for a website, the draft brochures the agency had sent, and she needed to make a list of things to do over the next weeks, but tonight she could not focus on any of this. Her thoughts kept turning like a carousel, whirling around the same images of the afternoon. The blonde girl, standing in the door frame of her father's old room, walking over the meadow to look at the house from a distance, shielding her eyes from the sun with one hand. And how she herself had walked over to his graveside, with the English woman next to her. She was even a bit shorter than she had remembered her. Her face showed some wrinkles around the eyes and her hair was about to turn silver... *Some people are like birds in the sky...* She heard it loudly in her head, as if she was still standing close to her.

She touched the wooden top of the secretary desk and followed the intarsia flower with her finger. This desk would move with her into her own little apartment. She would have to make space in it; the drawers were needed for all sorts of documents. Perhaps she could keep herself busy with sorting some papers. She started with the small caskets in the front. Some of them had not been used in years; she hardly remembered what she kept in them. She started with the one on the very left. It was blocked at first; one needed to hit a specific angle to pull it open. When she finally got it right, it shot out with force, spilling a pile of cut-out newspaper pieces over her desk – little squares with black frames, all of them. It took her a moment to remember where these were from. They were obituaries she had cut out of the Sunday paper, years ago. On Monday morning, when no one cared about yesterday's paper. For many years, the obituaries had been the only thing she read. It was her only comfort, that there were other people out there who had lost a loved one too. She had looked at the dates and calculated their ages, read their names and the number of children and siblings, and imagined what they looked like. Those that touched her, she cut out. A mother who had died very young and left four daughters behind, or a professor who died at the age of 102, leaving behind twelve grand- and great-grandchildren. She had imagined him to be the happiest man on earth. Others she kept merely because she liked the psalms and poems people chose. During her leepless nights, she had sometimes gone through her collection, reading them again and again. *Like a bird in the sky*, that was it! There was one like that! She found it easily. The names and the dates were insignificant: an old man, leaving a wife and two children behind. She had kept it for the beauty of the poem. She had known it by heart once. It had felt important, but then she had forgotten.

Alma leaned back in her armchair, closed her eyes for a moment. The darkness was soothing and, out of impulse, she switched off her desk lamp. When her eyes had adapted, she found the room covered in a silver-white glow. It was a clear sky, with a silver moon. One or two days more and it would be full circle. The moonlight painted long black shadows in the grass, shadows with sharp edges. As if tonight, God had forgotten to switch off the light. Or rather, as if he had installed one of those night lights, which parents put up for their little children, so they never feel scared when they wake up.

"Like a bird in the sky," she said aloud once more. And then she knew. She knew exactly what to do. The one thing left to do before she could rest. He would love this idea of his old mother's. The thought had formed slowly at the back of her mind when she was standing next to that tiny woman, staring at the stone plate. That place of stone that she had always hated visiting, nothing but a cold thorn in her heart. Even on good days, sunny days, when she sat outside on the terrace and listened to her birds chirping, all the sun could do was fight against that cold gust coming over from the graveside.

*

It took her two days to plan everything. She needed to get to the graveyard when it was likely that nobody would see her. She was not sure whether what she planned was a criminal act according to someone's book. It was her family's grave, after all, but in any case, she did not want people to know about this. Her first attempt was in the early morning, right when the priest opened the cemetery gates at 7.30am. But she was disappointed. She found herself among a group of silver-haired ladies, some equipped with flowers, and chatty, as if they were meeting for one of Clara's senior fitness classes, although Alma was the only one carrying a sports bag. They glanced at her from the side, then at her bag; probably they knew better who she was than the other way round. How naive, she of all people should have known that old ladies have a hard time sleeping. So why not visit the dead, who took your sleep in the first place, at the break of dawn? Amidst this crowd, her plan wouldn't work.

"*Padre* Giuseppe," she addressed the priest, who turned to her with a smile.

"*Signora* Carneggio," he said in the kindest voice, "how very nice to see you here! How are you?" The very man she had turned down several times when he attempted house visits to console the grieving widow, still smiled as if they were close friends. Perhaps out of grandeur, perhaps because she continued to smell like a possible source of generous donations. Anyway, there was no time to think about this now.

"Thank you, *Padre*, I am very well. I hope the same is true for you." After a further exchange of pleasantries, she finally managed to ask her question: "*Padre*, I would like to come to pray at the graveside, but I would like to enjoy the silence of the place. When is the best time to come and find the cemetery empty?"

"Ah, yes, the mornings are quite lively and so are the afternoons. In that sense, you should come at noon, directly at noon. People go home for lunch and siesta and there is basically nobody here."

Alma thanked him, promised to come to Sunday Mass soon, and called for a taxi again. It was too long to wait until noon and too hectic for her to go a second time this day – she would have to come back.

*

The next day, she was at the cemetery gate exactly at noon. And indeed, the cemetery was deserted. Her heart was pounding in her chest, fearing that something or someone might still jeopardise her entire plan. The inside of the family grave was not more than a small space between the compartments, half of it taken by a gigantic flower bouquet. The third from the right in the middle column had her son's name inscribed on the white marble – thank God it was low enough so that she could reach it. The marble was quite a bit heavier to open than she thought, but there was a technique to it; she had seen cemetery staff handle it before. With the right push, it gave way and she could reach for the urn. It looked like a decorative vase but with a lid, in black with golden edges. She placed the urn carefully in her big sports bag and left the cemetery as quickly as possible. The bottom of the bag was sagging towards the ground now, but thank God she did not meet anybody on the way out.

The real challenge began at home. The lid of the urn unscrewed after she used a small towel against her sweaty hands. But inside, the ashes were not just floating around. They were sealed in a small metal capsule, like a tuna can. She had expected some resistance; urns were not the same as Tupperware. Anticipating this, she had gotten a hammer from the den and hidden it in the library. She waited for Flavia and Maria to leave, then opened the library door to the terrace. The moonlight was even brighter than it had been a few days ago. She took two candles with her, and that was enough for her to see. There was a light wind, but not enough to blow them out.

She placed the urn on the stone tiles and took a deep breath. Could one burn in hell for what she was about to do? She vowed to donate a considerable sum to *Padre* Giuseppe, to be on the safe side, and then swung the hammer over her head and down on the metal can. It was the first time she had held a hammer, and the first hit was much too subtle. It made a gentle 'ping!', more like someone wanting to give a speech at a banquet. The can remained unharmed. The second time was better. The hit left a mark in the lid. And with the third hit, she had gathered enough courage to tear a hole in it. With the fourth, the hole was big enough to pour out the ashes. She had been terrified of this moment. What would it be like to see or touch her son's ashes? Would it haunt her so much that she would have to abandon her plan? But she could not relate this grey mass to her child; it was much less than she had expected, and so light. And there was no going back now. She kneeled down for a moment and prayed. Then she walked back into the library and took one of his drawings and placed it on the terrace. She turned the capsule on its head, and amidst the canvas was now a pile of light grey dust.

Then she lifted the canvas over her head and started to walk over the grass, up and down in front of the house. Every now and then, she shook it lightly to whirl up the ashes and spread them over the park. She watched them blow up in a silver cloud in the moonlight before they settled down or disappeared in the night sky. When the canvas was empty, she was out of breath and her heart was pounding so hard, she had to sit down by the candles for a moment. When she could breathe again, she recited the poem in a low voice, just for herself to hear:

'When you awake in the morning's hush
I am the swift uplifting rush
Of quiet birds in circled flight.
I am the soft stars that shine at night.
Do not stand at my grave and cry;
I am not there, I did not die.'

And now it was true, as true as she could make it for him. Lighter than air, exactly as he had always wanted to be. In honour of the man who died as well as the man who got buried alive. For the dead to live, and the living to love on.

For exclusive discounts on Matador titles,
sign up to our occasional newsletter at
troubador.co.uk/bookshop